THE HOOKUP

MOONLIGHT AND MOTOR OIL

KRISTEN ASHLEY

ROCK CHICK
PRESS

The Hookup
By Kristen Ashley

This book is a work of fiction. Names, characters, places and incidents are a product of the author's imagination or are used fictitiously. Any resemblance to actual events, locales, or persons, living or dead, is coincidental.

Cover Art and Interior Graphics: Pixel Mischief Design

MATLOCK, KENTUCKY

MOONLIGHT &
The Hookup
EST 2017
MOTOR OIL SERIES

KRISTEN ASHLEY

ONE
PANTIES

Izzy

I woke up to the sound of a ceiling fan.

I did not have a ceiling fan.

Obviously, this made me open my eyes and do it fast.

Which brought to my brain the fact that I was lying on tan sheets. They had a slight sheen to them. I could feel them too, and they were soft. They looked and felt expensive.

But they were not my sheets.

The pillow my head was on was not my pillow.

And the nightstand next to the bed that had three used condom wrappers, some change, a cell phone, an alarm clock and a lamp was not my nightstand, my cell, my alarm clock or my lamp.

Stupidly, I stared at the alarm clock.

I still had the same alarm clock that my mom bought me when I went to college. It was square, pale pink and had a mirrored face.

Even though it was over a decade old and it had been super cheap, it was still cool and better yet, girlie. Best of all, it still worked.

The alarm clock I was staring at looked modern, complicated and expensive.

I was not in my bed, in my home, with my alarm clock.

I pushed up to leaning on a hand, realizing I was naked (I *never* slept naked). I yanked up the sheet to cover me as it all came crashing in, even before my eyes swept the interesting (so interesting even in my state it had to be noted) space until it hit a wall of windows on the opposite side of the bed outside which stood a man.

Johnny.

Johnny Gamble.

My stomach pitched in an enjoyable way just at the sight of him.

But the sight of him also brought back memories of him and the night before.

His name was impossible. No man in real life had a name like that.

That was the name of the superhero in his everyday existence when he was not being a superhero. Or the suave, talented con artist who eventually falls for the girl and gives up the grift. Or the slick cat burglar who smiles into your eyes as he's sliding the diamond off your finger.

But that was his name.

Even more, that man standing out there was not a John with the "ny."

However, that was how he introduced himself.

"I'm Johnny. Gamble. Johnny Gamble," he'd said last night at the bar, smiling into my eyes and not sliding a diamond off my finger, because I didn't have a diamond on my finger, but more, he just wasn't that guy.

That man outside might be a John or a Dirk or a Clint or an Adonis.

John*ny*, no.

Except looking at him, having said his name repeatedly to him, moaned it while he was inside me (amongst other times), he was absolutely *Johnny*.

He was outside now, with his coffee.

No, he was outside now, standing on his balcony wearing nothing but a pair of gray sweats, so long they gathered at his ankles and covered his heels, the hems of them loose with notches at the sides. He was bent into his forearms on his balcony, holding a heavy white mug between his two hands. He was twisted partially at his trim waist so I had a clear view of his muscled lat and shoulder.

I also had a profile view of his face.

He had black hair, a great deal of it—thick with waves and flips and curls—and right now a lot of it was hanging over his forehead.

He also had a black beard. It was not bushy but groomed. Not trimmed close and overly groomed but it wasn't lumbersexual or ZZ Top either. It stated he was a man who wore a beard before it was trendy, and he'd continue to have a beard when it was not.

I couldn't see them from where I was, but he also had black eyes. Dark as tar.

The beard didn't hide his strong jaw. And nothing hid his large, straight and aggressive but somehow classic and cultured nose. Or the heavy brow that shadowed his eyes, the thick black eyebrows that seemed at a glance to be ominous, but if you spoke ten words to him, you'd know they were anything but.

He was anything but.

He was tall. He was built. Broad shoulders. Veined forearms. Ridged stomach. Bulky thighs.

Last, he was the most handsome man I'd seen in my life. The kind of man you'd expect to turn on the TV and see. The kind of man you'd think you'd walk into a movie theater and he'd be even larger than life on the screen. The kind of man you'd open a magazine and expect to see pictured wearing fabulous clothes at the wheel of a sleek speedboat on the Mediterranean, advertising cologne.

Not the kind of man standing on a wooden balcony behind whom—I squinted—rotated a water wheel.

A water wheel!

This fact, the fact that he was that handsome, not the fact that he lived somewhere with the impossibility of a functioning water wheel, was not the reason I was in his bed in his home in the middle of nowhere, a home that had a water wheel.

To be honest, this was part of the reason.

But not all of it.

Bottom line, I didn't do that kind of thing.

I wasn't the kind of girl who had a hookup.

I didn't frown on it. My mother taught me it was not my place to judge. Not anything. Not anyone.

"You never know, Izzy, what the story is," she'd told me more than once. "You never know what's deep inside a soul. You just never know. And since you don't know, you're never, not ever, in the position to judge."

So yes, I'd learned not to judge.

But I didn't do that kind of thing, meeting a man at a bar, having a few drinks with him and then going home to have sex with him (lots of sex), sleep naked with him and wake up in his bed while he was outside wearing not much and enjoying a cup of coffee.

I'd often wished I was that kind of girl.

In fact, my mom was that kind of girl.

And until she'd gotten married, my sister was too.

I just wasn't.

I was too shy.

To be honest, I was also a hint of a prude. I tried to drive that out of me, the need I felt to be proper, modest, *good*. However, I'd learned from a young age what "bad" could bring you, and my inherent shyness and that lesson didn't allow me to be anything else.

I'd also learned at a not-young age the way men could be, falling into a trap that from my history (and my mother's) I should have seen from a mile away.

So I wasn't just shy. With men, these days especially, I was skittish.

But not with Johnny.

Not Johnny Gamble.

And not just because he was so handsome.

It was also not just because he bought my drinks. Though it was partly because, between drink three and drink four (all of which he bought me), he'd stopped the waitress and said, "Could you bring my girl here a glass of water?"

That said that he didn't want to get me drunk so he could then have his way with me. He didn't mind me feeling relaxed and loose, but he didn't want to take advantage.

That also said a lot of good about him. But it wasn't just that either.

And it wasn't just because he listened. He didn't talk much, but he listened and he did it in an active way, asking questions as I talked about my job, my mom, my sister, my pets, my house. He was interested. He was following everything I said. His gaze didn't roam to other women at the bar or the game on one of the television sets.

His attention was all on me.

It also wasn't just because he had a great grin and an even better smile. His grin was broken, hitched at one corner, creasing one side of his face in a way that made his dark eyes seem like they were twinkling.

His smile was more. Big, bright and white in that dark beard, curving those full lips, it was sweet and it was sexy, both achingly so, both in equal measures.

And he gave me both a lot, his grin and his smile, which was also another reason why I was right then naked in his bed. He thought I was funny. And I liked that. It felt good to make him grin and smile, and definitely chuckle (something he did a lot of too).

Adding all this together, after drink four, when he'd leaned into me and asked in his deep voice, "You wanna get outta here?" I said yes.

I didn't hesitate.

I nodded and verbalized my agreement with a shy, somewhat breathy but still definite, "Yes."

That earned me another smile.

I would find it only got better after that.

It started with the fact that he opened the door to his truck for me.

And after I was in, he closed it behind me.

Then, as he started us on our way and it hit me it might not be the smartest thing to do, to get in a strange man's car and go to his house, I looked at his profile in the dashboard lights, the timidity hit me along with some panic, which made me blurt, "Am I...uh, going home tonight?"

He didn't ask my opinion on the subject. He also didn't hesitate.

He just said, "No."

At that point, after I experienced a pleasant trill down my spine, I pulled my phone out of my purse and told him haltingly, "I just... need to text my friend. I have dogs. Cats too. And some, uh...other animals. She lives close to me. I want to ask her to pop around in the morning to feed them, let the dogs out."

"First, I think it's cool you've got a mind to your pets, and second, I'd think you were stupid if you didn't have a mind to yourself and let a girlfriend know where you were and who you were with."

That was his response. He knew why I was calling Deanna, and that reason wasn't only because I wanted someone to have a mind to my pets. And like getting me a glass of water between drinks, it showed that he, too, had a mind to me.

So yes, definitely yes, he started out great and kept getting better.

I texted Deanna with this information, and although the anxiety sheared away at his earlier comment, it came back because we went out of town. I lived out of town in the opposite direction on three acres with my house, my small stable, my two dogs, three cats, two birds and two horses, but I didn't live as far out as he did.

Deanna might have my text but she wouldn't know who he was,

where he was taking me, and as he turned into a dirt road that was surrounded entirely by woods I wondered what I'd gotten myself into.

Serial killers, I was sure, lived on dirt roads in wooded areas.

And maniacs that forced you into underground bunkers and kept you captive while forcing you to make babies so they could build armies (or whatever) also surely all lived on dirt roads in wooded areas.

When his headlights finally fell into a clearing that had a two-story building made of stones in varying shades of mellow cream, tan and brown (the water wheel was on the other side so I hadn't seen it), flanked by a large creek, I felt nothing but the panic because we were in the woods, nothing around us, and I had a long way to run to get to anything if I had to run away.

And he was tall and fit, he had very long legs, so I had the distinct feeling if I had to run, he'd catch me.

He got out, came around and opened my door (mostly because I was frozen in my seat).

He also took my hand, and when I turned my head, I could feel through the dark that he was looking into my eyes.

It was then he said softly, "Izzy, baby, there's a good possibility I'm gonna bite you. But just to say, trust me, you'll wanna get outta my truck, because I can guarantee you're gonna like it."

A tingle drifted between my legs that must have been a lot more powerful than it felt, because it forced those legs to the side.

Johnny got out of my way as I got out of his truck. He guided me to some wooden, open-slat steps at the side of the building, and he stopped me halfway up to kiss me.

The rest was a haze of nothing but goodness.

During that goodness, on more than one occasion, he had bitten me.

And he'd been true to his word.

I'd liked it.

And after three times of having sex (but four orgasms for me), I fell asleep naked in his arms.

Now there I was, still naked in his bed, and he was deep in contemplation of the creek and woods that surrounded his home, cocooning it in nature, looking a part of it with his bearded-man-because-he-was-a-man-who-wore-a-beard, sweats-wearing, coffee-drinking casualness in his space.

I looked away and spied my panties tangled with my jeans on the floor by his bed, and not far away from them was the T-shirt he wore last night.

I scooched to the edge of the bed, holding the sheet to my chest, and kept scooching, and reaching, as I extended out a leg as far as I could stretch, toes pointed, to drag his T-shirt my way.

I managed this, leaned over, grabbed it and pulled it over my head.

Only then did I get up.

I was tall. He was taller but I was tall. He had very broad shoulders, so the shirt bagged at mine and down my chest, but it barely covered my rump.

That wasn't the only reason I bent and nabbed my panties.

I slid them on, surreptitiously looking out the windows only to see Johnny had moved, but only to be in the act of lifting his coffee mug to his lips. His eyes were still trained to the distance, his back partially twisted toward me.

Thus I took in the room, which was one big room (huge actually) with kitchen, dining area, lounging area, a reading area, and bed. But there was a mouth to a hall to the right of the kitchen.

I headed that way seeing three doors down the hall, two to the right, one to the left.

The first to the right was open. I glanced in and saw a big long room that had a lot of stuff. This stuff was a furnace, water heater and a Wi-Fi setup, but also a bunch of man things. Jackets and fleeces on hooks. Boots and running shoes in an untidy pile on the floor. A gun rack with four places for rifles, only two of them taken. What appeared to be a bound up tent and some folded camp chairs in the corner. A camp stove. Camp lanterns. Fishing nets. Fishing poles. A big backpack.

I walked a couple of steps down the hall and looked into the room at the left.

The bathroom.

I entered and was astonished.

The front room I hadn't fully taken in. The ceilings, however, were wood. The walls, stone. It was a room you would expect in this building made of cream, tan and brown stone that had a water wheel.

The bathroom had been completely redone, and even to my inexpert eye I could see it was recently.

And it didn't look like it belonged in this building.

All white.

Everything.

Shiny white, subway tile walls. A large shower (actually mammoth, with five sprays, two slanted in at the top sides, one at the ceiling, and two more coming from the walls). A white with gray veins marble-topped double sink with illuminated mirror. A toilet behind a half partition that hid it mostly from view. And a big (actually huge) corner tub with a narrow platform built around it where it met the wall, where a woman would put candles, plants, decorative jars with bath salts.

The last I knew because there was that there. The only thing on that narrow platform. A decorative glass jar with a handsome chrome top half-filled with blue bath salts.

This was not Johnny's.

This was someone else's.

Right just then I didn't want to think of the possibility of "someone else."

I looked away from the bath salts and the fabulousness of this huge, clean, gleaming, gorgeous bathroom that was any woman's fantasy and so incongruous to the furnace/water heater room that was a mess of men stuff and outdoor gear, and I used the facilities. I washed my hands. I opened Johnny's drawers until I found some toothpaste and used my finger as a brush. I rinsed and stared at the mirror into eyes that really needed the makeup removed, and in a further quick and as noninvasive as I could make it perusal, I searched for facial care products that might go with the bath salts.

There were none.

There was, however, some mouthwash so I used that.

I wanted to leave the bathroom, but after seeing it in all its glory, curiosity overwhelmed me, taking me to the door at the back between the tub and shower. A door that was closed.

But I couldn't do it.

Johnny Gamble had bought me four margaritas. He'd brought me to his home. He'd then given me four orgasms and held me in his arms while I fell asleep (this didn't take long, then again, I'd had four margaritas and four orgasms).

I owed him privacy.

If he offered me a tour of his home, I'd take it.

But those bath salts notwithstanding, there was no indication from him or anything else that I needed to pry just in case he was hiding something.

He might have a woman who was off on a girl's weekend or away for work and he felt safe to go on the prowl and in doing so, being as he was, looking like he did, knowing he'd get lucky, he'd hidden the evidence and forgot the bath salts.

But if he had a woman who used bath salts, there'd be a lot of evidence to hide and there wasn't even an extra toothbrush, much less a stray tube of mascara he missed. Not in my as-non-invasive-as-I-could-make-it perusal that I'd seen.

Maybe he was a man who liked baths or he took them after a massage, when everyone knew you threw in some Epsom salts to help leach out the toxins.

Perhaps he liked to smell good.

He embodied and defied the name "Johnny." He was a man who

knew precisely what he wanted in bed, so he took it, and if he had to drag it, position it, stretch it, flex it, brace it, he did.

He could take as many scented baths as he wanted.

I walked out and saw him still at the railing at his balcony. He was standing straight now, but braced into a hand on the railing, holding the coffee mug aloft, close to his mouth, but not sipping, eyes still contemplating the view.

Quickly, I took in his space.

Mid-century furniture everywhere. Not stuff he'd inherited when he moved in. It was new. Handsome. Clean lines. Boxy. No nonsense. In tweeds and leathers and light wood. Everything, including the bed, the copious bookshelves (filled with copious books) and the easy chair in the corner was sparse and sleek, like Johnny had hit an auction of the dressings of the *Mad Men* sets and furnished his home with his buys.

It was unbelievably *cool*.

The kitchen he'd worked with as it was. It had nothing trendy. No cement, granite or marble countertops. No fancy swoosh-closed cabinets. There were butcher-block countertops that were so old, they were smooth everywhere, warped in places, wavy in oft-used spots. Stark-fronted cabinets and open shelves.

Though he'd replaced the appliances with a stainless-steel dishwasher, fridge and stove that were high quality and expensive, if not top of the line.

I spied the coffee. I saw the white coffee mugs on an open shelf above the coffeemaker and a bottle of creamer out on the counter.

I went there and made myself a cup.

As I moved toward the balcony, I saw Johnny was no longer in peaceful contemplation of the verdant surroundings of his water wheel, brilliantly furnished with bathroom-to-die-for home.

He must have noted my movement, maybe even noticed I was out of bed and had gone to the bathroom. But regardless, his regard was now aimed through the wall of windows.

At me.

I opened the glass door and walked out, shutting it behind me and looking back to Johnny, only to stop because he was looking at his T-shirt on my body.

Perhaps the intimacy of that, and me helping myself to coffee (and bathroom, toothpaste and mouthwash) wasn't welcome.

I'd never hooked up. Not in my life. I dated. I had a firm five-date rule before even groping (this mostly due to shyness, but also my prudishness, which I had reason to believe I held on to because it assisted in me being so shy), so I obviously hadn't slept with a man hours after meeting him.

I didn't know the protocol when you woke up in a mostly strange man's bed, no matter how handsome, gentlemanly or what a good listener he was.

"Although I appreciate the unadulterated view of those legs, not to mention that hair, I'd prefer you get your ass over here, Izzy."

This amused command jolted me out of my apprehension and I slowly moved on my bare feet through the cool early summer Sunday morning toward Johnny Gamble.

He hadn't taken his hand from the railing but he did put his coffee cup to it so he could have a free hand to curve around my waist.

This he did, pulling me up tight to his side and dipping his chin into his neck to look down at me.

I liked that. Being tall, I didn't get that often, a man looking down at me, having to go to such lengths to do it as to shift his chin into his neck.

This had to put Johnny at six-two, maybe even six-three.

Yes, I liked that a lot.

I also liked the warmth of his body. I'd noticed just how warm it was in bed last night and it helped things (that his talents really didn't need help with, but still), and it helped them in nice ways.

And last, I liked the solidness of him and this didn't come just from him being built. It came from him looking right into my eyes, taking hold of me right away, making me feel welcome there, like he was glad I used his toothpaste, his mouthwash (even though he didn't know that...yet), helped myself to a cup of coffee, woke up naked in his bed.

He wasn't going to load me up in his truck and take me back to my car in town and be done with me, not looking back.

This was something else.

This was...

It was the beginning of something.

I relaxed in his hold.

"Hey," I whispered.

His mouth hitched.

"Hey." He slid his hand down my side to my hip as he asked, "Sleep good?"

I nodded because I had but also because the movement of his hand had so much of my attention I couldn't speak.

It got more attention when his fingers met the hem of his shirt I was wearing and pulled it up.

Therefore, it came out kind of squeaky when I asked, "Did you? Sleep good, I mean."

I also felt my cheeks getting warm and Johnny didn't miss it. I knew this as his black eyes started twinkling even as the tips of his fingers found the waistband of my panties.

"I slept great," he murmured, and then didn't hesitate to go on, "Panties?"

"Sorry?" I asked, confused at his question perhaps because his fingers were trailing along the waistband of the item of clothing we were oddly discussing and it felt nice.

"Panties," he repeated, not in a question this time.

"Yes, those are, uh...my panties," I confirmed.

This got me the bright, white, beautiful smile. "Babe, why'd you put on your panties?"

I blinked up at him.

His fingers slid inside the waistband to lightly cup one cheek of my behind.

My lips parted.

"Sweet, shy Eliza," he muttered like he was referencing me to someone else even if he was gazing right into my eyes. "Gonna have to break you of that."

Yes.

Oh God, please let it be yes.

This was the beginning of something.

"You hungry?" he asked conversationally.

I nodded, not really knowing if I was or I wasn't. Mostly knowing I liked the warmth and possessiveness of his hand down my pants.

"Wanna fuck before or after I feed you?" he inquired.

My legs wobbled.

He felt it, I knew because that got me another smile, this one less sweet and oh-so-much-more sexy.

"Both," he whispered, his head coming toward mine. "Starting with before."

"Johnny," I whispered back, but I did it with my lips moving against his.

His eyes were open, they were close, because I'll note again, his lips were against mine, when he answered, "Yeah?"

"My coffee," I noted idiotically.

Sadly, his lips went away.

Then my coffee went away and was set on the railing by his.

Then his lips were back.

"I haven't even taken a sip," I announced, again looking in his eyes so close, I could count the (abundant) eyelashes.

"Make you three pots after I make you come," he mumbled then moved infinitesimally closer.

"Johnny," I said urgently, again waylaying the kiss for no reason at all.

He was a good kisser. The best. The best I'd ever had.

By far.

Still, I was me.

So I was nervous.

"Izzy," he replied.

"Yes?" I asked.

"Shut up."

I shut up.

And then, finally, he kissed me.

TWO
THE CODE TO HIS PHONE

Izzy

I t was me that switched it up.

It was me who made him let me take over.

I didn't know why I did it. I didn't know that I had it in me to do it. I didn't even think about any of this stuff.

I just did it.

The night before, Johnny had dragged, pulled, shifted, hauled and anything else he wanted to do to get me where he wanted me to be. On my back. On my knees. On his face.

That morning, it started out the same way. It started out like it had continued after the first time the night before.

The first time being fast and hungry and urgent and spectacular.

The rest of it was slow and hot and unhurried and spectacular.

That morning, it was the second kind.

Until I switched it up.

Until I took over.

It was when I was naked and he was naked.

It was when I was sopping wet and he was rock hard.

It was when every inch of me buzzed, and that buzz shimmered deeper from anything he did—a touch, a kiss, a lick, a nip—but also just looking at him, the harshness of sex set in his face, the dilation of his black eyes taking them from bright to blazing.

It was then I pushed him to his back, and at first he allowed it since I could tell he wanted it, because he was willing, for that moment, to go with my flow in order to move me into his new flow.

But when I held his shoulders down, straddled him, feeling his hard cock graze the damp curls between my legs, and I looked into his face, he stilled.

I did not.

I bent to him, sweeping my lips from his neck down to his collarbone up to his shoulder, thrilling in the warm silken skin over hard muscle my lips encountered.

I found his hand, laced my fingers in his and pulled it away from his body. After that, I trailed my lips down his arm, stopping to kiss the bulge of his biceps, moving on to lightly nip the skin at the inside juncture of his elbow.

Then I sat up abruptly, taking his hand with me.

I unlaced our fingers so I could flatten his hand against my chest, my eyes locked to his. Slowly, I drew his hand down my chest, between my breasts, over my belly.

And he held my eyes.

He didn't look at his hand. My body.

He looked into my eyes.

God, I loved it that he kept looking into my eyes.

At my final destination, I twisted our hands, curled them in. My middle finger over his, both of them I took inside.

My head fell back.

His hips jerked.

"*Izzy,*" he growled.

My eyes were closed and I didn't open them when his other hand curved around my breast, his calloused thumb rough as he dragged it across my nipple.

I started panting, feeling his finger move both of ours inside me, lifting my other hand to cover his at my breast to feel his movements there as he engaged his finger with his thumb and started rolling.

"God," I breathed, rocking into our fingers, feeling the back of my hand slide over the underside of his hard cock.

"Look at me," he ordered gruffly.

I didn't look at him.

It felt so good, everything, I arched into his hand at my breast as I rode his finger inside me.

He stopped rolling with one, thrusting with the other, and I heard, "Eliza, *look at me*."

I tipped my head down and slowly opened my eyes.

"I'm inside you, Iz, any way I can be inside you, you *look at me*," he demanded thickly.

"Okay, Johnny," I forced out.

"Ride it," he commanded. "Show me."

I rode it. I showed him. I helped him fuck me with his finger and tug at my nipple until the beauty it was causing had me whimpering, my movements desperate, my eyes floating closed.

He drove deep with our fingers, planted them there, and my eyes shot open.

"Eyes on me," he growled.

"Yes," I whispered, swaying into him when his finger moved again, the desperation turning to violence, urging him to fuck me brutally with our fingers, something he did, slamming my clit into the apple of his hand.

"Christ, sweet, shy Izzy, skittish as a cat, hides the wild of a sex kitten," he murmured.

"I'm a prude," I pushed out nonsensically.

I was barely able (but I did it, mostly because each and every one of them were exactly that good) to catch the flash of the white of his now seriously sexy smile before he replied, "Remind me of that so I can laugh when my dick's not about to explode watching you take yourself there on my finger."

I caught that too, *just* barely, not nearly enough to be embarrassed by it because I'd taken myself there on his finger.

I arched. I cried out. I ground into our fingers panting and whimpering.

In the middle of it, I lost them and was on my back in the bed.

I heard a drawer open, the wrinkling of foil, then I got him back.

Not his fingers.

His cock.

The first time the night before had been fast and hungry and urgent and spectacular.

This time we had started out slow and hot and unhurried and spectacular.

But right then, it was burning and rough and savage and totally uncontrolled.

And *spectacular*.

Circling my wrists with his hands and yanking them straight over my head, pinning them to the bed with his weight to hold me down at the same time giving himself leverage, Johnny hammered into me. *Drilled* into me. Crashing the base of his cock into my clit, pushing me over the edge yet again so I had no choice but to clutch him with everything I had available, hold on for dear life, and chant his name at the same time begging him not to stop, never to stop.

And I did this while my orgasm carried on and on, until it completely overwhelmed me and I couldn't speak at all. I could just hold on and feel the magnificence of the climax engulfing me—us—as he groaned into my neck and powered through the jolts of his final thrusts.

When mine was waning and his was done, he collapsed on me, all his weight, his fingers manacles on my wrists, still pinning them to the bed.

And I didn't mind.

I took his weight, his heat, his captivity because he was a man who had a great smile. Who had a way with interior design that was masculine and confident, interesting and cool. Who had a water wheel. Who opened the door on his truck to let me in and closed me in after. Who didn't look at pretty girls who passed our barstools while he listened to me. Who made me feel sexy. Who made me feel pretty. Who made me feel so unencumbered by all the weight I carried that I'd be moved to take over, to slide his finger inside me and ride it while he watched. Who let me take over and draw him inside and ride him while he watched. And who got off on that so intensely, he'd been moved to take me rough, pinning me to his bed.

I was that girl with him.

That girl who could flirt with a handsome man and set him to scoring through four condoms. That girl he couldn't even let her take a sip of coffee before he had to kiss her and whisk her back to his bed.

I was free and I was easy and I was sexual and I was desirable and I was funny and I was *worth something*.

I wasn't Eliza Forrester, the straitlaced daughter of a hippie, the prim and proper and responsible older sister of a wild child.

I was Izzy Forrester, free and easy and sexual and desirable, who could hook up with a handsome man with a fabulous house in the woods who couldn't get enough of her, and after one night chatting in a bar over margaritas and beer, they were starting something.

As I gloried in all of this, it slowly became clear that he wasn't moving.

This was strange, and in a flash of panic I thought it was just my luck that I would kill the most gorgeous man I'd ever seen, much less slept with, after intense, amazing, pounding sex.

Did I give him a heart attack?

"Johnny?" I called tentatively, and a little wispily, seeing as I was accommodating his weight.

Instantly, he moved. Not letting go of my wrists but shifting them down so my elbows were bent, the position more comfortable, at the same time taking his weight out of his hands and also miraculously some of it off me.

His face was in my neck but he moved his lips to my ear where he asked, "You okay?"

"Yes," I whispered.

He finally lifted his head and I liked that the harshness of sex was gone, the laziness of satisfaction had taken its place, but he still had an expression of concern.

"Rode you hard, baby," he murmured.

"Yes," I agreed.

His gaze scanned my face.

"I'm good," I said quietly and then gave him a small smile at the same time I gave him a hug the only way I could, tightening my legs where I had them wrapped around his thighs.

I didn't know him, at all—well, biblically, one could say I knew him relatively well—but otherwise I didn't know him. Still, I could swear I saw the flash of unease in his eyes before he muttered, "Gonna take care of this condom."

After that, he slid out, let go of my wrists, disengaged, and with no further ado, got off me, out of the bed and walked naked toward the hall.

No kiss.

No cuddling.

No tender caresses and soft murmurs.

I lay in bed staring after him and continuing to stare after he disappeared into the bathroom feeling a hint of frost come. It came like in the movies, when the bad things come and the chill comes with them, at first invading a corner of a window, starting slow but then moving quickly, covering and crackling over the window, the whole house.

Except this frost swept over my body.

It took but seconds to realize that I might not have tons of experience but I did have enough to know it didn't take years for a man to dispose of a condom.

And for this reason, I shot to sitting in bed, searching for something to cover me.

I saw my panties on one side of the bed, on the other his T-shirt, sweats, and the rest of our clothes from last night.

I didn't have time to fully dress so I rolled toward the clothes, grabbing up his T-shirt and tugging it on at the same time dashing around the bed to snatch up my panties.

I was settling them on my hips when Johnny appeared back in the hall.

He went right to his sweats, and I tried to take it as good he glanced at me as he did, not avoiding me, my presence or even eye contact.

He nabbed them and yanked them up as he asked, "You like eggs and bacon?"

"My mother was a vegan."

He stopped in the process of tying the drawstring under his navel and stared at me.

His hair was even messier now, falling over his forehead and nearly into his eyes.

It made him look disheveled and more handsome than ever, especially my firsthand knowledge of and participation in how it got that way.

"I'm not," I went on.

He kept staring at me.

"A vegan that is," I shared. "I tried. About seven times. Even vegetarianism didn't stick. So uh...yes. I like eggs and bacon."

He slowly finished tying the drawstring on his sweats as he asked, "There a story behind all that information?"

"No, just, my mother wasn't a vegan. She was a militant *vegan*," I told him.

"Ah," was all he said in reply, but he did it lifting his chin.

"And my sister was a vegetarian for years and years, until she met a guy who thought that was stupid and he introduced her to cheeseburgers." I shrugged. "The rest is history. I had long since been a lost cause, but my mother never got over that."

I was blathering and doing it mostly because I was beside myself with relief that he asked me if I liked bacon and eggs, which meant whatever strangeness I felt after we finished didn't mean he was going to ask me to take off his shirt and put on my clothes so he could take me back to town and be rid of me.

"Not sure there's a vegetable in this house, unless you count a bag of frozen corn," he said.

I couldn't stop myself from looking alarmed.

Johnny of course didn't miss it and any of the cold I had left at the strangeness of how he left me in bed melted away when he burst out laughing.

I'd heard him chuckle. It was throaty and rich and lovely.

His laughter was that times a thousand.

But still, there was something about it that sounded...

Rusty.

"I'll get the mugs," I said in order not to do something stupid, like watch him laugh like a besotted teenager seeing her first boyband crush in concert.

I turned to the doors but turned back when he called, "Iz."

My eyes met his.

"You eat a lot of vegetables?" he asked.

"Three quarters of your plate should be vegetables," I answered.

"She eats a lot of vegetables," he murmured through a white smile.

"I *really* need coffee," I blurted.

"Then get our mugs, babe. I'll get cracking on breakfast."

He moved toward the kitchen.

I moved toward the deck.

I came back with the mugs and he was at the stove, but I knew he heard me enter when he ordered toward the stove, "Dump that out, we'll get fresh."

His cup maybe only had one last mouthful in it. I hadn't even taken a sip.

"I'll nuke mine," I told him.

"Dump it out," he returned.

"It's okay. I nuke coffee all the time."

And I did. I nuked coffee. I found creative ways to use leftovers. I slammed my lotion bottles on countertops to force down the last dregs.

What I didn't do was waste, and I didn't waste partially because I was an environmentalist but mostly because I grew up with government cheese in the refrigerator. When you didn't have a lot, you not ever wasted what you had.

"It's been sitting outside for almost an hour," he stated.

"It's still good," I replied.

I made it to the kitchen, seeing he had a fancy drawer microwave in his island.

I was heading there when I stopped because I was divested of the mugs in my hands.

I watched Johnny go to the sink and dump both cups. He rinsed them, shook them out and then went to the coffeemaker.

"How do you take yours?" he asked.

"Just cream."

"Little, lots or in between?" he asked.

"Little," I answered.

He poured coffee while I watched. He then turned and put both cups by the stove. After that, he turned again, came to me, put his hands to my waist and shifted me around, then backward. Finally, I had to bite back a surprised cry when he lifted me up (without even a grunt of effort) and planted my behind on the counter next to the mugs, but removed from the stove where there was already a clump of strips of bacon cooking in a skillet.

Once he had me settled, he nabbed my cup and handed it to me.

He then grabbed his, took a sip and set it back down on the countertop. He went to a drawer, took out a fork and moved to the skillet in order to separate and straighten the bacon.

I guessed I was drinking fresh coffee.

And I guessed I was doing it sitting on the counter while he cooked, keeping him company.

"You put your panties back on," he noted while I was swallowing my first sip.

"Uh..." I mumbled, not saying anything more.

His mouth hitched in the direction of the skillet before he put the fork down and went to the fridge.

I took another sip of coffee and looked around his room.

It was then I noticed that the massive TV hanging on the wall hung on the wall opposite the bed, but the couch, oblong coffee table and two flanking armchairs had their backs to the TV.

I guessed he watched TV in bed.

Or not much at all, considering the number of books practically falling out the many bookshelves and covering the table by the chair in the corner with the fabulous tripod floor lamp beside it.

"How long have you lived here?" I asked.

The utter silence this question received made my shoulders instantly tense and my gaze move directly to Johnny.

He had eggs out and was taking down a bowl from some shelves over where he was working.

What it appeared he wasn't going to do was answer what I thought was a non-intrusive question.

It then came to mind our conversation last night at the bar.

A conversation that I hadn't noticed until right then, thinking back on it, was one-sided.

I was new to town. I had to move there for reasons I didn't like to think about. But I'd moved there because Deanna was there, she'd moved there years before, right after she married Charlie, and she was always talking about how fabulous it was. How friendly. How community minded. Added to that, property values were way cheaper than in the city. You could get so much more for so much less.

The one downside was that the commute was long and could be horrific if traffic got backed up. But I'd learned in the two months I'd been there that it was worth an hour's (and often longer) commute every day.

That said, Deanna and Charlie were the only people I knew in town and I'd decided, with spring turning to summer, it was time to be more social, get to know my neighbors.

So I went to the one and only local bar, On My Way Home, known as Home. It was a drinking establishment like any other, with a rectangular bar in the middle, tables around, TVs all over the place. I'd heard they sometimes had bands but most times it was just a quiet place to catch a game or meet up with friends, have a chat and throw some back.

I'd actually seen Johnny pulling into the lot at the back when I'd finished parking. I'd glimpsed his magnificence through the cab of his truck. I'd even heard his car door close as I was walking in the back door of the bar.

And I'd barely sat down when Johnny had come up beside me.

He didn't look at me, just slid into the space between me and the stool beside me.

He'd received instant attention from the female bartender whereupon he'd said, "Usual, Sally, and whatever she's having."

It was not the most original pick up line ever.

But it was the best one ever used on me, only because Johnny used it.

Thus ensued him sitting next to me and asking my name.

"Eliza. I'm Eliza Forrester. But everyone calls me Iz or Izzy."

Sharing that got me my first grin.

And for the next couple of hours, I shared a lot.

Johnny had asked questions as I did. But when I'd done the same with him, he deflected them, bringing the conversation back to me.

Sitting on his counter in his kitchen after having sex with him four times in eleven hours, it occurred to me very belatedly I didn't know a thing about him but his name, he drove a truck, he lived in a house with a water wheel in the middle of some woods and he was an exceptional lover.

Uncomfortably, I sipped my coffee, casting my mind frantically out for a conversational gambit that might actually work.

In the midst of failing at that, he answered, "Three years."

I looked to him not because he answered but because it sounded torn from him.

"It's a great place, Johnny," I said quietly.

"Been in the family generations," he shared, cracking eggs into the bowl. "Dad kept it up so folks who came to visit us had their own space. Wasn't like this though. When I moved in, cleaned it up, fixed it up, updated some shit. Now it's home."

"It's very attractive," I told him. "And peaceful."

"Yeah," he agreed.

"The water wheel is cool," I remarked.

"Yeah," he repeated.

"Is it still being used for something?" I asked.

"Place was a gristmill. Now it's not," he answered in a way that was that and there would be no more.

Time to try something else.

"You don't have pets," I noted.

"Nope."

And that was that too.

He turned the bacon. Got out another skillet. Put it on a burner. Walked to the double door pantry at the edge of the kitchen and got out a loaf of bread.

He brought that to me and set it by my thigh on the opposite side of the counter from his mug. He pulled a toaster from the wall.

"You wanna be in charge of toast?" he asked, his gaze finally coming back to me.

I nodded. "I think I can manage that."

His head tilted to the side. "You know how to cook?"

"I was a latchkey kid. My mom worked and I was the oldest. So yeah, I know how to cook." I smiled at him. "And I definitely can make toast."

His impassive face softened before he reached up beside me and pulled down a plate.

He gave me a knife and the butter.

I grabbed the bread.

"How many pieces do you want?" I asked.

"Two," he answered.

He reached across me to grab the butter, shoved a huge pat of it in the empty skillet, then reached back across me to replace the butter.

I slid the lever down on the first two slices of toast just as a cell phone rang from somewhere in the vicinity of his bed.

"That's my tone," I said.

"Mine too."

Another sliver of information about Johnny, he had an iPhone.

He moved into the room and I watched him toss his jeans aside and come back with my purse, which was ringing.

He handed it to me.

I dug out my phone.

He took the purse from me and set it on the island as I took the call and he went back to the stove.

The call was from Deanna.

"Hey there," I answered.

"Where are you?" she replied.

"I'm, well...still with, uh...Johnny," I stammered.

"Okay, then, just so you know, went by your place and took care of your menagerie. All fed and watered, including Serengeti and Amaretto."

Serengeti and Amaretto, my palomino and bay horses, respectively.

"I'm still here," she went on. "Letting the dogs have a good roam. I'll bring them back in before I go, but could you call me when you get home?"

I suspected, since this was not my done thing, and she'd lived through my last nightmare with me (and others besides), she just wanted to make sure I was not only okay right then, but that I got home okay.

"Sure," I replied. "And thanks."

"Not a problem, babe. Later," she said then r
found a little odd.

I mean, she knew I was there with Johnny so sl
girlie gab at that particular moment about my hookup,
seemed matter of fact to the point of being blunt.

Maybe it *was* a problem I asked her on a Sunday morning to go
look after my babies.

I made a mental note to bring over some treats as a show of gratitude
some time that week and definitely call her when I got home as I brought
the phone down and saw the notifications had come up after the call.

Three texts from Deanna that came in unnoticed sometime
during the activities last night (or this morning).

Call me.

Babe, call me.

As soon as you can, call me.

Oh God, maybe she really couldn't look after my babies but had
to because she hadn't heard from me.

I engaged my texts, typed in, *I'm so sorry. I didn't get your texts. If
it was an inconvenience to look after my zoo, I apologize. I got caught
up in things. It means the world you took care of them anyway, I can't
thank you enough and I'll totally make it up to you.*

I sent the text with a whoosh and Johnny asked, "All cool?"

"I think so," I answered uncertainly.

"What's the thinking part of that?" he queried.

"I don't know, but it might be that Deanna had something on and
I didn't get her texts after I'd texted last night so she went over, but
still, it seems like something's up."

My phone binged and I immediately looked down to see Deanna's response of, *No, no, it's cool. Totes cool. All good. No worries. Just
call me when you get home. No biggie. Just want to chat.*

I relaxed.

"Okay?" Johnny asked.

I looked at him and nodded. "Read it wrong. She's cool."

"Good," he muttered, turning his attention to pouring the eggs in the skillet.

The toast popped up.

Johnny finished up the eggs and bacon and I finished up the toast. He served up and I hopped off the counter to toss my phone in my bag and warm up our coffee. He took the plates to a small, round dining room table with highly polished wood that radiated out beautifully from a center circle and space-age angled legs that had four scoop-backed chairs around it.

My mind screamed when he didn't get a placemat before he put the plates down on that wood but I kept my mouth shut. I brought the mugs over. He returned to the kitchen and came back with the toast, a bottle of ketchup and a jar of grape jelly.

"Sit," he ordered, putting all that on the table and going back to the kitchen.

He'd set the plates on the curve next to each other and he'd dished up equally, so I just picked a seat and sat.

"No, Iz, other plate," he said, coming back with cutlery.

"Sorry," I muttered self-consciously, shifting to the other chair.

"Better view, baby," Johnny murmured close to my ear as he set a fork and knife next to my white plate.

I looked from the flatware to the room to see I was positioned facing it, and the windows, so he was right.

It was a better view.

I felt my chest warm as he took his seat.

Johnny grabbed the ketchup and squirted it all over his eggs.

I picked up my fork and stuck in.

I ate, alternately looking to my plate to get food and chewing it while staring out at the lush leaves dappled in sunlight beyond his wall of windows.

"Quiet," he remarked suddenly and softly.

I looked to Johnny.

"Sorry?"

"You're being quiet," he noted.

"These are good eggs," I told him.

His lips hitched. "Eggs are eggs, babe."

I nodded, though they were actually good. Fluffy and light and well-seasoned.

Then I said, "Thanks for letting me have the chair with the view."

"I got a chair with a view too," he replied, his eyes on me telling me what his view was. "And mine's better."

I felt warmth in my cheeks and looked to my plate.

"Watched you walk into Home last night, no...giving you the honesty, watched your ass walk into Home last night, my plans of havin' a few and relaxing after the week went up in smoke. Got up next to you, you looked at me, thought you were gonna bolt. Shocked the shit outta me you told me your name when I asked it," he declared while I turned my attention back to him. "Maybe margarita courage that kept you where you were, just you in the beginning though. Now you're here, you keep putting on your panties when you know I'm just gonna take 'em off, which means you gotta know I'm into you but you still can't take a compliment for shit."

"I'm sorry," I whispered.

He shook his head slowly, not taking his eyes off me.

"It's your thing and you got no clue, and I seriously don't know if I should give you one but I'm gonna. You work it, Izzy, so don't apologize for it."

I ducked my head and grabbed a slice of toast.

Johnny chuckled.

"Yeah, it's your thing," he muttered.

I tore a bite of toast off, eyes to the table, chewed it, swallowed and announced, "I used your toothpaste."

"Seeing as I kissed you after you did it, that kinda wasn't lost on me."

My gaze flitted to his to see him taking a bite of his bacon. "I didn't use your toothbrush, though."

He swallowed before he stated, "Iz, you've spent time sitting on my face. Do you think I give a shit you use my toothbrush?"

I was somewhat appalled. "That's kind of gross."

"Sitting on my face?" he asked, though I could tell by the sparkle in his eyes he was teasing.

"No," I said swiftly.

"Since you didn't use it, I don't have to be grossed out by it."

"True," I mumbled, putting my toast on my plate and picking up some bacon.

"I understand," he said quietly and I looked again to him while I chewed bacon. "You had to go through my stuff to find toothpaste. You don't want me to think you got nosy. But I got nothing to hide, Izzy."

I nodded.

This all seemed very weird, complicated with a good deal of it contradictory, but at least that was good to know.

"Your bathroom is really nice," I observed and it came again.

He turned off, looked at his plate.

Shut me out.

The Izzy I was normally would ignore it, find some way to move around it, but something made me ask, "Sorry, I...you...am I stepping where I shouldn't?"

His black eyes came direct to me and they weren't entirely impassive. There was something in their depths. I just couldn't read it.

But surprisingly, he gave it to me.

"Left my old place, sold the place I grew up, fixed up this place and moved in after my dad died."

"Oh God, Johnny, I'm so sorry."

"There's shit in my life I'm not big on talking about. Was tight with my dad. So that's some of it."

I nodded. "Of course, sorry. So sorry."

He nabbed another slice of bacon. "You didn't know so no need to apologize."

"Right. Okay," I replied quickly.

But even though this was an explanation, something niggled at me because I found it odd if he was still so deeply affected by his father's passing, why he'd chosen to be in a place that daily, hourly, each second he was in it, reminded him of that in such a way it clearly bothered him.

I knew what it was like to lose a parent because I'd lost both. How that came about, I'd had no choice but to let them go and I'd lost each in entirely different, but not equally agonizing, ways.

I knew how hard it was. I knew how painful. No matter what way you lost them.

I also knew escaping anything that brought additional pain was a good coping mechanism.

So I wondered, no matter how fabulous this space was, why he didn't find his way to that.

I did not ask this as it became clear even if I'd asked, he more than likely would not tell me.

This made something else clear.

This was not a getting-to-know-you date.

This wasn't a date at all.

This was a hookup.

This was not something beginning.

This was something else.

Not just sex, as such.

But something I'd never encountered.

And as handsome as he was, as nice as it was that he gave me the best seat (and all the rest), even if I wanted that to be the type of girl I was (and I actually did), that wasn't the type of girl I was.

I always wanted more.

Sitting there I realized with more pain than it should cause, I wanted this maybe especially from Johnny.

"Baby."

That came gently and I turned my attention to him.

"Not sure I like the look on your face. It seems a lifetime ago but also like yesterday. Most the time, I just live with it. But sometimes I have bad days. This is one of those days."

This was one of those days.

A sunny early summer morning in his house...with me.

"My mom died of cancer, Johnny, so I get that."

He stared at me.

"Ate her up. She was dead in six months," I shared.

He blinked.

"I miss her every day, and if I let it in, I miss her every second."

"Iz," he whispered, a wealth of meaning and understanding and a lot more in his saying my name, all of it, for his sake on a bad day where I was sharing that day with him thus him having that understanding didn't make me feel real great.

I didn't focus on that.

"But that wasn't the meaning behind the look on my face," I told him, surprising myself at my candor.

"What was the meaning?" he asked.

I didn't know what was happening. What this was. Where it led.

I just knew I liked him a whole lot for a whole lot of reasons, the most recent him being thoughtful enough to give me the seat at the dining room table in his own home that had the best view.

But it seemed he liked me mostly because he could have sex with me and I amused him with my shy ways in the midst of me having lots of sex with him.

He let me talk about myself, and he listened, because that was easier than sharing about himself, something it had become clear he didn't intend to do. Or at least not without a goodly amount of effort on my part and with little elaboration when he gave me something.

He shared his body and his talents in bed without a problem though.

So I might not have a lot of experience with a hookup, but one and one were equaling one in this equation, not the path to there maybe being a two.

"I need to go home. Deanna took care of my animals but I have things to do today," I declared.

This was somewhat a lie. I had one thing to do, which would take me ten minutes.

He put his fork to his plate and sat back in his seat, eyes on me.

"So do you mind, after I help you clean up, taking me back to my car?" I asked.

He studied me pensively as he answered, "You don't have to help me clean up."

"I don't want to be rude."

He didn't respond to that.

He tipped his chin down to my plate and asked, "You get enough to eat?"

"Yes, thank you."

"You ready to go now?" he queried, even though neither of us had cleaned our plates and that so went against the grain for me, it was difficult to give him my answer.

But I did.

"Yes, that probably would be best."

"Right, Eliza," he said on a curt nod. "I'll get this soaking. You get dressed."

"I can help," I offered.

His eyes came to me. "Get dressed."

That hurt. It shouldn't. It was me putting an end to this.

But it did.

I got up and went to gather my clothes. I took them to the bathroom and got dressed.

By the time I came out, the dishes were cleared, soaking in the sink, jelly and ketchup still on the table.

"Be out in a second," Johnny muttered, moving by me to go down the hall.

He disappeared in the bathroom.

I felt the sudden need to cry.

Instead, I went to his wall of windows, leaned a shoulder against one and looked out.

It was then I knew why he didn't give up this place that reminded him of his dad.

The creek was wide and meandered slowly. Some of the trees grew straight out of it, their wide trunks serving as banks. Even that early in the summer, there was so much foliage, the sun struggled to get through but the power of it was such it cast streaks of bright against leaves and trunks and glimmered in the clear water and stone creek bed, making it appear magical.

I could stand out there with coffee every morning for fifteen minutes, half an hour, ages, just letting the peace of it and the gently turning water wheel calm me.

I wouldn't have that opportunity, then or ever.

Johnny called from behind me, "Ready?"

I pushed away and looked to him to see him in another T-shirt and a different pair of jeans, wondering inanely (knowledge I'd never get either), where he got his clothes from, and I nodded.

I went to the island to get my purse, made sure my phone was in it, then followed him out the door.

He didn't lock it behind him.

I moved at his back toward the truck, feeling a melancholy steal over me when he walked right to the passenger side door.

He opened it.

I started to shift around him to get in position to climb in but stopped when he slammed the door and turned to me. Hooking an arm around my waist, he pulled me around, put his hand to my stomach and pushed me against the truck.

My heart started beating hard as I tipped my head back to look up at him.

"You just got your fill or what?" he asked coldly.

"Sorry?" I whispered anxiously.

"Is that your play?" he demanded to know, the ice still in his tone.

"My...play?"

"Cut the crap, Eliza. What the fuck?"

I stared up at him.

"I don't know. I'm not a woman," he went on. "Only know the different reasons a man goes alone to a bar. The reason I hit Home last night was not the way it turned out to be. But I figure, one of the reasons men go alone is one of the reasons women go alone. So is that it? You went to find yourself some cock. Found it, got your fill, now you're done?"

I felt my eyes get wide.

"You don't owe me dick," he continued. "I got it good so I'm not complaining. But assuage my curiosity. What the fuck?"

"I've never...not ever..." I trailed off, not knowing if I was offended, hurt, angry or all three.

"You've never what?" he pushed tersely.

"This," I said, throwing out an arm to my side.

His heavy brows shot together. "You tryin' to tell me you were a virgin?"

"Of course not," I answered fast.

"Then what?" he pressed.

"Hooked up," I told him.

"You've never hooked up," he stated, making it clear he didn't believe me.

"Well, I've hooked up but not *hooked up* hooked up. Like, you know, what we did. Meet a guy, and then, you know, leave with him and then, well...what came next."

He glowered down at me.

"I don't know the protocol," I blurted.

The glower wavered as he asked, "The protocol?"

"I don't know how to act. What to do. I mean, what do you do when a hookup is obviously coming to an end?"

"Jesus," he whispered, now staring at me like he'd never seen a woman in his life.

"I...in there...you were...you've been..." I stuttered then changed courses, "This isn't like a get-to-know-you date. I know how to do those. This, I don't know what I'm doing."

"You want some insight?" he inquired.

By the look on his face, what I knew was I did not.

Even though I didn't, I tentatively nodded, such was the only response I could give due to that look on his face.

I was wrong, that hooded brow with those thick eyebrows *could* be ominous.

"When the man you've outstandingly fucked four times opens up enough to tell you he's havin' a rough time because his dad died three years earlier, *on this day*, this being the reason he went out to get a few drinks the night before, you don't immediately set about scraping him off so you can get on with your day."

"Oh my God," I whispered.

"Yeah," he shot back.

"I didn't know," I pointed out gently (and it must be said, since that look was still on his face, carefully).

"And that makes it okay?" he asked.

"Well, um...no. But, in my defense—"

"You've never hooked up and don't know the protocol," he finished for me.

Right then, that totally sounded weak.

I pressed my lips together.

He studied me a few seconds before he asked, "Honest to Christ, you've never picked a guy up and fucked him before?"

I shook my head slowly.

"You're a prude," he stated.

"Well, not recently, but, um...yes," I confirmed. "My mom wasn't and my sister *really* wasn't, so someone had to be around, you know, to feed the dogs and get in the car and pick them up when they got in situations and, uh...other stuff. Though, that said, it really just comes naturally, until, like I said but you already know since you were there, recently."

"Why am I pissed at you and still wanna laugh my ass off?" he asked curiously.

"Because I'm being an idiot?" I asked back in answer.

"Yeah, that's why," he agreed.

I fell silent.

Johnny didn't break the silence.

I couldn't take the silence so I surged ahead.

"I can cook, like I told you, but, I don't want to brag, I'm actually really good at it. So, to make up for being an idiot, if you want, you can take me to my car and I'll get stuff sorted to make you dinner and you can come over later. Meet the babies. I'll feed you and then maybe do some other, you know, *stuff*, to um...make up for being an idiot when you're having a rough day."

"So what you're saying is you'll feed me, introduce me to your pets and then fuck my brains out."

I got a becoming-familiar trill down my spine, looked to his throat and muttered, "Something like that."

"Iz."

I looked into his eyes.

"I got a tradition for tonight that I do by myself. But tomorrow, I'll be over."

My heart skipped a beat and my lips formed the word, "Really?"

He hooked me at the waist again, pulled me from his truck, opened the door, and after I climbed inside, he tossed his phone at me.

I bobbled it but caught hold of it while he said, "Code, eight, nine, one, two. Program you in. Call yourself. Program me in. I'll call you later."

Then he slammed the door and started around the hood.

I didn't know what he did for a living.

But I did know the code to his phone.

I bent my head to it making the herculean effort not to do it smiling so big, I broke my own face.

He climbed in beside me, roared the truck to life and I looked up from programming myself in his phone in order to catch him put an arm around my seat so he could twist to see where we were going as he reversed in a big arc in the huge space beside his house.

Johnny Gamble then set us on our way to my car.

We were well down the dirt road, I was done with all my programming, when I said softly into the cab, "I'm sorry I messed up so big over eggs."

"Don't worry about it," he replied.

"I lost my mom so I know—"

His fingers curled tight around my knee and he cut me off. "Put it out of your head. Only things I want in your head are you getting inspired about what you're gonna feed me tomorrow night and what you're gonna give me after."

"Do you like chicken enchiladas?"

"Yup."

"Do you like olives?"

"Yup."

"Do you like sour cream?"

"Yup."

"On a scale of a little bit of cheese goes a long way to cheese fanatic, where do you sit?"

"Fanatic."

We had something in common.

"Do you want beer or wine or something else?"

"Beer."

"Well, that's dinner sorted," I muttered.

He burst out laughing, slid his hand up my thigh and kept it resting there.

I let out a relieved breath.

Johnny stopped, checked, then pulled out of the dirt road onto the paved road.

And he took me to my car.

THREE

BE

Izzy

When I got in my front door, my dogs attacked me.

This wasn't surprising. Except for me going to work and out to an occasional social engagement, they usually had me all to themselves.

After I gave them rubdowns, I let them out and went in search of my cats.

They were far less excited to see me.

I still gave them scratches.

I looked in on my birds and then went to the back porch. I took off the cute sandals I'd worn to the bar last night, dropped them on wood and pulled on my Wellington boots that were black and had big pink roses, blue leaves and tiny yellow flowers on them.

I headed to my stable with my dogs at my heels and my phone in hand.

I now had three things I had to do that day. Call Deanna. Change the sheets on my bed. And go back into town if I needed anything to make dinner for Johnny tomorrow night.

My schedule was this free, my time just my own, because I'd lived a disorderly life with a hard-working, hard-playing, hard-loving, hard-knock mother who, through choice and situation, taught me that stability was people, not places and things.

The way my mind worked, it violently rejected that idea. So when I left my mother's home, I sought order and stability in almost every aspect of my life to the point I planned times when I'd allow the former of those two things not to be available.

Along the line, I'd hit on the perfect model in which to order my life when I read an article somewhere about how to use useless time in order to free up useful time, make it non-stressful, but most of all, *free*.

This was, get chores out of the way during time you'd likely just waste sitting in front of the TV, so when the weekend came, it was yours.

To that end, one night a week, I dusted. Another, I vacuumed. Other nights, I cleaned the bathrooms. I did one load of laundry a night until it was done. Every two weeks, I added doing the ironing. And if I had to run errands, I divvied them up and ran them after work in the city before I got home. Except grocery shopping, which I did every Friday evening, hitting Macy's Flower Shop first —which stayed open late on Fridays—so I'd have fresh flowers around the house for the week, before going to the store and then home.

The only thing I left was changing the sheets on my bed every Sunday, so when, in the evening, I'd had a long hot shower or soaked in a long hot bath, given myself a fresh manicure, pedicure and a lengthy facial, I could then eat the extravagant meal I cooked myself while reading, coloring or watching a movie, and after, slide into cool, clean sheets.

For a person who craved order, having this schedule was like nirvana. The only weekend chore was Saturday morning's mucking out of the stalls and then I was free.

Free to be disordered.

Free to putter in my garden and with my flowers in the summer months.

Free to bake breads and make jellies and infuse flavored vodkas and gins.

Free to go back into the city and wander in a mall or down a shopping street, get a lovely lunch or treat myself to a nice dinner.

Free to linger over my Sunday facial, the only thing my mother kept scheduled and ordered for all us girls (if she was off work that was), saying, "If you take care of nothin', my beautiful queens, take care of your skin."

Of course, she made our facials back then out of oatmeal, honey, bee pollen and avocados she carefully scrimped and saved to afford.

But we had girls' night facial nights every Sunday she wasn't at work, and on the rare occasion Mom was in the black and could also afford a bottle of fingernail polish after we'd run out of the one before, we did manis and pedis too.

This meant when Mom died, instead of doing it at age forty-six and looking forty-six, she did it at forty-six, and until the pain and poison aged and withered her, she'd looked thirty.

Tops.

This was why her boyfriend at the time had been thirty-two.

I wondered how old Johnny was.

Perhaps a question he'd answer tomorrow night.

I hit the stables. The dogs began to roam and sniff the space like they'd never been there before when they were there daily. I was sure to secure the gate behind me before I moved toward Serengeti's stall in order to let her have some time in her pasture after I hit GO to contact Deanna.

"Izzy?" she answered.

"Hey, I'm home," I told her.

"Okay, well...how are you?"

How was I?

Johnny's behavior explained by the sad fact it was the anniversary of his father's death, but still explained, and he was coming over for dinner the next night, not to mention, after not being affectionate (at all, unless you counted sitting me on the countertop, which I kind of did) after the last time we'd had sex, he made out with me at the door of my car for a good, long, *happy* while—I was great.

"I'm great," I told her, opening Serengeti's stall and moving in, lifting a hand to pat her jaw while she moved her nose to snuffle my neck and blow at my hair.

"Damn," Deanna muttered.

My hand arrested on Serengeti and I focused on Deanna.

"What?" I asked.

"Damn," she repeated.

"Damn what?" I asked.

"Well, just to say, Johnny Gamble is *Johnny Gamble*."

A specific area in my chest squeezed at the way she imparted that obvious but still confusing information.

"What's that mean?" I asked.

"He's Johnny Gamble of Gamble Garages. Did he tell you that?"

No he didn't tell me that.

And suddenly I was embarrassed about something that I hadn't liked all along.

But it was worse since Deanna knew more about a man I'd slept with than I did.

Serengeti was getting fidgety, so I used my hand on her to lead her out of her stall, and once in the corridor, she trotted out the open bay at the back, directly into her pasture.

I moved to Amaretto as I shared with Deanna, "No, he didn't tell me that. I mean, we talked but we were also doing other things." I let that lie. It did, weighty between us on the phone, before I went on, "I don't know what that means."

Even though it seemed like I did. Something seemed familiar about that.

"You haven't lived here long enough," she murmured while I opened Amaretto's stall and moved in for some quick pats before I let him loose. Louder, Deanna said, "You know the gas station in town?"

Oh yes.

That was where I'd seen it.

"He owns that?"

"That and seven more of them across three counties. None in the city, just in the counties. Some of them are like mini-mart stores. All of them sell gas and do work on cars."

Wow.

That was impressive.

"He inherited it from his dad, who inherited it from his dad," Deanna told me.

No less impressive.

Following Amaretto to the pasture, I stopped at the side of the open bay, leaned on it and watched my horses, reunited, nose each other familiarly.

"I'm not sure why this would earn a 'damn,'" I shared.

"Because Johnny Gamble is also the Johnny part of Johnny and Shandra."

I stilled.

Johnny and Shandra.

The bath salts crystalized in my mind, clear to the point it was almost like they shimmered in the air before me.

"Sorry?" I whispered.

"Total movie, romance movie, but one written by a man seeing as it did not have a happy ending."

Oh God.

"He's gorgeous. She was a knockout," Deanna continued. "When they got together, not sure anyone was surprised. He was into her. She was into him. When I say that, he was *into* her and she was *into* him. We're talking Romeo and Juliet. Lancelot and Guinevere. Scarlett and Rhett."

My stomach sank.

"With the crappy ending to match," she carried on.

"What happened?" I was still whispering.

"No one knows. One day, it was just over. She was gone, he

remained. No one's seen her since. But we'll just say everyone *freaked*. That was not the ending they thought would come of that. Everyone, including me, was sure there'd be mini-Johnnys working in his garage who would grow up to set all the girls' panties on fire, and mini-Shandras he'd treat like princesses who would grow up to be prom queens and break all the boys' hearts. When this didn't happen, I think even Pastor Thomas thought God had dropped the ball."

My stomach still in my boots, my heart started beating really hard.

"Since then, again no big surprise, and it's been years, there's been no one for him. Every female in Matlock steers clear. Not like he goes out trying to bury his sorrow in every soft spot offered up to him. Just that, the first few who went there in hopes they could mend the broken heart, soothe the savaged soul, got seriously burned."

Got seriously burned.

I'd just finished being seriously burned but not by a guy like Johnny. By a guy like my dad.

I hadn't had the experience, but I suspected having it happen from a guy like Johnny would be worse.

By a lot.

"You said it's been years?" I asked.

"Babe—"

"Maybe he's—"

"Baby girl, listen to me," she whispered fiercely. "After what happened with Kent, if you found a guy, I'd be at your back, rooting for you, glad you're back in the saddle, hoping for the best because you deserve it. I'm not sure I know anyone who deserves it better. So this conversation is not easy to have."

"Do you think he—?"

"I think you're sweet as sugar, cute as a button and he's a man. He gets a load of you, he's not gonna think, 'Best be careful I don't mess with this one. She's sweet, cute and sensitive as all get out and my ex burned me so bad I'll never recover, so I should leave well enough alone.' He's not gonna know about that sensitive as all get out part. So he's just gonna go forth to get him some."

"He's coming over for dinner tomorrow night," I blurted.

"Say what?"

"He's coming over for dinner tomorrow night. I'm making him Crock-Pot chicken enchiladas."

"You're pulling out the enchiladas, which means you dig him *and* he's good in bed."

He was very good in bed.

I also dug him.

"They're easy to make, Deanna, they just taste like they aren't."

"They're the kind of thing any normal girl, like you, would make any normal guy she likes so he'll think, 'Man, this woman can cook. I get all that sweetness in my bed and before that I get to eat like this? I better grab hold and do it tight.' But just to say, Izzy, this guy is not a normal guy. This guy is a guy ruined for all other women by a knockout of a redhead with long legs and big boobs who was almost as sweet as your sugar, but I only say that because I know you and I didn't know her except in passing. A redhead who he'll be hung up on forever, even when nature calls and forces him to settle down in order to procreate. The next one will be *numero dos*. Runner up. Second best."

Runner up.

Second best.

I did not have red hair.

I was blonde. Of a sort. It was dark blonde, like an amber-ish blonde-brown.

But I was not a redhead.

I did have relatively large breasts and long legs though.

"They were that in love?" I asked quietly, my voice tight.

"I love Charlie with all my heart and soul, you know it, baby girl, but any time I saw those two together, they were so happy, so close, so damned sweet, they gave me a toothache I wanted for myself. So yeah, they were that in love. The air turned hazy and pink around them, they were that in love," she answered gently, her voice kind.

I looked to my boots.

"Izzy?" she called.

"I like him," I told my boots.

"I only know him in passing too, but I still know he's that guy. The kind you can't help but like. He's solid. Dependable. From good people. His brother took off before Charlie and I got to town and I heard he's a bit of a wild one. But I knew the man, and Johnny Gamble's dad was like that too. Those men are men who fix your car even if you can't afford it and let you make payments that won't bite too deep. They sponsor Little League and girls' softball and Pop Warner teams, and even coach those Pop Warner kids. Heard somewhere there was this ex-con, local screwup who no one trusted, but he gave him a job and the man stayed on the straight and narrow, probably doing it just to give loyalty to a man who took a chance on him."

She paused.

I waited.

And after she took an audible breath, she kept going.

"And he might like you too. It might be that time where he's decided he needs to move on from the love of his life and find someone to settle down with. But I'm not Johnny Gamble's friend. I'm *your* friend. And you deserve to be the love of someone's life. Not the one who followed that first act, and you get it good because you got yourself a good man, but you don't get it how you deserve it."

I looked unseeing to the pasture. "He had bath salts in his bathroom."

"He had what?"

"He's really, you know, *a guy*. And he had this pretty glass jar with blue bath salts in his bathroom."

Deanna said nothing.

"Do you think they're hers?"

"I think this is...when you found out, and you'd find out, it just sucks that it's me who has to tell you...the kind of question you'd be asking yourself a lot if things go far beyond this dinner tomorrow with Johnny Gamble."

"Should I...do you think I should tell him I know about this and talk to him about it?"

"I don't know. Did you guys hook up or did you guys connect?"

I knew what she was asking and answered honestly, "I don't know."

"You'd know, Izzy," she said softly.

I would.

I would know.

He told me about his dad and he gave me the code to his phone and he got mad when he thought I was scraping him off.

But he also talked to me about not wearing panties more than once, and at the time it just seemed sexy and thrilling and flattering, but it could just have meant that he didn't want any obstructions when he was ready to get back to the real reason he was spending time with me.

"Honestly, Izzy," she said carefully, "I was hoping you'd get my texts last night so I could stop you from letting anything happen. I've seen the man. I'm chocolate with a taste for nothing but chocolate but I still can see clear that man is *fine*. And if I knew you to be a girl who could go out and get herself some without her head getting in a tangle about it, I wouldn't have texted back anything except not to worry about your menagerie. But you're not that girl. You might want to try it out but that's an outfit that will never fit. Like me and skinny jeans. They look *tight* on other sisters, but I look like someone squirted me into denim sausage casings."

I wanted to smile.

But with all she was saying to me, there was no chance of a smile.

"So I'll just say, be careful," Deanna continued. "You're a sweet chick but you aren't stupid. You'll see things as they are, especially now that you got all the info that you need. Take care of you and just play it by ear. But most important in that is, take care of you. There's a man out there for you, Izzy, who's gonna be your Charlie. He's gonna treat you like the queen you are and you should accept nothing less. If I'm wrong about Johnny Gamble, I'll be happy to pour barbeque sauce on them and eat my words. Just...be careful."

"I will."

"You want me to come over?" she asked.

Deanna said I was sweet but she was even sweeter. She liked to say I was white chocolate. Take a bite of me, I'm so sweet, I'll make your jaw ache. And she was bitter chocolate, take a bite of her and get a caffeine rush.

But she wasn't.

She was the finest truffle you've ever tasted. The kind you let melt in your mouth, and as it does, you pray it'll never melt away.

"No, I'm good. I just...well, with Kent doing the things Kent did and me not being the kind of girl who does this kind of thing, now this, I don't know. I mean, we had a night together, he made me breakfast. He's coming over for dinner tomorrow. We exchanged numbers. But he didn't ask me to be the mother of his children and pledge the rest of his life to me. I haven't even known him twenty-four hours."

"You're also not a risk-taking girl. It took you five seconds flat to decide to adopt Dempsey but it took you six months to research buying your new car. God willing, you'll have Dempsey far longer than you will that Nissan. I'm hoping you get what I'm saying, so I'll repeat, be careful. Treat Johnny Gamble like your Nissan. Do not adopt him like a member of your menagerie because they're glad to have a home, someone to love who loves them in return. Not sure that's what Johnny Gamble is looking for, but bottom line, that isn't all *you* should be looking for from a man."

My eyes were on the boxer mix I got as a puppy a year ago. Dempsey. He had white feet and a white flash on his chest that slid up to his white snout, the rest of him was red fawn.

He was grown up now, beautiful, all mine, and one of the reasons

Kent had lost his mind eight months ago and broke down the door to my house.

The other reason was that Kent was creepy, stalkerish, pathologically possessive and possibly insane.

I'd adopted Dempsey when I was with Kent, so somehow Kent got it into his mind that when I ended things with him and refused to start them back up he should have Dempsey, so he set about taking him.

Sadly for Kent, not so much for me, Dempsey didn't like Kent breaking down the door, shouting down the house (anytime he did that), but evidently Dempsey was fed up with it that night. To wit, Dempsey mauled the heck out of Kent's arm while my other dog, Swirl, attacked his leg. All this as I was frantically talking to the 911 operator.

After the "attack," Kent then tried to make me have Dempsey and Swirl put down.

Fortunately, the cops saw Kent for what he was, what with the breaking down of my door and all, thought Dempsey and Swirl were the bomb and refused to press the issue.

Unfortunately, Kent got an attorney.

Fortunately, the judge saw it the cops' (and my) way.

Unfortunately, Kent continued to be such a nuisance, I had to sell my little house and move to Matlock.

Fortunately, it meant I had my horses not stabled elsewhere but right outside my back door.

Unfortunately, all this meant I headed into Home last night and met Johnny Gamble who I'd like to think could be someone special in my life but who might just be a really great memory.

"Izzy, are you there?" Deanna called.

"I'm not thinking I'm made out for the hook-up kind of life," I muttered.

"Oh, baby," she crooned. "You sure you don't want me to come out there?"

"No, but maybe next Saturday you and Charlie can come over so

I can make you something a whole lot better than chicken enchiladas to thank you for taking care of my zoo today."

"You don't have to do that."

"Yes I do."

She let that sit for a moment before she replied, "Yeah, you always do."

Deanna and I worked together. Deanna and I met at the office. Deanna and I moved up the ranks together. Deanna and I were both directors of different departments now.

I'd been at the hospital with her after her mother had her stroke. She'd come to the hospital with me repeatedly when mine was dying of cancer.

I'd also been there when Deanna met Charlie. I had stood at her side when she married him.

She'd been there when I met Kent. And she'd stood at my side while we stood about five feet behind Charlie's back when Charlie stood in my doorway with a baseball bat and told Kent if he showed at my place *one more time* he'd cave his head in with that bat.

Deanna was very black, very round, very beautiful, and even though I adored the younger one I got by blood, Deanna was also the big sister I'd always wanted to have.

Needless to say, with my life, and Deanna's, me wanting to have it together so bad it was an obsession, her having it together naturally, there were a lot of thank-you dinners from me to her in our past and there probably would be a lot more in our future.

"See you tomorrow at work and we'll be there Saturday for one of Izzy's delicacies," she told me.

"Great, doll. See you tomorrow."

"That you will, later, babe."

"Later, Deanna."

We hung up but I didn't move, watching my horses roam their space, my dogs doing it with them, Dempsey with Swirl, my old boy, the senior member of my zoo, my Bernese mountain dog mix I'd rescued about a year after I graduated from college.

I'd come to Matlock thinking, after losing Mom, after my sister married a loser, after what happened with Kent, that I'd hit this little farmhouse on three acres and hit heaven.

Johnny and Shandra.

Well, there it was. Johnny was probably removed not only because he was having a rough day, which was the anniversary of his dad's death, but because he was remote so as not to let anyone think they were getting in there because my sense was he was that kind of guy. He might have burned a few women after Shandra, but he'd know that and in future have a mind to it. I could only guess that was true, but with his gentlemanly manner, I figured it'd be a good guess.

So it was what it was. I'd had my first hookup, which wasn't going to be a one-night stand. That soothed the inherent good girl in me but ravaged the dreamer I wouldn't ever let myself be.

I stared at my horses and dogs.

This was my dream.

This was mine.

This was my heaven.

It was ordered and it was pretty and it was filled with love. It reminded me of what I had with Mom and my sister, but without all the bad parts mixed in.

Would it be better with Johnny or a Johnny-type person in the mix?

Maybe.

But this was what I had now.

And it was beautiful.

So I'd take it.

And do what my mother always told me to do.

Just be happy.

I'D ALREADY EXFOLIATED, had just ripped the charcoal strip off my nose and was about to slather the facial sheets on my skin when my phone rang.

I looked down to my bathroom counter and saw it said, JOHNNY CALLING.

I took the call and put the phone to my ear.

"Hey."

"No bullshit with you, rings twice and I get a 'hey,'" was his reply.

I stared at the curlicue, ivory wire bathroom accessories on my countertop. "Sorry?"

"Nothin', Iz," he said, sounding amused. "Have a good day?"

I wandered into my bedroom straight to my iron bed with its acres-of-material white coverlet, large, gorgeous sage-green crocheted throw draped along the bottom, lacy white euros at the top sprinkled with dusky flower-printed toss pillows, and climbed in while answering.

"Did a recon of the kitchen because you're getting dessert tomorrow night too. This necessitated a trip to the store in town. Came back, rode Serengeti. Got my tomato and strawberry pots sorted and planted some herbs. Looked at chicken coops. They're not that expensive, but the ones that aren't so expensive only allow two chickens or four bantams, so I think I need to do more research since I want at least six. Maybe eight. And I want standards. Now I've got the lasagna in the oven and I'm in the middle of my regular Sunday night facial. So all in all, it was really good."

Johnny said nothing.

"So, well...I hesitate to ask," I filled the silence, "but how was the rest of yours?"

"Strawberry pots?"

"They're biggish pots with lots of little openings that strawberries grow out of," I explained and when he made no reply, I shared idioti-cally, "Mine are dark blue ceramic. I have five of them."

His voice sounded funny, tight, like he was choking when he asked, "Chicken coop?"

"We had chickens once growing up. Mom didn't eat them but my sister and I did, and fresh eggs are hard to beat. Plus, chickens have funny personalities. They have brains the size of a pea, but they still have personalities."

Johnny again was silent.

He was this for so long, I called, "Johnny?"

"Sounds like you had a full day," he noted.

"I guess so."

"You guess so?"

"Well, I mean, it was just a day."

"Strawberry pots. Chicken coops. Horseback rides. Grocery stores. And lasagna," he oddly ran it down.

"And my tomatoes, and I'm half into my facial. And then, of course, there was breakfast and, uh...other things with you."

He let out a sharp bark of laughter that sounded so nice it tingled through my ear down my neck and parts south.

"What's funny?" I asked softly.

"Watched you walk from that sleek, burgundy Murano without a speck of dust on it in those sweet jeans with that cute top and all that hair, and I would not have pegged you as a woman who wanted chickens and planted herbs."

"It was car wash day yesterday," I informed him. "My Murano is usually coated in dust and specked with mud."

"I'll believe it when I see it."

"Well, that would be about now since it's been sitting at the front of my house all day and it's dusty around here. I don't have a garage."

"Probably should consider that before a chicken coop, babe," he advised.

"Perhaps," I mumbled.

He chuckled.

That tingled down my neck too.

Since he was chuckling, I didn't want to ask. But I'd mucked things up earlier that day, so I had to ask.

"You okay?"

"Don't do my thing until later. Movin' out in about an hour."

"Okay," I replied and didn't pry about what his "thing" was.

"What time you want me over there tomorrow?"

I stared at my beautifully crocheted throw.

I got off at five but usually hung around to make sure my staff met their goals for the day and were off themselves. The commute was an hour, if traffic cooperated. The chicken cooked all day and it was only a matter of separating it, tossing in more stuff, and letting it cook a little longer, but there was that little longer.

He lived close to town and had a garage in that town (not that he'd shared that last with me).

And he was a small-town guy with a blue-collar job. Or at least he owned garages that were blue collar, if perhaps owning them made him not so much that.

Maybe he wanted dinner on the table at five thirty, which was an impossibility.

"Six thirty?"

"It's you gotta be ready for me, Iz, so don't know why that's coming at me as a question. That give you enough time?"

"I work in the city."

"Again, that give you enough time?"

"It'll probably be more like seven."

"How 'bout you call me when you're ready. It's earlier, I'll come earlier. It's later, I'll come later."

"That sounds like a plan."

"Text me your address and I'll bring the condoms. You don't have to worry about that shit."

I blinked at my beautifully crocheted throw.

Was he coming for dinner?

Or for sex?

"Okay?" he prompted.

"I'll text you my address," I replied.

"Great, babe. Now I'll let you go so you can finish your facial, eat your lasagna and read A through F of the encyclopedia."

"Sorry?"

"Izzy, you do more in one day than a lot of people do in a year."

"Hmm..." I hummed because I never thought of it, but that was probably true.

Mom taught me that. Even when we lived in apartments, she had herb gardens in the kitchen window, tomato pots on the balcony, front or back stoop, as many animals as the landlord would allow (and some they wouldn't), and in the rare occasion we had extra money, she cooked up a vegan storm doing things with tofu, beans and lentils that made my mouth water at the memory.

Our house was never exactly tidy but whenever she scored skeins of yarn, she also knitted and crocheted. She'd hoard bits and pieces everywhere she could find them to get the stuff to make all her own cards and saved up to make huge scrapbooks for any occasion (all of which I had in my bookshelf in my office). She meditated, journaled, read anything she could get her hands on, sometimes wrote poetry or lyrics to songs she'd read or sing to us. She'd often spend hours doodling or turn the music loud and make us get up and dance with her, or sometimes she'd just take us outside, anywhere outside, and lay us down on an old blanket to look up at the stars.

I always thought it was because we couldn't afford a TV.

But I was beginning to wonder, even if we could, if she'd have had one.

"You camp?" Johnny asked into my thoughts.

"Is that have I or would I?" I asked back.

"The last," he clarified.

"Well, just to say, it's yes to both."

"Take you camping."

My heart leapt.

"You free next weekend?' he asked.

My heart leapt higher.

Then my brain kicked in.

"I'm having friends over for dinner Saturday night."

"That's cool. Maybe another time."

"I could see if they'd do Friday," I offered.

"You're up for that, Iz, we'll head out Saturday morning."

We'd head out Saturday morning.

And I was sure he'd bring condoms.

But if you camped, you didn't do it just for an alternate place to have sex.

You did it to spend time with nature.

And whoever you were with.

"I'll change dinner," I told him.

"Great, babe. Now I'm gonna let you go."

"Okay. I hope, well…whatever you're doing, I hope it brings you some peace."

He didn't say anything for long moments before he said, "It never does, but that's still sweet, Izzy."

"Sorry, Johnny," I whispered, then knowing he wanted to let me go, I finished, "Take care and see you tomorrow."

"See you tomorrow, Iz. Later."

"'Bye."

We hung up and I stared at my beautifully crocheted throw.

We were having dinner tomorrow and then spending the weekend camping.

I wondered if he'd let me bring Dempsey and Swirl.

I'd still have to ask Deanna and Charlie to look after the rest.

Another thank-you dinner.

That wouldn't be hard.

And Johnny wanted to take me camping.

He'd probably camped with Shandra.

However, next weekend he'd be camping with me.

Maybe I was an idiot.

But I didn't care.

He hadn't asked me to mother his children and he hadn't made any promises of any sort, except that he'd be there tomorrow and we'd be camping next weekend.

I could live in the moment.

I had the info I needed.

I could enjoy Johnny.

And I could let him enjoy me.

I was Eliza "Izzy" Forrester, daughter to Daphne, sister to Adeline, and if my mother and sister taught me nothing (and they didn't, they taught me a lot, good and bad, but mostly good), they taught me to enjoy everything I could.

So I needed to stop obsessing, ordering, *thinking*.

I needed to just let things...

Be.

FOUR

UNICORN

Izzy

"So can you do Friday instead of Saturday?"

I was in Deanna's office and had just told her about camping with Johnny.

And after I finished talking, I studied her face. She was a couple of years older than me, but at times she felt decades wiser than me, and I was trying to get a lock on what she thought of this latest development.

"That boy isn't playing any games," she replied rather than answering my question.

"Sorry?" I asked.

"Charlie said the same thing yesterday when I told him what was going down. Said if this guy was playing you, he'd not be coming to dinner tonight. He'd be calling you two days from now at around nine thirty and setting up a booty call. Now he's called you and set up a whole weekend together on top of dinner. So yeah...this boy isn't playing any games."

"I'm not sure I understand," I told her.

"That's 'cause you had a long dry spell before Kent, and also 'cause Kent was a successfully disguised psycho, so when you met him neither of us saw he was a successfully disguised psycho and we just thought he was into you. But, you'll remember, we met Charlie at that bar and I gave him my number, and he made me wait three days before he called. When he did, I didn't pick up. I waited two days to call him back, and when he answered the first thing I said was, if he pulled that crap again we wouldn't even get to our first date. He didn't pull that crap again. He *was* a player and he admitted it to me on our first date. But he saw what he wanted in me and the games ended. This Johnny, he's not playing games right off the bat."

I wanted that to feel good.

Instead, I said, "I don't think it matters."

"Uh...what?" she asked.

"He wants me for sex."

She stared at me.

"And I'm good with that," I told her.

She kept staring at me but she did it this time looking freaked.

"I mean, don't get me wrong," I continued. "He likes me. But I've been thinking on things and he's making it clear this might be about spending time together, but it's mostly about having sex. He's not giving me the wrong impression. He told me not to worry about tonight, he'd bring the condoms. He didn't ask if he could bring a bottle of wine and he didn't ask if maybe I might want to rent a movie to watch with him after dinner. He assured me he'd bring the condoms. So I know the lay of the land and I'm good with that."

Her eyes narrowed and she asked, "You sure?"

I nodded. "Totally."

She stared at me again and didn't hide she didn't believe me, and she did this by beginning to look alarmed.

"I'm not getting a good feeling about this," she shared.

"I am," I replied. "Because, listen, like I said, I've been thinking on things and after Kent, this is perfect. I mean, I get to feel pretty and funny and spend time with someone that doesn't have feathers or fur or a mane or isn't my best friend in all the world. I also get to have unbelievably good sex. When it's time, he'll move on and maybe we can still be friends and then maybe he'll give me discounts on oil changes or something."

"Did Johnny Gamble perform an invasion of the body snatchers through orgasms this weekend?" she asked.

I grinned at her. "No."

"This isn't the Izzy Forrester I know."

"It's the Izzy Forrester my mom raised and with what went down with Kent"—and with my dad but Deanna knew all about that so I didn't have to remind her of it, just myself, so I wouldn't find another Kent, or another Dad—"this could be the best thing that could happen to me."

When it looked like she was going to say something, I hurried on and did it quietly.

"I'll find the guy for me and it won't be a lunatic like Kent and it won't be a loser like Addie's husband. It also won't be some guy who settles for me, might fall in love with me the way he can, even if most of his heart belongs to someone else. But I'm thirty-one years old, Deanna. Since I can remember, I've done everything right. I've researched everything, not including Kent, to the point where I'd never put any foot wrong, never make a mistake, never mess up so bad all I worked so hard to get was lost. It's time now to have a little fun. It's time now to do something just because it feels good. I know where I stand with Johnny. But I like him and he likes me. I like having sex with him and he wants to have sex with me. So I know where I stand and I'm good with that."

"Okay then, babe." She lifted two coral-tipped fingers to her eyes then turned them to me and stated, "But I'll be watching."

I grinned again. "I'd expect nothing less. So are you good with changing to Friday?"

"Totally. And looking after your menagerie while you're camping. *And* we're doing lunch this week. I wanna know all about this unbelievably good sex."

I was still grinning when I replied, "You're on." I started to the door, saying, "Gotta get back to work. Lunch tomorrow?"

"I'm in."

I gave her a wave, left her office and I went back to work.

I'D MESSED THINGS UP.

As I drove up to my house that evening, seeing Johnny lounged in the wicker rocking chair on my front porch, one knee bent, one leg stretched out, two six packs of bottled beer on the deck beside him, his truck parked off to the left so I had a clear view of him, all my calm of understanding where I stood with Johnny Gamble flew out the window and the nerves settled in.

I was late.

And I'd made him wait.

Which was rude.

I kept my eyes on him in a state where I couldn't let it filter through how good Johnny looked coming out of my wicker rocking chair on my little porch with its pillow festooned porch swing, standing, curlicue, iron candleholders with the crystals floating down, the big and small pots filled with flowers, the amazing fretwork at the corners of the roof supports and in the screen door (it might be crazy, but that fretwork was one of the primary reasons I bought the house).

I had to park, shut down the engine, grab my purse then practically merge with the cushion of the passenger seat while I felt under it for my phone.

I'd called him when I was twenty minutes away, telling him he could show in forty-five and I did this sharing that I was almost home but had to stop for beer.

He told me he'd bring the beer and see me at my place in forty-five minutes.

And then all hell broke loose, part of that hell meaning my phone slipped under my seat so I couldn't call him and share about said hell, and that I'd be late so he shouldn't be there in forty-five minutes.

I found my phone, nabbed it, straightened, got out of the car, slammed the door and expertly motored through the gravel of my wide front drive on my spike-heeled pumps toward him now standing and leaning against one of my fretwork festooned posts, staring down at me.

I did this talking.

"I'm sorry. I'm so, so sorry. After I phoned, some idiot who looked like he was texting swerved into my lane and I had to swerve to avoid him, and my phone flew across the car, settling under the seat. This means I couldn't get to it to call and tell you that they set up construction sometime today out on 32 and traffic was backed up forever. Then I had to take a detour that I thought might take me five minutes out of my way but took me *twenty* minutes out of the way, and now I'm late and you've been waiting for me."

I could hear the dogs barking in the house and I'd made it to the foot of the three steps that led up to it but stopped when I stopped talking and also when I noticed Johnny giving me a top to toe.

"Working girl," he murmured so low, I almost didn't hear him.

"What?"

His gaze went from my shoes back to my eyes.

"You a lawyer?" he asked.

I stared up at him.

I'd told him where I worked over margaritas at Home.

"I work at Milo-Corp Data Security and Management. I thought I told you that at Home."

"You did. Are you a lawyer for them?"

"No, I'm Director of the Data Management Department."

His lips hitched. "That explains it."

I was wearing tailored black trousers, which were simple and classic. At the waistband though, I had a trim, shiny gold belt that I found at a vintage clothing store that cost close to nothing but looked like a million bucks.

I was also wearing a black blouse with a slit that fell sideways at the neck but tied in a big bow at the side collar, which even I had to agree was fabulous because it was, but also because I got it on sale (the only way I purchased clothes) but still paid a mint for it.

I further had on a pair of simple, stylish black pumps with a suede upper and a sleek, glossy, slim, tall heel. Shoes that cost a fortune (also on sale) but I took care of them better than many women would take care of their children.

In my life I had to have three wardrobes: casual every day, work around the house and stables, and business attire. I spent as little as possible on all of them even if I worked hard finding pieces that would last and make me feel cute. Or, when it came to work, last, be stylish, and make me look professional and serious even though I *was* cute as well as young for someone in my position.

I took one step up, murmuring, "I'm sorry I'm late."

"Iz, your place is only half a notch down from the mill on the scale of sheer awesomeness, so it was no hardship sittin' here soakin' all this in," he told me. "Except I felt bad for your dogs seeing as they've been going crazy I 'spect since my truck pulled up."

I loved it that he thought the same about my house as I did (though his mill was fabulous I'd disagree that my place was half a notch down, they occupied the same notch with maybe my acres being slightly higher).

But on that reminder, I said a swear word under my breath and hurried to the door.

I opened the screen, used my key then opened the door.

Dempsey and Swirl bounded out it a flurry of furry glee that Mom was home.

I did not worry about Johnny being there. Both my dogs had no issues with strangers unless I had an issue with a stranger, and usually they just acted protective and alert until I gave them the vibe they could be friendly.

This, obviously, didn't include Kent who they hated, but they were allowed to do that for obvious reasons.

That said, neither of them had been overtly friendly with him even before he showed his psycho side (this included Dempsey when he was still a puppy, but definitely when he became a full-grown dog), but I'd already made a mental note to assess my dogs' reaction to anyone in order to make better choices about who I allowed to spend time with me...and them.

Thus they shuffled around me, panting, licking and wagging with their violently moving tails, and seeing company they shuffled around Johnny, adding sniffing to their panting, licking and wagging.

Apparently, Johnny got the stamp of approval.

"Friendly," Johnny muttered, bending to them to grab as many head rubs and ear scratches as their excitement would allow.

"The mountain dog is Swirl, the boxer, Dempsey."

"Hey, boys," he rumbled, low and rough and sweet.

He didn't have pets.

But he liked dogs.

That tingle again slid down my spine.

It became clear to Johnny at the same time it did to me that the dogs were ignoring the call of nature in order to get pets from a stranger back and forth with saying hi to Mom, loathe to go off and take care of business when all this goodness was on the porch.

So before I got to it, Johnny lifted an arm, snapped his fingers, pointed down the steps and commanded, "Go."

They looked up at him, ears perked then they went dashing down the stairs, and it was noses to the ground as they looked for the perfect spots to take care of business.

"Let's get inside," I said, bending to grab the handle of one of the six packs.

"Babe, do not even think about it."

Half bent at the waist, I twisted to look at him.

"Sorry?"

That got me a full, white smile before he said, "Leave them. I'll get 'em. Just get your ass inside."

I nodded, straightened and went inside.

My cool, dim foyer closed around me as Johnny entered behind me and I threw my keys and purse on the table at the side.

I also spied Kelly, my fat, fluffy ginger cat, sauntering across the foyer.

She stopped, took me in, dismissed me entirely, took in Johnny, then walked to him, slid the side of her body across the leg of his jeans, then showed him her backside.

"That's Kelly. She's a flirt. Jill and Sabrina are around here somewhere. Sabrina's the sleek gray. Jill's the scraggly, long-haired gray and black tiger with a white chest. She's tiny and she's shy. You probably won't meet her."

Unless he came again. Jill got bolder the more a scent filtered into her sphere.

I felt his regard, so I looked from Kelly, who was not too pleased he was ignoring her invitation to scratch her booty, then again she didn't understand the concept of him carrying two six packs, to him to see him staring at me.

"You named your cats after Charlie's Angels?" he asked.

"They don't fight crime. They mostly just shed, eat, nap and make me feel inferior. But they're still beautiful."

The white flashed through his beard again as he slowly shook his head.

I turned toward the hall, ordering, "Follow me. We'll get those beers in the fridge and I'll get the Crock-Pot sorted. Then I'm sorry, but I have to change, go out and get the horses in. But after I do that, I'll get down to the guacamole so we'll have something to snack on while we wait for dinner to finish up."

"I can get your horses in."

I was at the kitchen counter, opening a drawer to get some forks out, but I stopped to look at him where he was, closing the fridge door on his beer.

"That's sweet, Johnny, and Amaretto is a love, but he's also protective of Serengeti, who's a diva. And she sometimes doesn't feel like behaving. So if she doesn't, he'll stick with her. That means it can be a pain to get them in."

"Grew up with horses, Izzy. We had them with Dad. Granddad had them too. Dad's last died six weeks after he did, a week before I sold Dad's place, or she'd have come to the mill with me. I'll be able to handle it, and if I can't, I'll just come back and get you."

Being good with keeping it just as having some company and sex with Johnny Gamble seemed easy when I was talking to Deanna.

It was a lot harder when I was actually with Johnny. Especially when I just kept learning more and more how wonderful he was.

I mean, he wouldn't even let me carry in a six pack of beer.

"That'd be great. And that'd mean we can get to the guac faster. My chicken enchiladas are relatively famous in my circle. My guac is revered."

He gave me his uneven grin and muttered, "Lookin' forward to that." His attention went to the back door, came again to me, and he said, "I'll be back."

I watched him disappear before I went to the Crock-Pot and took the top off.

But I didn't immediately dig in to separate the meat.

I looked out the window and watched Johnny saunter in his faded jeans, which fit somewhat loose just hinting at all the goodness they covered, and dusty boots, but he'd put on a denim shirt, which was a nice touch. It said he was coming over to a woman's house for dinner and he made the kind of effort the kind of man Johnny Gamble was would make, but he wasn't going to show in a T-shirt.

I also watched when he stopped to welcome both dogs with firm rubdowns when they found him, and I kept watching as he carried on his way, the dogs dancing beside him, toward the stables.

I did this thinking it took me from probably fifteen to thirty minutes to get the horses inside and settled in for the night, depending on how cooperative Serengeti felt like being.

So I did this thinking that if there was a Johnny-type figure in my life, it would be really nice.

I loved my horses and never thought a second about the time it took to take care of them.

But having someone help would be lovely.

I'd never lived with Kent. Perhaps subconsciously knowing something wasn't right about him, and Charlie stating about two months into the relationship, "Sorry, Iz, there's just something off about that guy," made me cautious. But even though we'd been together for over a year, we never took it to that place.

I'd never taken it to that place with any guy, not Kent, not the two longish-term boyfriends I'd had before him.

Maybe I'd find someone like Johnny who knew how to deal with horses.

Maybe I'd find someone who wouldn't mind throwing in a load of laundry too.

And maybe I'd find someone who also wouldn't mind throwing it in the dryer and folding it after.

Or someone who didn't mind vacuuming the floors.

Whatever it was, even before I struck out on my own, with Mom working all the time and my sister a crazy person, from before the time I really should have been taking it on, I took on the bulk of the responsibilities of running a house with people and animals in it.

It would be pretty amazing to have someone help shoulder the chores.

Johnny and the dogs had disappeared into the stables when I realized ruminating on this wasn't getting the chicken separated.

Fortunately, it fell apart easily like it always did after cooking all day.

And fortunately, I had the corn tortillas already cut, the real English cheddar already grated and the olives already drained so I could toss them in, stir them up, sprinkle more cheese and olives on top and then put the lid back on for it to finish its magic.

I got the black beans out, opened them up and poured them in a pot on the stove, ready to heat up before I dashed out of the kitchen and up the stairs to change clothes so I didn't have to do that when Johnny was around.

He could chat with me while I made guacamole. But after he'd waited for me to arrive, I didn't want to make him hang alone while I changed clothes.

I'd mentally planned my outfit so it took no time at all to get rid of the trousers, blouse and pumps and put on a pair of crop boyfriend jeans with wide cuffs and the green printed blouse with its cute, ruffle, barely-there sleeves.

I took off my gold bangles, my slim watch, left in my gold studs, and went barefoot down the stairs, lifting my hair in order to fashion a band around it in a big messy topknot.

I hit the kitchen and looked out the window, not seeing Johnny. I considered going out to check on him but instead decided to give him time and I grabbed the avocados.

I started on the dip, my eyes straying to the window often, so I saw it when, not five minutes later, Johnny and my dogs ambled out of the stables.

It was then I realized I liked the way he walked. There was a confident, masculine grace to it. He just was who he was. He looked the way he looked. He moved the way he moved. The fact that all of that was amazing didn't factor to him.

It was just...

Him.

I'd scooped out the avocados and thrown in some salt and was mincing the onion along with the cilantro and chilies when Johnny and the dogs walked in.

"Serengeti felt like being a diva," I guessed, looking over my shoulder at him and in the process of mincing, so I just swayed my legs against their bodies to say hi to my dogs when they came to say hi to me.

"Your dogs like strangers. Your palomino, not so much," he answered.

"No, she does, when she feels like doing it. She just felt like being a diva tonight."

He gave me an amused look and headed to the fridge. "You want a beer?"

"I don't drink beer. But there's an open bottle of white in there. If you could pour me some of that. Wineglasses are over there." I jerked my head to the opposite wall.

"Gotcha," he muttered.

"This won't take long, and then we'll sit out on the back porch and munch while the enchiladas finish up."

"You gonna make me eat vegetables?" he asked.

I smiled at him. "You're a big boy, not sure I can make you do anything, but I am making a big salad. If you don't want any of it, I won't be offended."

"We'll test it and see if my body will accept something healthy fed to it."

I laughed softly, decided against chiding him because I knew intimately that somehow he took care of that body or it wouldn't be the body it was, and went back to my guac.

I was squirting the lime juice in in preparation for mixing when Johnny remarked from behind me, "Sweet kitchen."

I looked over my shoulder at him to see him leaning in a hand on my island, a beer bottle in his other hand, his attention to me.

"Luckily it mostly came this way. I put the farm sink in, got a deal on the marble countertops because some lady ordered them and then decided she didn't want them. Other than that, I just painted, put some new handles on and *voilà*."

"It's sweet. It's cute. It's you. But I feel my balls shrinking just standing here."

My body jolted and I burst out laughing, doing it looking at the cream painted cupboards, the green glass handles and knobs, knowing below the sink was a fabric curtain of roses and leaves against a cream background. There was a narrow flowery print over the window that was above the sink. There were shelves around the sink with the green milk glass pieces I'd inherited from Mom (who inherited them from her mom) with others I'd been picking up for years, intermingled with pink. Even my KitchenAid mixer was mint green. All the rest was cream or elaborate wire. And definitely every inch of it was feminine.

"I'll be done in a second and we'll get you out of the danger zone and on the back porch."

"Babe, your back porch looks more comfortable than my living room. There are more pillows on that loveseat out there than on my bed. You even got a lamp out there."

"I like to be comfy," I told the guacamole.

"I'd hazard a guess you succeeded in fulfilling this desire."

I again laughed softly then moved to the cupboard to pull down my chips and salsa bowl.

"You can go on out," I told him. "I'll dish this up and pour out the chips, and I'll be out in two seconds."

"Got your wine," he replied.

"Thanks," I said.

I dealt with the dip and chips then, to mess with him, I searched for the pink paper napkins I'd found at an antique shop that had a frilly corner, like a doily. I'd been saving them up for a special occasion, a party or something, but decided now was the perfect time to use them.

I located them and took a bunch out with the bowl.

Johnny was in my loveseat, both dogs roaming around the screened-in porch, deciding where to settle as I settled myself beside him, throwing down the napkins and placing the white chip and salsa bowl on the table in front of us.

"Jesus," he muttered, eyes to the napkins.

I giggled.

Dempsey came up and stared hopefully at the chips.

"No, baby," I murmured.

He gave me an adorable look then Swirl came up and stared hopefully at the chips.

"No to you too, handsome," I told him.

He gave a whine then rounded the table to slide with a groan to his belly by my feet.

Dempsey picked Johnny, partly because with Swirl where he was there was no more room on my side. But mostly because Swirl was older, he'd learned a long time ago my no categorically meant no. Johnny was an unknown entity, and he might be a pushover with the chips.

"They get treats later, not chips now," I told Johnny.

"Right," Johnny replied, leaning forward to load a chip with guac and doing it looking at Dempsey, muttering, "Sorry, buddy."

Dempsey looked sad.

Johnny sat back and I leaned forward to do the same thing he did.

It was then he touched me for the first time that night.

He did this by putting a warm hand on the small of my back, the heat of it melting into my flesh, traveling up my spine and down over my bottom.

"Christ, Iz, this is the best guac I've ever had," he stated.

I was glad.

I was also glad for the reminder of who we were with his touch at my back.

I hadn't thought about it, but he hadn't given me a kiss when we met on my steps. He hadn't touched me or even come close to me. He also hadn't gotten close in my kitchen. Even as small as it was, he stood removed at the island. Indeed, there were no touches, pecks on the cheek, brushes of lips on my neck.

There was no intimate or even familiar affection at all.

We were going to have food now. Sex later.

He might not even spend the night.

That was where we were. Who we were. What was happening here.

And Johnny getting the horses in and teasing me in my kitchen didn't change any of that.

I sat back to eat my chip and lost his hand as he immediately leaned forward again and got more.

After I swallowed, I said, "Glad you like it."

"Need this recipe," he told me.

"Sorry. I'm only giving it to my daughters, but only after they vow to give it to no one but their daughters."

Johnny turned his head to the side and gave me a look from sparkling eyes.

Then he went back to the guac.

I leaned forward and grabbed my wine.

When he finally nabbed his beer and sat back, I shifted into the corner, crooking a leg to the seat, which meant my knee was pressed to his thigh, something he didn't react to at all, but that was where we were.

And now it was time to get some things out of the way.

"Can I talk to you about something that might be awkward?"

Dempsey was sitting by him, leaning against his side of the seat, and Johnny's attention went from scratching Dempsey's head to me.

He looked guarded but said, "Sure."

I held my wineglass in front of me and carried forth the decision I'd made after talking to Deanna that day.

"I moved here not long ago. I did because I have some friends who live here and love it. They've been here about five years. They're a couple, Deanna and Charlie. Deanna's actually my best friend. She's the one who came out to look after my animals."

"Okay," he said when I stopped talking.

"Well, I told her I was with you and she told me you own Gamble Garages."

He seemed to relax and leaned forward to grab another chip and load it with dip, saying, "I do."

"She said there are a lot of them," I told him.

He popped the chip in his mouth, chewed it, and sat back to look at me.

He swallowed and replied, "Depends on what you consider a lot. We got eight shops. Circle K has over three thousand."

His response wasn't defensive, just informative.

It was still odd.

"No, what I mean is, that's impressive."

"Granddad had a wife and three kids to feed, a boy and two girls," Johnny shared. "Then, it was just the garage, the one here, in Matlock. He saw the writing on the wall and knew he'd never make it, have something to give to his son, if he didn't grow. You sell more gas, you can buy it cheaper. You change enough filters, you buy in bulk, you get better prices on supplies. You diversify, adding Big Grabs of chips and fridges filled with pop, you got additional sources of revenue. He opened shops two and three. Dad took it up to seven and I added the eighth."

I nodded.

"But I'm a mechanic," he announced. "I got a GM who deals with all that shit because I can't be bothered with it. It bores me sick. I look over his reports. I meet with him once a week so I can okay his decisions. And I'm the only one who can sign checks because I'm not a moron. The rest of the time, I repair transmissions and replace brakes."

"I...are you upset?" I asked, because I couldn't tell with the utter emotionless and matter of fact way he was imparting this information if he was or wasn't.

"I'm not upset. I'm wondering why you'd think talking about my garages is awkward."

"That's not the awkward part," I shared carefully.

"Then how 'bout we get to that part," he prompted.

I decided it best to do it quickly and get it over with.

"My friend also told me about Shandra," I said quietly.

I also watched him closely.

But nothing changed in the utter emotionlessness of his face, except perhaps the skin around his mouth tightened a bit, but I couldn't really tell considering it was covered in beard.

"Matlock, pretty much anyone in it who was around when I was with Shandra, decided what that was when not a one of them, but Shandra, knew dick. So don't listen to that shit."

"I just wanted to say that if she's the reason that—"

"I lost my dad three years to the day before I met you, Eliza. That's where I was at yesterday. Don't listen to that shit."

"Okay," I said hesitantly. "But can I just say that...well, I thought you should know. You should know that someone told me. You should know I know. I didn't want to...I mean, you don't live in a bubble and you know I don't either, so I can imagine you'd guess I'd talk to my girlfriends about meeting you. But I also think it's uncool to talk about you, learn things about you, know things about you that you haven't shared without letting you know I know."

He said nothing to that.

So I finished, "So that's it. That's the awkward." I flipped out a hand in a way that was just as uncomfortable as I felt and concluded, "That's done."

"I loved her," he stated.

It was me who said nothing to that.

"Thought I'd make babies with her and spend the rest of my life with her. That didn't happen. We've been over for a while. She's nowhere near Matlock and she's not coming back. Did that fuck with my head? Yes. A man decides to spend the rest of his life with a woman, make a family with her and it ends, that's gonna happen. But it happened. She happened. And now it's done."

"I'm sorry that happened," I said gently.

"You weren't a virgin before I had you so I reckon I'm not the only one sitting here with history like that."

"I've never been in love," I shared quietly.

"Avoid it," he advised resolutely. "It sucks."

And again...

There we were.

"I hate you feel that way," I told him, still quiet. "My dad was a hard act to follow. Not the same way I'm guessing, but still, he was.

Mom never recovered. She tried though, a lot, and she did it hard. So even though I've never felt anything like that, I get it in little ways, what you're saying, watching her search for something that wasn't to be had. Because sometimes I wished she'd avoid it so she could find another way to be happy."

"You've changed," he declared.

I felt my head give a slight twitch in surprise to his comment.

But I suspected he said it in order to change the subject.

"Yes, I ran up when you were in the stables and got out of my work stuff," I confirmed.

"No," he said firmly. "Yesterday, you were nervous and unsure of yourself, unless I had you in bed. Sweet, when you weren't letting your nerves run away with you, which made you do stupid shit, but shy as fuck. Now, you're not."

"I'm in my space now," I explained.

"It's not that," he returned.

"I've also already been a total idiot in a pretty bad way, so I broke the seal on that so you won't be as surprised, or angry, if I do it again. Which I might, just saying. I can be confident when I'm serving up my famous guacamole because as you can tell," I waved my wineglass at the bowl, "it's confidence worthy. The rest of the evening, fair warning, anything could happen."

He said nothing again.

"And camping, which I assume will be Saturday to Sunday, just be aware, with that much time, I could cause a mini-Johnny-Izzy Armageddon."

His mouth twitched.

"But you're good through the enchiladas because those also rock," I assured.

"You got plans Wednesday?" he asked.

My heart jumped. "No."

"My turn to dazzle you with my cooking."

A slow smile spread on my face. "You're on."

He leaned toward the guac again and did it speaking. "Just to say, babe." He loaded up a chip, sat back and looked me right in the eyes. "It's appreciated, you being honest with me. You're right. It'd be totally uncool you knew shit about me you didn't share. So thanks for that."

He then popped the chip in his mouth.

"You're welcome, Johnny."

He jerked his head to the bowl. "Am I gonna eat that all by myself?"

I grinned at him and shook my head, leaned toward the bowl and took my own chip, saying, "Nope."

I sat back and shoved it in my mouth.

It was when I was washing it back with my first sip of wine when his hand settled on the side of my knee that was pressed to his thigh.

I felt the tingle and swallowed the cool wine.

"Now," he murmured, and I looked at him. "You honestly gonna make me ask for a freaking kiss?"

He wanted a kiss.

"Nope," I whispered, bent toward him, put my own hand on his thigh and my face close to his.

He slid his fingers into my hair as he wrapped his hand around the back of my head and pulled me closer.

I kissed him but he kissed me too.

Then he let me go, I sat back and we ate up all the guac and chips.

LATER, after enchiladas, after Johnny declared my apple pie à la mode was better than my guac, after Johnny helped me clean up, after I let Johnny give the treats to the dogs, I led him upstairs and moved forward into my room where I'd guided him.

I stopped because I sensed he stopped.

Enchiladas went great, though Johnny agreed, as great as they were, the guac was better (this was before he had my pie).

And the half a plate of salad he served himself didn't make his body slide into shock.

Also, things were relaxed, they were easy. We were getting to know each other, perhaps not sharing deeply, but I now had the info Deanna gave me confirmed that he had a brother, but I also knew he used to have a dog named Ranger. I further knew he was thirty-four years old and didn't go to college. He went to mechanics school but knew most everything they taught him since he'd been working beside his dad (and before he died, his granddad too) at the garage since he could see over the fender of a car. And he was totally okay with Swirl and Dempsey going camping with us.

Through all that I didn't make an idiot of myself.

But that time was nigh. I could feel it.

Because Johnny had made no bones about what we were doing after cleanup and dog treats, and he'd done this by looking at me and saying, "Now, Iz, where's your bedroom?"

So now we were about to have sex.

So now I was nervous as a cat.

I looked back at him to see him staring up at the old-fashioned, droopy crystal chandelier I'd found at a garage sale and bought for a song because it was messed up. But I cleaned it up and now it was fabulous.

"Johnny?"

His chin tipped down and his eyes sought mine. "You have a chandelier in your bedroom?"

I grinned, the nerves beginning to glide away.

I also shrugged.

"Am I gonna walk outta your house tomorrow morning coated in glitter dust?" he asked.

My heart sang and the nerves took flight.

He was spending the night.

"I don't think so," I answered.

"Best get to fucking you before I turn into a unicorn or something," he muttered.

I burst out laughing.

I stopped doing this when Johnny charged me with a purpose, this purpose ending in us both bouncing on my bed, him on top.

And then he got to fucking me.

I'd find he'd brought a string of five condoms.

But before I passed out naked in his arms in my bed, we'd used only three.

Still, it was good he came prepared.

"Iz."

I turned from the sink and looked to Johnny.

He was standing in the kitchen doorway, his hair a mess, his jeans on, done up, belt not done up, shirt on, not buttoned up, feet bare, boots in his hand.

His eyes were drowsy and they were on my shoulder.

"You're awake," I said.

"Babe," he replied.

"What?" I asked.

"What the fuck is on your shoulder?"

I looked down at the orange canary perched on my shoulder.

That canary sang.

I looked back at Johnny. "That's Wesley."

He stared at me.

I gestured to the yellow canary hopping on the countertop. "That's Buttercup."

"Jesus," Johnny muttered.

"They keep me company while I make breakfast," I told him, moving to the coffeemaker. "You want coffee?"

"Babe," he said.

"What?" I asked, looking to him again to see his eyes aimed to the floor.

"What's on your feet?"

I turned my attention to my feet then back to him.

"Wellies."

"Why?" he queried.

"Why?" I repeated after him.

"Why do you got boots on with your pajama bottoms?"

"I had to go feed the horses and then let them out."

His gaze slid down my fitted T-shirt to my pajama bottoms, which I had rolled at the waist, to my wellies and back up.

"I'm here, you get my ass up to go turn out the horses."

My belly flip-flopped.

"Okay," I whispered.

"I don't know what time it is but I know I don't want to know what time it is. You get up this early every day?"

"I have a lot to do in the mornings and a long commute."

He dropped his boots on the floor, strolled into the room and came right to me.

He didn't kiss me or touch me.

What he did do was lift a finger.

Wesley hopped on it.

Johnny turned his hand to his shoulder and Wesley hopped there.

My whole world trembled, because although it was arguable, that might be better than a morning kiss.

I felt it, as I would.

I also ignored it.

Then Johnny grabbed the pot out of the coffeemaker at the same time he took one of the cups hanging on hooks under the cupboards.

"Go do what you do to morph into working girl. I'll make breakfast."

"Working *woman*," I corrected.

His still sleepy, beautiful eyes cut to me.

"Don't bust my chops at three o'clock in the morning."

"It's five thirty, Johnny."

His attractive and sometimes ominous thick brows shot up.

"What'd I say about not busting my chops?"

I grinned up at him.

"Go," he rumbled.

I kept grinning, turned on a Wellington-clad foot and headed to the back door.

I took the boots off, tossed them on the back porch and headed out of the kitchen but stopped at the door and turned back.

Johnny, with Wesley still perched on his shoulder, was peering into the open fridge, one hand on the handle, the other hand held up to his side with his long, strong fingers wrapped around one of my heavy cream coffee cups.

"Johnny?" I called.

He twisted to me but didn't close the refrigerator door.

"You didn't turn into a unicorn," I pointed out.

"I still got the equipment to drill you so if you don't wanna be late to work, you best stop being cute at the same time you're being a smartass and get on with morphing into working *woman*."

"Message received," I returned, smiling hugely at him.

"Izzy, no human on earth who's normal smiles that big at three o'clock in the morning," he growled.

"It's five thirty," I repeated.

"Baby?" he called.

"Yes," I answered.

"Get the fuck upstairs."

I kept smiling at him.

After I did that for as long as I thought he could take it, I turned and dashed up my stairs.

FIVE

GHOSTRIDER

Johnny

He took the call even though he didn't know who was behind the number that showed on his screen.

He shouldn't have.

After answering, she spoke in his ear.

"Johnny?"

He closed his eyes.

Three years.

That voice was back after three years.

Christ, would this never be done?

"Johnny," she said softly.

He opened his eyes.

"You have got to be kidding me," he whispered.

"Johnny," she whispered back.

"Don't," he ordered.

"I'm coming to town."

"Don't," he repeated.

"I need to see you."

"Three years," he stated.

She had nothing to say to that.

"And you call and say you're coming to town and you wanna see me?" he demanded.

"We need to talk."

"You made your decision."

"There are things I need to say to you."

"I don't give a fuck."

"It was out of my control."

"It wasn't."

"You didn't understand."

"I understood. I understood you walked out my fuckin' door a week after my father died."

"You know why. I had no choice."

"I told you your choices, you just chose the wrong one."

"You couldn't ask me to do that."

"You're not remembering it right. I could. I did. And you gave me your answer by walking out my door."

"He's my brother. What was I supposed to do?"

"Not go on the lam with him."

"You know how it was with us," she said quietly.

"I knew. So...what? Now you're calling and wanna talk, tell me he did the right thing, turned himself in, he's serving his time and you're free of his shit?"

"He...I don't know where he is."

Johnny closed his eyes again, muttering, "Right."

"I've...it's over."

Johnny opened his eyes and repeated, "Right."

"I'm done with him. He's had his last chance."

"You need money?" Johnny asked.

"No." She sounded struck. "Of course not."

"So why are you calling, Shandra?"

She was back to whispering. "Johnny."

"You destroyed me."

She didn't whisper.

She said nothing at all.

"Dad died. Toby was being his usual Toby. Your asshole of a brother was pulling his usual felonious shit. He needed you. I needed you. And you chose him."

"I asked you to come with us," she reminded him.

"On the lam with an asshole who'd robbed a bank?" he asked incredulously.

"You could have talked some sense into him. He listened to you."

"He didn't listen to anyone, Shandra, except the voice in his head that drove him to do stupid, selfish acts of assholery."

"He was all I had."

Christ.

Christ.

Why did that still burn?

"Yeah, in the end he was, because you made it that way."

She sounded wounded. "Johnny, you know what I mean."

Oh, he knew what she meant.

"So you can't forgive me," she said, sounding sad now.

"I forgave you five weeks later, the day I had to put Lace down, which also happened to be the day I finished that fucking bathroom you designed that you loved so much and couldn't wait to use so bad, you put that jar in it to start decorating it before I got the damned thing done. It was then it became clear to me your dad was a dick, your mom was a piece of shit, and growing up, all you had was your brother. Until you met me. But when it came down to it, your loyalty was to blood. I get that. I still put up with Toby's shit, so I get that. That doesn't negate the fact the choice you made communicated where I stood. And from your choice, where I stand hasn't changed."

"You had to put Lace down?" she asked, not masking this news was upsetting, as it would be. She'd loved that horse. They all had.

He saw her, her red hair streaming behind her, the smile she'd aim down at him from under her hat, astride Lace while he and his dad sat on his dad's porch, grinning like idiots because Johnny had done what his father had failed to do.

Found a good woman who loved him more than anything on the earth.

One good thing about his father dying before she took off.

He never knew that wasn't true.

"He went, she declined so fast, it was like she knew and didn't wanna be in a world without him in it."

"Oh God, Johnny," she said gently.

"Can we be done with this?"

"I...still have Ranger. He's good. Healthy and happy. But I think he still misses you."

That was outside her norm. That was close to making her a bitch.

He'd told her to take his dog. He couldn't be there to protect her from whatever her brother got her caught up in. But he could leave her with Ranger.

She'd cried, sobbed, told him she wanted him to go with them, and if he couldn't then she couldn't take a dog from his man. She couldn't do that to Ranger. She couldn't do that to him.

But he'd said if she had to go she had to go with Ranger, and she knew him well, to the bone, to his soul. She knew he'd set her free if that was what she needed, but he wasn't letting her walk out his door without someone to look after her.

So she'd taken his dog.

"Uncool," he muttered.

Again with the hurt. "I thought you'd want to know."

"Now I know."

She gave it a beat before she pressed, "I want to come and see you."

"For what purpose?"

"You know."

"I know so the question remains, for what purpose?"

And again with the wounded. "Can't we just talk?"

He had an excuse not to "just talk."

He was seeing Izzy.

"Seeing" was a loose term after the short time they'd had, but they had plans to make that short time longer and he was the one who set that up.

They'd fucked a lot and had one date but he still knew if there could ever be a one again, that woman gave every indication she'd be that one.

But one was one and there couldn't be another one.

For Johnny, because she'd walked out his door three years earlier, there also couldn't be the one.

When it came down to it and a decision had to be made, he wouldn't decide on a woman like Izzy.

No, a woman like Izzy with her frilly pillows on an outside loveseat and her flowerpots and birds singing on her shoulder, and her guacamole and her honesty, and her stories about her dead mom needed a whole man who could give her his whole self, not half a man who'd given half of himself to the wrong woman.

Shandra didn't get to have any part of Izzy.

Izzy knew about Shandra.

But Johnny would never pollute all that was Izzy with the mess that became of him and Shandra.

"No," he answered.

"Dad's sick," she told him.

"Don't know a man who deserves being that more than him."

"I understand why you feel that way. It's hard to wrap my head around my need to do my duty as his daughter when I understand why you feel that way better than you. I still have to come see him."

"After the choice you made with your brother, if you think this surprises me, it doesn't."

"I might be moving home," she shared.

Fuck.

"I wish you wouldn't."

"I might not have a choice."

"Then avoid me."

"Johnny—"

"Shandra, just *don't*."

She gave that a few beats.

Then Shandra was all Shandra was.

Gently, tenderly, she said, "Okay. I won't. I have to come home, but I'll avoid you, Johnny."

"Obliged."

"Tell me one thing. Are you happy?"

He was not happy.

His shot at happy walked out his door with his dog and went on the lam with her brother exactly one week after his father died.

You didn't turn into a unicorn.

"Yes," he answered.

"I...okay." He could almost hear her swallow. "Good."

She wouldn't ask. Not about another woman. Not because she didn't want to know. But because she was Shandra. She did the worst to him and it cut her up just a little less than it did him, that little less being all she needed to go through with it.

She wouldn't put him in that spot.

She wouldn't infect what he had with another woman.

She wouldn't do that.

But she could guess.

And Johnny reckoned she was guessing.

"Take care of yourself," he bid.

"You too," she whispered.

"Goodbye, Shandra."

"'Bye, Johnny."

He didn't hesitate to disconnect.

He also didn't hesitate to do what he did next, something he knew he shouldn't do after he got done talking to Shandra for the first time in three years.

He went to his texts, a specific number, and typed in, *You remember how to get to the mill?*

He moved to the car he was working on but didn't get the chance to get stuck in because Izzy texted him back.

It's driving yonder until you hit a dirt road and then you drive on that until you hit a stone building with a water wheel.

Yes, he shouldn't have texted her after he spoke with Shandra for the first time in three years.

This was because the smile her text gave him felt wrong, twisted, corrupt.

He had to exit her life.

He had to do it tomorrow night over dinner.

Hell, he should ask her to meet him at Home and tell her there, not make her come all the way out to the mill for him to share what hadn't really started and could never have been was over.

He didn't change their plans.

You missed about three turns, he texted back.

Whoops, she replied.

Oh yeah.

He had to exit her life.

Save me from happening onto a lunatic with an underground bunker who's going to hold me captive and force me to make babies so he can build a flock of crazies and send me directions, she went on.

Fuck yeah.

He had to get the hell out of Eliza's life.

Johnny texted directions.

Then he texted, *Be there whenever you get there. I'll make something that works with that.*

I have to stop and let out the dogs and deal with the horses.

Leave a key under your mat tomorrow and I'll go do that after I'm done at the garage. His thumbs arrested, then they moved on without his permission, *And I'll get Swirl and Dempsey and bring them to the mill.*

Jesus.

What was he doing?

Fabulous. I'll be with you around 6 or 6:30, she returned.

Bring a toothbrush.

Jesus.

What the fuck was he doing?

Roger that, Ghostrider.

The smile that got didn't seem corrupt.

It was still wrong.

Smartass, he replied.

She shot him a toothy-grinned emoji and *I'll bring wine.*

I'll get wine just bring you.

I'm kind of picky about wine.

I'll get a lot of it so you'll have your pick.

I can just bring what I like, Johnny.

Baby, so we're not texting up until the time you're gonna show at my house tomorrow night, just...bring...you. I'll get the fucking wine.

Okeydokey.

Go back to work.

YOU go back to work.

I'm spanking you tomorrow night.

No text came in for long moments, and he knew she slid right into the shy she could forget when she was with him and they were both fully-clothed and sex wasn't imminent or after he got his hands on her, before he got, *This is my technologically clad vow to be good from this point forward.*

The woman couldn't be bad with a gun stuck to her head.

Unless she was naked.

Then she was anything he wanted her to be.

Jesus.

See you tomorrow, Iz.

You betcha, Johnny.

He shoved his phone in the back pocket of his coveralls and leaned over the car.

He did not see the engine.

He saw Izzy at her sink wearing a light-purple top that clung to her tits, purple, green and pink striped pajama bottoms, the most ridiculous boots he'd ever seen on her feet, her huge mass of tawny hair piled up in a mess at the top of her head, an orange bird on her shoulder.

He then saw her in those black pants that clung to her ass with that sharp shirt that made her look badass, wearing those pumps he wanted to fuck her in, ruining all that with her huge mass of tawny hair tumbling over her shoulders making her not look like a professional businesswoman but instead a sex kitten stripper in her fake professional businesswoman's outfit before she tore it off.

Then he saw her on his deck in his tee, holding a coffee mug looking uncertain and shy, and sleepy and gratifyingly thoroughly fucked, and so cute he still wondered how he managed not to tackle her to the wood and bury his cock up to her throat.

That vision turned into her last night, holding on to the top curve of her iron headboard, her neck twisted, those clear blue eyes directed at him hazy with sex and turned on as fuck, her lips swollen from his mouth and moist from her tongue running along them as she took his cock from behind and begged him to give it to her harder.

His final vision was altogether different.

Years before, Shandra sitting at his father's table, her beautiful face filled with laughter, the sound of it mixed with his dad's, ringing in his old man's dining room.

He'd wanted to hate her.

He'd never managed that.

He'd wanted to put her behind him.

He'd never managed that either.

He needed to exit Izzy's life.

She knew about Shandra and he'd tell Izzy she was coming back to town.

And he'd make her dinner tomorrow night and take her camping on the weekend and share how it was.

She seemed to understand a lot of shit. She even seemed to understand about Shandra.

Maybe he wouldn't lose her.

Maybe they could be friends.

Maybe she'd have him over when she had her other friends over, he could eat her guacamole and get her cute and shy and smartass and know he was taking it in a way that was healthy for her, which was something that would cut. But it was something he could live with better than what he could do to her if he didn't exit being in her life that way or not having her at all.

And maybe he was a selfish dumbfuck.

But whatever way it went, he'd explain things while they were camping.

After that, it was her choice and that was the best he could do.

It always had been.

SIX

TIGHT

Izzy

"Pull me out."

I heard Johnny's growl but chose to ignore it.

And I chose to ignore it because he had his back to the pillows shoved up against his headboard, his knees cocked, feet in the bed, thighs spread wide, both his hands in my hair, and his cock was in my mouth.

He looked amazing like that, spread out for me, offered up to me: his broad shoulders, cut collarbone, wide chest with its sprinkling of black hair across his pecs, large nipples, the boxes of his abs standing out like he was doing crunches instead of getting a blowjob, the dark hair on his forearms, dense on his thick thighs.

He felt amazing in my mouth, silk over steel.

He tasted awesome, like musk and man.

And I loved who I was right then, kneeling between his legs, sucking him off, feeling what I was giving to him as his hips jerked uncontrollably, the noises that rolled up his chest and out of his mouth abrasively, his strong fingers clenching in my hair restlessly.

I was the woman who could make this man react like that, feel the way he was holding back from thrusting into my mouth, but I knew he needed it and it was costing him, because he liked what I was doing so much he wanted to take more.

And I was the woman who was dripping wet between my legs, fighting the trembling that threatened to overtake me because I liked the taste of him, the look of him, the feel of him, the knowledge of how much he got off on what I was doing to him with just my mouth, the power all that sent surging through me, vibrating in my clit, knowing in that instant he was all mine.

I wanted to take him there. I wanted to kneel between his legs and watch him explode for me. The ones I'd caught, he was beautiful in orgasm, almost agonizingly so.

And I wanted that, spread out for me, offered up to me...all mine.

I kept at him, sucking harder, adding a hand wrapped around him and stroking tight.

"Iz, pull me out," he grunted.

I kept at him.

"Eliza, *fucking pull me out.*"

I lifted my eyes to his, pulled him out of my mouth, but stroked him harder with my hand and felt the shudder score through me at the dark hunger carved in his handsome face.

Suddenly, I was flat on my belly in the bed. A quiver ran over me when his knees pressed against the insides of my thighs, spreading them so wide I felt the pull in my muscles.

I whimpered through the sound of crinkling foil and then whispered, "Johnny."

Fingers dug into my hips as they were hauled up.

I started to come up on all fours but Johnny planted a hand in the middle of my back, shoved me back to the bed and growled, "Down."

That didn't cause a quiver.

That set me to shaking.

And it set my sex to soaking.

He then caught my hair, twisting it in a fist so it pulled at my scalp and I whimpered again as I trembled before him, now offered up to him.

And *loving it*.

"Keep your knees wide," he ordered, gave a rough but gentle yank on my hair and drove inside.

My neck arched, I cried out and instantly started coming.

"Like my cock?" he asked harshly, thrusting deep and fast.

"Yes," I moaned through my orgasm.

I felt his thumb circle my anus and my legs locked, my hands clenched his sheets and my climax stuttered.

"Johnny," I whispered.

"No, baby?"

"No."

His thumb slid away to become his hand sliding across the cheek of my behind. He grasped my hip, kept pounding, and the climax shot back so forcefully, I was panting into the sheets.

"Arch your back," he commanded.

I did as told.

"Give me more," he grunted, the sound of our flesh connecting getting sharper, each slap coming faster.

I reared back into him, spread so wide, taking him hard, feeling exposed, now all his.

All Johnny's.

And that was better.

Another orgasm began to rock through me and I gasped as it came.

"Yeah," Johnny growled, sounding turned on and pleased, and close himself to coming.

He went faster, twisted his hand in my hair, "Now up, Izzy."

I came up on all fours, my head back, my spine arced to the bed, my body slamming back into his drives, my climax still burning, making me do all this with full body tremors.

"God, fuck, Izzy, *fuck*," he groaned.

I glanced back at him to see him watching me take his cock and another shudder tore through me.

He let my hair go, seized my hips and forced them to connect with his brutally as he took me through his orgasm, his grunts exploding in the room.

I whinnied through them, a series of hums, pants and soft cries, until he slowed, the power drifted out, gentleness drifted in, and then he finally seated himself deep and I dropped back down to the bed, my cheek against his soft sheets.

I felt it as he glided one finger lightly along my spine from where it sat between my shoulder blades, through the arch, up the small and it kept going, skating between the cheeks of my behind. My hips twitched and his finger trailed out and he flattened both hands on my bottom and pulled out.

He tipped me to my side.

I tilted my eyes up to him. He looked in them then exited the bed, flicking the sheets over my body.

I watched him walk to the bathroom, only Dempsey following him (Swirl had settled in somewhere for the night) and I was too spent to think of the steaks he'd broiled for us earlier that had some strong garlic and herbed cheese crusted on top and were utterly delicious. Or the fact he'd bought ten bottles of wine for me to choose from, four red, five white and one sparkling, all the whites chilled in the fridge.

I also didn't think of the sated but remote look in his eyes that I caught before he left me in his bed. Nor did I think about how he said not a word after we shared the most intimate thing a man and woman could share before he took off to go deal with the condom.

This last was his way. He'd done the same thing at my house.

Though at my house, when he'd come back, he'd teased me about my girlie bathroom, focusing on the pink wire basket shelves on the wall filled with corked bottles of girlie pamper stuff and thick wash cloths and natural sponges and loofahs and pink cotton balls.

I had a feeling I couldn't tease him about his bath salts.

I watched him come back, semi-hard, condom free, all beautiful. He flipped a switch on the wall during his return, which put out the canister lights in the ceiling around his kitchen and pendants that hung over his island, lights he'd dimmed before he'd taken me to bed.

Dempsey followed him, and Johnny gave him a distracted head scratch as he watched me while he finished walking back to me. When he made it to the bed, I scooched away. He lifted the sheet and slid in.

Dempsey took a hint and wandered off.

Johnny dropped the sheet, settled back against the pillows with his shoulders high against the headboard, and only then did he reach for me, hauling me up so I had a cheek to his chest.

I slid an arm around his stomach and rested there.

I didn't snuggle in. Johnny wasn't mine to snuggle.

But when he pulled me to him, I allowed myself to relax into it.

"You okay?" I asked softly.

"I tell you to stop sucking my cock, babe, you stop sucking my cock."

I blinked at his chest.

His fingers were trailing on my lower back, light, sweet, even tender but his voice had been mildly ticked and very firm.

And it continued that way as he carried on.

"I went for your ass. I felt it even before you said no. I asked, you said no. I stopped. I tell you to pull me out, you pull me out."

"I'm sorry," I whispered, now not feeling his fingers lightly, maybe even tenderly trailing. Only feeling the burning ball of humiliation that was blazing through my body.

I didn't know what to do. I'd never done something so wrong in bed and then been called on it like that. I didn't know how to proceed.

And worse, I'd loved what I'd been doing and thought he had too.

But apparently, he had not.

I stared beyond his chest at my clothes on the floor and I whispered, "Maybe I should—"

"You're thinking of bailing and I'm just saying it like it is. No need to get sensitive about it. Just don't do it again."

"Okay, I'm sorry." I was inching away. "But I still think maybe I should go."

Johnny stopped trailing his fingers along the small of my back, yanked me up his chest, took one look at my face and went completely still.

"I really..." I stopped and started again. "I didn't think about it, but I have to wake up even earlier to get home and see to the horses and get ready for work, so maybe I shouldn't spend the night."

"Christ, Iz," he murmured, still staring at me.

"So I'm just gonna do that, go home, I mean," I said, bracing to push away from him.

I saw his hand heading my way like he was going to cup my face at the same time I saw the gentleness settle in his expression.

But I now had a plan, which was mostly a mission that didn't include allowing Johnny to be gentle with me, to touch my face in a way he never had and wasn't allowed to do with who we were. So I darted up a hand and pushed his away at the same time I shoved into the bed to launch myself over him.

However, in the midst of this, I somehow found myself on my back in the bed with Johnny on top of me, and that hand I'd pushed away was tenderly cupping my face.

"Izzy, baby, I'm so sorry. I should have found a way to deliver that more gentle," he whispered.

"No, that's okay. I mean, no...you should feel free to be frank with me. But just to say, you know...again, that I probably should get going."

"That was spectacular," he said softly.

"I'm glad you thought so. Now, I know you get mad when I get like this but this time I really kinda need to go."

"The way you took me, Izzy, it was so beautiful, watching my cock sink into your pussy that was so goddamn wet, it was sleek. Your face, Christ. Your face. You're so damned pretty but when you get like that for me you're unbelievably beautiful. I wanted to claim all of that. I wanted to be inside you every way I could. So I went for your ass."

"It's okay. I mean, that's all very nice and thank you for that, it means a lot and it means a lot too that you listened to me during, you know...what you were going to do with your thumb and felt I wasn't there. I'm sorry I didn't give you that when you were communicating about what you didn't want but now I need to—"

Johnny cut me off. "You swallow?"

The question was so bizarre, for a second I forgot my mortification and stared at him.

"Sorry?"

"Cum. Do you swallow?"

Oh dear Lord.

"Um..."

His eyes got even softer.

"I didn't think so," he murmured.

"Johnny, I—"

"Ten more seconds of your mouth, babe, you wouldn't have had a choice but to swallow."

I felt my eyes get big. "Oh."

"Yeah." His lips hitched. "Oh. You do know that's what happens when you give phenomenal head?" he asked.

"Phenomenal?" I breathed and his eyes warmed.

"Baby, you knelt between my legs, worshipping at my cock. You were so into it, never had that in my life. It was beautiful. Top that, you got talent. So yeah, but maybe phenomenal doesn't cut it. Outstanding. Superior. Stupendous. Unbe-fucking-leivable. Take your pick."

"I wanted to watch," I whispered.

"What?" he asked.

"I wanted to...not, um, with my mouth. I was going to finish with my hand and I wanted to watch."

His eyes warmed a different way, his body shifted on mine and his voice sounded kind of growly when he asked, "You wanted to watch me blow for you?"

I nodded.

"And who was going to take care of you?" he inquired.

"I hadn't...well, thought of that part, but it was kinda going the way that it would have, um...happened naturally."

He gave me his sexy grin before he bent his head, flicked my earlobe with his nose, kissed my neck, lifted his head and caught my eyes again, but when he did he was a lot closer this time.

"You think you could come just by watching yourself make me come?"

"Evidence was suggesting that," I told him uncomfortably.

Another sexy grin. "How 'bout, if we do that, you kneel to the side so I can get a hand between your legs and help with that?"

"I think that sounds...doable," I breathed.

It was then that something slid over his face that wasn't sexy or warm or sweet, but seemingly alert, like he'd just remembered something. Then uneasy, and if I read it right, it ended remorseful before he bent in to touch his lips to mine and pull away.

"Dogs need to be let out before we settle in?" he asked quietly.

"I think Swirl's down for the night but Dempsey probably could take a wander," I answered then began to make an impossible move, the impossibility of it being me lying under him. "I'll do it."

"I got him," Johnny said, sliding his thumb across my cheek before pulling away from me.

He put on his jeans and nothing else before he whistled, and I looked to the room to see Swirl lift his head from his spot camped out on Johnny's couch but otherwise not move, but Dempsey trotted Johnny's way.

Man and dog went out the door and I heard them clamber down the stairs.

I pulled the sheet to my chest wondering about the unease and remorse I thought I saw in Johnny's face.

Then I pushed the sheet aside, got out of bed, found my panties and tugged them on. I also tugged on the rust-colored T-shirt Johnny had discarded that had a very cool, faded, peeling away yellow decal that was designed to look kind of like an old-fashioned, fifties motor oil ad that said, ON MY WAY HOME, THE ONLY PLACE TO BE.

That done, I went to my purse and took it with me to the bathroom.

I grabbed my toothbrush out of it, used it. I then unearthed the travel-size facial cleanser I'd brought with me and used that too. Finally, I found the travel-size moisturizer and I used that as well.

I tucked everything in my purse and found Johnny and Dempsey were back when I returned.

His eyes were on the T-shirt and his lips were now curled up at both ends.

"You just can't help yourself, can you?" he teased.

"I can't brush my teeth naked, Johnny," I returned.

His gaze came to mine. "Yeah you can."

I rolled my eyes, dumped my purse on his island and headed toward the bed.

Dempsey came up and rubbed against me, so I stopped to give him some pets before I headed toward the bed where Johnny stood close to it, not taking off his jeans, just watching me with my dog.

But when I got close, he hooked me around the belly and pulled me into his front.

He then wrapped his arms around me loosely.

I put my hands to his chest and tipped my head back to look at his face.

"I'm a guy who likes to control what he gets in bed."

My body jerked against his in surprise at this announcement and his arms tightened.

"I'm thinking that isn't lost on you," he carried on. "And maybe it also isn't lost on you that I got rules. You come. Then I come. That was not the way things were going. I was gonna blow before I gave it to you and that is not acceptable to me. I liked what you were doing. Too much. It was taking my mind off where I needed to be at, that being seein' to you. I got slightly pissed about that and didn't communicate that very well. I was unintentionally a dick, but I was still a dick and that wasn't cool. I said I was sorry but I want you to know, Iz, that I really am."

This moved me a great deal.

And maybe this was why he'd looked remorseful.

Something that relieved me a great deal.

"Thank you, Johnny," I said softly.

"You can wake up when you normally wake up. I'll follow you home and deal with Serengeti and Amaretto, get the dogs sorted, feed your cats and make you breakfast so you don't have to miss any sleep."

I relaxed into him.

"You don't have to do that."

"I know I don't but I'm gonna."

I smiled at him, and my hand, of its own accord, was sliding up with the intent to cup his jaw, my feet itching to roll up on my toes to kiss him, but I stopped both.

I ended up squeezing the spot where his neck met his shoulder instead of doing something more affectionate, more familiar, not where we were or who we were. But I hid my disappointment I couldn't have that, couldn't give that, by continuing to smile.

"Are you saying we're done having sex?" I asked.

He returned my smile. "Had my big workout today, babe, and you gave me my second one, so it sucks, but yeah. I'm wiped."

I gave his shoulder another squeeze. "So you *do* do healthy things."

"This body is not a miracle of nature."

"Do you eat vegetables?"

"Protein shakes but there's an occasional green smoothie," he admitted.

"I knew it."

He chuckled.

Then he let me go, shoved me gently toward the bed and his hands went to the button on his jeans.

I crawled into his bed with his T-shirt on.

He joined me and reached out to turn out his light while I did the same with the one on my side.

I settled in and didn't have time to begin to wonder if he would hold me on an occasion where I didn't pass out in his arms due to lots of insanely good sex.

He pulled me into them, tucking my back to his front and curving his body into mine.

"You need me to set the alarm?" he asked.

"Isn't it set?"

"It's set for six thirty, not five."

I was usually on the road to work at six thirty.

"I have an internal alarm," I told him.

He kept hold of me with the arm under me but rolled his body away. I heard a beep and then he was back.

"Just in case," he muttered.

I hated it that I totally could fall in love with this man...but I couldn't.

I hated it that he was all mine and I was all his...but only when we were having sex.

I hated that I knew when it was over that I'd miss this and miss it badly...but I'd rather have it while I could than not have it at all.

But I had it now and it was beautiful.

It was also guiding my way to understand what to look for that was right and good for my future.

The problem with that was, I was terrified what was right and good was only right there in that bed with me and nowhere else on this earth.

I didn't hate that.

I didn't allow myself to think of it.

If I did, I didn't know what I'd do.

I DIDN'T KNOW what woke me.

I just woke.

I also didn't know how I knew instantly Johnny wasn't with me.

But I did.

I rolled to my back, tentatively reaching out an arm to his side of the bed.

He wasn't in it.

I heard a whine, and as my eyes adjusted to the dark, I saw Dempsey at the door in the wall of windows.

Outside it, I could barely make out Johnny's chest where it was positioned at the railing, his face as well, his bottom half and hair blended in the night because his hair was dark and he was wearing something dark down below.

He was turned, looking toward the creek, like the first time I woke up in his house.

I rolled back and looked at the clock.

It was just past two in the morning.

I didn't know what to do.

However, my body did.

It scooched to the side of the bed, and with experience, my feet carefully found their way to the floor, knowing Swirl would be asleep there beside me so I'd have to find my way without stepping on him.

He was there.

I felt him move to lift his head and murmured, "Shh, baby. Just going to check on Johnny."

He settled back in and I got out of bed.

Dempsey came to me.

I gave him some head scratches then headed to the door.

I saw Johnny more distinctly from closer as I opened the door and his head turned to me.

I shoved my body in the narrow crack I'd opened the door, so Dempsey wouldn't come out, and called softly, "You okay?"

"Come here."

"I don't want to intrude if you need—"

"Come here, Eliza."

Keeping Dempsey back, I slid out the door, closed it and moved to him.

Even though I was only going to position myself close enough to have a conversation with him, weirdly, powerfully, almost violently, the instant I got close enough for him to reach out to me, he did, yanking me into his arms and holding me tight.

Not loose.

Not casual.

Not sexual.

Not nonchalant.

Tight.

Oh my God.

"Are you okay?" I whispered, rounding him with my arms too.

"I'm a dick."

"What?"

"I'm a dick."

"Johnny, if you mean what happened earlier, it's okay—"

"Shandra called yesterday."

My body turned to stone.

"Out of the blue, haven't heard from her in years, she calls."

Again of their own accord, and I didn't stop them this time, my hands slid up his back over his shoulders so I could curl them around either side of his neck.

That neck bent so he could stop looking over my head and instead look at my face.

"Her dad's sick. She's coming back."

The blow that caused after two breakfasts, two dinners, one phone call, one text exchange and lots of sex was far more extreme than I was ready for.

But I withstood it without letting on I endured it.

And I did that for him.

"Okay," I whispered.

"I should have changed our plans and met you at Home. Shared it there. Let you go back to your place knowing where things were at. I shouldn't have brought your dogs here, made you come here, fed you and fucked you and acted like a dick to you and let you be cute and sweet, all this making me a total dick."

"You want her back," I surmised.

"Fuck no," he stated tersely.

The pads of my fingers dug into his neck.

"No?"

"Babe, she left me for reasons I can't get into and she took my dog with her. The reason she left is still out there, even though she says it's gone. I'm not setting myself up for her to gut me again."

"She stole your dog?" I asked in disbelief.

"I let her have him. She needed someone to protect her."

God.

From what I was learning that was so very *Johnny*.

"Regretted it the instant she walked out my door. Ranger was a great dog. Missed him so much, never got another one. But it was still the right thing to do."

"Okay."

"I can't give you what you deserve."

I endured that without my body reacting as well, like lurching, moving like it suffered the blow that it did.

Instead I said gently, "I know. I've known since the beginning. I only understood when Deanna told me about Shandra. But I know, Johnny. You aren't a dick. You told me without saying anything where we were, and I like you, so I made the decision to stay there so you shouldn't feel bad. I get it. I totally get it. I always got it. I knew where we stood. So please, don't feel bad about it."

His arms pulled me even closer as his forehead came down to rest on mine.

"You're an amazing woman."

Now I was understanding all those women who complained

when men broke up with them and said things like that making them wonder, if that was the case, why they broke up with them in the first place.

I'd never been broken up with. I'd always done the breaking because I'd always chosen poorly.

I guess in a different way I was still doing that.

I gave his neck a squeeze and got up a bit on my toes to press my forehead deeper to his. "And you're an amazing guy."

"I'm sorry I went through with tonight."

I pulled my forehead from his and forced a bright smile on my face. "And deprived me of garlic cheese encrusted steak and fabulous sex? Now, if you'd done that, that would make you a dick," I teased.

"Fuck," he whispered, his arms spasming around me.

My voice got soft again. "Johnny, it's okay."

His voice was soft too. "I wish I met you before she fucked me up."

"It didn't happen that way. It happened this way. And from how you're talking, it was good for you like it was good for me. So let's have that and not bring anything bad into it. It is what it is and we had what we had. I'll go, and if you ever want some good guac or to hang out with Wesley, you know my number and maybe you'll swing me a deal on my next oil change."

"I still wanna take you camping."

I melted into him.

"But I'm not gonna take you camping," he whispered.

He wasn't going to take me camping.

Why, after two breakfasts, two dinners, one phone conversation, one text exchange and a lot of sex did that sound like someone cancelled Christmas *forever*?

I pushed up to him, kissed him, pressing my lips lightly against his, harder, opening my mouth. His opened, I slid my tongue inside. He sucked it deeper for a second then slid mine out as his tongue invaded my mouth.

We kissed like that, gently, unhurried, for a long time in the chill of an early summer night by a creek with a water wheel splashing behind us.

After we were done, he led me to bed and he held me close, and I wanted him to make love to me but he was not that man. He would hold me but he wouldn't take any more from me than he already had.

I fell asleep before he did.

But I also woke before he did.

And as quietly as I could, I got dressed. I found a pad of paper. I wrote him a note. I refused to look at him asleep in bed as I propped it on his nightstand. I got my dogs. We got in my car. And we drove home.

It wasn't until Buttercup was on my shoulder, Wesley hopping on my counter chirping, that my phone also on the counter chimed with a text and I glanced at it, seeing the whole text under his name on the screen.

You too.

My note to him had said, *You're the best. Thank you for being that.*

I finished up making breakfast and eating it, and I did all that silently, gently, unhurriedly crying.

AFTER WORK THAT EVENING, walking up to my front porch, I wasn't resolutely thinking about catching up on all the chores I'd missed being with Johnny as I'd made myself resolutely think about all the way home.

I was staring with some dread at my wicker rocking chair.

When I made it to the chair, I stood in my high-heeled shoes staring down at the seat.

On the gingham pad, propped up against the floral pillow, was a Ball jar filled with water and overflowing at the top with pale pink peonies.

I'd noted vaguely the night before, in my excitement to get to

Johnny, that the fat peony bushes that hugged the back of his mill had gone full bloom.

And they were all pale pink.

In front of the jar was a rolled up piece of rust-colored material.

I took it up, unfurled it and a piece of paper fell out.

It was the On My Way Home T-shirt I'd slept in the night before at Johnny's.

I bent down, picked up the paper and read,

IT'S A GOOD MEMORY.

I hope.

For me it will be, Izzy.

Always.

~J

HE DIDN'T MEAN to be cruel, I knew it. He meant it to be what I hoped one day it would become.

Sweet.

And when I bunched the T-shirt to my face and smelled he'd laundered it, I knew he meant that to be sweet too.

But I wished he hadn't washed it.

I allowed one tear to fall, soaking into the material.

Then I sniffed, pulled the T-shirt away from my face and moved to my door in order to let out my dogs.

SEVEN
MARGOT

Izzy

I t was exactly two weeks and one day after Johnny and I ended what had never begun.

I'd gone home from work, let the dogs out, changed from heels to boots, checked the horses but left them in their paddock, put my heels back on, grabbed up my purse and keys but also my journal, selecting a few colored pens to go with it, and I headed out.

I was going to The Star. A very nice but not fancy (I was told) steak joint about ten miles out of town that Deanna and Charlie had been rhapsodizing about for years.

Deanna demanded all her birthdays be celebrated at The Star and Charlie hogged her birthdays, letting people celebrate it with her on the weekend (or the next weekend day if her birthday fell on a weekend), so I'd never been there.

And instead of continuing to mope about coming to terms with the fact that I would not ever be my sister or mother and thus be able to grab on to life and take what I wanted without giving too much in return, simply enjoy myself and what life offered without wanting more, I was going out to have a nice steak.

In other words, continuing to mope about the fact that Johnny and I had ended something that could never begin.

Or precisely, moping about the fact that what I wanted with Johnny could never begin.

The last steak I'd eaten, Johnny had cooked for me.

I didn't allow myself to think about that.

That said, I knew part of me was breaking that seal or I'd get to the point I'd never eat steak again.

My mother would smile down from heaven at that.

But as much as I wished I didn't, I loved steak.

So I needed to break the seal.

In the time since it happened, I also hadn't allowed myself to spend too much time in town.

I'd been in Matlock for months, but steaming into summer, it was waking up. People were out and about, the big square was setting up to have what Deanna and Charlie had explained were nearly weekly weekend events of bands or festivals or open air plays, or whatever (I'd even been to a concert in the past, and their Memorial Day food festival, which was happening that weekend). And if he happened to be one of those people waking up, out and about, I didn't want to run into Johnny.

Instead I'd caught up on my chores and planted my big garden and given up on the idea of a chicken coop, because Johnny was right. I should save up to build a garage. I'd be happy I had one for a variety of reasons and chickens just offered up fresh eggs.

I was nearly at the restaurant when it came on the radio.

And it was just my luck it would.

Bonnie Raitt's "I Can't Make You Love Me."

I pulled into the parking lot of The Star, my fingers on the steering wheel adjusting to change the channel or completely wind down the volume.

Something made me not do that.

Instead I parked and sat in my car with goose bumps on my arms, staring unseeing out my windshield toward the rough, unpainted clapboard at the side of The Star, listening to the whole song.

When it was done, I switched off the car and said to the windshield, "It was two breakfasts, two dinners, one phone conversation, one text exchange and lots of sex. Get over yourself."

With that, I grabbed my clutch, my journal and got out of my car.

I went in.

I asked for a table.

I got one.

I selected a seat with my back to the door so I could focus on my journal and not people watching.

I perused the menu and ordered a glass of Malbec.

I put my journal on the table and pulled out a couple of the pens.

I opened it up to the crazy doodles and wonky writing that slanted this way, then that, or went straight across, or curled around word for word from a circle in the center. Short notes, long meanderings and drawn flowers or balloons or whatever sprang to mind.

My journal was the only thing I allowed to be truly disordered in my life.

My mother's journals had looked like that. Just like that. Except without all the colored pens because the only pens we had were ones she picked up wherever they gave out free pens, and she didn't have the luxury of bringing color to her innermost thoughts.

The wine was served, I ordered my filet with no potato but instead steamed broccoli and roasted asparagus and had been bent back to my journal for maybe two minutes before I heard an achingly familiar, "Izzy?"

My head shot back and I stared into Johnny's black eyes in his beautiful face staring down at me looking stricken and searching and gentle and gorgeous.

Those eyes slid to the empty chair opposite me then back to me and he asked, "Are you here alone?"

Was he?

Oh God.

Or was he there with Shandra? She was back and they were cele-brating their reunion with steak at The Star.

"I...uh..." I stammered.

"Who's this?"

My attention zipped to a woman who appeared at Johnny's side.

She was in her sixties, maybe seventies. Hair dyed a light, becoming red and set in a lovely, soft style that suited her immensely. She had makeup on even though the battle against wrinkles the rest of her put-together-self told me she'd valiantly fought was the inevitable loss it was meant to be. Regardless, her makeup was subtle and attractive. She was wearing a pretty shirtwaist dress with a full skirt in a green and white pattern with a fabulous rectangular bag with a short strap on her forearm.

And she was wearing pearls, real ones it seemed to my inexpert eye. A string of them at her throat and one at her wrist with plain but large and magnificent pearl studs in her ears.

Her eyes were locked on me.

"Leave it to you to find the prettiest lady in the place."

This came from a man who materialized at the woman's back. He was bald on top, his gray hair cut very short on the sides. He was wearing a shiny blue golf shirt and nice trousers. He was also in his sixties or seventies, very tall and quite good-looking. Sharing that, shave a decade or two off him, he'd been exceptionally handsome.

And speaking of exceptionally handsome, Johnny was wearing clothes I didn't even imagine he could own. Black on black—a delec-tably tailored black shirt over deliciously tailored slim-fit black trousers that made my mouth water more than anything I saw on the menu (way more).

"Johnathon, darlin', who is this fetching creature?" the woman asked.

"Margot, Dave, this is Eliza," Johnny rumbled.

"Iz or Izzy, my friends call me," I whispered, sounding like someone was choking me.

Johnny's gentle gaze came back to rest on me.

First Bonnie Raitt and now this?

Bonnie was hard enough but Johnny in that shirt (and those trousers) might be the end of me.

All right.

I was never leaving my acres again.

"Izzy. Now isn't that sweet? Unusual. But sweet," Margot declared.

"You know this gal?" Dave asked Johnny.

"Yeah, we—" Johnny started.

"We're friends," I put in firmly, straightening my spine and finding my inner Daphne, the piece of my mother she left me that could make it through anything. "I'm kind of new to town. We met at On the Way Home a few weeks back and Johnny kept me company helping me break in the local tavern."

Both Margot and Dave turned speculative eyes to Johnny.

Unfortunately, Margot got over her speculation way too quickly and looked back at me.

And when she did, she declared, "No girl as cute as a button as you are wearing a dress that pretty eats alone. You're joining us for dinner."

Oh God.

No!

"I've already ordered," I told her.

She turned directly to the tall man behind her. "David. Find someone and tell them to hold this pretty girl's dinner and serve it with ours." She turned back to me. "If you're hungry, darlin', we'll order you an appetizer."

"I—" I started.

But Margot now had her attention on the hostess who was hovering with them, holding their menus. "You can take us to our booth now." Her attention came back to me. "We always get a booth. They're roomy."

"You can also ask the chef to hold making this lady's dinner, if you would," David said under his breath to the hostess as Margot spoke.

"Of course," the hostess muttered.

Was this happening?

"Help Eliza out of her seat, Johnathon," Margot ordered, turned her head, tipped up her nose and flounced after the hostess.

This was happening.

I had a feeling Margot got what she wanted, but it was a definite it would be tremendously rude if I didn't join them even if the very last thing on earth I wanted was to join them for dinner.

More aptly, to sit at dinner with a Johnny with gentle eyes wearing that shirt and those trousers.

Seeing as I had no choice, I closed my journal, dropped my pens in my clutch and slid out of my chair only to run right into Johnny.

"You don't have to do this, Izzy," he whispered, his lips at my ear sending that damnable tingle down my spine.

And it got worse.

He was wearing cologne, and it was amazing cologne so he even smelled fantastic.

I turned my head and caught his gaze.

"It's okay, honey."

His eyes melted with warmth and regret and compassion and all that looked good on him before he reached out and grabbed my journal off the table.

He handed it to me, reached again and nabbed my wine, then put his free hand to my elbow and guided me after Margot and David.

"She seems like she's a firebrand," I muttered to Johnny.

"David and Margot, my dad's best friends. Dave started working for my granddad when he was about seventeen. That's how him and Dad met. Dave's about a decade older than Dad and he took him under his wing back then. And whatever grew between them meant they were inseparable until they had no choice but not to be. Dad was fifteen when he was best man at Dave's wedding. Dave said the eulogy at Dad's funeral."

How beautiful.

And how sad.

"Right," I said softly.

"Margot's a pistol and I don't remember a time when she wasn't. She's the only mom I ever really knew. She was a tough one but the best a kid could have."

My head turned, and I stared at his profile in shock at getting this news about Margot and his apparent lack of his own mother as he guided me the rest of the way.

He stopped me and I turned to see Margot scooting into a booth. She barely got settled before she was sweeping her hand imperiously across the table.

"Get in. Get in. Johnathan knows better than to seat a lady on the outside of a booth to be brushed by waiters and busboys and patrons as they pass," she announced.

So Margot was the reason I got the seat with the view at Johnny's house.

I scooted in and tucked my purse and journal against the wall beside me as Johnny followed me in.

"You journal?" Margot asked in a way that made it more like a demand I offer up this information she already had to know since she'd seen me doing it.

"Yes," I told her. "I never did until my mother died. She did, journaling, I mean, and after she died, I took it up. I don't know why but it makes me feel closer to her."

Margot's piercing regard completely disintegrated and her commanding voice was nothing of the sort when she queried, "You lost your momma?"

I nodded. "To cancer."

"I'm sorry, darlin'," Margot murmured.

"Me too," Dave put in quietly.

I nodded to him and gave him a little smile.

Margot's head jerked up and turned left and she then hit David's arm lightly but repeatedly with the back of her hand. "Get that boy.

We need bread. Izzy needs something to snack on since we're delaying her meal."

David's eyes searched for "that boy" as Margot looked back at me.

"We'll order some of their stuffed mushrooms. They're *divine.* Have you been to The Star before?"

I looked around at the interior that didn't fit the unfinished clapboard exterior. It was mostly decorated in rich reds and golds, the décor unobtrusive, just classy and warm, and then I looked back to Margot.

"This is my first time," I shared.

Her pretty face split into a smile. "How wonderful we get to share it with you."

I felt Johnny's fingers drift down my thigh, there and gone, sharing he was sorry and he knew it wasn't so wonderful for me.

"So, are you a lawyer?"

This question, which I'd heard before, coming to me from David startled me.

"No. I work for a data management and security firm," I told him.

"How exciting!" Margot declared as she clapped her hands elegantly in front of her.

I grinned at her. "I think you and I are probably the only ones who think data is exciting."

"You get to wear that dress to work, and those shoes, darlin', are *fabulous.* Any job you get to dress like that has to be exciting," she returned.

"Gotta say, it's a knockout of a dress," Dave muttered.

Johnny made a noise in his throat that was muted and low, but it was the kind I'd only heard when he was in bed with me.

This so surprised me, my head floated around to look at him but I was arrested in this endeavor when Margot asked, "Now you said you were new to town. Where did you come to us from?"

"The city," I shared.

"So not far," she replied.

I shook my head. "No."

"I bet you like it out here better than there. All that dirt and noise and graffiti, and all those *people*," she stated, like *people* meant muddy, stinky livestock and she might eat beef, but she had no interest in how it came to be on her plate.

"I do." I nodded. "I have some land, and I can have my horses close and my dogs love it and it's calm and quiet. So yes. I very much like it here."

Her eyes slid toward Johnny when I mentioned my horses and dogs but came back to me before I finished.

"You got kin close?" Dave asked and I looked to him. "Said you lost your momma, child, but hope you got blood around."

"I have a sister but she got married and moved south. She's about a five-hour drive away so not too far but a lot farther than I like it. We're close but now it's more, after she had my nephew."

"Ooo, a nephew, lovely. How old is he?" Margot queried.

I looked down to my clutch and pulled out my phone, answering, "He's seven months now. He's adorable. His name is Brooklyn." I came up with my phone. "I call him Brooks."

"I'd call him Brooks too," Margot murmured delicately, sharing while not sharing she disapproved of my nephew's name.

I turned on my phone, went to All Photos and found a picture of Brooks that I took. I turned it around to show Margot.

"That's him a few months ago. I'll have to pull up Addie's texts to get one that's more recent. But I love that photo. It's my favorite of him. He's been a goof since birth and he's being a goof in that picture."

He was, giggling so much his chubby pink cheeks took over his eyes so all he looked like was pink cheeks, pink mouth, pink gums and blond baby fuzz.

Her shimmery-bronze tipped fingers came out and snatched my phone out of my hand.

"My, oh my, look at this child. He's *adorable*." Her head turned to Dave. "David, my love, find a waiter and get me a martini. I don't know what's taking them so long but Izzy is going to get a bad impres-

sion of The Star if they don't sort themselves out." She looked back to
my phone and went on like she hadn't interrupted her compliments
to my nephew by giving her husband another order. "You could just
eat him up with a *spoon*," she cooed.

I started giggling.

I stopped giggling when Johnny rested an arm behind us on the
booth.

Uninvited, Margot started flipping through the photos on my
phone by sliding her finger across the screen.

"I see your horses. They're *gorgeous*. And this cat is so *sweet*.
Now who's this? Is this your sister's husband?"

She turned the phone around and showed me a picture of Kent.

I instantly tensed.

Johnny instantly tensed beside me.

"No," I forced out.

"So, your brother?" she asked, shaking my phone side to side in
front of me. "Do you have a brother?"

"No," I pushed out.

"Margot," Johnny rumbled at the same time Dave said the same
thing.

Her face changed, her hand with my phone moved back slowly,
and she whispered a disappointed, "Oh."

I didn't like her disappointment or her face falling so I stated
quickly, "That's Kent. My ex."

This was not a good move.

Not in the slightest.

And it was only going to get worse.

She brightened but looked to me and asked, "If he's your ex,
darlin', why do you keep his picture? I always say, if you're movin' on,
move 'em out, leave 'em in your dust and start with a blank slate."

This seemed not only directed at me, but even if her eyes
didn't slide to Johnny like they had when I talked about my
animals, it was not lost on anyone it was mostly directed at
someone else.

"Margot," Dave growled, and Johnny shifted uncomfortably beside me.

But in order to comfort me, he wrapped his hand around the back of my neck.

Which did not comfort me at all.

"Well, I—" I began.

"Do you want me to delete it?" she asked helpfully, finger poised.

"*Margot*," Dave clipped.

"*No!*" I cried.

A death pall spread over the table.

"I can't delete it. It's evidence," I said swiftly and felt something else spreading over the table, coming from all directions, but especially Johnny.

I'd started it and from the avid attention I was getting from all quarters, I had no choice but to carry on with it.

"The police told me to save it. That milk glass he's holding was my mother's. Actually my grandmother's. He broke in, stole it, sent me that picture and then sent me the next one where he'd smashed it."

Woodenly, Margot shifted the picture to the next one and I watched her face pale.

"I should have put it on my cloud but I haven't gotten around to it. But, um...he's a big reason I moved to Matlock," I finished weakly.

As I spoke, all the time I spoke, Johnny's hand on my neck got tighter and tighter...

And tighter.

"Evidence," Margot whispered, staring at my phone.

"He kind of didn't want me to break up with him," I told her.

"Oh, child," Dave murmured.

But Margot's eyes narrowed.

On me.

"What else did he do to you?" she snapped.

"Excuse us," Johnny growled.

And they had no choice but to excuse us because Johnny was out of the booth and his hand capturing mine and dragging me meant I had to get out of the booth too.

Once I made my feet, he twisted our hands so they were held tucked to the side of his chest, which meant I had no choice but to be tucked tight to his side as he marched me out of the restaurant, straight out the front door, down the walk to the far side of the front where he whipped me around. He let my hand go, put his to my belly, shoved me against the clapboard and moved in so the rest of the world disappeared and the whole of mine became Johnny.

He then made a noise that I'd never heard come from any human before, a low, rolling, reverberating, hushed—what could only be described as—*roar*.

My eyes drifted up his throat to his just as he bit out, "*Kent?*"

"Did you just drag me out of a restaurant?" I whispered.

"Your ex broke into your house to steal something that meant something to you just so he could destroy it?"

I turned my head to look down the path and ascertained for myself that he did, indeed, just drag me out of a restaurant because there I was.

Outside the restaurant.

"Look at me, Izzy."

My eyes snapped back to his at the unerring command in his tone.

"Why didn't you tell me that shit?" he demanded.

"I—"

"Are you safe now?"

"Well—"

"You said the cops know. Did they do something about this fuck?"

"It's a little—"

"Do these friends know? The ones you say live close to you."

He was in such a state, I couldn't stop myself.

I arched into him, putting the fingers of both my hands to both of his bristly cheeks, and whispered, "Johnny."

A blaze of black fire continued to sear me for a moment before his eyes closed.

They opened and he asked a lot less terse now, "Did he hurt you?"

I dropped my hands from his face.

"He was just a nuisance."

"A nuisance doesn't break into your house and steal shit from you. A psycho does that."

I decided against telling him he'd broken down my door to steal Dempsey.

Or any of the other stuff.

"The cops know. I have a restraining order against him. Deanna and Charlie also know. The last time I saw him, Charlie was in my doorway with a baseball bat explaining that if I saw him again, Charlie would cave his head in with that bat. I think he took Charlie at his word, which is good because I have a feeling Charlie was serious and I don't want him in trouble. But I haven't seen or heard from Kent since. I'm not even sure he knows where I live. It's been months. It's over."

Johnny stared into my eyes before he looked at the clapboard over my head.

"It's very sweet you're concerned but—"

His gaze cut down to mine and he interrupted me.

Shockingly.

And breathtakingly.

"You look good. You smell good. That dress is so fucking hot I want to haul you around to the back, shove the skirt up, rip your panties off and fuck you against The Star."

My mouth dropped open.

Johnny wasn't done.

"Eat dinner beside you knowin' you can't put on your torn, useless fucking panties and I'll keep them in my pocket while you eat steak that isn't half as good as the one I made you, sitting beside me feeling thoroughly fucked."

"Johnny," I breathed, not right then feeling thoroughly fucked, alas, but definitely suddenly thoroughly *wet*.

"I thought I'd give it some time and come back, build something different with you, but I'm not thinking this friend thing is gonna work, Iz."

"Please don't say that," I begged.

His forehead came to mine, one hand went high on the wall beside me and his other hand slid down my side over the ruched, soft, stretchy white fabric of my dress that skimmed my figure from neck to knee, had no sleeves and even I had wondered if it was too sexy to wear to work (guess I had my answer).

"He comes back, you call the cops then your next call is me," he ordered.

"I can't promise that. Charlie already made me promise my next call would be him."

"Then you call this Charlie guy and *then* you call me."

"He won't come back, Johnny," I assured.

"You call the cops, Charlie and me. Say it, Izzy."

I stared up close into his eyes.

"I call the cops, Charlie then you, Johnny."

He didn't move.

I didn't either.

But eventually my mouth did.

"Is she back?"

"Oh no. Hell no." His forehead rolled on mine as he underlined a negative I thought I understood, but when he went on I would find I did not. "She doesn't get this. She doesn't get us. We've talked about her all we're ever gonna talk about her. She doesn't get to be a part of whatever it is that's gonna be the me and you we become."

My breath caught.

What did that mean?

"How're the dogs?" he asked.

"They're good," I forced out.

"The horses?"

"Good."

"Wesley still singing?"

He was *killing me.*

I nodded.

"Good, baby," he whispered, his gaze no longer focused on mine.

It had dropped to my mouth.

Oh God, he was going to kiss me.

Oh God, I was going to kiss him!

This couldn't happen.

I wanted it, boy did I want it.

But it took a huge effort of will to survive it ending after two breakfasts, two dinners, one telephone conversation, one text exchange and lots of sex.

If there was kissing, more sex or more *anything* like that, I might not.

We needed to be friends.

We could *not* be lovers.

"Oh shit, son, sorry." Both our heads turned (and I will note they did this without our foreheads disconnecting) to see Dave walking backward, hands up. "Could see you were shaken up at gettin' that news about Izzy. Margot could too. She sent me out to check on you but now I've done that and you two look like you're, um...good. You, uh...just get back to what you were doing."

Johnny made another noise, kind of like his subdued roar of earlier, but this one was not indication of enraged fury but instead indication of enraged frustration.

After making it, he lifted his forehead from mine and called, "We're coming back in, Dave. Tell Margot it's good and I hope you all ordered the mushrooms."

"Got you a beer, boy, mushrooms ordered, just take your time," Dave replied, moving sprightly back to the front doors and through them.

There was a couple standing outside the doors, both looking our way.

"Hey, uh...Johnny," the man called.

"Trev," Johnny returned and it sounded like a grunt, a loud one that carried, but a grunt nonetheless.

The woman Trev was with gave a hesitant wave.

Johnny ignored her.

I waved hesitantly back.

That got me a hesitant smile.

I hesitantly smiled back.

"Babe," Johnny clipped.

I looked back to him to see that he might have lifted his forehead but he was still close.

"That's Francine and she's the biggest mouth in Matlock," he shared.

"Oh dear," I murmured.

"Yeah," he agreed. "She's good people but good people with a big damned mouth."

"Hmm," I mumbled not wanting to be the talk of the town linked with Johnny when Shandra came back (if she wasn't already).

"I'm thinking we need another conversation about where shit's at with us," he declared.

Oh my.

"Johnny, it's the man you are to be protective but don't let what happened with Kent color where we—"

"*Kent* is whatever the fuck Kent is. That dress is why we need another conversation."

It really should be noted that I liked how much he liked my dress.

Even noted, I shouldn't and furthermore, couldn't.

I needed to tell him where I was with this.

"I'm not sure I can do just sex," I whispered.

"Right," he muttered.

I kept whispering. "I could do just friends."

"Right," he repeated.

"So maybe you can unpin me from the wall and we can go have dinner with Margot and Dave," I suggested.

His hand that was resting on my hip slid up and I thought it would slide *up* but it only got to my waist before he squeezed in, let me go and moved away.

I guessed he was going to make a stab at being friends.

That devastated me.

It shouldn't.

That didn't change the fact that it did.

But he caught my hand and held it as he led me back to the table, and I found it odd as just friends that Johnny held my hand and when we were lovers, he hadn't.

He stood solicitous to the side as he let me scoot in and he followed me immediately, but Margot wasn't wasting a second.

"Do you have the situation with this unsavory ex-boyfriend of Izzy's in hand, Johnathon?"

"It's in hand, Margot. Izzy has it sorted and we have an arrangement if something comes up. So you can chill," Johnny replied.

Her irate eyes turned to me. "I cannot *tell you* the number of times I've shared with Johnathon and his brother Tobias that I have not, do not, and never will *chill*. If a woman is upset they should listen and assure her and do whatever they can to sort the situation that's troubling her. Not simply tell her to *chill*."

"I do kind of have it sorted, Margot," I shared.

"Kind of is not *sorted*, Eliza," she retorted in a tone that made me fight back laughter, because she sounded like she'd known me all my life, not maybe twenty minutes, and she had the right to boss me around.

"Well, Kent's proved to be a guy who does what he's going to do but now I'm calling Johnny should he do more of it, so I think I'll be all right, don't you?" I assured her, not adding the cops and Charlie because I got the impression she thought Johnny could handle just about anything and that would help her to chill.

"Well then," she huffed, reaching to her martini glass that was nearly frosted the liquid was so chilled and had three big fat olives in it, making me wish I wasn't driving so I could have a martini. In that moment I sure the heck needed one. "I see it's actually sorted so fine."

"Is that vodka or gin?" I asked, reaching for my wine.

"Vodka," she answered.

"If you like flavored vodkas, I make them and they're really yummy. If you want to try them, I'll bottle some and get them to you."

She took a sip with her eyes on me the entire time I talked, and when I was done she slid my phone across the table to me with one hand, the other hand swinging her martini to the side like I would imagine a sultry bombshell from the sixties would do the same thing.

Except cooler.

"Then it's good I already programmed myself into your phone. I also called myself so I have your number. So there'll be no delay in you phoning me to invite me over for a vodka tasting."

I hadn't invited her for a vodka tasting but I didn't share that because I loved the idea of doing that. Deanna would too. And she'd think Margot was a hoot.

"I'll set that up right away," I said.

"Excellent," she answered, lifting her glass to me.

I lifted mine to her and we both took a sip.

"That right there, Johnny boy, you witnessed it. Your girl here accidentally just participated in the ritual that enters her right into the coven," Dave declared.

Johnny chuckled.

Margot sliced narrowed eyes to her husband. "I wish you'd stop referring to my circle as 'the coven,'" she stated.

He bent his face to hers with a smile on his. "The voodoo that you do, sweetheart, I've been addicted to for forty-eight years. That wasn't an insult. But I've been a man bewitched for nearly five decades. Johnny here hasn't even lived that long, so it *was* a warning. And you and me both know that when that voodoo you do spreads to your acolytes, he needs that."

Johnny draped his arm across the booth again.

I felt a tingle again.

I also sighed.

Margot's face softened as she looked into her husband's eyes.

The waiter arrived at our table with the mushrooms.

Margot looked to him. "Well, *finally*."

I giggled.

Johnny's hand curled around the back of my neck again.

I let out another sigh.

Margot looked to me. "Now, Eliza, *do* tell me where you got that dress and those shoes, because I'm thinking we'll go shopping at these places first and *then* return to your home to taste vodkas. Don't worry. Dave is a very experienced designated driver. He comes to pick me up after a lot of coven activities, his way of referencing them, not mine. So we can be thorough in our sampling."

I grinned at her.

She grinned back, her blue eyes sparkling.

Johnny reached for the mushrooms and served me first, pushing four of them on my appetizer plate, before he handed them to Dave who pushed four of them on Margot's, and only then did he take some for himself then hand the remainder to Johnny.

I reached for my fork.

And made plans to go shopping and drink vodka with the only woman who'd been a mother to Johnny Gamble.

EIGHT

MORE IMPORTANTLY

Izzy

"Let me get this straight," Deanna said.

It was the next morning at work, and I wasn't certain I wanted to let her get this straight. Whenever Deanna performed the lengthy process of "getting something straight," that something emerged in logical clarity your illogical mind refused to allow it to have until she'd straightened it out, and sometimes that wasn't a good thing.

I had the feeling if she got this particular thing straight, that being what happened the night before with Johnny, it would absolutely not be a good thing.

Because the promise of it actually *being* a good thing and that not coming to fruition would be cataclysmic.

"Deanna—" I tried.

"So," she spoke over me, "three long, agonizing, heartbroken years and Johnny Gamble gets a call from his ex, his Juliet, his Guinevere, his Scarlett, but he has a date planned with you. After this call, he knows he's got no choice and is gonna end it between you two but for some reason that's out of character for this guy, he goes through with the date anyway. He also buys you ten bottles of wine to choose from during said date so you have a better shot at having exactly what you want."

He'd, of course, done that. It had seemed sweet at the time.

It seemed sweeter now.

I continued to stare across my desk at her sitting in one of the chairs opposite me and tried again, "Deanna—"

"During this date, he has sex with you, knows it's wrong, in fact *so* knows it's wrong and he's so cut up about it, he can't sleep. You wake up and he delivers a tortured speech about how he's done you wrong and how his ex messed him up so bad he can't be all you'd need him to be if things went further with you. You two decide to be friends, but he doesn't then take you to your car, load up your dogs and give you a kiss on your cheek, telling you to drive safe home. He makes out with you then leads you to his bed and sleeps with you tucked close."

He'd done that too. And it had also seemed sweet at the time but definitely sweeter now.

And as she talked I was realizing, as much as I loved her, that maybe I shouldn't share so much with her.

"De—" I started but that was as far as I got.

"You don't see him, hear from him, then he shows at The Star and he doesn't walk by you, give you space, take his seat with his second father and the only mother he ever knew, tipping his chin to you if he catches your eye in that hot way hot guys have of saying pretty much anything when they don't feel like speaking. He stops and he doesn't say hey or how's it going. He right off the bat asks you if you're alone."

I felt my heart start beating harder because I hadn't thought about that.

And I gave up trying to interrupt. Deanna was getting something straight and I should have learned a long time ago just to let her.

"Which says, obviously, he was thinking you might be on a date and one could read into that he might not like that much," she went on. "*At all,*" she stressed.

Yes, one could read just that.

"So then," she carried on, "the only mother he ever knew invites you to dinner—"

"She didn't invite me, Deanna. She pretty much just told me I was eating with them," I cut in to share.

Deanna kept talking like I didn't.

"And he's Johnny Gamble, *all* that's Johnny Gamble. He could find a way to make that not happen but he doesn't. He doesn't even begin to fight it. He just gives you an out should it be bothering you so much you can't go through with it, sharing he'd take care of it...but only then. Other than that, he doesn't say boo."

I bit my lip.

He'd done that too.

Deanna kept at it.

"The situation with Kent comes out, Johnny loses his mind, drags you out of the restaurant, demands you phone him if something goes down then tells you he wants to do you against The Star and take your panties as a souvenir."

My clit pulsed at the reminder.

Yes, I definitely needed to share less with Deanna.

"And when you bring *her* up," she continued, "he won't even allow you to speak about her. Not because he doesn't want to talk about her but because he refuses to allow her to get between whatever you two are to each other."

My heart pulsed at that.

"Yes," I whispered when she stared at me and said no more.

At this point she said more.

"And you're barely through the door home before he texts you."

I was.

Last night, I'd barely gotten through the door before Johnny was texting me.

"Yes," I repeated.

And then it came.

The declaration.

And the pulse it gave me was more like a shockwave throughout my system.

"This guy is into you."

"Deanna—"

"I don't wanna say it," she told me. "Heck, I didn't even think I ever *would* say it. But I'm saying it. Johnny Gamble is into you. Nope, that isn't it. That man is *into you*."

"Shandra's back or coming back or—" I started.

She shook her head, lifting her hand shaking that too, and interrupted me.

"Make no mistake, that boy's messed up. She's got him twisted still and he's in a bad way about it. But that hold she's got on him is in its death throes, Iz. He got jacked by a stupid woman who threw away probably the best thing she was ever going to have and that tore him up. And then he met you."

I was feeling warm inside. So warm I felt it everywhere and it was beginning to burn.

"I told him I couldn't do just sex and he agreed with that, Deanna," I reminded her. "So it's clear he wants sex without anything weighing on that or just to be friends."

"Yeah, nonverbally he agreed. Also nonverbally he held your hand all the way back to the table, served your mushrooms first, kept touching you all through dinner, walked you to your car and texted you almost the minute you got home."

Definitely needed to stop sharing so much with Deanna.

"It doesn't mean anything," I said softly.

"I got men friends and none of them squeeze my neck, rest their arm on the back of the booth we're sitting in, touch my thigh, tinker with the bracelet on my wrist or walk me to my car even before I had Charlie, who would break their neck if they tried any of that shit."

The first thigh touch wasn't the last one last night.

And the tinkering with the bracelet thing had come after

Margot had said she'd admired it. I'd told her it was my mother's and about ten minutes later, after the dinner plates were swept away and before the dessert Margot insisted we have was served (and when I said I was too full, she decreed I could share Johnny's, and when his arrived, she demanded I share Johnny's, so I shared Johnny's) Johnny had become fascinated with it.

Which meant I exerted some effort not to become fascinated with Johnny's fascination with it.

By the way, I failed at this.

And by the way, Margot didn't miss any of it.

Margot's machinations weren't hard to decipher. She elongated dinner to the point we'd closed the place down and she'd done it in an effort to get to know me better and force me to spend time with Johnny.

Dave hadn't resisted, because Dave wouldn't only throw his hanky over a puddle so her shoes wouldn't get wet, he loved her so deeply, he'd throw himself bodily over that puddle.

That said, Dave was totally on board also to force me to spend time with Johnny.

Johnny hadn't resisted for reasons I refused to think about.

That was, he hadn't resisted until it became clear Margot didn't care they were setting up the restaurant for lunch the next day and wanted us gone. She'd have talked to the wee hours of the morning if she could get away with it.

But I'd yawned.

I'd tried to be inconspicuous about it but Johnny had seen it.

Within two seconds the night was over.

No, I refused to think about any of his reasons.

Until now when Deanna was making me think of them.

"You need to ride this out," Deanna advised quietly.

"Doll—" I began.

"Baby girl, no way I'd set you up for this kind of fall if I didn't think it was worth the risk."

"Three weeks ago you were telling me to be careful of getting in too deep with Johnny Gamble," I reminded her.

"That was before the ten bottles of wine and the communication of his desire to do you against the wall of The Star."

It was indeed before all of that.

She wasn't finished.

"And three weeks ago Shandra hadn't called him and forced him to take a good look at his life and what he had in it. You been spending the last two weeks cut up about something you wanted that was never meant to be. I think last night states clear Johnny Gamble spent the last two weeks the same exact way."

"I can't think of it like that. We're friends. It may take some work to get to that place but we're just going to be friends," I stated firmly. "He heard about Kent and got protective because he's that kind of guy." I paused and then added, "And I had on a pretty dress."

"Babe that dress is *fine*, and you look *fine* in it, and Johnny Gamble could want a piece of that action but Johnny Gamble would never go for that, say one word about it. For you and your peace of mind, to keep things where they need to be between you two, he'd control the urge, put it in the back of his mind and keep on keepin' on. That is, he'd do that if he didn't want a piece of what was in that dress because of *who* was wearing that dress. He might not have consciously intended to make you think about him doing you against the wall of The Star all through dinner, but I don't think he's too cut up about knowing you spent half that dinner thinking about him doing you against the wall of The Star."

"That's not Johnny, he isn't like that," I told her somewhat heatedly, the heat coming from defending Johnny.

"Precisely," she retorted, reading the heat.

Sometimes I really hated when Deanna got things straight.

"My advice doesn't change," she announced. "Be careful. Look after you. But it also has changed because I know you, Izzy. I know how beautiful you are right down to your bones. I know that runs so deep, it spills out everywhere. I don't know Johnny Gamble to throw him but I know enough to know the man isn't stupid. He caught that. He caught your sweetness and he definitely caught your honesty, and he caught you being gentle about understanding where he was at and not ending it ugly but ending it compassionately, trying to salvage some part of what both of you felt brewing between you. Again, I don't know Johnny and I also don't know what happened to him and Shandra. But just like anyone else in Matlock, I paid attention because it was just something you pay attention to."

She paid attention because she was nosy.

I didn't interrupt her to share that. I also didn't have a chance because she again wasn't finished.

"And what I've seen of that man, what you've said, he's a gentleman. He wouldn't play you. He might have dinner with you and the family he's got left in an effort to start this friendship you think you two are building. But he'd never, *never*, Iz, mix his signals like he did last night with you. He might be twisted up still, but he's not playing games. His heart is telling him something and it seems to me he's listening."

"I can't do this," I whispered.

"Then don't," she replied. "If Johnny gets his head sorted and decides he's gonna make that play, all I'm saying is, let him do it."

I decided not to respond.

But my heart was still beating fast, warming up my entire body.

"I love you, doll, but I need to quit thinking about this and get back to work," I said.

She nodded. "I hear you. But did you hear me?"

I nodded.

She gave me a gentle smile and stood, but she leaned into a hand on my desk and did it holding my eyes with her warm brown ones.

"Just to finish up, I was wrong about something else. You got your hands on a stray, baby girl. Lost and alone, maybe cast aside, definitely done wrong. And you're Izzy Forrester. No one better at taking the stray out of the stray and giving them home. And also, Scarlett wanted Ashley. He went for Melanie. And Melanie was the finest being in that book. Even Rhett adored Melanie. Scarlett gets all the attention because the woman is the diva to end all divas. But there ain't nothing wrong with being Melanie. Far from it. She was just as strong as Scarlett but a whole lot quieter about it, which is strength in itself. Johnny isn't Ashley but I'm thinking he isn't Rhett either. I'm thinking that Johnny Gamble is realizing that and because of it he's realizing Scarlett wasn't the one for him. He's thinking he's all about Melanie."

"You need to stop it," I told her quietly.

"So I will." She grinned, pushing away from my desk. "Just to say, I'm also thinking this is going to be fun." She kept grinning as she shook her head. "Don't worry, I still got my eyes on you and I'm always here. This is still going to be fun."

"Not from where I'm sitting," I muttered.

"Then, Izzy, start paying attention."

With that, she sashayed out of my office.

I watched until she disappeared.

Then, stupidly, I dropped my eyes to my phone and lifted my hand to it.

Leaving it sitting on my desk, I engaged it.

And I went to Johnny's text screen.

I scrolled up and started reading.

You too. Johnny from weeks ago.

You home okay? Johnny from last night.

Yes, Johnny, thanks. And thanks for dinner. Me, because Johnny and Dave got in a minor fight but definitely the word "fight" was apropos about who would pay. Although I went so far as to get my wallet out, they didn't even acknowledge I'd done that, ignoring me so completely I had no choice but to put it back in my purse without having a chance to utter a word.

This fight had unsurprisingly been sorted when Margot waded in, stating, "Split it, boys. That way, David, you're taking care of me and Johnny's got Izzy."

Johnny's got Izzy.

They agreed immediately.

God, I *hated* it when Deanna got things straight.

No problem, babe. Going to the festival? Johnny texted.

Yes. My first big thing as a resident of Matlock, I replied. Then, drunk on an evening spent with Johnny and two people he cared about who cared about him, at the same time disconcerted about it and not thinking straight thus being an idiot, I added, *Though I've been before with Deanna and Charlie.*

It's a blast but go early and get out early. Out of towners come in the afternoon and traffic is a bitch.

Thanks for the advice. Are you home?

Yup.

How? You had farther to drive than me.

I followed you, Iz. You need to take driving lessons from Margot. Dave calls her AJ Foyt. You drive like you're behind the wheel of a Buick and just celebrated your ninth decade on this earth.

I laughed at his joke, wandering my house, letting the dogs out, checking the cats, covering the birds, getting ready for bed, through it all phone held in hand like a lifeline, texting Johnny Gamble.

Not surprised Margot drives like an Indy car driver, I'd shared.

He's being nice. It's more like demolition derby. Her car is in my shop more than any in three counties and not because she's big on keeping her oil clean.

That made me laugh again.

Right, you got work tomorrow so I'll let you go. Dogs in? He'd asked.

That made my belly flip-flop and I answered, *Getting them now.*

Lock up tight after you. Windows too, baby.

Baby.

I'd missed that.

Two breakfasts, two dinners (now three) and the little there was of the rest and I'd missed *him.*

A lot.

Now I was getting more of him.

A lot more.

And liking it.

Too much.

I will, Johnny, I'd replied. *Sleep well.*

And he'd ended it the way it had ended before.

But this time it didn't seem an end at all.

You too.

I stared at the screen of my phone, scrolling up and down idly with my finger, reading and rereading, so lost in it, I let a small smile spread on my face and I nearly jumped out of my chair when the phone I was staring at rang.

The screen changed from the text string with Johnny to announce Johnny was calling.

Oh God, what did I do?

My mind didn't know.

But before it rang twice, my hand decided it did and it snatched up the phone, took the call and put it to my ear.

"Hey," I greeted.

"Hey, got a sec?" he asked.

I didn't. I'd barely gotten any work done that day.

"Sure," I answered.

"Got a friend who has a horse. He and his family are going on vacation and the person who used to look after him has left town. He's way out there, about a forty-minute drive away or I'd look after him. I noticed you got a couple of open stables. Wondered if you'd be cool stabling his horse. Not more work for you, Iz. I'll come and deal with him."

I sat staring at all the work on my desk I should be doing but wasn't since I was talking to Johnny, and I did this thinking of Johnny coming out to my house every day to take care of a horse.

This was a good thought.

"So?" he prompted when I said nothing. "Will Serengeti be able to handle company?"

"I...well, I've got to take care of Serengeti and Amaretto anyway so you don't have to—"

"While Mist is there, I'll deal with Serengeti and Amaretto too."

He'd take care of my horses too.

"Johnny—"

"You'd help him out. He's in a bind. Everyone he can find is charging a shit ton. He'd pay you, bring his own feed, make sure you're covered for hay and time. But I'd deal with the rest."

My mouth made up my mind for me. "I don't think that would be a problem."

"Fantastic, *spätzchen*, I'll tell him."

"*Spätzchen?*"

"What?"

"You called me *spätzchen*."

Johnny made no reply.

My heart convulsed.

Whatever that meant, he'd called her that too.

"Okay, whatever. Just let me know when—" I began.

"My granddad called my grandmother that. She was German. He met her over there when he was in the service. Married her there."

"That's sweet," I forced out.

"She used endearments too. She called me *häschen*," he went on with sharing.

"That's...sweet?" It was a question this time because I didn't know what that word meant.

He chuckled. "It means little hare. She called my brother *mäuschen*. That means little mouse."

"Yes, sweet," I murmured.

"*Spätzchen* means little sparrow and no, she never got that," he stated bluntly, reading my thoughts, and my breath arrested. "Iz?" he called when I concentrated on forcing myself to breathe.

"I'm here."

"I wouldn't do that to her," he said.

Of course he wouldn't.

"Right," I whispered.

"More importantly, I wouldn't do that to you."

My breath arrested again.

More importantly?

"We clear on that?" he demanded to know, sounding like he was ticked.

"Are you angry?" I asked.

"I wouldn't do that to you."

"Okay," I said softly, realizing he really just wouldn't.

"I didn't call her anything I got from Grams."

"Okay, Johnny."

"We clear on that?" he repeated, definitely wanting to make sure we were.

"We're clear on that," I told him.

"So that doesn't happen again," he declared.

"Sorry?"

"That kind of shit, it doesn't enter your head."

"Johnny, I don't think this is—"

"Say it, baby. Let that shit go," he coaxed gently, definitely wanting me to do that too.

"It doesn't enter my head," I whispered.

"Good," he stated. "I'll talk to my bud, call you about Mist."

"Okay."

"Have fun at the festival," he bid.

"Are you, um...going?"

"I always swing by. The garage sponsors a tent that makes money for Pop Warner. I think this year it's a hog roast. Or ribs. Or something. My GM sets it up but I gotta make an appearance."

That was all he said. Not that he'd meet me there. Not that we could hang there for a while then go to Home and hang there for a while, and then maybe go to his place, or mine, and fuck each other until we pass out.

So maybe him calling me a pet name as derived from his German grandmother, something he didn't give Shandra, wasn't what it might seem to be, especially to Deanna if she knew about it (which she wouldn't, I was learning).

And anyway, I'd just promised not to let that enter my head.

It wasn't my business.

They were who they were and would be whatever they became.

And we were who we were and would be whatever we became.

And Johnny clearly did not intend for the twain to meet.

"Oh, okay," I replied.

"Have a good day at work and talk to you later."

"You too, Johnny."

"Later, babe."

"'Bye, Johnny."

We hung up. Our texts came back up. And I stared at the screen, confused at what had just happened.

Deanna would sort it out.

But I was not telling Deanna.

I also wasn't going to take her advice, though part of it I was.

I wasn't going to pay attention. I wasn't going to read into things to see if Johnny intended to make any play, then let him make it, possibly getting my hopes up only for them to be dashed.

What I was going to do was be careful, look after me and do what I'd told myself I was going to do weeks earlier when this all began.

I was just going to *be*.

As I DROVE up my drive that night, I stared at the yellow Ford Focus parked in front of my house, my heart thrumming a mad beat.

The dogs were out and they avoided my car as I parked, but they were on me the minute I opened my door.

I loved my babies.

But it was only cursory pets I gave them before I ran to my front door, the screen shut, the door behind it open.

Me and Swirl and Dempsey pushed through and we barely got two steps in before I shouted, "Addie!"

My sister appeared at the back of the hall coming out of my kitchen, my nephew on her hip.

"Jeez, the drama," she drawled.

I raced down the hall and threw my arms around her and Brooks.

She only had one arm but she wrapped it around me and held tight.

Brooks pulled my hair.

I shifted a bit away, not letting her go, and declared happily, "I can't believe you guys are here!"

"Well we are, in the flesh," she returned.

I smiled at her, turned and gave Brooks a sloppy kiss on his neck. He tilted his head toward the kiss and squealed. I looked back to my sister.

"Where's Perry?" I asked after my brother-in-law.

Her face shut down.

Oh no.

My enthusiasm at her surprise visit started to dissolve.

"What's happening?" I queried gently.

"Nothing," she answered, pulling from my hold but then depositing Brooks right in my arms before she moved back into the kitchen. "Brooklyn and me just needed a little vacation. We can't afford a five star on the Riviera so we came to the next best place." She stopped at my island and turned back to me. "Here."

"And Perry couldn't come on this vacation?" I pushed.

She shrugged one shoulder.

Brooks attacked my necklace.

I turned my attention to him, lifting a hand to carefully disengage the chain from his grip. "No, baby. That's delicate and it was Grandma's," I whispered.

He looked at my face like I swear he understood me then giggled so hard, his roly-poly body bobbled in my arm and his attention shifted to the floor when Swirl trotted in.

Brooks squealed and reached toward my dog.

"The chicken is in the brine," Addie declared and I looked to her. "I'm making my famous chicken parmigiana."

"It's *my* famous chicken parmigiana," I corrected her.

"Even if someone steals something, they've stolen it so they have it so it's theirs," she returned.

"But I still have it so it's mine."

"We can share it," she replied.

I didn't want to talk about chicken parmigiana.

I wanted to talk about why my sister and her son were in my house without warning and Perry wasn't with them.

"Addie—" I began.

"Put him down. The dogs love him and he loves them. He'll be fine," she ordered, moving toward the fridge.

"Addie—" I tried again.

"And get changed. I brought two bottles of tequila and the makings for *my* famous margarita mixer, and that *is* mine even though *you* stole it and you can't say it isn't."

She was right. That was hers and I totally stole it, her margaritas were that marvelous.

"We're eating, putting Brooks down and getting loaded," she finished.

I decided to wade into the Perry situation after she'd had a margarita or two.

"It's the Memorial Weekend Food Festival in Matlock tomorrow," I shared.

She sent a smile my way.

A smile that was not her usual devil-may-care Adeline Forrester smile.

"Awesome," she decreed.

"I take it you want to go," I noted, bending to put Brooks on the floor.

Dempsey instantly moved to him with Swirl not far behind.

Brooks shrieked when he got doggie kisses and then started giggling.

"Sun, copious amounts of food, my baby and my sister? Heck yeah I wanna go."

"Great, doll," I murmured. Louder, I told her, "I'm gonna run and get changed. I'll be right back."

"Right on."

"Did you get your stuff in?" I asked.

"We're all sorted," she replied, whisking eggs in a bowl.

"'Kay. I'll get on margaritas when I get back."

"That's a deal."

I left the room and was putting my purse that had been over my shoulder through all that on the hall table when it rang.

I pulled out my phone and saw it said JOHNNY CALLING.

I let it ring more than once that time because I didn't want to be in earshot of Addie when I answered.

She was going to tell me about Perry, I'd make sure of it.

I was *not* going to tell her about Johnny. If she knew about Johnny, she'd drug my margarita, take me to the mill herself and put me in his bed.

"Hey," I answered when I was halfway up the steps.

"You driving?" he asked.

"No, I'm home and my sister's here. Surprise visit."

"She bring Brooks?"

He asked about Brooks like he'd not only met him but helped raise him.

"Yes."

"Cool for you, baby," he murmured.

"Yes," I agreed, and it was. I loved my sister. I hated her living so far away.

What I didn't love was knowing something was up. Something she wouldn't tell me.

"I won't take a lot of your time then," he said as I entered my room. "Talked to Ben. They're taking off next Saturday. I'm gonna go get Mist and bring him to you that day if it's good with you."

"It's good with me," I replied distractedly, flipping off my shoes.

"You sure?" Johnny asked.

"Of course," I answered.

"I'll bring feed and muck out his stall after he goes back home, which'll be the next Saturday."

I juggled my phone in the crook of my neck as I went for the belt on my slacks. "It's fine, Johnny. Serengeti and Amaretto were stabled with a bunch of horses before we came out here. They like company."

"Fantastic, babe. Now I'll let you get back to your sister."

With my belt undone, I gave up on my slacks, sat on my bed and blurted, "Her husband isn't here."

"Say that again?" Johnny demanded.

"Perry. Her husband, who I want to like, I've tried to like, but I can't like because he's a loser, isn't here. She's here. Brooks is here. And Perry is not here. She's not telling me why. She's keeping something from me."

"Shit," he muttered.

"Yes," I agreed.

"How's this guy a loser?" he queried.

"He can't hold a job because he's convinced himself he's the next Chris Robinson and has to be available for gigs that never materialize since he's no longer even in a band. But he's okay watching TV, drinking beer and going out with his buds while she holds one down and does overtime. They had Brooks, and for Perry it was about someone giving him something to play with. Not the responsibility of raising a child and all that comes with that like diaper changes, feedings in the middle of the night, looking after him because he can't fend for himself, and oh, I don't know...contributing to the household to keep a roof over his head."

"Shit," Johnny repeated in a mutter.

"Yes," I repeated my agreement.

"Where are you?" he asked a strange question.

"At home," I answered.

"No, *spätzchen*," he said quietly with gentle humor. "Where are you that it seems like you can talk without her hearing?"

"I'm in my bedroom. She's in the kitchen."

"So you can talk without her hearing?"

"Yes, Johnny."

"She needs to dump this guy."

I blinked at my bare feet at his frank and inflexible decree after I'd shared the little I'd shared about Perry.

"He's her husband and the father of her child," I reminded him.

"Don't give a shit. She's there, that's good. Something's going wrong at home, she's the best place she can be. With her sister. With family. With someone who'll take care of her, look out for her and have her back. There's a scale of assholes to dipshits. Murderers and rapists are at the top of that scale. But men who don't look after their wives and kids aren't closer to the dipshit end. They're up top. She needs to scrape him off, and since you got her, you need to guide her to that."

"She loves him," I shared.

"Love isn't everything. When it comes to this kind of thing, love is nothing. I can see those people who stay together for their children because they both love their kids and they both want to work at giving them a good home. I can't see those people who stay with someone who's a fuckwit because they love him."

"This makes sense," I murmured, even if his declaring at all that "love was nothing" was a tad alarming.

"Izzy, baby, there are good guys out there. She scrapes this one off, she'll find one of those guys."

"My mom didn't," I told him.

"My mom left, my dad didn't find a good one either. But he had fun trying. And she gave him two things that meant everything to him. His sons. So your sister, she's doin' all right. She's got you and she's got her boy and whatever comes after that comes. We all gotta settle in with what we got and just rejoice if life gives us more or gives us better. She not only has more, she's got her son, so she's got better."

I wanted to know about his mom. I wanted to know about his dad. I wanted to know about his brother. I wanted to know why he seemed to have all the time in the world to listen and advise about a possible problem with my sister that even I didn't know what was happening.

And I wanted to tell him how much it meant to me that he'd listen and advise but also that he was the kind of man who would say the kinds of things he was saying.

But being careful and looking out for me, I wasn't going to give myself any of that.

"We're having a margarita night so maybe I can pry something loose and give her your honesty," I said.

"My experience with you is that margarita nights lead to really good things, so I'm rooting for you, baby."

I again stared at my feet as those particular words made my toes curl.

"Now I'll let you go be with your sister. Take care, Iz."

"You too, Johnny. 'Bye."

"Later, *spätzchen*," he murmured then he hung up.

It was then I realized he didn't say "bye," he said "later," and that was a version of "bye" but it could also mean something entirely different.

After realizing that, I realized that I was paying attention and picking apart some nuance that Johnny had given me instead of just letting whatever we were becoming be.

Anyway, I had to change clothes and get down to my sister. She didn't live close so I didn't have near enough of her.

And she wasn't talking but I knew she needed me.

NINE

A REUNION

Izzy

"We'll get a patch of grass, stake our claim and then we can go back and start sampling," I suggested to Addie as we wandered down one of the many crisscross walks in Matlock's town square late the next morning.

She was pushing Brooks in his stroller and we'd made a loop to check out all the booths and tents.

This year's festival was bigger than the one I'd been to, some of the stalls going down alleys and one of the streets off the square shut down so food trucks could roll in.

There was everything a festival could have that was all about food but also all the festival vendors with all their wares on display, not to mention the face painters, hair braiders, flower laurel makers, balloon animal sellers, and then some.

The place wasn't yet packed, but it was busy and festive.

But I was in hell.

My hell was due to three reasons. Drinking too many margaritas the night before. Staying up until four in the morning talking to my sister. And the fact she'd firmly avoided any chat about Perry, but I'd spied she'd obviously loaded up her car to the gills and brought it all to my house, mostly Brooks's stuff.

I didn't have a kid and I knew when you had a baby you didn't have the luxury to travel light.

But you didn't have to travel like she'd done to spend a few days off with her sister.

She had a portable crib, a portable high chair, a ton of his clothes (and hers by the way), several bags of diapers, wipes and the rest, what had to be every toy he owned and enough food to last a month.

So as we wandered I was tired, hungover and very worried, and to top that off, the sun was shining bright. The day was the warmest we'd had that year so far, and all I felt like doing was lying down and taking a nap or shaking my sister and demanding she tell me what was happening.

But I knew my sister. She wasn't one to hold things in forever, she shared when it was her time. I just had to wait it out.

I didn't like it but it was my only choice.

"How about here?" I asked, motioning to a wedge of grass shaded by a large tree, the surrounding areas quickly being taken up by other festival goers.

"Works for me," Addie replied, looking rested and alert, something I found annoying but then she was a mom and she was a waitress at a high-end restaurant. She was used to late hours and lost sleep and being run off her feet.

I dumped the basket I was carrying that had napkins, plastic cups, real forks, spoons, knives, wet wipes, treats for Brooks and a bottle of sunscreen for touch ups, and I slid the plaid blanket out of the handles, unfolded it and flicked it out to lay it on the grass.

"I can't believe you have a picnic basket like that," Addie remarked.

I looked at the double door basket with its pink and white gingham lining rimming the edges then at my sister. "I got it at a garage sale for twenty-five cents. It was dirty but in perfect condition.

Except I had to replace the lining, and that material I bought at a yard sale for five whole cents."

She fell to her knees on the blanket and twisted to a sleepy Brooks in his stroller at its edge, saying, "That's my Iz. If there's a deal or a steal, she'll find it."

I said nothing because I considered that a high compliment.

Addie looked to me. "Except for dog food, cat food and bird seed, you ever pay full price for anything?"

"No," I answered, and I had no problems with that either.

"Right," she muttered, turning back to Brooks and pulling him out of his stroller, still speaking. "I blame Dad for a lot of things and that's one of them."

"Sorry?" I asked.

She set Brooks on the blanket and he immediately but drowsily crawled to me so I dropped to my knees so when he reached me, he could have me.

"You always wanted things. That's who you are and that's cool because pretty much everyone is like that. Mom wanted peace on earth and a fresh manicure every other week. I wanted him," she motioned to Brooks, "and more like him. You wanted things."

"I didn't want things," I said, feeling stung.

"You liked clothes and you liked shoes and you liked purses and hair stuff and your space just so. Mom bought that plastic wineglass for you that birthday and I swear, for months, you never drank out of anything but that."

"I was a little girl and it was fancy," I explained.

Her eyes locked to mine. "We're allowed to want things and not only earn them and work for them and fight for them, but have someone maybe once in a while *give* them to us because they love us and they want us to have what we want."

I stayed silent and held her gaze, letting her get it out.

She then got more of it out.

"Mom would have lassoed the moon and brought it down to us if it was in her power, and we wanted it. I'm not surprised she died so young. I think of it a lot, every day, and I think that cancer she had was Dad and it was always with her even before they found it, eating away at her every time she couldn't give us something. Every time she had to do without so we could have stuff we just plain needed, not wanted, *needed*. She had to stomach so much of that, it's not surprising it burned through her, wasted her away."

"Don't think of it like that," I whispered, lifting up Brooks and holding him tight to me but never taking my eyes off my sister.

She glanced at Brooks in my arms before looking away and declaring, "I'm getting souvlaki."

"I'll go with you."

She turned back to me. "You stay. Save our place."

"The Greek tent isn't in Africa. We won't be gone a week. Our stuff will be okay here."

"Iz, I hate to break this to you," she started, swinging out an arm, "but bad stuff, *really* bad stuff, happens. Even in Mayberry."

I didn't think of Matlock as Mayberry.

With the gazebo in the square and the cute shops and handsome buildings with their bright bunting all around it, I thought it looked more like Stars Hollow.

"No one is going to take an old picnic basket," I told her.

"People are capable of anything. They don't know you cleaned it up and lined that picnic basket yourself, and if you had to replace it with something new you couldn't, because you have horses to feed. They just want it so they'll take it and they don't think for a second that it means something to someone else and it's not theirs to have in the first place."

"Addie—"

"And anyway, I love him more than my life but it wouldn't suck to take a walk in the sun and get some souvlaki without pushing my boy in front of me."

I knew she had very little of that. She had a neighbor who ran a small daycare center in her house who also loved Addie and Brooks, so she did a lot of extra watching him because Perry couldn't be bothered to do it. Even when he wasn't working.

But if Addie wasn't working, anything that had anything to do with taking care of Brooks was all on my sister.

I held her boy closer. "Brooks and I'll stay here."

"That's my Izzy," she murmured, again locking eyes with me. "If what happened to Mom ever happened to you, you'd waste away in seconds, not able to give the people you love everything they want."

"Addie," I whispered.

She rolled to her feet. "I'll be back."

I rested on my knees and watched her go, disappearing quickly in the fast-growing crowd.

I had her on my mind and all she said. I also had a sleepy Brooks in my arms. It was naptime for baby boys, and sleepy Brooks was reminding me I needed a nap and badly.

With all this, at first, I didn't notice it.

But then I did.

People were watching me, and when I caught their eyes, they didn't look away.

Some smiled. Some lifted their chins. One woman even waved. So tentatively I waved back.

I would think this was friendly but they weren't doing it to other people.

It was just me.

It was me because of Francine.

And it was Francine because of what she saw happen at The Star between me and Johnny.

Crap.

I fell to my hip and curled my legs around, cradling a snuggling Brooks in my arms and trying to ignore the attention I was receiving.

"Okay, well," I began in a half hum, half coo to my nephew while rocking him gently side to side, "the good news is, it seems I have the town's approval when it comes to me and Johnny. The bad news is, it seems the town thinks there's something to approve of."

Brooks's eyes were drooping but that wasn't the only reason he made no reply.

The sun dappled the picnic blanket, the big trees over us offering shade and coolness that wasn't to be found on some of the paths that were in the sun and I decided to put Brooks down so he could settle in.

I also decided to have a bit of a rest myself. I told no lie, the souvlaki was not in Africa and Addie would be back in no time.

So I put Brooks on his belly on the blanket. I was careful to tuck around my bum the full (but knee length) skirt of my black sundress with its stark red, orange and yellow flowers intermingled with teal peacocks print, subtly ruffled short sleeves and plunging vee neckline (so, okay, the possibility I'd run into Johnny crossed my mind while dressing that day, sue me). I curled my legs in their dusty cowboy boots up to cocoon Brooks as much as I could. I then rounded him with an arm, resting my head on my other arm that I stretched out.

In that position, I watched my nephew drift off to sleep.

I thought I might doze, but Brooks was out and Addie would be back shortly, we'd be okay.

And I didn't keep track because I fell asleep, but that was the last thought I had before I fell asleep.

I WOKE in the much the same position.

But with profound differences.

Therefore I opened my eyes and I saw Brooks's body lying atop a yellow-gold T-shirt. That T-shirt was what my head was lying on top of too. Under it, I felt soft and hard. And beyond it at a downward angle there was a flat area covered in T-shirt with my arm wrapped around it. Beyond that were very, *very* faded men's jeans with a man's lower body inside them, one of his legs cocked, knee to the sky, the other one of his legs straight, my legs wrapped around it.

What on earth?

In order to support a little of my weight, I pulled my arm up from where it was trapped between me and some solid heat and tilted my head back to look right into the beautiful black eyes of Johnny Gamble. Eyes that were shadowed by a beat-up baseball cap.

Brooks was dead to the world with his face tucked in Johnny's neck opposite where I'd had my face tucked in Johnny's neck with my head further supported by the crook of his arm, since he had one arm holding Brooks steady and the other one bent so his head could rest on his hand.

Never...

Never...

Never...

Was he more beautiful.

"Hey," he whispered.

"What's going on?" I asked.

"You were out," he stated.

I blinked at him.

"He was out too, but he's a mover," he told me, gently jostling Brooks who didn't flutter an eyelash. "Kept my eye on you two, he got out from under your arm, you didn't feel it. So thought it best to move in and make sure it was all good."

"So you laid down on my blanket and cuddled into me?" I asked.

"No. I *sat* down on your blanket, until *you* cuddled into *me*," he answered. "That was when I laid down."

Oh man.

He was close, very close, my body still pressed to his side, my arm still wrapped around his stomach, my legs still tangled with his, and suddenly I lost track of the conversation.

"You look good in that baseball cap," I told him and his lips hitched.

"And you look good in that dress, *spätzchen*. But just to say, you look a lot better in that dress than I look in this cap."

"I'm not sure that's true," I replied.

"I am," he returned.

And there came the thrill down my spine.

"Margarita night got out of hand," I shared and got a white flash through his black beard.

"That tends to happen with you."

That got a tingle and not along my spine.

"I needed a nap," I defended myself.

"I kinda noticed you like to crawl back into bed after you crawl out of it after you down some margaritas."

That got a shiver.

Johnny felt it and took pity on me, gently jostling Brooks again.

"He's cute," he noted.

I moved my attention to my nephew, took my arm from around his stomach, laid my hand on Brooks's diapered booty and whispered, "He's the whole world."

A change came over Johnny. I knew it because I felt it since I wasn't looking at him.

Then I saw it when I lifted my eyes back to Johnny and the whole world became something else, and that something else started and stopped in the infinity of Johnny Gamble's black eyes.

"You want some?" he whispered.

"Yes," I whispered back immediately.

"How many?" he asked, still whispering.

"Fifteen, but I'll take one if he's healthy and happy."

His heated eyes warmed a different way. "Fifteen is a tall order, *spätzchen*."

"Thus me being happy with just one."

His eyes dropped to my mouth and his voice became a growl. "Fuck, I wanna kiss you."

Some sanity returned and I started to pull away, but his hand came from under his head so he could round me with his arm and keep me where I was.

"Johnny," I breathed.

"We need to talk," he decreed.

"I'm not sure—"

"Which is why we need to talk. It'll give me time to make you sure."

Oh man!

"Johnny—"

"After your sister leaves."

"Jo—"

I cut myself off that time because he'd mentioned Addie.

"But I'd like to meet her while she's here," he went on.

I wasn't listening.

My head drifted around and I saw that the festival had grown a great deal during my nap. I also absently noticed I—and now Johnny and I—still had a lot of attention.

What I didn't notice was my sister anywhere.

I shot up to sitting on my hip as panic bolted through me.

Johnny came up with me, holding Brooks tight to his chest.

"Iz?"

"Addie," I whispered.

"Izzy," he growled, obviously feeling my change in mood, and my eyes cut to him.

"How long was I asleep?" I asked.

"I don't know," he answered.

"How long have you been here?"

"Watched you maybe five minutes. Been with you and Brooks fifteen, maybe twenty."

"Was I asleep when you first saw me?"

"Yeah."

"The souvlaki guy isn't that far away."

"Say again?"

I leaned into him, lifting a hand to press it tight to his chest, the tips of my fingers at the base of his throat, and said, "Addie. She went to get souvlaki. She said she'd be right back. It might take fifteen minutes to get souvlaki but it doesn't take longer."

"Maybe she's having a wander," Johnny suggested.

"She was in a bad mood when she took off. Not mad, just...whatever is happening I think was getting to her."

"Call her," Johnny ordered.

That was a good idea.

I turned to the picnic basket, which also held my phone, this move necessitating me untangling my legs from Johnny's. I dug it out. I looked to Johnny and he held my nephew and my eyes as I called my sister.

She didn't answer.

"Where are you?" I said into her voicemail. "Call me."

Then I hung up, broke eye contact to bend my head to the phone and text.

"No answer?" Johnny asked.

I shook my head and texted.

When I looked to him, he said, "Pull up a picture of her, give me your phone. I'll give you this little guy and you look after him while I go look for her."

"You'd do that?" I asked.

"Fuck yeah," he answered.

"Okay, I'll...okay," I mumbled, head bent to my phone again to find a photo of Addie. I turned the picture I found to him and said, "That's her."

"Almost as pretty as you," he muttered, reaching out to the phone and taking it at the same time shifting like he was going to hand Brooks to me, but I didn't go for Brooks.

I was so relieved Johnny was there and I could stay at the blanket and wait for Addie should she return but he was going to go out to look for her that I didn't think.

I just did.

And what I did was lean in and press my lips hard to his.

I did it grabbing tight to the side of his neck, and when I was done, I left my hand there.

"Thank you," I said with feeling, giving his neck a squeeze.

"Welp, Mayberry seems to have a good effect on my sister. I go to get some souvlaki and goody two-shoes here scores herself a hottie."

I jerked my head back, my hand on Johnny staying where it was, and I saw my sister with a little cardboard tray in one hand, a huge soft drink cup with straw in the other, standing at the edge of the blanket.

"Where have you been?" I asked, finally letting my hand fall away from Johnny.

I might have done that but his free arm moved when I did to curl around my hips.

Addie didn't miss his movement.

She also ignored my question, shifted her attention to her son and back to me. "He go down okay?"

"Where have you been?" I repeated, my panic gliding away and my focus returning.

And what I was focusing on was that her hair was in a haphazard pony when she'd left, but now it was in a significantly more haphazard pony that, knowing her as I did, stated a variety of things, all of which, again knowing her as I did, I knew to be true.

She didn't have a taste for souvlaki.

Harking back, she'd eyed up the man in the Greek tent and he'd eyed her up in return.

She had a taste for the Greek guy in the souvlaki tent.

She'd been a wild one but she was true to Perry. I knew it. She loved him, adored him, against all my advice married him. And she told me everything (eventually). If she ever strayed (which she wouldn't do and not simply because now she didn't have the time), she would have told me.

Unless there was a reason to stray and that straying had happened so recently, she hadn't yet had her shot to share.

"Addie," I snapped.

She dropped to her knees, planted her soda in the grass, fell to her hip and took up the plastic fork in her tray, but she didn't take a bite.

She skewered Johnny with her eyes.

"And you are?" she demanded to know.

"Johnny Gamble," he rumbled.

"I was thinking you'd answer Magnus McHotterson but that works too," she quipped, finally digging into her pork. "So, I know my sister and she wouldn't score a hot guy and start making out with him in my thirty minute absence, so my guess is that someone wasn't entirely forthcoming during margarita night last night," she noted conversationally.

"That makes two of us," I retorted.

She whirled a fork with pork stuck in its prongs in the air and then shoved it in her mouth.

She barely swallowed before she asked, "How long you been seeing each other?"

"We aren't—" I began.

"Three weeks," Johnny declared.

I looked to him to see his entire focus was on Addie.

"I'm taking his response," Addie stated, and I looked to her to see her focus was on me. "You don't suck face with someone you aren't seeing."

"We weren't sucking face."

"Girl, if you grabbed tighter hold on him, your fingers would have fused with his neck," Addie returned.

I felt heat hit my cheeks and started glaring at her. "Let's stop talking about Johnny and me."

She arched her brows. "So there's a Johnny and you?"

I ignored that. "Let's talk about where you've been."

"Uh," she pointed with her fork to the paper tray, "souvlaki?"

"Getting souvlaki gives you sex hair?" I asked sharply.

Johnny burst out laughing, doing this using his arm around me to snatch me closer to him, fitting me tight to his side.

Addie's eyes narrowed. "We're not talking about this in front of your new boyfriend."

"He's not my new boyfriend."

Johnny's arm spasmed and Addie didn't miss it.

She looked to Johnny. "Only Izzy would be in hot guy denial. She was practically dateless all through high school and convinced herself it was because she was ugly when it was because the guys were pissed at her because they wanted to date her but she refused to put out."

"Addie, stop sharing stuff with Johnny," I snapped.

This time, Addie ignored me.

Spearing more pork, she shared, "She's probably convinced you're only hanging around because you want to be her friend."

"We've had sex eight times, Addie," I informed her stiffly.

Her eyes sliced to me. "Eight? You're counting?" She again looked at Johnny. "Well done. Three weeks, eight goes. She usually makes a guy wait for a year before she gives him the goods."

Johnny chuckled and I turned to him. "Stop laughing."

"Right, *spätzchen*." He gave me a squeeze and his body kept rocking but he beat back the audible of his humor.

So it was now him I was glaring at.

"*Spätzchen?* What's that mean?" Addie asked.

"Nothing," I answered.

"Little sparrow," Johnny answered.

"Cute," Addie said through a mouth full of pork and a grin. "And so you," she added, her blue eyes twinkling at me.

"I don't make a guy wait a year," I bit out.

She jabbed her fork at Johnny. "Apparently not anymore. Then again, for that," she started swirling the fork, also at Johnny, "I wouldn't wait five minutes."

"Oh my God, someone kill me," I said to the roof of leaves over our heads.

"Not gonna happen," Addie replied cheerfully.

So I turned to Johnny, carefully pulled Brooks from his arm into my own, and decreed, "I'm going for a walk and I'm taking Brooks with me."

"Don't take Johnny. We have all sorts of fun things to talk about," Addie said.

I speared her with a look.

She grinned through more pork at me.

And it was then the most adorable white Labrador in the world bounded toward us then to us, invading the blanket and jumping all over Johnny.

So the exuberant dog wouldn't wake Brooks, I leaned away but then I stilled.

Completely.

Because Johnny was stilled.

Completely.

The dog danced around Johnny, kissing his neck, his bearded cheeks, butting him with his snout and bending to nose his hand, and Johnny just stared at him.

I also stared at him.

All of a sudden, Johnny took his arm from around me, lifted his hands and captured the dog's head between them both. Dog and man stared into each other's eyes before dog took his shot and licked Johnny from jaw to temple.

This was Ranger.

This was his dog.

This was his baby returned.

This was a reunion.

A happy one.

"Boy," Johnny murmured with such immense feeling, my stomach that had twisted into a painful knot warmed even through the pain.

Ranger's tail was wagging so hard, his entire body wagged with it.

Finally, Johnny's eyes lifted and mine went in the direction he aimed them.

And there she was, maybe ten feet from our blanket.

Tall.

Buxom.

A mane of wild, beautiful, dark red hair.

A killer outfit that fit close to the one Johnny was wearing, a slim-fitting, black baby doll tee with what looked like a heart from a playing card on it with some wording in it, seriously faded jeans, worn in cowboy boots and lots of silver at wrists, ears, fingers and neck.

And a face that could start wars and end them.

She was so beautiful, I envied her on sight with such intensity it felt like I shriveled sitting there on my picnic blanket next to Johnny. Shriveled and shrank until I felt two inches tall.

Her face was stricken, pained, *tortured*.

And then she ran. Like a heroine in a romantic movie, with the grace of the beauty that was just her, she turned and raced through the crowd, bobbing and weaving, her hair flying out behind her, catching the sunlight with a ruby glow.

I was watching her so I didn't know how it happened but Ranger made a choice and raced after her.

He stopped though. Stopped, looked back at Johnny, and with what looked like a "come on!" jerk of his head toward Johnny that sent his floppy ears flying, he turned and bolted after her.

And I sat frozen in agony on a picnic blanket dappled with sun on a summer day, holding my nephew as I felt the sudden movement beside me when, without a word, Johnny Gamble surged to his feet and sprinted after the both of them.

TEN

A MEMORY

Izzy

I was on the back porch pulling on my wellies the next morning when the door to the house opened.

I looked up and saw my sister standing there with bed hair, in her jammies, looking both just woken up and still tired, with an expression on her face that I was sure I wore the night she arrived and the morning after when I'd looked at her.

"Hey," she said gently.

"Hey," I replied strongly.

"You okay?" she asked.

No.

No, I was not okay.

"I'm fine," I lied.

Her hand came up and in it was my phone.

"He's calling again," she said.

She'd turned the ringer back on.

I wished she hadn't done that.

I didn't even look at the phone.

"I'm going out to feed the horses and let them loose. I didn't get to muck their stalls yesterday morning so I'll come back in, make you guys breakfast, change, but then I have to go back out and do that."

"I'll help you when you do."

"You don't have to."

"I will," she stated firmly.

"Someone has to look after Brooks," I reminded her.

"He can hang in a stable. Kids for millennia have been hanging around horses and eating dirt and whatever and they survived. Plus his favorite place on earth is with his mom and his Auntie Izzy, so that's where he's gonna be."

I shrugged, bent to my boots and finished putting them on, saying, "If it's okay with you, it's okay with me."

I started toward the screen door of the back porch when she called my name.

I turned to her.

"You should talk to him," she urged quietly.

Not going to happen.

She liked him. A brief conversation on a picnic blanket and she'd liked him.

This was unsurprising.

He was Johnny.

I nodded, muttered, "Maybe later," and took off out the screen door.

I headed to the stables trying not to think about the fact that Johnny had called when we were in the car on the way home from the festival yesterday. And we'd headed home from the festival approximately ten point eight seconds after he'd hauled ass after Shandra.

Worse, we'd packed up and hightailed it out under the kind and sympathetic eyes of the many spectators to the reunion of Johnny and Shandra, a reunion that was mere minutes after he'd been cuddling on a picnic blanket with me.

A reunion where he'd raced after her, not looking back.

I didn't take the call because I knew why he was calling.

He was Johnny. He was sweet. He was a gentleman. In the throes of the situation, he could forget me. But he'd see to me when it hit him what he'd done, and he'd be as kindhearted about it as he could when he explained the way things needed to be.

But I didn't need that.

I knew where I stood even before that happened.

It was nice and all, but unnecessary.

I had to admit, the text that came in seconds after I didn't answer his call was a surprise.

I also had to admit the repeated calls and texts, none of which I took or looked at, were a surprise too.

However, after I'd phoned Deanna and Charlie and lied through my teeth that I was hungover, couldn't hack the crowd, noise, smells and heat and we'd headed home so we wouldn't meet them when they hit the festival later as planned, I'd turned my ringer off so I wouldn't have the constant reminder that I'd been smart not to let myself think I could have Johnny.

But knowing now without any doubt I couldn't have Johnny still hurt way, way, *way* more than it should.

Addie had tried once to coax me to pick up the phone and talk to him. But when I refused, she let it go. Do onto others as you would have them do onto you, our mother taught us the old proverb and she'd done it frequently. Addie lived that, as I did too.

I hit my stables, went through the gate, latched it behind me and set about feeding my horses.

I was dog-tired. I'd slept even less the night before. Still hungover but mostly sick to my stomach about what had happened, not to mention the whole town (well, some of it) witnessing it. Thinking it was not (exactly) what it was. Not knowing I hadn't let myself get in too deep (though, if I was honest, I had). Thinking I was just another one who'd fallen hard then gotten burned in the aftermath of Johnny and Shandra.

The last one, but still.

I'd be the object of compassion, I was sure. And that would not be fun, seeing as it would serve as a reminder of what had happened whenever I'd hit Macy's Flower Shop or the grocery store, or if I ever (which I probably wouldn't, at least for a while) hit Home again.

But I'd endure.

I'd get through it.

I'd get over it.

And I'd carry on.

Like my mom, in the many and varied ways life could bring me to my knees, I was just going to get back up and keep going.

Mostly because I had no choice.

After I fed my babies, I decided to check supplies of feed and hay. I always carefully calculated the needs of both, because I bought in bulk due to the discount I could get and also bought them both at the same time due to the fact the feed store delivered at a flat rate no matter how much you ordered.

I was low on feed but had plenty of hay.

I could stack extra outside and put a tarp around it, use it first so I didn't have to haul it in and put in the hay room only to haul it back out again for the horses.

After closing the door on the hay room, I turned to go to Serengeti to see if she was finished eating and ready to head out to her paddock and stopped dead.

Johnny was standing inside the closed gate, his eyes locked to me.

This could not happen and it could not happen for a number of reasons.

First, I couldn't deal with it. Not then. I needed at least a whole day, more like a hundred of them.

Second, this wasn't fair. I knew he wanted to do right by me, let me down easy, explain his head was messed up and that was why he was leading me on, try to make me understand in order to make himself feel better while doing it.

But it was my thought in this particular scenario that *I* got to pick the time that would happen, if it happened at all.

And last, in a fit of heartbroken stupidity I refused to allow myself to dwell on considering it had only been three dinners, two breakfasts, several phone and text conversations but not years of togetherness and a path of broken promises, I'd gone to bed wearing the T-shirt he'd given me.

Therefore right then I was standing before him wearing that tee, an old, threadbare pair of men's pajama bottoms that I'd cut off at the knees and pulled on to go to the stables, and my wellies.

My hair was a mess.

And I knew I had to look fatigued and perhaps was wearing my heart on my (actually his) sleeve.

So this wasn't just too soon and unfair.

It was a disaster.

I tore my eyes from him, immediately started moving to the tack room for reasons unknown since I didn't have to go to the tack room, I had to go to Serengeti, doing this shaking my head and talking.

"You don't have to do this, Johnny."

I sensed him on the move but didn't look at him.

"Izzy, I need you to listen to me."

I kept shaking my head at the same time averting it. "It's okay. I get it. You know I get it. You don't have to do this."

"Iz, baby, stop for a second and listen to me."

I hit the door to the tack room, stopped and twisted only slightly to allow myself to look at his chest, a view I had because he'd gotten close.

He had a new tee on today, blue that had a faded American flag all in white on the front.

It was fabulous.

"Honestly, it's okay. I'm fine. I expected that to happen," I told him, though I didn't expect to have to witness it.

"What to happen?" he asked.

I ignored that.

"And I'm still good with Mist coming here, if you are. I'll go get him though and take care of him. It won't be hard. Don't worry. Just text me the address. I know someone who'll let me use their horse trailer and Charlie has a truck that can haul."

"Iz—"

"Thanks for coming, Johnny." I started to open the door to the tack room. "It was sweet." I lifted my eyes to his bearded chin and wanted to kick myself because my voice was starting to sound husky when I finished, "Be happy."

I was going to disappear through the door but I didn't.

The door that I'd opened nary three inches was slammed shut in front of me, and then I was turned around with a hand on my upper arm and I found myself backed up against the wooden wall to the tack room with a hand in my belly.

I looked up at Johnny.

He was angry.

I felt my wounded heart start beating rapidly.

"Need you to shut up, baby, and *listen to me*," he growled.

"You really don't have to do this," I whispered.

"You really *do* have to *shut up*," he returned sharply.

I stared into his angry eyes.

He was telling me to shut up.

And he was angry.

He was invading my land, my stables, my *space* with the driving bent to do the right thing and not thinking how *I* might feel, and he was getting angry that I wouldn't let him.

And that made *me* angry.

"Don't tell me to shut up," I snapped.

"Izzy, I'll repeat one more time, you need to listen to me."

I got up on my toes to put my face in his and retorted, "I don't need to do anything."

"Right," he bit off.

Then his hand was no longer in my belly.

It was an arm wrapped around my waist, his other hand became fingers bunching my hair tight in his grip, and his mouth slammed down on mine.

He kissed me.

I went still for a second in shock before I tried to push at his hold.

My hands encountered broad, strong shoulders and that was it.

I wasn't Izzy.

I wasn't in my stables.

I wasn't angry at Johnny.

I wasn't heartsore from him either.

My sister wasn't up at my house with my nephew dealing with whatever it was she was dealing with at the same time having a mind to what was happening with me.

Shandra Whatever-Her-Last-Name-Was didn't exist.

She'd never even been born.

I was something else, somewhere else, something foreign entirely.

But he was Johnny.

Johnny holding me and kissing me.

And I had become pure *need*.

I opened my mouth, his tongue slid inside with a groan that drove the burning hunger deeper into my flesh, the marrow of my bones, straight to my soul, and I couldn't have stopped myself from acting on it if I'd tried.

My hands left his shoulders and went to the drawstring on my bottoms. I pulled it and the baggy material fell to my ankles.

I then went for his belt.

He broke the kiss, lifted his head and looked deep into my eyes.

Then he made a noise, that muted roar of his that now wasn't angry or frustrated, but ravening.

If I wasn't already drenched between my legs, that would have done it.

But instead, it made me sopping.

I worked his belt as he lifted my shirt and hooked a thumb in the side of my panties, his other hand reaching behind him.

He pulled my panties down to low on my hip, the nail of his thumb digging into my flesh, the feel of that reverberating right up my pussy, as he pulled his wallet out of his back pocket.

I got his belt undone and went for the button.

I heard his wallet plop to the dirt before he put the edge of a wrapped condom between his clenched teeth and brushed my hands aside.

I focused on my panties, tearing them farther down and shimmying them until they fell to rest with my bottoms at my ankles.

Johnny dragged his jeans over his ass and the condom disappeared from his teeth.

Within seconds, his hands were at my ass, mine were to his shoulders, and I jumped up.

He kept hold, securing me aloft, taking a step in, pinning me to the wall.

Then he was inside.

I gasped.

He groaned.

And through all of this our eyes stayed bonded.

He started moving and I rounded his hips with my legs, using my calves and heels to dig in, giving me leverage, undulating into his strokes. My hands moved, one clasping hard at the back of his neck, one clenching tight into the thick waves of his hair.

He rounded my bottom with an arm, and his other hand bunched my hair tight against the back of my neck.

His labored breaths clashed with my wisping ones as he stared into my eyes and rode me.

There was nothing while he did.

Nothing for me in the whole world but his eyes and his cock and his hold tight on me and all the amazing, beautiful, wondrous things he was making me feel.

My wispy breaths came faster, whimpers eking through and his grunts started to sound as his thrusts grew in strength and velocity.

My hand at the back of his neck slid around and I caught him rough at its side when all I was feeling, all he was giving me made me start moaning.

"You there?" he grunted.

My arms shot around him, circling his head, yanking it to me, stuffing his face in my neck, and I cried out loudly and bucked in his arms when a climax, exquisite in its purity and intensity and the magnificence of its beauty, tore through me.

"You're there," I vaguely heard him whisper before he beat into me faster and rougher, and seconds later I heard and felt the rumble of his long, deep groan against my neck.

He slid in and stayed in, tremors shuddering through his long body, and through them he held me pinned to the wall, impaled on his cock.

I held his head in my arms, face shoved in my neck, my legs tight around his hips.

In Johnny Gamble's arms. Connected to him. The only place I felt safe. The only place I felt right. The only place I felt free to be whatever me I wanted to be.

And then the world came crashing in.

I'd just fucked another woman's man.

I was so mortified and utterly horrified that I'd done this, it didn't even occur to me he'd fucked another woman being some woman's man.

It was just me.

Me doing the wrong thing. Me hurting a sister. Not even thinking of the consequences. Me taking what wasn't mine.

I unlocked my arms from around his head and put them to his shoulders.

"Let me go."

"Izzy," he whispered against my neck.

I turned my head to the side, away from him, not able to deal with this, not even able to be in my own skin.

It was dirty. Wrong. Revolting.

"That wasn't right."

"Baby—"

"Let me go."

His lips found my ear. "*Spätzchen*, you need to listen to me."

"That wasn't right. You're not mine. You're hers."

His body grew solid all around me. "What?"

"You ran after her."

"I ran after my dog."

I blinked at the dirt-floored corridor between the stalls.

He touched his lips to my earlobe and then kept them there, saying gently, "I knew you'd think that but I couldn't correct you when you wouldn't answer the fucking phone."

Slowly, I turned my head his way, and slowly he lifted his to look into my eyes.

"You...ran after...your dog?"

"Ranger's home," he stated.

I blinked up at him.

He gently slid me off his cock and I took the hint, unhooking my legs from his hips. He set me to my feet but held me close, still pinned to the wall until he knew I was steady on them.

He moved away only enough to hitch up his jeans and then he bent and grabbed my panties.

I automatically lifted a hand to take them but he didn't offer them to me.

He shoved them in his jeans pocket.

My lips parted.

He bent back and grabbed my pajama bottoms. He shook them to get the dirt off, his brows drew together as he gave them a look, then he handed them to me.

Brushing Johnny repeatedly because he stayed in my space, I put them on.

I was tying the drawstring when he said, "Trash."

It was a statement that formed a question.

"Tack room."

That was my answer.

He took my hand and shifted us to the tack room, opening the door. He walked with his jeans undone, dragging me with him.

He then treated me to the intimacy of him disposing of a spent condom in my trash.

There was something about this, something huge, something powerful. A shift in our relationship where the veil was pulled down and it was no longer about guarding important secrets until you knew they were safe to share or just getting to know each other a little better.

It was about fitting into each other's lives.

He righted his jeans and belt then looked into the room.

"Jesus," he murmured.

I looked into the room.

The tack was mounted on two opposite walls in a fashion that wasn't only organized and orderly, but attractive. The narrow floor space between had a clean, oval, braided rug on it. In the two back corners, at angles to each other, were two armchairs. A faded chintz one I got in a yard sale for two dollars. And a fabulous, mahogany leather club chair I bought at an estate auction for twenty-five. The light fixture was tin, antique, beat up and fabulous and cost me a buck fifty at an antique store, and a margarita night plus my guacamole for a girlfriend who was an electrician to rewire it.

On the back wall there were four precisely placed pictures, two on either side of a big window, and I'd paid a small fortune to have each one of them professionally framed in the exact same frame.

All of them with huge mats surrounding cheap, drugstore produced snapshot pictures of the day Mom took Addie and me to a state park and we rode horses on a trail. One picture of Mom and Addie. One of Mom and me. And two of all three of us together, standing in front of a horse, smiling, goofing and looking happy.

"Trust you to have a tack room that's nicer than most folks' living room," Johnny muttered.

I looked from the room to him.

"Johnny."

He looked to me, said firmly, "Right," then grabbed my hand and dragged me to the leather club chair.

He sat in it.

Then he sat *me* in it, that being me in his lap.

"Caught up with her and my dog," he began without preamble.

I sat in his lap, and unsure I wanted to, unsure of anything, I listened.

"Since I wanted my dog back, told her we needed to find a private place to talk. She wanted the mill. I agreed to the mill because that way I could just let Ranger in his new home when we were done and I didn't want to drag shit out by discussing where we were going to discuss shit. She followed me there in her car. I called you on the way there." His expression turned annoyed. "You didn't answer."

"Um..." I muttered.

"Needless to say, when I got there and told her I wanted my dog back, this did not go over well. I'd told her we weren't going back, what's done is done, but apparently that didn't get through. Me saying I wanted her to return Ranger made it get through. She was upset and I couldn't just tell her to get gone but leave my dog. I did find times to call and text you during her being upset. But again, you didn't answer."

"Uh..." I mumbled.

"Things degenerated, because she couldn't miss me trying to call and text you so she wanted to know about you, and since I wasn't giving her a shot, she jumped to conclusions about Brooks bein' our kid. Assuring her that didn't happen but not assuring her that you and I weren't what she assumed we were didn't go over very well either. When it came out that it had only been a few weeks and she'd actually called right after we met each other, things degenerated further with a lot of her asking what ifs about if she'd just called a couple of days earlier. And again, it didn't go over very well when I said what if was moot since I found someone, the connection we have runs deep, we're both intent on exploring it and I was all in for that happening."

I stared at him, no longer feeling unsure about listening.

I was listening hard to every word he said.

He kept saying them.

"It would have ended there and I would have come to you, except folks talk, and they were talking, so by the time Margot and Dave got to the festival, what happened on that picnic blanket with the three of us was running rampant. Margot got in a snit, Shandra isn't Dave's favorite person either, so they decided to load back up in their car, show at the mill and give Shandra a few pieces of their minds."

"Oh boy," I whispered.

"Yeah," he agreed. "Margot laid into her and the result was mincemeat. She ground her to a pulp. I'd tried to be as cool with her as I could, but in that situation there is no way she'd think I was being cool. So Shandra had already taken a few lickings from me, and with Margot wading in she became a mess."

"Yikes," I murmured, beginning to feel sorry for Shandra.

I hoped Margot never was moved to make mincemeat of me because I figured she had a talent with that.

"Yeah," he again agreed. "But Margot wasn't done, because she jumped to conclusions about the fact Shandra and me were at the mill and she had a few things to say to me too. About Shandra and about you. Shandra hearing from Margot the depths of the wreckage of me she left behind meant she got it in her head that she might be the only one to salvage them, and even shredded she gave that a go. Me *and* Margot disabusing her of this considering you'd entered the picture and did it with staying power was insult to injury. She lost it, took off, and I spent the rest of the afternoon and most the night looking for her to make sure in her state she didn't wrap herself around a tree while alternately trying to get you on the phone. I found her late, got her back to her folks safely, left her there and decided to sort you out this morning. You being you led us to straightening shit out the way we straightened it out, which, *spätzchen*, I'm not complaining since what we did against that wall was hot as fuck. And here we are."

There we were.

That seemed very definite coming from Johnny, and all he had to say was illuminating and, if I allowed it to be, hopeful.

But even if I was right where I was, I didn't know where *we* were.

"Where are we?" I asked.

His brows shot together and again they turned from manly and attractive to downright sinister.

Then he looked around my tack room, to me, both his arms curled around me and did it tight so he could give me a firm shake, and he asked, "Where the fuck do you think we are?"

I didn't know.

That was why I asked.

But I made a guess.

"I'm not sure I can do this," I told him carefully.

"Do what?" he asked angrily.

"Come after her. I don't want to be—"

"Don't fuckin' say it," he growled.

I closed my mouth.

"She was three years ago, Eliza. I loved her. That fact doesn't change. I loved her and she wrecked me when she left because that was how much I loved her. I'm not going to apologize for that or deny it or walk on eggshells with you about it while we figure out what we got and why it's so fuckin' good and so fuckin' intense and so fuckin' everything."

I blinked at him again.

He thought we were...

Everything?

He carried on speaking.

"I'd think you'd want that. I'd think you'd wanna know the man in your life could feel that deep for the woman he decided to spend the rest of his life with. But with her, *that didn't happen*. She left. I wasn't Sleeping Beauty, unconscious and unmoving, waiting for her to return. Life happens and it happened. I met you. She's a memory that's bittersweet and now back in my sphere, and unfortunately since you've taken firm residence in my sphere, yours. But the fact remains, she's a memory."

"She's beautiful," I told him something he was sure to know.

"So?" he asked.

"I...well, she dresses like you. You guys...you two..." I swallowed and finished, "*Fit.*"

"What do you want me to say?" he asked. "Her rocker-cowgirl gig is hot. Always was. But I'm not fucking her. I'm fucking a girl who wears a dress that reminds me how much I like her tits with that neckline, baby, which isn't hot. It's smokin'. A dress that has fuckin' birds on it and still, it's so sexy I took one look at it and wanted the skirt around your waist, or better yet, the whole dress lying on the floor by a bed, my bed, your bed, I don't care. But just saying, this isn't the way it's gonna be where I gotta reassure you that I'm with you because I wanna be *with you* and I'm not with her because of history. I'm not with her because I wanna be *with you.*"

I withdrew without physically withdrawing, and I knew by the irritable look Johnny gave me (or the *more* irritable look) he felt it.

Still, I couldn't help it.

"So you wanna fuck me," I said, and I couldn't keep the injury out of my tone.

"Well, *yeah*," he bit out. "You're the best lay, bar none, Iz, I've ever had. No one even comes close. You're not on a higher level. You're reinventing the highest level."

Well that was a kind of compliment.

"I also want more of your guac," he decreed. "And I wake up every day now at fuckin' five in the morning because I can't keep sleeping knowing you're out here," he threw out an arm to indicate the stables, "taking care of these horses all by yourself. I go to bed at night, every night, Eliza, jacking my junk thinking of you and wondering if you're touching yourself thinking of me. Except that night after The Star. I didn't sleep that first wink, not able to get it out of my head you're alone out here and some fuckwit is messing with you. I cannot tell you how relieved I was to hear your sister was with you. For you, because I know you love her, and because you're not alone out here with no one to look after you."

I sat still on his lap in his arms staring at him and forgetting how to breathe.

Johnny didn't forget.

He took a breath and kept at me.

"I spent a lot of time the last two weeks bein' pissed at Shandra, not because she took off on me but because she called and fucked things up before I could take you camping. And I spent a lot of time wondering if you got your peonies and tee and wondering if I should have done that at all or if it made things worse and needing to talk to you about it. So, to end, I spent a lot of time just thinking about you and yeah, some of it was thinking about what I wanted to do to you to make you come, but the rest of it wasn't."

"So, you like me," I whispered breathily.

He scowled at me like he wanted to strangle me then his head dropped to the back of the chair and he stared at the ceiling.

"I'll take that as a yes," I muttered.

His arms tightened around me so tight, they curled my thighs into my torso so I was a little ball of Izzy tucked tight against his chest as his head came back up and he clipped, "Yeah, I fuckin' like you."

"Okeydokey," I mumbled.

"I know your sister is here but I wanna spend time with you today and then I want you comin' back to the mill with me to spend the night."

"She's in a rough spot, Johnny, and she's always had the mammoth share of taking care of Brooks."

Something closed down in his face I didn't quite understand but that wasn't the reason I said my next.

I said my next because I wasn't finished speaking.

"But she'll get it. She tried to get me to talk to you so she'll be, uh...glad things are where they, um...are. Though, I'll need to be with her tomorrow. Every diaper change I do with Brooks, I swear, after I'm done she wants to kiss me."

Whatever clouded his features cleared, he nestled me closer and he asked, "You got tomorrow off?"

I nodded.

"Your sister and Brooks can come over to the mill and I'll grill for you."

"That'd be sweet," I said on a smile.

He looked to my smile then his eyes wandered down farther and his arms loosened.

"I...well, liked the tee, uh...obviously," I shared. "And also the peonies," I added.

His gaze came back to me.

"The bottoms?" he asked.

"Sorry?" I asked back.

"Whose are those?"

Uh-oh.

"Uh..."

He gave me another shake and said a warning, "Iz."

"They're not Kent's," I felt it safe to share.

"So whose are they?"

I could tell him I had a man's pair of pajama bottoms because I found them comfy.

But that would be a lie.

"The guy before the guy before Kent."

"Okay. Then you can wear 'em back to the house but after that, lose them, Izzy. And by that I mean I'd prefer you burn them but chucking them in the trash works."

I stared at him again.

He took in my stare and stated, "Right, we're doin' this so no more fucking around. I'm that guy. I got a sense of the type of woman you are, it'd be hard not to. You made all this. You keep all this like it is. You dress like you dress. You got it together. You can take care of yourself and a lot more than that. You're smart, sharp, successful and independent. I like all that or I wouldn't be here. I'm still that guy and you gotta know that. And part of that guy is being a guy where his woman doesn't wear another guy's pajama bottoms, even if that guy is history. You want some, I'll dig out some of my own, give them to you and have at it. But those are gone. Now, you got a problem with that?"

"Not really."

He relaxed all around me, muttering, "Good."

"Can I say something?" I asked.

"Can I ask why you'd ask if you could say something?" he asked back.

I felt my mouth quirk before I got serious.

"I'm sorry you had to go through all of that yesterday, honey. It sounded like a rough day and I feel bad that I made it rougher by not talking to you."

His face got soft and it also got closer to mine.

"It was messed up all around," he stated. "Now it isn't. Thanks for saying that, *spätzchen*, but it's done and we're moving on. You with me?"

I nodded then asked, "Are you going to give me back my panties?"

"Hell no," he answered.

I felt my brows draw together. "Why?"

"Babe, do you have even a little clue how hot it is, you sitting in my lap after we fucked like we fucked and I know you're not wearing panties because I got them in my pocket?"

I squirmed in his lap.

His face then got something else entirely when he growled, "Yeah."

It took a second for us both to have our moment before his lips hitched and I should have prepared but I didn't.

So when he said, "You thought I'd bagged on you and you went to sleep in my tee?"

My eyes narrowed on him.

That got me a white flash in his beard.

I tried to push off, mumbling, "I need to make breakfast and then muck stalls."

His arms tightened again and he returned, "You can make breakfast, babe. For three. I'll muck the stalls."

I stopped pushing against him. "I can muck my own stalls, Johnny."

"No doubt. Just that today your sister is here and so am I, so I'm gonna muck the stalls and you're gonna spend time with your sister. Then you're gonna feed me. After that, I'm gonna go home, shower and come back. We'll spend the day together and after dinner, I'll take you home with me so I can fuck you without you worried about anyone hearing and I'll bring you back in the morning. I'll go out and get shit to grill and you guys can meet me at the mill. We got a plan?"

I forgot my pique because I liked that plan so much I just smiled at him and agreed, "We have a plan."

Johnny's face changed back to what it had been before, my body responded to the change and then I was shoulders to the arm of the chair and he was making out with me.

When he lifted his head, he said, "Soon's your sister leaves, date night and you wear that dress you wore to the festival because I didn't get near enough of it, *spätzchen*."

"'Kay," I breathed.

He knifed out of the seat, taking me with him and putting me on my feet.

Feet he looked at as he draped his arm around my shoulders.

Feet he was still looking at when he muttered, "I cannot believe I fucked you in those boots."

Heat rose in my cheeks.

His arm angled down and his hand cupped my bottom as he rolled me into him and stared down at me, grinning.

"You sliding my finger inside you, baby, was seriously hot but you dropping drawers after half a kiss was seriously fucking hotter."

And now I could actually feel the pink get more pink in my cheeks.

"Can we not do audible replays?" I requested.

"Why not?" he teased.

"It was—"

"Hot."

"Yes and also—"

"As fuck."

I slapped his arm. "Johnny."

He brought his lips to mine. "Okay, *spätzchen*, I'll just do mental replays."

I glared at him even as I melted into him.

He kissed me again. It turned into a short make-out session. Then he guided me with his arm around my shoulders to the door, through it and pushed me gently toward the gate.

"Breakfast," he ordered.

"Okeydokey," I replied.

I headed out the gate and latching it, looked back to see Johnny was already to Serengeti, getting her ready to let her outside to roam.

I didn't think about how much I liked that visual.

I didn't think about how much had just happened and how huge it all was.

I didn't think about the fact that life might have just changed in major ways and just how much possibility now lay before me, all of it embodied by Johnny.

I went to my house, slid my boots off outside the door (and I did this grinning) and I walked in.

My dogs bounded to me.

My nephew sat in a high chair by the island with a bib on and my sister bent over him, shoving baby cereal in his mouth.

Her head turned to me.

"You might have seen that Johnny pulled up and—" I started.

She straightened.

Brooks screeched when his food got farther away.

Addie spoke.

"Yeah. He came to the door. I told him you were in the stables. He didn't say a word, turned on his kickass boot and stalked to the stables. And to say the man can stalk is to say the man can *stalk*. I watched with what I will admit was avid fascination until he disappeared around the corner and I couldn't watch anymore. He seemed pissed and worried. I went with the worried at first then I got worried about the pissed. So I went out to make sure everything was okay. And just to say, you getting drilled by a hot guy against a wall in a stable is something I cannot ever unsee."

My entire chest depressed.

"Though," she bent back over Brooks and shoved more cereal in his mouth, "after my eyeballs stopped burning, objectively I could see it was seriously hot and I'm glad for you."

"He's mucking out the stalls and spending the day with us," I said quietly.

She turned her head to me again.

"Good," she said strongly.

"It wasn't the woman. It was his dog," I told her.

"You got until he gets done in the stable to fill me in on all this stuff you wouldn't talk about last night and you kept from me the night before. But just to say, it wasn't lost on me how into you he was. It was just lost on you, until he drilled you against the wall in the stable. Still, I wanna know all the dirt, so get cracking on breakfast, Iz, and spill."

"Do you think he'll want pancakes or eggs?" I thought for a second and added more options, "Or waffles or French toast?"

"When I turned on the ringer of your phone this morning, I saw he'd texted twelve times and phoned eleven. I think that man would eat sawdust, it was you serving it up to him."

Twelve texts.

Eleven calls.

So fuckin' good and so fuckin' intense and so fuckin' everything.

It seemed Addie might be right.

I smiled at her.

She rolled her eyes. "Spare me the post-coital bliss, cook and fill me in. Man like that will have two stables mucked out in less than twenty minutes."

This might be true.

So I got cracking (I picked pancakes).

And I filled my sister in on what was happening.

But I couldn't quite beat back or even hide my bliss.

Johnny

JOHNNY GOT out of the shower and reached to grab a towel.

When he did, his eyes fell on the jar by the tub.

It had been sitting there so long he didn't even see it anymore.

But he saw it then.

He rubbed his hair, gave his body a cursory wipe and then wrapped the towel around his hips.

He secured it and went to the jar.

Ranger got up from lying on the rug in front of one of the sinks and came to him.

Johnny grabbed the jar but bent with his free hand to give his dog's head a scratch.

He then walked with his dog at his heels to the kitchen. He opened the cabinet that hid the trash bin and tossed the jar in.

He closed the cabinet and bent fully to his dog.

Grabbing his head, he asked, "Wanna go to Izzy's with me?"

Ranger tried to lick his face.

Johnny smiled at him. "I'll give her a call. See if Dempsey and Swirl are good with company."

He rubbed Ranger's head and moved back to the bathroom to his jeans on the floor. He dug his phone out, called Iz and was not surprised with her answer.

So he pulled a comb through his hair, put on deodorant, clean shorts, jeans and tee, tugged socks and his boots on and he grabbed his wallet, phone and keys.

Then he and Ranger headed out the door to his truck in order to get back to Izzy.

ELEVEN
YOU

Izzy

Hearing a ceiling fan, I opened my eyes and saw tan sheets.

I rolled and saw Johnny in sweats and nothing else at the railing on his deck holding up a cup of coffee.

Ranger was lying at his feet.

Dog and man looked comfortable in their morning repose.

That was, dog and man looked comfortable in their morning repose until Johnny's head turned and he looked through the windows at me.

He then lifted up his free hand and crooked a finger, also at me.

Like I was mesmerized, I threw back the covers and tossed my legs over the side, pulling myself out of bed. I walked like I was in a dream (because mostly I was) to the door and through it.

Ranger shot up and came to me and I gave him some distracted pets as I made my way to Johnny.

He held his arm out.

I walked right in, pressing my front to his side.

His arm wrapped around but his hand kept moving, pulling up

his tee that I'd put on before collapsing in his bed then gliding down, fingers in my panties.

I shivered.

He put his coffee mug down on the railing.

"Passed out on me, *spätzchen*," he murmured instead of saying good morning.

"I didn't sleep well the last couple of nights," I explained.

"You sleep well last night?"

The day before I'd learned a lot about Johnny Gamble.

I'd learned he had a quick wit and could match Addie quip for quip, a lot of the time doing it even better than her.

I'd learned he didn't only muck stalls, he did dishes, refilled drinks without being asked, and proved to be an excellent sous chef when you're cooking.

I'd learned he changed diapers.

I'd learned when his head wasn't messed up necessitating he convey a message so your heart wouldn't get broken, he was exceptionally affectionate and sweetly teasing, but there was more.

He was appreciative.

With his eyes and facial expressions, sometimes touches, sometimes murmured words, he showed and told me he liked how I moved. He liked my legs. He liked my hair. He liked my behind. He liked listening to me talk. He liked watching me laugh. He liked seeing me tease my sister. He liked watching me respond when she teased me. He liked the little mini-dress I'd put on (Johnny *was* coming over to spend the day so I absolutely made an effort) that was a blue and white print with a blousy top and short sleeves and a flouncy short skirt.

He liked me and didn't hide it in any way.

In fact, I'd never had the admiration of a man aimed at me the way Johnny did it. It was casual, spontaneous, but definite. It was a part of who he was and how he felt about me, not a path he was taking to get what he wanted.

After dinner and after after-dinner conversation, which both involved wine, and Johnny taking me back to his house, I'd barely made it up the stairs and walked a step inside when his lips were at my neck and he said, "Get your ass to bed, baby, before you curl up on the floor and fall asleep."

I'd turned drowsily to him, eyes to his chest and mumbled, "Tee."

He took his tee off.

I took my dress and bra off and put it on.

Then I climbed into his bed and went right to sleep.

And having the day I'd had the day before with Addie and Brooks and Johnny, learning all I had about Johnny, I'd slept like a baby.

"I slept great," I whispered.

He bent his head, brushed his lips against mine and lifted up.

"Did you?" I asked.

"I didn't have the best nights' sleep the last few nights so yeah. It was good to sleep solid."

I nuzzled into him, turned my head, put my cheek to his chest and stared at the sun glinting off the creek.

I felt fur slide down my calf as Ranger slid down my leg to lie down at our feet.

Ranger had a lot going on, what with being back with Johnny then spending the day with new dogs, new people and a baby.

He didn't seem to miss Shandra.

But once things settled down and he realized this was his permanent reality, he would.

I sighed.

"What's on your mind?" Johnny asked, the tips of his fingers idly tracing the curve at the bottom of the cheek of my behind.

"Nothing."

"We don't do that, baby," he admonished gently.

I left my cheek to his chest but still tipped my head back to catch his gaze.

"Don't do what?" I asked.

"Especially not with a beginning like we had that was rocky," he went on.

"What?"

"Something bothering you?" he asked.

"No," I answered.

"You made a noise like something was on your mind," he stated.

"It isn't bothering me."

"And I asked what was on your mind. You said nothing when it was something. And we gotta stay open and out there so we don't fall into shit that might keep things rocky."

I lifted my head, turned it back to him and put my hand on his chest.

"I was just thinking that Ranger probably doesn't get that things have changed and he'll miss Shandra when he does."

His hand cupped my behind. "So you were thinking about her."

"No, I was thinking about Ranger."

"And Shandra."

"Well, kind of," I allowed.

"Not kind of," he returned.

"A dog can't communicate like we do, but they can communicate and they have feelings and change is rough for them just like it is for anyone."

"He'll be fine," Johnny assured shortly.

"I know he will," I replied, also shortly.

"You need to get her off your mind," he ordered.

I felt cold penetrate and I pushed a little away, stopping only when the pads of his fingers started biting in, and retorted, "No. It seems to me *you* need to get her off *your* mind."

"I didn't bring her to the balcony, Izzy."

"I didn't either, Johnny."

"We gotta make sure this doesn't infect what we've got or what we got isn't gonna stay good."

"I'm all in for that, but just to say, you also need to let me worry about your dog because he's cute and he's sweet and he loves you, and he gets along with Dempsey and Swirl and he thinks Brooks is awesome and I like him and that's me. I'm an animal freak. If I see a humane society commercial with pictures of animals that have been abused, I won't be able to sleep. I once stole a neighbor's cat and took her to the vet to be fixed because the neighbor kept letting her out and she'd get pregnant and have babies, and the neighbor would just take the kittens to the shelter every time and that's not right."

Johnny stared down at me.

"Don't worry," I told him. "I gave her back after she'd recovered. Said she got stuck in my garage. Her baby had her belly shaved and she probably figured it out but she never said anything. For her, free neutering. For me, I didn't want to shoot her with BBs every time I saw her load a box full of kittens in her car."

He kept staring down at me.

I kept blabbing.

"You know, it was better when you were being sweet and I could just think about how much I liked it that you don't mind changing diapers. So can we have a nice morning, and to have that, can I ask that you stop annoying me?"

"Changing diapers?" he queried.

"Men don't get it. If they knew how much women liked it when they took care of babies, the moms wouldn't get anywhere near their child."

His lips hitched. "You liked it when I changed Brooks's diapers?"

I shrugged.

His hand still in my panties moved from my behind to my hip.

"What else did you like?" he murmured, his voice having changed entirely.

But I was still annoyed.

"I liked it that you didn't let Addie give you any shit."

"She's fun," he said.

"She's a smart aleck."

His hand shifted to my hipbone and my attention on our conversation stuttered.

He dipped his head closer and asked "What else did you like?"

I tried to stay focused at the same time wondering where his hand was going to go next.

"I...I, uh...like it that you're easy to cook with."

"Yeah?" he murmured, his eyes dropping to my mouth and his hand sliding even farther.

"Yeah," I whispered, my eyes also dropping to his mouth.

Seriously, I really loved his beard.

And his lips.

"What else you like, baby?" I watched his lips whisper back, his fingers skating across the curls between my legs.

"Um..." I mumbled.

"Hmm?" he hummed against my lips and then his fingers slid over my clit and my hips jerked. "You like that?" he asked.

"Yes," I breathed.

He repeated the gesture and my hand at his chest slid up to hold on to his neck as I pressed into him.

"How much?" he asked.

"A lot."

He stroked me between my legs, barely grazing my clit and I started panting.

"Does your man always gotta ask you to kiss him when he's wanting a kiss or are you gonna learn to get with the program?" he inquired.

"I'm gonna learn to get with the program," I whispered but was so entranced with him, I made no move.

"Then give me that mouth, Izzy," he demanded.

I kissed him.

He pulled me closer, giving his hand more room to move and his fingers scored firm against my clit before he bent into me so he could glide one inside.

I whimpered into his mouth.

He separated his mouth from mine and slid his finger out.

"Get inside," he growled. "And get naked."

"'Kay," I pushed out.

He let me go.

I turned immediately and moved on jellied legs into his house.

Johnny followed me.

Ranger came with us.

But I had no mind to Ranger.

I went to my side of the bed and tore his T-shirt from me.

And I watched in turned-on confusion as he went to his side of the bed and pulled his sweats down.

I watched his hard cock spring free and it felt like it took ten years to yank my panties down my legs.

He bent to the bed, shoved the pillows against the headboard and climbed in.

I watched.

He settled with his back to the headboard, one leg straight, one leg cocked but falling to the side and then...

Then...

Then he started lazily stroking his cock and his eyes locked on me.

"What you gonna do to me, Izzy?"

Oh my God.

Ohmigod!

If I was completely in control of my limbs, which I absolutely was not, I would have scrambled in bed and taken that beautiful cock in my mouth so fast, I'd be a blur.

Instead, I was shaking with anticipation so it was deliberately, my gaze to him, that I put hands then knees to the bed and crawled his way.

He watched me do this and I got his sexy noise, this one lower, rougher, the one that carved through me, leaving me open, exposed, wanting, *needing*.

I positioned between his legs and stopped.

His eyes burning black fire, I was again mesmerized by Johnny.

But I didn't miss him stop stroking his cock so he could cup his balls, use his other hand to angle his cock from his stomach and offer it to me.

Oh...my...*God*.

"You gonna stare at it, beautiful, or are you gonna suck it?" Johnny asked gruffly.

My attention went from his shaft on offer to his face.

For a second.

Then I moved in, put a hand to his chest, trailing it down as I dropped my head, kneeling in front of him, positioning to worship his cock.

My closed lips touched the tip, I let it spread them then I drew him deep.

Johnny hissed out a breath.

I drew him out and sucked him back in.

I found his nipple with my thumb, rubbed it, felt it tighten under my touch, but my focus was what my mouth was doing, how far I could take him, how hard I could suck, how fast I could go.

His hand was in my hair pulling it back and I felt him take it, like it, become agitated and tense under my movements.

I gave him a break, laved him, stroked him with my free hand while I gently licked the tip.

Then I went back in, sucking hard, moving fast.

I felt him begin to strain around me, his big body getting tighter. Tighter.

Tighter.

Then it broke him and he started thrusting and I liked it so very much that I didn't put my fingers between my legs the way I needed to because I didn't want to miss anything.

I sensed him squeezing his balls and instinctively I knew.

I released him, surged up and put my forehead to his, curling my hand around his cock and jacking him tight.

His gaze glued to mine, his breath harsh, he wrapped his hand around mine and guided the way, loosening at the bottom but going in hard and tight at the top.

My mouth open, my breaths coming fast and shallow, I covered his hand at his balls.

"Squeeze," he grunted.

Gently I squeezed his hand over his balls.

"Fuck yeah," he bit off, his eyes closing. They opened and they were on fire. "With both, baby."

I squeezed with both.

"Don't miss it, Iz," he warned.

Leaving my forehead on his, I tipped my head down and watched the both of us working him, his hips restless, half thrusting, half writhing.

His hand on his shaft tightened tight, his other hand shifted so it was on the outside and I was cupping his balls skin to skin.

"God, beautiful," I breathed reverently, my hips mimicking his, my wet so wet, it was dripping down the inside of one thigh.

"Fuck," he ground out. "*Fuck*," he groaned.

And then he blew.

His powerful body strung tight and his cum jetted up his chest. His hands manipulating mine in a rough, tight, fierce way I'd never begin to touch him, it seemed he forced the cum out of his cock, squeezed it from his balls, and I whimpered and whinnied through my panting at the splendor of it.

"You're...just...*beautiful*," I breathed.

I barely got that out when my hands were pulled away and Johnny slid under me, taking me off my knees.

I landed on him and he pulled me through his cum as he hauled me up his chest. When he could, he grasped my hips and yanked me higher.

I gasped as I made my knees, exposed over him, and grabbed the headboard as his hands gripped my hips and he planted me on his mouth.

My head fell back and I ground into his face in a way that might have dawned on me was too much if his hands at my hips weren't pulsing me into him.

He was tongue fucking me, sucking my clit, biting it and I was rolling into every move, breathless, riding his face like I'd ride his cock.

My hand moved to his at my hip, and like he'd done to me, I showed him the way, pushing it back, curling his fingers in until the tip of his middle found my anus.

He growled up my cunt and then I was off, on all fours beside him on the bed.

But only for half a second.

He pulled me back on his face but with me facing the other direction, a hand between my shoulder blades shoving me down.

His cock was still hard.

I gobbled it in my mouth.

He grunted up my pussy, yanked me down to his mouth and I felt a wet finger gently pressing up my ass.

I lost him with my mouth as my neck arched back, a cry escaped me before I forced out a breathy, "*God, yes,*" and when he started to slide his finger out, I went back to his cock and again sucked it deep.

He ate me rough, fucked my ass gentle and I sucked his cock hard, cupping his balls, squeezing, feeling his grunts just as I heard them, taking his thrusts when he started driving up into my mouth, grinding my pussy in his face.

I just had the presence of mind to wrap my hand warm around him when my entire body arched up and back, smothering his face with my cunt.

I moaned, loud and long and low as he shoved his finger up my ass and ate me through an overwhelming climax that shook me from head to toe, leaving me blinded to all but his mouth, gasping for breath, straining into him, lost.

I vaguely became aware his hand was again around mine on his cock and he was pumping and it was fortunate I vaguely became aware of that because I did just in time to watch him come again all over his belly.

The gushes were weakening, he was using both our hands to milk himself dry, and that was when I collapsed on him, my cheek to the junction of his thigh and hipbone, my hair falling everywhere, my face nuzzling his shaft and balls, a soft sound escaping my mouth when he tenderly pulled out of my ass.

Johnny shifted my hair off my cheek and kept running his fingers through it as he ran his lips along the inside of my thigh.

I trembled on top of him.

He sank his teeth into the inside of my thigh.

I jolted and then melted into him.

"Iz?"

I shifted just enough to nuzzle the area between cock and balls.

"Iz." That sounded gruffer but also amused.

"Mm?"

More amused than gruff. "You goin' to sleep?"

"Mm."

"As much as I like your pretty pussy and the idea you can fall asleep with it in my face, you wanna roll off?"

It took effort but I rolled off.

He shifted me around so I was righted in bed and rolled on me.

I looked at his handsome, sated, amazing face.

He was smiling.

"Okay. Good to know that you can get hotter than jumping my junk in a barn," he declared.

"I didn't jump your junk," I mumbled, physically incapable of offering more than a mumble.

"Baby, you hopped right up and nearly planted yourself on my dick."

"Whatever," I muttered, finding I had the energy to trail my fingertips up and down his back, so I did that.

His amusement didn't flee but it got warmer and sweeter.

His voice was warmer and sweeter too, when he asked, "You wanna know what I like?"

"Can I guess?" I asked back.

"Shoot," he offered, still smiling.

I expended the effort to lift my head to touch his mouth with mine and found it took it all out of me, so I let my head plop to the pillows and wrapped my arms around him.

"You like blowing for me."

"Oh yeah, I like that," he agreed.

"I liked it too," I shared.

"I noticed," he replied.

"Like...a lot," I told him.

I felt him chuckle. "Yeah. I noticed."

"A lot, a lot, alotalot," I unnecessarily confirmed.

He smiled again. "You wanna know what else I like?"

"Me riding your face."

His smile got bigger. "Yeah, baby. Definitely. When you totally lose it and become all sex kitten, it rocks my world."

"Good," I muttered.

"Iz," he called.

"Yes?" I answered.

"You're covered in my cum, baby," he whispered.

"Hmm," I hummed, deciding to expend more effort and I did this by lifting my head and running my nose along the side of his neck.

Then I let my head plop back.

His thumb started rolling circles on my temple.

"You haven't guessed it, *spätzchen*," he told me.

"Guessed what?"

"What I like."

"I thought you liked blowing for me."

"I do."

"And me riding your face."

His voice shook with laughter. "That too. But that's not all."

"You like my guac."

"Yeah," he whispered, and the way he did made my sex haze dissipate.

I looked into his eyes and I saw humor there, for sure, warmth and sweetness, definitely.

But something more.

No.

Everything more.

"What else do you like?" I asked quietly.

"You," he said simply.

Me.

"Johnny," I breathed.

His face disappeared in my neck and he said there, "The sex kitten you who nuzzles my dick after I blow for her twice, and I haven't done that shit since maybe I was thirteen. And the working woman you. And the take-care-of-her-sister you. And the miss-her-mother you. And the thinking-Margot-is-sweet-instead-of-bossy-and-controlling you. And the love on your dogs, my dog, your cats, your horses and letting birds jump all over you you. The you in that blue dress yesterday and the you in the jeans I met you in and the you in that white dress at The Star and the you in my tee in the stables."

His thumb was still drawing circles on my temple opposite where his face was in my neck so I turned my head and kissed his wrist.

He lifted his head and I turned mine back.

"I don't mind changing diapers, baby," he whispered.

"I'm glad," I whispered back.

"I do mind my cum drying on you."

"It's okay," I told him.

"It's not."

I gave him a squeeze. "I really don't mind."

"I do 'cause getting it off you gives me an excuse to wash it off in the shower."

My eyes got bigger.

His eyes got hotter.

And then he was off me and I was being dragged across the bed to my feet whereupon I was promptly being tugged down the hall toward the shower.

I WAS BRUSHING my teeth in the basin Johnny didn't use in his bathroom, wearing his tee, no panties (I tried to put them on but Johnny was too close and he ripped them from my fingers, threw them in the middle of the bed and shook his head at me, saying, "Babe, would you get with the program? Your man likes easy access," after which he'd sauntered off in nothing but a towel and disappeared in the bathroom).

We'd obviously had our shower.

After, and after I'd pulled his tee back on, when I'd joined him back in the bathroom and rooted through the bag I'd brought to get my toothbrush, I found out what "easy access" meant.

This did not mean he did me braced against the basin.

What it did mean was offering me another nuance of how Johnny could be appreciative.

This being me brushing my teeth, Johnny coming up behind me, lifting my T-shirt (so I stopped brushing my teeth because I froze) and then running his hands across my behind while he watched his hands move and I watched him moving his hands in the mirror.

If I worshipped his cock, he was right then worshipping my behind.

It was sexy as all get out.

It was also somehow piercingly sweet.

When he was done, he slid his hands flat from my hips across my belly with the shirt still up, wrapping his arms around me so he could kiss my neck. He tipped his head back and looked into my eyes in the mirror.

"Sweetest piece of ass ever and not just because she likes it fucked," he muttered. He kissed my neck again, gave me a squeeze and then said, "I'll bring you some coffee."

He walked out still in his towel, Ranger following him.

It took me a while to get myself together to start brushing my teeth again but then it happened.

I saw it.

Or I didn't see it.

And I stopped brushing.

The pretty jar of bath salts was gone.

I heard a phone ring, and since Johnny and I had the same ring, it could be either of ours, so I spit, rinsed and was wiping my hands to dry them when Johnny strolled in wearing just his towel, phone to his ear, cup of coffee in his hand, dog at his heels.

He came to me, put the coffee down by my sink, leaned a hip against the counter and said into the phone, "Not sure, I'll have to ask."

By the way, he did all this, from the second he entered the bathroom, looking at me.

"All I can do is ask, Margot," he continued.

Oh boy.

Margot was in the mix.

Johnny kept going.

"Yeah. It's fine." Pause then, "Yeah, like I said, it's fine." His lips hitched at me. "It's good." Another pause then through a chuckle, "You wanna ask her? She's standing right here in my bathroom wearing nothing but my tee."

I instantly grew horrified.

"Johnny!" I snapped, slapping his chest.

He captured my hand and held it flat against his chest.

"Yeah, it's *that* fine," he stated. "And yeah, her sister is here, and she and her kid are coming over and hanging with me today and I'm gonna grill for them tonight. But no, you can't come over unless I ask Iz and make sure it's okay."

I felt my eyes get big.

Johnny took them in smiling and talking. "Right. I'll call you back." Pause then, "No, I haven't shopped yet, so if Izzy says it's okay I'll buy enough for you and Dave." Another pause then, "Margot, Christ, I love you. I'd take a bullet for you. I'd give you my kidney. But no, don't make your cherry pie *right now* because I don't know if you're comin' over here for them to eat it." He listened for a second then said softly, "*Ich liebe dich auch, mein liebling.*"

After that, he hung up.

I was feeling residual warmth and a newfound adoration of the German language when I asked, "Do you speak German full stop?"

"Enough I could go to Germany and get myself around."

That was impressive.

I let that go and continued with my questions.

"Do you know what kind of hell we'd both be in if Margot and Addie got together?"

He let my hand go, both of his came to my hips, they turned me, pulled me to him and only when I was resting against him with my hands on his chest did he answer.

"We can hack it."

"Johnny, your house is one room. I don't know if I can be in the same room with Margot as the room I did what I did to you this morning." I paused and added, "And the other times I've been here."

"Margot loves Dave more than he loves her, and I know that sounds impossible but trust me, she does. They had three kids. I think she knows what men and women do together when they like each other."

"Especially now that you told her I was in your T-shirt and nothing else."

He grinned. "Sometimes shock therapy is the way to go with Margot."

Why did I not find that surprising?

"Johnny—"

He pulled me closer. "Izzy, baby, we can't chose the way our lives go and shit got sorted when your sister is here and Margot is horning in because she's worried about me. Where I was at when Shandra left was not lost on her. Where I was at with you sitting beside me at dinner was not lost on her either. She thought from the story, like everyone thought when they heard the story, that I'd blanked you to go after Shandra. She wants to make sure I'm okay but it's more, she wants to make sure *you're* okay. And you can say no and I'll tell Dave who might be the only one who could stop her from coming here anyway. But I don't know why I'd do that since your sister loves you, Margot loves me, she likes you a lot, she'll feel the same way about Addie and she'll adore Brooks. So it's gonna be a big Memorial Day cookout. And it's probably gonna be fuckin' fantastic."

"If Addie offends Margot so much she tries to make you break up with me, you have to promise right here and now to stand strong."

He pulled me even closer. "I can promise that."

My gaze drifted to his shoulder and I muttered, "I'll tell Addie to behave herself."

"Will she do that?"

I looked again at him. "Absolutely not."

He burst out laughing, doing it clutching me to him.

Yes, when Johnny wasn't holding back, he was very affectionate.

I fit myself to him and wrapped my arms around.

When he quit laughing, he asked softly, "So can I call her back and say she can make her cherry pie?"

"I was going to make my chocolate silk pie," I told him.

"We'll have both," he decreed.

Perfect.

I smiled.

"Best call her and then get you home to your sister."

I nodded.

Johnny kissed me.

After he finished doing that, he called Margot. We got dressed.

And he took me home to my sister.

I made French silk pie, got dolled up, loaded up my dogs and my family.

And we went back.

TWELVE
LOOK AT HER

Johnny

Ranger perked up as Johnny was slipping the meat into the marinade.

He watched his dog run to the door so he turned to the sink, rinsed his hands, dried them and moved that way.

The minute he opened the door, Ranger sprang out and rushed down the steps.

Johnny went a lot more slowly and not because he didn't want to get to the burgundy Murano parked thirty feet from the foot of his stairs (she hadn't lied, it was now covered in dust) but because going slow gave him the opportunity to enjoy the show.

As usual, Izzy didn't disappoint.

He watched as she got out of her car.

That day, she was wearing a cream dress with big lilac flowers on it that had long, loose sleeves, a short flowy skirt, which hit her at mid-thigh, and a low vee dip that offered up a hint of her tits.

With it, she was wearing a pair of simple, flat, fawn suede sandals that had a wide strap across her toes but notched up the sex-kitten factor with the tasseled strings that snaked up her calves.

Another dress he wanted the skirt of it up to her waist.

But that was after he took her out somewhere. For a burger. For drinks at Home. To Margot and Dave's. Somewhere for dinner with his friend Ben and his wife Cait.

Sit by her side in that dress. Walk by her side while she was wearing that dress. Have her on his arm whatever way he could while she was in that dress.

When he was sitting across from Dave in The Star, he'd finally got it. He'd finally got why, all Johnny's life, it seemed whenever Dave was with Margot, he stood straighter, walked prouder.

Because that was how Johnny felt sitting next to Eliza at The Star.

She wasn't his then, exactly, but anyone seeing them would think she was.

And he sat straighter, moved prouder as the man who caught that woman's attention. The man she let be in her life.

She tipped her head, with her huge seventies-style sunglasses over her eyes, up his way and smiled.

He started to smile back but it ended in soft laughter when she was nearly bowled over as both her dogs jumped out after her.

That was his Izzy. Sexy as fuck and cute as hell.

Swirl and Dempsey greeted Ranger with dog abandon and went off to dance around each other, heading toward the creek.

Johnny headed toward Izzy.

She'd shut her door and met him halfway, holding a pie up in one hand, some kind of felt material bunched up under it, a little bag with a long strap dangling off her shoulder.

He rounded her with an arm and marveled how she could make those ridiculously huge sunglasses cute.

The same way she could make those just plain ridiculous boots she had cute.

He bent and touched his mouth to hers before muttering, "Hey."

"Hey," she muttered back.

He gave her a grin then let her go and moved right to Addie.

"Hey," he said. "Welcome."

"Yo, Magnus McHotterson. Boss pad," she replied.

He shook his head, still grinning, and since he'd made it to where she was pulling Brooks out of his car seat in the back, he took the kid. Then he took the big bag she had slung on her shoulder. He planted Brooks on his hip and Brooks went right for his beard. He then planted the strap to her bag on his shoulder.

He turned to her.

"Got any more?"

She was staring at him.

"Addie?" he prompted.

"Just his highchair in the back," she answered quietly.

"Leave it. I'll come back and get it when we need it."

With that, he turned toward the steps to see Izzy standing at the foot of them now wearing a brown floppy hat that was so fucking adorable and so fucking ludicrous, he felt his dick start to get hard at the same time his stomach burned with the need to bust out laughing.

She was also smiling so huge he thought her face would break.

"The dogs'll be okay, get your ass upstairs," he ordered.

"Roger that, Ghostrider," she returned.

To that, he let himself laugh.

He got them all in, dumped the diaper bag on one of his armchairs, kept the kid held to him and headed to the kitchen, saying, "Think I got all you need to make your guac, *spätzchen*, so get on that."

He jerked his head to the ingredients he'd left on the island, the stuff he saw her use when she'd made it.

She was twisted toward him, inside the door of his fridge, putting the pie in, and she'd taken off her hat and sunglasses.

She looked to the island, again to him, and she smiled.

Her smile, aimed at him from her standing in the open door to his fridge, hit him like a rocket.

Christ, if there was a definition somewhere of the whole package, she would be it.

The pie she put in his fridge he had no doubt would be fantastic. She never failed to make him want to fuck her in whatever she wore, even if it was another man's pajama bottoms. She'd made her home on her own, stamping it with all that was her in a way that was confident so it was also impressive. To have that, she had to be good at what she did at work. Her sister was loving and loyal and their relationship was tangibly close and strong. She treated her pets better than some people treated their children. That smile could brighten the depths of a mine shaft. And she was a woman who got off on letting him fuck her ass as he ate her pussy and she sucked his dick, losing herself so much in it, after he'd taken her there, she nuzzled his cock with the same adoration she sucked it. She did that, and when they weren't in that zone, she was shy and prissy.

He'd almost lost his shot at that.

He'd almost fucked it up.

And holding her nephew and taking in her smile, Johnny swore to himself he wouldn't do dick to let the promise of her slip through his fingers again.

He swore that and he swore he was taking his woman camping the first chance he got.

He forced himself to turn away from that smile, held Brooks to him as the kid tried to pull his beard out by the roots, and put the lids on the containers of meat and shoved them in the fridge.

"So he doesn't leave bald patches on your hot guy cheeks, give him to me. We're checking out that fab-you-*las* water wheel. That way, you can suck face with my sister and I don't have to witness it. With that over, we can get on with our day," Addie declared, pulled Brooks out of his arm and gave her sister a jerk of her head Johnny's way before she walked across his space, out the door and down the balcony toward the water wheel.

He was watching her sister, but that wasn't the only reason Iz took him by surprise as she bum rushed him into the corner of the countertop in the kitchen. Mostly the reason was that he didn't think she had it in her.

Another part of the whole package.

Eliza Forrester was full of surprises.

He was smiling down at her and just sliding his hands from her waist down to her ass when she took hold of his head on both sides, pressed into him, got up on her toes and laid a wet, heavy one right on his mouth.

Johnny took over, yanking her deeper into him and up, using her ass to do it. He took the sweet, little noise she made down his throat and the kiss got serious.

He was semi-hard but fully cognizant of the fact he had no place to do it and not enough time to offer her a quick fuck when he pulled his mouth from hers.

"Whatever I did to earn that, you gotta tell me, baby, so I can do it again," he muttered.

She stared right into his eyes and replied, "You're the best, Johnny Gamble."

He had a feeling he knew what this was about so he skated his hands up to wrap his arms around her waist but kept holding her close when he whispered, "I just carried him up the steps, Iz."

He knew he'd got it right when she said, "Her shoulders are sloped from lugging that diaper bag around, honey. Something little to you is something big to her and she's my sister so it's big to me too."

He gave her a squeeze. "You can pay me back by making your guac."

"Oh, I'll pay you back, but the guac will only be part of it."

That got her another squeeze and he put his lips to hers. "Lookin' forward to what you got planned, *spätzchen*."

"Okay, ugh. *Hurl.* Your time is up," Addie announced, and he looked beyond Izzy to see her sister coming in the door. "And just to say, it's dog bath day since those beasts have decided to frolic in the creek."

"Oh no," Izzy murmured.

He gave her another squeeze before letting her go, setting her gently away and telling her, "Don't worry, babe. I'll hose 'em down when they're done messing around."

She gave him a grateful look and moved toward the island.

"I need a bowl, a knife, a spoon and a cutting board," she declared.

He got her what she needed as well as another big bowl. He grabbed the bag of chips that was also on the island, opened them and dumped them in.

"This place is da bomb-diggity-bomb-bomb," Addie stated, and he looked to her to see that Brooks was motoring around the floor of Johnny's space and she was at the island. "But not to cast aspersions on your manhood, how do you not only have the most kickass furniture I've ever seen but also," she pointed to the large white chip bowl with its uneven top edges, "kickass stoneware?"

"The furniture, me. The other shit, Margot showed one day and declared the plastic stuff I bought at Walmart when I moved out of my dad's place at nineteen had to go, and I had no choice since she'd already made it gone and this shit was in its place."

Addie took a chip, shoved it in her mouth, and while chewing looked at Izzy. "I already dig this chick."

Izzy threw him a look and he caught it grinning.

"You want a drink?" Johnny asked Addie.

"Is it *su casa, mi casa?*" she asked back.

"Today it is," he answered.

"Then I'll get my own," she replied, moving to the fridge.

"Iz, babe?" he asked.

"I'll grab something when I'm done with this," she said, scooping out avocado into the bowl.

Johnny decided to let Izzy do her thing, Addie do hers, and he moved across the room, out the back door and located the dogs.

They were soaked and chasing each other around the huge grassy patch outside the mill.

He left them to it, found when he came back inside that Brooks had followed him to the door and bent to scoop him up.

Then he collapsed on the floor with Brooks squealing out giggles. He put the kid on his chest, tickling him and Brooks screeched more, arching and squirming and crawling all over Johnny.

"This sucks. He's yours and I totally wanna bang him," Addie stated loudly.

Johnny smiled at her son.

"There is the small fact you're married," Izzy put in.

"Huh," Addie grumbled.

Johnny twisted his neck to look at Iz to find her looking at him.

She gave him a scrunched nose.

With no words, that scrunched nose shared the reason for Addie being there had yet to be revealed.

He smiled again, this time reassuringly.

The front door flew open.

His gaze went there and he saw Margot swan in, Dave at her back carrying a pie.

She stopped, did a sweep of the place with her eyes, it halted on Izzy in his kitchen and her expression shifted straight to sheer bliss.

"Eliza!" she cried. "My darling girl! Could you *be* more adorable in that dress?"

As Johnny rolled up to his feet holding Brooks to him, Margot swept in, latched onto Izzy and hugged her like she was her favorite daughter who'd married a Russian who'd whisked her off to the cold of Siberia and she hadn't seen her in a decade.

"Totally...dig...*this chick*," Addie murmured.

Johnny moved their way as Margot let go of Izzy, assessed Addie, and Dave moved into Iz and gave her a hug, muttering, "Great to see you again, child."

"You too, Dave," she said back.

"You must be the sister," Margot decreed.

"That I am," Addie replied. "And you must be the awesome Margot."

Margot arched a brow. "Awesome?"

"Izzy thinks you're da bomb."

"Did she use that vernacular?"

"No, she said, 'I can't wait for you to meet Margot. She's class on a stick.'"

Margot's face grew smug and she aimed a look Izzy's way, murmuring demurely, "Darlin'."

Izzy was blushing.

Johnny waded in.

"Let's finish this up. Dave, this is Addie, Izzy's sister. And guys, this is Brooks." He lifted the baby a couple of inches. "Addie's boy."

"Oh...my...*word*! Look at that handsome child!" Margot lifted both hands his way. "Give him to me immediately, Johnathon."

Johnny gave him to her and then turned to Dave. "I'm gonna drag the deck furniture and camp chairs down by the creek. Izzy's making her guac, and you can thank me for the ingredients and worship at the chip bowl as gratitude to her. The dogs are a mess. They've been in the creek, so I gotta hose 'em down. I'll grill later."

"Works for me, son. Help you with the chairs and the dogs."

"Thanks, Dave," he replied and turned to Izzy. "Be back, baby."

She was mushing guac. "All right, honey."

"Who's handsome? Who's sweet? Who's a precious boy?" Margot cooed, swaying Brooks side to side.

Brooks slapped her face and giggled.

"Who's a naughty little monster?" Margot asked through a huge smile, capturing his hand and pretending to bite it.

Brooks arched and squealed and then patted her lips when she stopped pretending to bite him.

"Just to say, classy babe," Addie put in quietly. "We try not to let him slap."

Margot turned her eyes to Addie, and when she did Johnny knew Izzy's sister had her approval.

"All right, darlin'," she whispered.

Margot grinned.

Addie smiled back.

Izzy squeezed lime into the guacamole.

And Johnny and Dave moved to lug furniture down by the creek.

HE WAS at the grill at the end of the deck and the women were in the chairs, with Izzy lying on the same blanket she'd had at the festival that she'd told him was still in her car, so he'd got it and spread it out.

She was again in her glasses and hat and she again looked cute, ridiculous, and with company, entirely too fuckable.

The chip bowl was empty, so was the guac bowl, both now in the sink.

Margot still had Brooks. Then again, except to allow him to motor around the grass for a while, Margot hadn't let go of Brooks.

The dogs were spent. Dempsey flat out on his side by Izzy, Swirl down on his belly at Margot's feet, but Ranger was curled at the foot of the grill with Johnny.

Dave was walking up the outside steps that led to the balcony.

"Need help?" he asked when he hit the deck.

"It's good. Later, you can help me carry everything down when this gets close." He indicated the grill with his head.

"Will do," Dave replied and got up close.

His attention was not on Johnny or the grill.

It was on the women in the grass.

"She's a great gal," Dave murmured, referring, Johnny knew, to Izzy.

"Yup," Johnny agreed.

Dave finally looked to him. "You seem...good."

"You tasted her guac. You've seen her dress. Her sister is hilarious. And you and Margot are here. What's not to be good about?"

"You know...you know with this one..." Dave didn't finish.

Johnny felt the back of his neck start to itch.

"Dave—"

"She's a fighter, I can see it. I can see it 'cause she's had so much to fight all her life, it's marked her. She can't hide it. Don't make her fight anything more, son."

Johnny fought back getting pissed. "You know I wouldn't take it there if I didn't intend to be right there with her."

"Your old man got his hands on a couple of good ones—" Dave began.

"I'm not Dad," Johnny returned.

Dave held his eyes. "Your mother, that woman...she was somethin'. Lance thought he won the Super Bowl, the World Series and the NCAA championship when he won her."

"Dave—"

"She shattered him."

Johnny shut his mouth.

"And I loved that man better than I love my own brother so it was hard to watch him destroy every woman that came into his life after that woman left it."

"That's not happening here," Johnny said tightly.

"Johnny boy," Dave murmured.

"My mother left my dad with two young sons and she didn't look back, Dave. She never looked back. Not a one of us saw her again. And I don't know why. Do you know why?"

Dave slowly shook his head and gave him the answer Johnny already knew.

"I don't know why, Johnny. Your dad didn't know why. He just came home one day to a note that you boys were with your grandma and all her stuff was gone. I think that's part of why she haunted him. He never knew why."

"Shandra made a choice," Johnny replied. "My opinion, it was the wrong choice. But she left me for a reason and I knew that reason. What happened with my mother is not what's happening here. I'm not haunted, wondering about whys. I let Izzy go when Shandra first told me she was coming back to town because I wasn't done grieving what I thought was supposed to be my life. But it finally hit me that wasn't what life had planned for me. Now I don't know if all along it had plans for me to find a girl who's got a way with wearing a dress and makes my blood burn with the need to take away the taste of whatever shit she's obviously had to consistently eat in her life. What I do know is she's what's in my life now and while she is, I'm gonna take care of her."

Dave just continued to look in his eyes.

"I mean, look at her, Dave," Johnny said quietly.

Dave's head turned so he could take in all that was Izzy.

"I don't know what was in Dad's head when he did all he did after Mom went away. If he was looking for her again and never found her. If some place inside him needed to be free if she came back. But Shandra's back and Izzy's on my grass with Margot, and knowin' she's gonna be right there to eat the food I cook for her makes me happy."

Dave looked back to him. "You got a long row to hoe with this, Johnny."

Johnny felt his brows snap together. "What's that mean?"

"Everyone in town thinks that—"

Johnny looked to the meat on the grill, stating, "Everyone in town can go fuck themselves."

"Boy," Dave said low.

Johnny looked to him. "I don't care what they think."

Dave lifted his brows. "You think she might?"

"I know Izzy's lived through a lot more than losing her mother and having a creepy ex-boyfriend. She hasn't told me yet what that is, but you're right. She wears it like a brand. So my guess is, she can live through a bunch of gossips in town intent on the romance of the decade playing out as they'd always hoped and Johnny and Shandra riding into the sunset. But the only person in my sunset right now is Izzy. If she's under my care, I'll make it so she doesn't give a fuck either."

"No offense but a son walks in his father's footsteps," Dave said.

"No offense taken, Dave, but sometimes that son watches instead then looks before he steps to make sure he doesn't walk the wrong path."

Dave nodded. "Gotta say, as much as it cut to lose him, I was glad he didn't have to watch you lose Shandra. Now it hurts, knowing he's not gonna see you get to the other side, finding Izzy."

Johnny looked to the meat and grunted the understatement of the century, "Yeah. That cuts."

"He would have liked her," Dave said softly.

Johnny again turned eyes to him. "A person would have to be insane not to like her."

Dave smiled.

"It's getting close, Dave. Can you make sure the women are topped up on wine?" Johnny asked.

"Do that right now, son," Dave replied.

He loped to the stairs and down them.

Johnny watched.

Then he shifted the chicken that was done to the top shelf and put on the steaks.

Margot, Dave and Addie were in the chairs back up on the deck.

Brooks was asleep in the middle of Johnny's bed, surrounded by pillows.

And Johnny was on his ass on Izzy's blanket. She was between his legs, resting her back against his chest. He had one arm around her, one hand up in both of hers and she was playing with it. The water wheel was splashing water gently not too far away and Ranger was lying on the blanket on one side, Swirl at their feet, Dempsey on their other side.

The man Margot raised knew he was being a bad host when most of his guests were up at the house and he was not.

Izzy right there, playing with his hand, Johnny didn't give a shit.

Though he figured, Izzy and him right there, the rest of them didn't give a shit either.

"Got plans next weekend, *spätzchen?*" he asked.

"I'm getting a horse to stable," she answered.

"Shit," he muttered.

He'd forgotten.

She wrapped the fingers of one of her hands around his and put them to her chest, turning slightly in his hold to look up at him.

"Why?"

"We missed a date to go camping."

She'd been relaxed, wine, food, pie, good company.

Still, he felt her ease further into him.

"Yes," she said softly.

"Take Mist back weekend after next, sometime in the morning. About twenty miles farther, there's a great camping and fishing spot. We'll drop Mist off and head out."

She put her free hand to his chest and slid it up to rest it under his throat. "That sounds awesome."

"You cool with hitting Home to have a few drinks with me after you have dinner with your sister tomorrow night?" he asked.

She nodded.

Johnny drew her up, slanted his head and bent his neck to kiss her lightly.

When he was done he didn't go very far away when she asked, "Wanna come over for dinner one night next week?"

"Absolutely."

He caught her smile in the waning light.

"Today was great, Johnny," she told him.

Started out spectacular and it was arguable, but he'd argue it only got better.

"Yeah."

"You have a way with meat," she said.

He chuckled.

"Well, you do," she affirmed.

"I'm a man raised by Margot, baby. I'm trying not to be crass."

It dawned on her and she mumbled, "Oh."

He pulled her up farther and gave her another light kiss.

Then he settled her back down, turning her so her back was fully to his chest again and he wrapped both arms around her.

"We're probably gonna have to go soon." She said it like she didn't want to say it.

"Yeah." He said that like he didn't want to say it either.

"How's Wednesday for dinner?" she asked.

"Works for me," he answered.

She fell silent.

Johnny held her to his chest.

Into the peace, she said hesitantly, "You haven't asked."

"What?"

It took her a moment to say, "Nothing."

He gave her a squeeze and reminded her, "Babe, we talked about this this morning."

She didn't reply.

"Iz, I haven't asked what?" he pushed.

"About sex."

"What?"

"Drinks at Home and dinner at my place and, well...you haven't asked where we'll fit in sex."

And again, Johnny fought against getting pissed.

"You can take it as given I want that from you whenever we find our shot, Eliza. But since it seems I haven't made it clear yet, I'll do that now. That's not all I want from you."

"Okeydokey," she replied quickly.

They fell silent again while Johnny continued to try not to be pissed.

"Uh...Johnny?"

"Yeah," he grunted.

"So, um...well, just to say, *I'd* like to know when we're gonna fit in sex."

For a second, he went still.

Then he busted out laughing.

She turned in his arms, pushed up and looked in his eyes.

"That isn't an answer," she declared.

Johnny kept laughing.

She started to pull away.

He pulled her back and gave her an answer.

"After drinks, we'll come back to my place and I'll fuck you stupid. And after dinner at your place, I'll spend the night and we'll be quiet."

She glared at him through the twilight.

"We got a plan?" he asked, trying not to sound like he was still amused but not succeeding.

"We have a plan," she answered, not trying not to sound like she was annoyed.

"Now I need to take you up to the house before I take you into the woods and fuck you stupid there."

She didn't sound annoyed, she sounded back to disappointed when she said, "'Kay."

Johnny gave her another kiss. He let that one linger. Then he brought them both to their feet, nabbed the blanket and walked her up to the deck with all three of their dogs trailing.

After a day like that day, goodbyes between all of them lingered too. But Brooks being asleep meant they eventually had to end, which meant with nothing but a peck on the lips, Johnny had to stand with Ranger sitting by his side and watch Izzy drive away.

When he lost sight of their taillights, he looked down at his dog.

Ranger looked up and tilted his head to the side.

"You like her, boy?" he asked.

Ranger got up on all fours, wagged his tail and licked Johnny's hand.

"Yeah, me too."

He slapped his thigh and moved to and up the stairs with his dog at his side.

They entered his house. Johnny got a beer, got his book and read with his dog lying at the foot of his chair until it was time to hit the sack.

He did that and he didn't jack his junk thinking of Izzy.

Because he'd have the real thing tomorrow night.

THIRTEEN
MOTOR OIL AND KITTEN FUR

Izzy

"Uh...*say what?*"

The last two words Deanna said were practically shouted so I quickly got out of my chair, dashed across the room and closed the door to my office.

I turned back to her.

It was the morning after Memorial Day. We were back at work.

And I'd just filled Deanna in on all that had happened that weekend.

She hadn't even sat down.

I probably should have waited for her to sit down.

"Deanna—" I started.

"You told me you were hungover, Iz. And just to say, we went to the festival. We heard the word going around. I knew you weren't hungover. But when you got something to sort, I know you. You need space to sort it. And anyway, Addie was with you so I thought she'd have you until you got to the point you wanted to share with me."

"I actually was hungover," I told her. And added, "As well," when her eyes narrowed on me.

"All the rest happened and you didn't phone your girl?" she asked, her voice pitching higher and higher with each word.

"I was kinda busy," I told her.

"Kinda busy having Johnny Gamble grillin' meat for his family and your sister, but what about the rest of your family, Izzy?"

"You guys went to Charlie's mom's," I reminded her.

"Charlie's mom works my last nerve, you know that. An excuse to bag on spending Memorial Day with her, listening to her tell me I didn't get the right amount of brown sugar in my beans and maybe I should work less and spend more time making and taking care of the babies I have as yet failed to give her son, I'd jump at the chance."

I knew this and immediately felt bad.

She crossed her arms on her chest. "How are things?"

"They're..." I hazarded a smile, "great."

She nodded her head once. "Mm-hmm. And what's next for you and Johnny Gamble?"

"We're meeting at Home for drinks tonight. Then he's coming over for dinner tomorrow night. I'm stabling a horse for a friend of his starting Saturday and Johnny's coming over to take care of him every morning, as well as Serengeti and Amaretto. And when we take Mist back, we're going camping for the weekend."

"Well, hells bells," she muttered. "That boy makes a decision, he don't dick around."

I grinned. "I think he likes me."

"Well, girl, strap in because that was not lost on the town of Matlock."

I blinked at her. "Sorry?"

She didn't make me wait.

"Now, the division between Shandra and Izzy is forming, baby girl, but far's I can tell, you're winning."

My chest started to feel funny.

"Sorry?" I repeated.

She put her hands on her hips and a foot out, settling in to sock it to me.

"Apparently, Johnny met Brooks," she said.

"Yes," I confirmed.

"Now, you see, you and Johnny and Brooks being all cozy got some hearts a'flutterin'. That new girl who owns the acres up north is a miracle worker, they say. She cured Johnny Gamble's broken heart."

"Wow," I whispered.

"Yeah, wow. Then Shandra shows and Johnny takes off after her and Matlock is in a tailspin. A little less than half of them thinking that's just the way it should be, and a little more than half of them ticked at Johnny for leaving a sweet thing like you in his dust as he raced after the woman who broke his heart."

"He was going after his dog," I told her.

"I know that and you know that, they do not know that."

"Does any of this matter?" I asked.

She stared at me.

"I mean, I know what's happening and Johnny knows what's happening and *you* know what's happening, so what do I care that they know what's happening?"

She continued to stare at me.

"Deanna, my earliest living memory is hearing scary noises coming from my parents' bedroom and walking in on my father beating the hell out of my mother. Do you think I care if people do or do not want me with Johnny?"

"Izzy, you grew up in the city. This is a small town. Things are different. You can escape things in a city that will be in your face in a small town," she explained.

"He said, 'Get rid of her.' And her nose was bloody, her face puffy and wet with tears, and she looked at me and said, 'Baby, go back to bed. I'll be in to tuck you in in a minute.'"

Deanna's face grew gentle.

"She was in when he was done with her, and she'd cleaned up and she tucked me in," I finished.

"Baby girl," she whispered, her voice thick.

"If things work out for me and Johnny, they'll get used to it. If they don't, I don't care. In the meantime, I don't care. He likes me, Deanna. He drops to the floor with Brooks and tickles him and he shovels shit right back at Addie when she's shoveling it at him, and Addie loves it, and he looks at me like I'm the prettiest thing he's ever seen. That's all I care about."

"You happy?" she asked quietly.

"I'm scared and I'm ecstatic," I answered.

She studied me for a while then she lifted her chin and warned, "I best be meeting this boy and soon, Iz."

I grinned. "I'll talk to him, but how's Saturday sound?"

"I won't talk to Charlie. I'll tell him his behind is at your place on Saturday and it's not a free meal. He's got a job. The job of sizing up your new fella."

Charlie would love Johnny. Two peas in a pod, just two different colors.

"That'll be great."

"If you're ecstatic, I'm ecstatic for you," she told me.

I grinned again.

"And if I hear anyone say anything, I'll set them straight."

I stopped grinning. "You don't have to do that."

"Still doing it."

I shook my head.

She raised a raspberry-tipped finger and pointed it at me.

"Now from here on in, I don't get news on a forty-eight hour delay. Am I heard?"

I was back to grinning. "You're heard, Deanna."

"Yeesh, we're gonna get fired things don't settle down with Johnny Gamble. We never get any work done."

I looked at my watch then told her, "It's eight twenty, Deanna, we're done with the update and I've already cleared my inbox."

"That's because you're an overachiever." I thought she was in the middle of making a quip but knew she wasn't with the sudden change in the way she was looking at me. "You didn't get much from your dad, but even if it was forged through adversity he gave you the drive to find something better in your life. That's yours. You work it. You own it. But he gave it to you. I'm not saying you should be grateful. You don't thank a rapist for teaching you how to be more careful as you walk to your car at night. But you own the strength you earned by getting through that even if it's all kinds of unfair you had to find that strength. He played a part in making you the Izzy you are, and you should be proud this is who you became when it could have gone another way entirely."

"Stop making me wanna cry when my makeup is this fresh," I retorted.

"Whatever," she muttered then asked, "Lunch?"

I nodded.

"And just saying, you're keeping Addie and Brooks from me too."

"I'll ask her to bring Brooks into the city for lunch tomorrow."

"Huh," she puffed out (which meant in Deanna-still-kinda-annoyed-at-you speak "okay").

With that, she strutted out of my office.

I watched her then went to my phone on my desk.

Deanna wants to meet you, I texted Johnny.

Almost immediately I got back, *Knew that was coming.*

She's good people, I shared.

Figured that, he replied.

Saturday at my place? I asked.

I'll be there, he answered.

See you later.

You absolutely will.

I smiled at my phone.

Then I got to work.

I HURRIED in the back door of Home and saw there was only a smattering of people, Johnny one of them, sitting on the stool he sat on the night we met.

It was not lost on me I had attention well beyond people turning to look and see who was coming in the door.

I just ignored it as I made my way quickly to Johnny.

"Sorry," I said, sliding between him and the stool where I'd sat when we met. "You been waiting long?"

"Babe, I'm at a bar with the game on. It's not a hardship to sit here and drink beer."

I grinned at him.

He stared at me.

"Everything okay?" I asked, setting my purse on the bar and hefting my behind up on the stool.

"You are totally not with the program," he muttered.

"Sorry?"

"Babe, *kiss me*," he ordered.

That sent the trill up my spine.

I leaned into him and touched my mouth to his only to have him cup the back of my head, making the kiss longer, sweeter, but keeping it light.

He let me go and murmured, "Have a good day?"

I nodded.

"You want a glass of wine?"

I nodded.

"What you want?" he asked.

My eyes trailed away as I mumbled, "Um..."

"Sally, you got a wine list?" Johnny called.

Sally, the bartender, looked at him like he'd gone crazy.

Johnny looked to me. "It's house red or house white, and maybe if you're lucky, house rosé."

"White," I said.

Johnny turned back to Sally. "Can you get my girl a glass of white?"

"Sure thing, Johnny," she said and moved to the wineglasses suspended upside down over the bar.

Johnny took a tug of beer.

After he swallowed, I asked, "You have a good day?"

He'd been positioned facing the bar through all this and only then did he twist on his stool toward me, put a forearm on the bar, fingers still wrapped around his beer.

"The goal for having a GM is that people bring in cars. I fix them. I know they're not gonna like how much it costs so I can tune that out. They drive away with something fixed. I work on the next car. In other words, being able to tune out the only shit I might take, I don't have to deal with any shit. So, *spätzchen*, it's rare I have a bad day."

I smiled at him. "That's cool." Sally put my glass in front of me and I turned my smile to her and said, "Thanks."

"Don't mention it," she murmured and moved away.

"News about Addie?" he asked.

I took a sip, put my glass down and told him, "She still hasn't shared."

"How long is she staying?" he queried.

"Maybe forever?" I replied in a question and saw his brows go up. "She hasn't said how long she's staying but she's gone so far as to unpack in my guest room and set up a makeshift nursery for Brooks in my office. And she brought a lot of stuff, Johnny. She's a waitress. It's at a high-end place so she makes a lot on tips. But she's hourly. She doesn't get paid for vacations."

"This isn't getting better," he muttered.

"No," I agreed.

"You good with her staying forever?" he asked.

"Totally," I answered.

His lips hitched. "Figured that was a stupid question."

I leaned toward him, scooting my wineglass closer, and grinned.

"You talk about your mom, Izzy, know your sister, what's up with your dad?" he asked.

I leaned back, scooting my wineglass away, and my grin died.

"Iz?" he called as I lifted the glass and took a sip.

I swallowed it and requested, "Can we keep tonight light?"

"Sure. But just to say, baby, I'd like to get to know you better and talking about your sister's possibly disintegrating, possibly already crashed and burned marriage isn't exactly featherweight."

"I don't see him," I declared.

"Your dad?" he asked.

"Yes," I answered.

"Your choice?" he asked.

"Absolutely," I answered. "However, there is the small fact that Mom took us, ran away from him, and after making her life miserable for about two months, we never heard from him again, so it was his choice first."

Johnny's hand came to rest on my thigh, the warmth of it immediately melting through my jeans.

It gave me strength.

So I shared, "This is probably because he found another woman to beat bloody."

I saw a flash in his eyes before he hid it and whispered, "*Spätzchen*."

"My grandfather hated my dad, ordered my mother not to marry him, and she rebelled. She was eighteen, head over heels in love, and pregnant, the last part my grandfather was *really* not hip on. She took off to be with the love of her life. That's just the way things go, I guess. Therefore, when Mom took us from him to them, my grandfather closed the door in her face. Apparently, he was that kind of guy. I don't know. I don't really remember him and Mom never talked about him. Though from the little I do know, mostly how my grandmother behaved, even though I didn't know her either, my mom found her father and married him."

"Fuck," Johnny clipped.

"My grandmother found us before we had to skip town and gave Mom her milk glass. Told her to sell it. Mom never sold it. It was the only thing she had of her mother. So she kept it. And Gramma would send cash as often as she could but it wasn't very often. Still, we were so poor, whenever she could, it helped."

"Izzy," he whispered.

"Government cheese," I said.

He leaned into me, his fingers digging in.

"*Izzy*," he hissed.

"She worked all the time. She'd find places close to school so Addie and I could walk if she couldn't take us. Every time we moved when we were young, she'd walk us back and forth, back and forth. 'Remember this, girls. Don't go a different route, my queens,' she'd say. 'And don't talk to strangers, not ever. Get yourselves home, fast and safe, and then you call your momma to let her know you're locked in tight.'"

Johnny said nothing.

"She'd open cans of soup so I could heat them up for Addie and me if I had to make dinner. Soup and cheese sandwiches. Night after night. All I could make but also all she could afford. She'd call to make sure I turned off the stove. I was seven."

His hand slid up my thigh as he got closer but he said nothing.

"I graduated to grilled cheese sandwiches when I was nine. You like my guac, you should try my grilled cheese. It's to die for."

"Don't make light of this, Izzy," he said gently.

"We were happy."

His chin jerked back.

"We had each other, and in the beginning Addie and I only knew she was safer without him so we were in a better place because she was too. When we figured out there was more to have, we'd already learned it didn't mean anything, so we stayed happy because we had each other. And then she died, and honest to God, Johnny, that was the first time after we left him that I was ever unhappy."

His eyes dropped down, he shoved my wine aside and he pulled my hand to him.

I was wearing my mother's charm bracelet again.

"It's cheap," I whispered.

He didn't look up.

"Those charms Addie and I bought her every birthday using some of the money we'd hoard that our Gramma would send us for our birthdays. I got the bracelet when we lost her. Addie has the two charms that say 'World's Greatest Mom' and '#1 Mom.' I got her her own bracelet when she had Brooks and gave it to her with them on it."

His finger fidgeted with the head of a horse charm.

"She made us dance with her in our living room, and she tried to get every Sunday off to do Sunday night facials she'd make out of honey and oatmeal, and she'd take us out to stare at the stars. She made a game out of doing laundry at the Laundromat, and she hid it really well those times rent was coming due but her paycheck wasn't and we were running low. She was sunlight and moonshine and honey and song and love. And I had her for a while and then God needed her with Him so I had to let her go."

His eyes turned to me and the pain in them, the pain for me, dug down deep. Deep inside me.

And settled there.

And I wanted it.

I needed it.

It was buried treasure.

"She was iron," I whispered. "Iron and steel and granite and everything strong packaged up in feathers and goose down and kitten fur and everything soft. She was the most precious gift I've ever received and will be until I have my own babies."

"Stop talking," he ordered gruffly.

I closed my mouth.

"I can't erase that," he stated and the blood started singing in my veins. "I can't make that better."

Oh my God.

"Johnny—"

"We fight wars over dirt and oil and ego when we should fight wars against men who force women to live that kind of life with their children."

"We were happy," I reminded him.

"You could have been happier," he said to me.

I again closed my mouth.

Johnny didn't break the silence so I asked, "Are you done getting to know me now?"

"Now?" he bit out. "Yes. Done? Not by a long shot."

My blood started burning.

"Do you...um...do you wanna talk about your mom?" I queried cautiously.

"She left when I was five, Toby was three. He doesn't remember her. I do. She was amazingly beautiful. And she was down to her soul selfish. I haven't seen her since. My dad never saw her again either. He also never got over her. I hate that for my dad, but her leaving meant Toby and I got Margot, so we had it better than we would have, I figure. And that's it."

"That's very succinct," I noted carefully.

"So it aptly describes her tenure as a mother," he returned.

"Honey," I murmured.

"I don't miss her and I don't think not having her made me miss anything. I don't feel loss. I had Dad and he was a great dad. The best. I had Margot. I had Dave. I had Toby. Toby's a wild one but it's not because he missed having a mom or was acting out, wondering why she didn't give a shit enough to stick around. Dad also didn't spoil him and Lord knows, Margot didn't. No one would say it to his face, but we all think it. He got a piece of her. But he also got a lot of Dad, so even though he hasn't yet found his way, he will."

"I hope so," I said softly.

"He will," he replied.

"Where is he?" I asked.

"Guiding fishing expeditions in the Florida Keys?" he asked, like I could answer him. "Training to be a ranger in Alaska?" he asked another question I couldn't answer. "Employed as a flight instructor in Phoenix? Who the fuck knows?"

"He can fly planes?"

"Toby can do anything."

"But can he, well...actually fly planes?"

"Yes. And speak German fluently since he had more of Grams, because I was in kindergarten when Mom left and shortly after, full-time school, so he had more time with her and she talked German to him all the time and kept doing it until she died. I would have lost half of what I had if Toby didn't try to get one over on me by speaking to me in German. Dad spoke it too, since Grams taught him, so he'd call him on his shit as well. Toby was captain of the football team, quarterback, and he got caught banging the homecoming queen in the locker room after the big game. The coach chucked him off the team. The town went nuts. So they ended up suspending him for two games. The only two games Matlock lost that season." He paused then said, "Golden boy."

He shook his head and any sting he might have felt about the next he said was taken away with his rueful but also admiring grin.

"No matter how much he'd fuck up, and he was a master at it, he'd come out smelling like roses."

"Did you play football?"

He nodded his head. "Tight end."

"But not captain?" I asked warily.

He looked confused. "Well...yeah." Then he grinned again. "And I was dating the homecoming queen and already banging her, so I didn't have to sneak a go in the locker room."

I rolled my eyes and reached for my wine.

After I took a sip, he said, "Dad was the shit."

I put my wineglass back and prompted quietly, "Yes?"

"He wasn't sunlight and moonshine and kitten fur, *spätzchen*. He was motor oil and beer and NASCAR racing. He didn't miss a single one of our games. He gave us the talk and told us he'd break our necks if we disrespected a woman. Then he gave us condoms. He also gave us Margot and Dave, and their sons were older than us so he gave us three older brothers and big Thanksgivings and Christmases and Easter dinners. He wept when his father died and sobbed when he lost his mother, but way before that he told us only stupid men hide emotion. There's strength in being who you are and feeling what you feel and not giving a shit what people think. He said one of the worst things a man could be is inauthentic. He told us never to willfully break a woman's heart because there'd come a time when a woman would break ours and we'd feel what we'd made her feel and we wouldn't be able to live with the guilt. He loved us and he showed it. He was proud of us and he showed it."

He looked to my wrist and slid his forefinger between my skin and my mother's bracelet, turned his hand and gently curled it around the inside of his first knuckle.

"And I wept when he died and every year on the anniversary, I take some of his ashes to the first place he took Toby and me fishing and I put them in the creek and feed the fishes in the moonlight," he finished.

"That's beautiful, Johnny," I said softly.

He turned his head to me. "I should have taken you with me. He woulda liked meeting you."

As my hand rose of its own accord, my body swayed forward the same way, and I curled my fingers around the warm, firm skin at the side of his neck and I pressed my lips against his.

I pulled back but I didn't go far.

"So I wish I'd had your mom and I wish you'd had my dad," he murmured.

"Instead, we found each other," I murmured back.

"Yeah," he said.

"She would like you but she would not like you grilling a chicken breast *and* a steak for five people," I informed him.

The white of his teeth cut through his beard. "Don't know how to grill tofu, babe."

"You sadly will never have the chance to eat one of her home-made veggie burgers. You might swear off beef for the rest of your life."

"I don't think that's true."

"They were really good."

"You didn't swear off beef," he pointed out.

"Mm," I mumbled.

He started chuckling.

He cupped the side of my head, kissed my mouth and leaned away so my hand dropped.

He took a sip of beer.

I took one of wine.

When I'd swallowed, he said, "Now's the time to take this shit light."

I gave him a small smile. "Agreed."

"So what's your favorite color?"

I started giggling.

Then I told him, "The rainbow."

He stared at me a beat before he burst out laughing.

When the laughter was waning, he asked, "How could I have guessed that?"

I tilted my head to the side and shrugged.

He shook his head and took another swig of beer, so I took another sip of wine.

When his bottle and my glass were back to the bar, I stated, "Let me guess. Red."

He looked at me and shook his head.

"Blue?" I guessed again.

He nodded. "Though there are stipulations."

My brows rose. "Stipulations to your favorite color?"

"Yup," he replied and went on, "Trucks, black. Dirt bikes and ATVs, yellow. Snowmobiles, black. Tees, they just have to be kickass. Jewelry I'll give a woman, gold. Lacy underwear with garters, black or red. Teddies, black, red and I'll throw in pink, which, babe, is the only way I like pink."

"I think I need to go underwear shopping," I muttered.

"This would not go unappreciated," he replied.

I averted my eyes and took another sip of wine.

He chuckled again.

When I put the wineglass back to the bar, he asked, "Ever been on a dirt bike?"

"No."

"Wanna try?"

"Yes."

"ATV?"

"No."

"Wanna try?"

"Yes."

"Snowmobile?"

I shook my head.

"Try it?"

I nodded my head.

His lips hitched.

"Do you have all of those things?" I asked.

"Drive my truck up under the mill in winter and that's where that stuff stays year round when I'm not using it."

"Ah," I said, not yet having wondered what that space was used for and glad I didn't have to start.

"You gonna nurse that wine until you die?" he inquired.

"In a hurry?"

"You goin' home tonight after I'm done with you?"

My nipples started tingling but I said, "I probably should, honey. If Addie's still up, she might want company."

"Then yeah, I'm in a hurry."

I took a gulp of wine and my eyes got big when I swallowed it.

He chuckled again, leaned in and kissed my neck.

He leaned back and shared, "You don't have to glug it, baby."

"We'll have to be quiet tomorrow," I reminded him.

"Yeah," he confirmed.

"So I have to glug."

Another lip hitch.

I took another gulp.

And when I did, Johnny burst out laughing.

JOHNNY HAD MOUNTED ME.

I was on my hands and knees and he was curled over me. One arm straight, hand in the bed, fingers linked with mine. One arm angled over my shoulder and slanted across my chest, his hand cupping my breast. He had his face stuffed in my hair that had fallen over my shoulder at my neck. He'd ordered me to touch myself, something I was doing. And he was thrusting inside.

It felt good, like it always did with Johnny. The best.

But it was more, surrounded by Johnny, the strength of him, the surety, the power, the safety of him, all of that covering me, penetrating me.

I had my head back pressed against his shoulder, my eyes closed, my lips parted, my breaths heavy, coasting on all he was giving me, letting it sweep me away, letting him take me there.

My climax was fast approaching.

I opened my eyes, about to call his name.

And that was when I saw us reflected in the windows to the balcony.

We were perpendicular in the bed, facing straight to the windows.

I hadn't noticed that before.

But now I couldn't tear my eyes away.

I could see the muscles of his shoulders moving with his thrusts. I could see his dark head stark against my lighter hair. I could see my thighs splayed wide in order to take him inside. I could see my face harsh with sex, filled with need.

We were beautiful.

God, *we were beautiful.*

Johnny must have felt the swift ride to climax I was taking had slowed as I watched him fuck me, getting off on yet something else he gave me, because his head came up.

And his eyes locked on mine on our reflection.

Instantly, that muted roar rumbled up his chest, so deep, I felt it beating down my spine, exploding between my legs.

"Fuck, you're beautiful," he growled.

No.

He was.

Suddenly, I was up on just my knees and fully exposed to my eyes, his eyes, watching myself take his cock as he moved his hands to cover my pubis in a V and then up my belly, over my breasts, where he gripped me on either side at the juncture of neck and shoulders and held me steady to take his cock.

That was even more beautiful.

I whimpered and started moving more desperately on him, meeting his thrusts, my breasts swaying with my movements.

"Look at my sex kitten," Johnny grunted, his eyes locked on our reflection. "She loves taking my cock."

"Yes," I breathed.

His hands came back down, one cupping my breast, fingers rolling my nipple, the other pushing my hand aside to dive in and rub my clit.

I moaned, and as much as I didn't want to lose the sight of us, I couldn't stop my head dropping back as my movements became frantic.

"Look at you," Johnny groaned. "Fuck. Christ." He squeezed my nipple and I gave a small cry. "*Look at you.*"

I felt my hair tickling my chest, tremors starting to flow through me, and I forced my eyes back to our reflection, seeing my body moving wildly on his, my knees spread wide, my sex exposed, everything exposed, slamming into his thrusts, watching his cock sink in, pull out and sink in again and again and again.

"Johnny," I gasped.

"Yeah, baby," he growled. "Yeah. You love taking my cock, don't you?"

"God yes," I panted.

"Work it, Izzy," he ordered thickly.

I was working it but I worked at it more. For me. For Johnny. For moments like this I'd do anything.

My back arched, angling him deeper, and I cried out again.

"Fuck," Johnny bit out, his face had been dark with sex but now it was cruel with it. Cruel and beautiful. "That's it, sex kitten, give it to your man."

"Just you," I forced out.

"Just me," he clipped off, his fingers at my breast curling and digging in almost painfully.

"Just you," I whimpered. "Only you. I'm only this for you."

I barely registered the look on his face changing before my head shot back, hitting his shoulder, my spine arced at an impossible angle and I came.

I did it hard, knowing Johnny was watching, knowing he could see *everything*, the shockwaves of a magnificent orgasm setting me to bucking my hips into his as he let out a far less muted roar and his thrusts grew violent.

And he completed the task of fucking me stupid.

"SEE YOU TOMORROW NIGHT."

We'd just finished making out with Johnny pressing me to the door of my car when he said that.

I was heading home.

I did not want to head home.

But as it was with my life, I had to.

"See you tomorrow night," I replied.

He unpinned me by stepping away and I'd just started to turn in order to open my door when he said, "Just a sec, *spätzchen*."

I turned back.

He moved back in.

I looked up at him.

His hand landed gently on my neck and slid up to cup the underside of my jaw.

"Gotta know," he murmured.

"Gotta know what?" I asked when he didn't elucidate.

"What 'just you' meant."

I stopped looking at him, though I was now looking at his ear so I was still kinda looking at him, just not *at him*.

"Baby," he whispered, giving my jaw a tender squeeze.

"I'm not like that," I told his ear.

"Like what?" he pressed.

"In bed." My eyes skimmed through his until I was looking at his other ear. "I'm not like that in bed with anyone but you."

He said nothing to that, and this lasted so long I chanced a glance at his eyes.

The instant my eyes met his in the moonlight, he asked, "How are you not like that?"

"I don't let go," I whispered, fighting back the heat that wanted to beat into my cheeks.

"You don't let go," he murmured.

"Like that...like...uh, the um, sex kitten. I don't...that's just..." I drew in a shaky breath. "You're the only one I've felt...that's made me..." I pressed out a heavy sigh. "That makes me like that."

"From the beginning?" he asked.

"Sorry?"

"Baby, you were hot and wild for me from our first night."

"Yes," I said softly. "From the beginning."

There was a tenseness to his frame, even a tenseness in the way his hand was at my jaw, and I felt something extreme in the way his gaze was boring into mine.

"So the sex kitten is all mine," he stated.

"I'm not really a sex kitten, Johnny," I told him honestly.

"Izzy, you watched your own show. You fuckin' are."

"Not...not, well...not like, *right now*."

"Thank fuck."

I stared up at him.

"What?"

"Always wonder how wise it is to clue you in to all that's you, but for you, Iz, I'll do it. Since you don't have a dick, you can't have any idea the man who's got claim to that body," his other hand came to rest on my waist, "that man bein' me, gets off on having the sweet, cute Izzy you give to the world knowing, when I get you in bed, you'll light up like that for me. Watch me fuck you. Let me take your ass. Watch me blow for you. And all the other stuff you give to me when I get you naked and you let go for me."

His face dipped close and I continued to stare in his eyes.

"It's an honor," he whispered.

"An honor?" I whispered back.

"That you'd give me that. That you'd feel that safe with me." His eyes changed in the moonlight. "From the beginning."

There was something profound in that, I knew it back then.

He didn't.

Until now.

And he definitely knew it now.

And he definitely liked what he knew.

I knew that because he kissed me.

Repeatedly.

Not deep and wet and hungry.

Soft kisses. Sometimes invading my mouth but just to stroke it with his tongue. Sometimes just brushing my mouth with his. Sometimes nibbling my lower lip.

Again and again and again.

I was holding on to his shoulders, my head tipped back, my mouth on offer to him. It was his and he could take it, kiss me like that until the sun rose, until the leaves turned brown, until the world stopped spinning.

The problem was he actually couldn't.

I had to get home to my sister. Sleep. Go to work the next day.

And he had to let me.

He knew that better than me because he quit kissing me and murmured against my lips, "Loved tonight, *spätzchen*. Text me when you're home safe. And see you tomorrow."

I nodded, my forehead bumping against his and I saw his eyes smile.

My body felt fluid, not entirely from the sex, but from his soft kisses and sweet words, when he moved away from me and I turned and climbed into my car.

I started it and waved at him and didn't worry that I looked like a dork.

I was his dork.

Johnny Gamble's dork.

His sex kitten.

His woman.

So I could wave like a dork if I wanted to.

I waved again as I drove away, looking into the rearview mirror at him standing and watching me go, Ranger sitting at his side.

And I drove home thinking I was still ecstatic about what was happening with Johnny.

But I was no longer scared.

FOURTEEN
THE VEIL DROPPED

Izzy

"Well, all right."

I looked from my computer to the door to see Deanna waltzing in after saying that.

She closed the door behind her.

I glanced back at the computer and again to Deanna before I said, "Addie and Brooks won't be here for lunch for another half an hour."

"Know that, baby girl, but just to say, heard the word," Deanna replied.

"What word?"

"The word from Sally, bartender at Home, who gave it to Norma, who owns Home, who had her hair done this morning by some chick I don't know, but at my hair salon, Image, where my stylist Crystal is. And Crystal knows you and me are tight. Crystal also overheard Norma telling her stylist that Sally was totally in the Shandra camp, until you did whatever you did with Johnny, being all kissy and sweet and then making him laugh real hard. Now Sally's an Izzy convert, and from this story, Norma's switched sides and Crystal too."

It felt vaguely good that I was winning the townspeople of Matlock over.

But mostly I didn't care.

"This doesn't matter, Deanna," I reminded her.

"Just came in to give you the thumbs up for a job well done," Deanna replied.

"It isn't a job. I was having drinks with my guy."

"*Your* guy?"

I grinned at her. "Well, he calls me 'his woman' so I'm thinking it's safe for me to call him my guy."

Her eyes started sparkling. "Yeah, I'd say that's safe."

I had a feeling my eyes were sparkling too.

We sparkled at each other for a while before she said, "You do know, Johnny Gamble hasn't been Mr. Happy-Go-Lucky since Shandra took off on him."

I felt my sparkle blink out.

"Sorry?"

"This is what Norma said to Crystal. He's a regular at Home. Not a barfly but he goes to catch a game. Throw back a beer with a bud. It's the only bar in town so even me and Charlie are regulars there, though they don't have martini glasses, so it ain't really my style. It's just my only choice unless I wanna mix my own drinks and sometimes, girl, I just am not in the mood."

"They don't have a wine list either," I shared something she probably knew.

"Dire," she muttered. "Anyway," she perked up, "Johnny Gamble has not exactly made it a habit to pick up some chick and canoodle with her at Home, but it's safe to say he definitely hasn't roared with laughter, those were Norma's words to Crystal, at all. Ever. For three years."

I found this alarming.

"He hasn't...laughed?" I asked for confirmation.

"I don't know. Probably no one knows. No one has spent twenty-four seven with the man. Seen him. When I did, he seemed normal,

not moody, but not bright and cheery either. He just seemed kinda...
detached. Like he was going through the motions."

I felt my body lock as memories of our first morning together hit
me like a shot.

Johnny, standing out on the deck, deep in thought, drinking
coffee.

Removed.

Then there was when we were talking about vegetables and I'd
been being a goof and he'd burst out laughing.

It was the first time I'd heard him laugh in our then short
acquaintance.

I remember thinking it was beautiful.

But rusty.

It didn't sound rusty anymore.

"Iz?" Deanna called.

I focused on her.

"Maybe I am a miracle worker," I whispered.

A slow, white smile spread across her beautiful face.

"Baby girl, I knew that a long time ago," she replied.

And as was her way, with a successful parting shot, she swayed
out of my office.

I LAY in bed on my side, the covers up over my hip, my eyes on the
little daybed in the raised alcove to the side of my bedroom where
one of the windows was.

On that daybed were three pairs of men's pajama pants. They
weren't threadbare but they were downy with use.

I sensed movement behind me and rolled to my back to watch
Johnny emerge from the bathroom wearing another pair of pajama
bottoms.

We'd found we had a new talent in bed.

We could be quiet and it still was spectacular.

His eyes roamed me in the pale-pink fitted, ribbed, knit camisole with the lace edging at the top, which I pulled on after we were done and he'd gone to the bathroom. His lips hitched before he put a knee to the bed, pulling the covers up and spying the all-lace, white panties I'd put back on after he'd taken them off.

He slid under the covers beside me and then claimed me, doing this by pulling me to him, gliding a hand down my spine, over my bottom and between my legs from the back in a way I had no choice but to glue my front to his front and hike my leg over his hip.

I looked up into his eyes. "I can't be without panties with my sister and Brooks in the house, unless, of course, I'm having sex."

The white slashed through his beard and he muttered, "Baby."

He lightly stroked the gusset of my panties and I squirmed.

I also whispered, "Are we gonna make love again?"

The white stayed in his beard as he answered, "No. Just like feeling the wet you give me."

"Oh."

His brows went up. "You can't take even this without starting to light up for me?"

I tucked my face in his throat.

He cupped me between my legs and said, "Okay, *spätzchen*."

I nuzzled his throat.

"Your internal alarm clock wakes you up, you wake me up, Iz."

I tipped my head back again. "Sorry?"

"I'll take care of the animals, make you breakfast. You just take care of what you gotta do to get ready for work."

"You don't have to do that, Johnny."

"Right," he said, shifting his hand out from between my legs, up and then down inside my panties where he gently cupped a cheek of my behind. "We're here again so I'll give it to you. I'm that guy as well. You got an hour-long commute. I got a ten-minute commute. It takes you six times the amount of time to get ready for work as it does me. It isn't that taking care of animals is man's work, which, babe, just to say, I'm that guy too so for me it is. But for me as the man in the life of the woman you are, it's about doing shit I do not mind doing so you can have an extra half hour of shuteye or just an easier morning. So when I wake up in this bed, Iz, I take care of the animals and breakfast. You take care of you."

I stared at him.

"We straight about that?" he asked.

I nodded.

"You good with that?" he went on.

I nodded again.

"Good," he said. "Tomorrow night, I'm letting you be with your sister. Maybe if you have some concentrated time with her, she'll open up about whatever's going on with her."

I didn't want concentrated time with my sister.

I did, of course I did.

I still wanted time with Johnny.

"Maybe," I said.

"Maybe," he repeated after me. "We can hope." He looked deep in my eyes. "She's degenerating."

I was surprised.

"You noticed that?" I asked.

"All spark and fire, better to hide she's dying inside. Now, she's just dying inside."

I pressed closer to him, loving that he caught that but hating he was right.

Addie was slipping into a state of despair with each passing day. She was becoming less of herself, more withdrawn. The only time she lit up was for Brooks. The rest, for her, was going dark.

"I'm more worried about her now than ever," I told him.

"Yeah. You don't hide that. She just isn't responding to it."

"Maybe concentrated time will help."

"That and I'm taking you two to a pizza joint in Bellevue Friday night. If you haven't been, you have to go. If you've been, you'll want to go back. I'll ask Margot and Dave if they'll look after Brooks, and if Addie is down with them doing that, we'll drop him off and go have pizza. Don't know what she's doing while you're at work but a lot of time alone kicking around your house with nothing but her thoughts and no contact with the outside world isn't helping. She needs to get out. Live life. Eat good pizza. Be a woman without her kid attached to her hip. I know she loves him but every parent needs a break. We'll come back to town, go to Home, throw a few back, get loosened up. Try to get some life back in her."

I was back to staring.

"That a plan?" he asked.

I nodded and told him, "She came into the city to have lunch with Deanna and me today, Johnny. And that didn't help."

"Well, she'll get a dose of just her sister tomorrow night and more of us showing we got her back Friday. She's the sharp edge to your soft touch. She's nearly as pretty as you, you look like sisters, but she couldn't be more different. Though deep down, she's got that iron you talked about that your mother gave both of you. We just gotta find ways to remind her of it."

"Yes," I agreed quietly.

"Talk to her tomorrow about it and about Margot and Dave looking after Brooks."

I nodded again. "I will."

"I'll be here with Mist around ten o'clock Saturday morning. Don't muck out Serengeti and Amaretto's stalls. After I unload him and get his shit sorted, I'll do it."

"Johnny—"

"You need to be with your sister."

I said nothing because I was again staring at his handsome face in his handsome head resting on my frilly white pillow.

"I'm done with the stalls, I'll take Brooks home with me. He can nap there. I'll give him lunch. We'll hang out. We'll come back for dinner with your friends. You look after your sister. Do your facials. Get her loaded. Whatever. Just try to break through without her having to worry about taking care of her boy."

"Thank you for the margarita," I blurted.

His expression grew perplexed. "What?"

I pushed into him so he was on his back and I was on him. I got onto my forearms in the pillow to hold his head at the sides in both hands.

"Thank you for the margarita," I repeated, my voice husky.

His hands were resting on my hips and he stared up into my eyes in a way I knew he knew precisely what I was saying.

"It was the best drink I've ever tasted," I whispered.

"*Spätzchen,*" he whispered back.

"I'm totally fucking you again now, Johnny," I shared, opening my legs and pulling up my knees so I could straddle him.

He grinned and both his hands dove into the back of my panties. "You gonna be able to be quiet?"

"We'll see."

He again slid his hand between my legs from behind.

I shivered on top of him.

"My Izzy's sweet, wet pussy," he murmured, stroking it.

I rocked gently into his hand.

"Need my jeans, baby, unless you got a condom close," he said.

"I'm on the Pill," I replied.

His black eyes went molten.

"Ungloved?" he asked low.

"When you blow, I want all of that," I answered.

He emitted his muted roar and drove two fingers inside.

I arched my neck back and rode them.

"Fuck," he muttered, and I felt his other hand working between us, untying his pajama bottoms, shoving them down, and then his hard cock was pressing against me and his hand.

He slid his fingers out.

I shifted up.

He yanked the gusset of my panties aside and guided his cock-head to me.

I bore down on it.

He hissed out a breath.

I sat up and took him deep.

Eyes half-mast, pussy full of Johnny, I gazed down at him and breathed, "Enjoy the show, honey."

Then I moved.

Johnny held my hips and did as bid, only shifting to start thrusting up into me when I was taking him there. He didn't even go for my clit, but he didn't have to since I gave that to him too, touching myself as I rode his cock and he watched.

When I came, I arced back and whimpered my climax through closed lips.

When he came, his groan forced its hushed way through clenched teeth.

I collapsed on him and his arms immediately circled me tight.

It took some time before I could say, "I'll go clean up."

His arms got tighter. "Don't fuckin' move."

I didn't move then, and I only moved when, many moments later he rolled side to side, holding me to him as he reached and turned out the lights.

He kept me planted on him in the dark as he grew soft and I lost him. And he kept me planted on him as I started leaking all over him.

"Johnny—"

"Go to sleep, *spätzchen*."

"Can you sleep like this?" I asked.

"Can you?" he asked back.

"Yes," I gave him the truth.

"Then yes."

I relaxed into him.

I felt something hit the bed and I looked through the dark as that something became a furry something curled against Johnny's arm.

"Jill," I muttered. "She's used to your scent so she's getting friendly."

"She's gonna get more used to it."

Thank you, God.

I smiled into his neck.

Jill started purring.
Johnny held me.
I fell asleep.

Johnny

AFTER MUCKING out the stalls Saturday morning, pulling off his work gloves and shoving them in the back pocket of his jeans, Johnny went to the little sink in the front corner of the tack room he'd seen when he'd disposed of the condom he'd used when he'd done Iz in the stables.

When he finished washing his hands, he turned toward the door and his eyes caught on the four pictures on the back wall that he'd noted the last time he was there, but it hadn't been the time to get a good look at them.

He moved that way and stared at the two photos to the right of the window.

Standing there, he got his first look at Izzy's mother.

And that first look rocked him straight to his boots.

If he didn't know the story, he'd have no idea the life she'd led from her face, her demeanor, the bright smile she aimed at the camera in the top photo where she was striking a pose, head thrown back, body in an arc, one leg kicked up behind her. Her arms were around an adorable little-girl Izzy who was standing straight and holding tight to her momma's middle, dazzling the camera with her smile.

A gleaming chestnut horse was behind them.

They looked what Izzy said they were.

Happy.

Not like people who needed government cheese.

The picture below was all three in a row: see no evil (a little-girl Addie with the fingers of both hands covering her eyes), hear no evil (Izzy's mother with her hands over her ears) and speak no evil (Iz with her hand over her mouth). They all had huge smiles on their faces (Izzy's he could see in her eyes). And that horse was behind them.

He moved to the other two and saw Addie with her mom up top, both of them striking a goofy pose. The three of them together at the bottom. Izzy's mom in the middle with her arms around her girls' shoulders, both of them with their arms around their mom's middle, all of them staring straight at the camera, looking like they were laughing.

That woman was not beaten.

That woman was not broken.

She'd made two precious beings and she was right where she wanted to be, happy as a clam.

He stared at her laughing face and he knew without ever meeting the woman that she left that man to save her daughters. She left that man to give her girls moments like that. She left that man to show them the path of their lives and it wasn't about things, it was about taking care of yourself and the ones you love, even if that meant sacrificing everything, that everything meaning nothing when you could hold the world right in the curve of your arms.

He'd never seen a more beautiful woman in his life.

Only looking hard did Johnny see the girls' cheap, plastic sandals. The decals on the front of their tank tops faded from many washings. The at-home haircuts that didn't really matter since they both had their mom's thick, long, tawny mane of hair. But still, none of their hair was styled, layered, like Izzy's was now. Just cut straight at the bottom and healthy.

He stared at Izzy's sandals and his palms started to itch, his throat started to burn, his gut started to roil.

So he forced his gaze to her face.

Her smile.

Her holding on to her mother.

The pictures were faded, square, small, from an old camera that took an antiquated type of film.

But the frames were top notch.

He took ten steps back and stared at the room.

The fabric on the flowered chair was faded, worn.

The leather of the other chair was beat up, there were scratches everywhere and there was a short split through the leather along the front side, under the arm.

He looked up at the light fixture, which was kickass right there in that room with the tack and those chairs.

But under that veil Izzy threw over it, it was a piece of shit.

Images collided in his brain as the veil was pulled off.

The chandelier in her bedroom had probably once been like that light fixture, except Izzy had made it something else with her flair and her care.

Got a deal on the marble countertops because some lady ordered them and then decided she didn't want them, she'd said about the marble in her kitchen.

Johnny had no doubt she rocked what she did at work. Her land was worth money. The farmhouse was solid. It had space. Three bedrooms. Two baths and a powder room downstairs. The stables added value. She took care of all of it and a bunch of animals including two horses. You couldn't have all that without the means to have it.

She'd made it magical using magic.

You just couldn't know what he now knew or look too close, because once the veil dropped, it all came clear.

He was a guy but he wasn't dead, blind or stupid so he'd heard of the concept of shabby chic.

Izzy had a master's hand.

She still made do.

She still surrounded herself with scraps of shit, other people's castoffs, because it was the best she could do to have what she needed to make herself feel safe and happy.

"That shit ends," he growled at the picture of her with her mother.

Johnny was rich.

He had six million dollars in checking, savings, property and investments. He also had eight garages with mini-marts that were locally-owned, priced right and had established customer loyalty over three generations, so they turned over a mint.

He'd picked his furniture at the mill and he'd fixed the place up himself, but he picked the furniture through an interior designer that cost a fortune. Her time and the furniture. His dining room table probably cost more than all the furniture on the first floor of Izzy's house, including the front and back porches.

He lived simple because that was the life his father taught him and his father's father before had taught his dad.

But if it mattered to him, he got the best.

And Izzy mattered to him. In her, he'd found the best.

So she was fucking going to have the best.

Addie had rallied the night before over pizza then copious beers at Home. She'd gotten loaded.

But with the troubled looks Izzy gave her sister as well as Johnny, he knew she hadn't *unloaded*.

Eliza and Adeline Forrester both were still eating shit.

"And that shit has to end," he said.

He turned on his boot and went up to the house, finding Izzy and Addie on the back porch, having late-morning coffee.

Izzy's eyes on him were bright, sweet and still troubled.

Addie's eyes on him were dull and dead.

He collected Brooks, his diaper bag, his lunch that came in jars, his schedule from his mother, and he strapped the boy in the car seat Addie had told him how to secure in the back seat of his truck.

He drove away with both sisters in his rearview and Brooks babbling in his back seat.

And Johnny drove away knowing he was going to shift the life course two sisters had been on.

With one, he knew how that was going to go.

With her sister, he had no clue.

FIFTEEN
IF IZZY WANTED TO GO, ABSOLUTELY

Johnny

Late that afternoon, after returning to Izzy's, Johnny stood in her backyard.

And he stared.

There was a long, wide wooden table under a tree. The table was covered with a filmy lace tablecloth. It had three little vases stuffed full of fluffy flowers and four squat glass things filled with little candles intermingled in a line down the middle.

At the end, surrounded by those squat glass things with candles, was a big tin bucket (with a dent in it) that was filled mostly with ice, some water, and in it there were three bottles of wine and six bottles of beer. A lacy-edged napkin dangled off the side. There was a bottle opener and a corkscrew discreetly tucked at the back.

The table was surrounded by chairs with ruffled pads on all of them, some wood with their paint chipping off, some miracles of curlicue iron.

When he sat his ass down, he was going for a wooden one.

The tree over the table now had a ton of Christmas lights in its branches with long strings of clear beads with crystals at the ends dangling down from it.

Needless to say, while he was hanging with Brooks, the sisters had not given each other facials.

He felt her come up beside him and looked down at her to see she was carrying a stack of melamine plates that were green with pink flowers all over them, a stack of pink cloth napkins laid on the top.

In that moment there was one thing he was not annoyed about.

She was wearing the dress she'd worn at the festival.

And knowing there was a good possibility he'd be taking it off her that night was the only thing she had going for her right then.

"Where'd that table come from?" he asked.

"The legs unscrew. I keep it in the hay room and pull it out when I want an outdoor party."

"How heavy is it?"

She cottoned on to the path of his questioning, gave him big eyes and pressed her lips together.

Right.

"The chairs?" he pushed.

"There's a shed beyond the stables. You can't see it from here. I keep the chairs there. And my Christmas decorations. My Halloween decorations. My Thanksgiving decorations and, um…" she faltered then rallied, "etcetera."

That shed had to be maybe thirty, forty yards away.

Yes.

Annoyed.

"The lights?" he pressed on.

"I had the idea and got the lights and crystals weeks ago, I just haven't had time to do it or the occasion to do it for. Today, Addie and I did it."

"You couldn't ask me to set that table up, bring out those chairs and get up in that tree with the lights before I took off?" he asked.

"I had Addie to help me. Normally I have to drag them out myself."

He felt his jaw get tight.

She hurried on. "And sometimes Charlie and Deanna come over to lend a hand."

He scowled down at her.

"You can help me take the table apart and put it all away," she offered.

"Do we need to have another chat about the kind of guy I am?" he asked.

She gave him a look and muttered, "Not anymore."

"Right," he grunted. "What else needs done?"

"I know you've had Brooks all day but can you keep an eye on him inside while Addie and I bring out the rest to set the table?"

"Wrong answer," he stated.

Immediately she adjusted her request.

"Can you bring out the rest to set the table while Addie and or I keep an eye on Brooks?"

"What do you need brought out?"

"It's all on the countertop, honey."

He turned on his boot and went inside.

On the counter he saw wineglasses, water glasses, cutlery and a pink milk glass pitcher with raised polka dots that was filled with ice and water.

He also saw, under a ribbed glass dome on a raised ribbed glass stand, a cake that was a miracle of rich, thick swirls of white frosting.

Addie was in the kitchen, Brooks in her arms, and she was cuddling him when Johnny came in, but her gaze was on Johnny when his went to her.

"This all the stuff that goes outside?" he asked, jerking his head to the things on the counter.

"Yep," she answered.

"You sure there's no unicorn statues, grenades rigged to explode glitter or nets of rose petals to hang to rain down on us when Iz pulls a cord?"

Her lips twitched but that was all he got from her before she said, "We didn't have that much time."

He nodded and set about taking the stuff to Izzy.

It took four trips to get it all out, and as he went back and forth with three canines dogging his steps, Izzy laid the table.

Addie wandered out with Brooks while Izzy was putting on the finishing touches and Johnny was opening a bottle of wine.

"If you're pouring, I'm drinking," Addie declared.

"I'm pouring," he confirmed.

She nodded to him, her face mostly expressionless. Not a woman who was looking forward to a dinner party with friends. Not a woman who was looking forward to anything.

Then she looked to her sister.

"Queso dip is bubbling, Iz," Addie told her. "I turned it down low and the skillet's ready to brown it in the oven."

"Thanks, doll," Izzy replied just as the dogs took off toward the front, only Ranger barking.

Johnny saw Izzy's eyes shift there and she visibly went from sure of herself, setting up an outdoor party, to flustered.

She was worried her friends wouldn't like him.

He finished with the cork, shoved the bottle back in the ice water and moved to her to sling an arm around her shoulders.

He then started her moving, murmuring reassuringly, "Don't worry, *spätzchen*. People like me."

"You're likable," she said, her eyes glued down the wide open space covered in neatly cut grass at the side of her house. "But they're family."

He gave her a squeeze. "It's gonna be fine."

He saw an African American couple emerging from a big, black truck that was a lot like his, except his was a Ram and theirs was a Ford.

They were vaguely familiar. He'd seen them around town.

The man was a good-looking guy, very tall, barrel-chested, hair cropped close at the sides, longer up top.

He was dressed like Johnny. Jeans. Nice button up. Boots.

The woman was top-heavy and coming out of her short skirt he saw she had legs that were nearly better than Izzy's, but the dark skin was shining, this something that made them so attractive, he almost couldn't move his eyes to her face. When he did, he saw she had strong, striking features under short hair that was artfully messy, with wisps of it hugging her cheeks and neck.

She was not dressed like Izzy. Her skirt, as he'd noted, was short. It was also tight and attached to the rest of a bright yellow dress that was loose up top and fell off one of her shoulders. She was wearing spiked heels with complicated ankle straps and walking through the grass without those heels sinking in, because he suspected she never wore anything but heels like those so she could walk anywhere in them.

Izzy's friend Deanna didn't hide she was sizing him up.

Her husband didn't either.

He felt Addie coming up behind them, Izzy beginning to make a move to separate from him to greet her friends, and he saw Deanna beginning to open her mouth, when another vehicle turned into Izzy's drive.

The dogs that were dancing around the newcomers looked that way then they headed that way, this time all three of them barking.

"Oh no," Izzy whispered as Deanna and Charlie turned to watch a beat-up, rusted-out, criminally-not-cared for, old, light-blue Mustang come screeching to a halt by Charlie's truck, kicking up the gravel of Izzy's drive as well as a fair amount of dust.

He felt something from Izzy.

He felt something more beating at his back.

He twisted to look at Addie to see her face was pale, her eyes were glued to the Mustang and she was holding on to Brooks like someone was trying to tear him from her arms.

Instantly, Johnny let go of Izzy and prowled forward as a tall, lanky man with a mess of dark-brown hair and a scruff of beard, wearing faded jeans with both knees split, a rocker tee and a pair of black motorcycle boots, got out of the Mustang not hiding his movements were agitated and aggressive.

Addie's husband.

Perry.

"You stupid fucking *bitch!*" he shouted, eyes on Addie.

Johnny felt Charlie come up beside him, but Perry was on the move and it was like the two men, both of them bigger than Perry, weren't between him and his wife, blocking his path.

He also ignored the dogs who were holding back from him, but on the alert, a *hostile* alert, all three of them having bared their teeth and were growling.

Fuck.

"Ranger, down!" Johnny called. "Dempsey. Swirl. Back!"

The dogs minded, but didn't.

They didn't jump Perry.

But they did follow him, front shoulders crouched low.

"You stupid *fucking bitch!*" Perry repeated in a yell, advancing quickly.

"Stop moving," Johnny growled, shifting quickly to block his advance.

Perry's gaze cut up to his as he tried to adjust to the side to round Johnny. "Get outta my way, man."

Johnny adjusted with him as Charlie flanked Addie's angry husband.

"I said, stop moving," Johnny warned.

Perry stopped and shouted in his face, "And *I said,* get outta my way, *man!*"

"You need to calm down," Johnny told him.

"You need to fuck off," Perry returned.

"Listen to me—" Johnny started.

"Kiss my ass," Perry sneered.

Johnny went on like he didn't speak. "You got one minute to turn around, get back in your car, go somewhere and cool off then make a meet with Addie when you're in a different frame of mind."

"And if I don't?" Perry asked snidely.

"I'll detain you while Eliza calls the police," Johnny answered.

"Fuck you." He shot to the side, yelling, "Addie!"

Johnny shot to the side and Charlie moved with him, both of the men crowding Perry and moving him back.

"Jesus, fuck off!" Perry shouted, bouncing his chest against Johnny's.

A low, pissed noise rolled up Johnny's throat and out his mouth.

"This is not the way this is gonna go."

A new voice in the conversation made all the men still.

Addie rounded at their free side.

The good news was that she was no longer holding Brooks.

The bad news was that she'd rounded at their free side.

"Get back, sweetheart," Johnny murmured, taking a step away from Perry but toward her.

"I'm fine, Johnny," she returned, but her eyes were on her husband.

Perry launched right in.

"Are you fuckin' serious with that fuckin' shit you pulled?"

"Are you serious, asking me that crap?" she shot back.

"You didn't give me a chance to explain," he retorted.

"Explain? Explain how I came home from work with a migraine and found our son in his crib without even a toy to pass the time, fretting and freaked, and you in *my* bed with some *skank*, pumping away at her?" she asked.

Johnny felt himself go solid and he felt something new beating at him from all around.

He knew Izzy was close to her sister even if he couldn't see her. Charlie was right there. But he had a feeling Deanna had disappeared with Brooks.

He didn't look.

He stared at Addie, avoiding looking at Perry so he wouldn't have the urge to break the man's neck.

"We need to have words," Perry decreed.

"*We* aren't doing anything anymore," Addie returned.

"You took my kid," he stated.

"Sorry, let me explain this to you, Perry," Addie began. "You see, when a sperm donor squirts, that's the start and end of it."

"I'm not a fuckin' sperm donor," Perry bit out right when Johnny sensed they had more company.

He looked to the drive to see another truck joining the fast-forming parking lot.

An old red Chevy with silver panels.

Johnny knew that truck.

Jesus Christ.

It was Toby.

He had no clue not only that Toby was coming to town but also how Toby knew where to find him.

At that moment, he couldn't think about it either.

"You apparently aren't a very good babysitter either," Addie noted casually, either so tuned to what was happening with her husband she didn't notice Toby arriving or so tuned to what was happening with Perry, she was determined to focus on it.

Perry was also either/or, proving this by replying, "I'm not a babysitter. I'm Brooklyn's father."

"A father bathes his child, Perry," she educated him. "He gives him bottles. He rocks him to sleep. And oh, another thing, he pays at least a few bills."

After Toby climbed out of his truck, Johnny gave him a short jerk of his head before he returned his attention to the situation at hand.

"You know I've been lookin' for gigs," Perry pointed out.

"I'm not sure how you'll find gigs camped out on the couch with a six pack or humping some chick in my bed."

"Addie, don't lay this shit on me. You haven't been giving it up for months."

"That's because I'm *tired*, Perry. I'm *exhausted*. I'm a single mother of a baby boy with a deadbeat dad who *lives with me*," she fired back, and Johnny knew she was losing it by the tone of her voice turning scratchy.

"I love my kid," Perry flung back.

"He's a toy, like I was a toy before I wasn't shiny and new anymore and life became a drag, but you didn't give me away. You tossed me aside and looked for a new toy just like I know you'll do with Brooklyn when he's not fun anymore," Addie replied.

Johnny saw Toby approach, not getting close but close enough to hear.

His brother's eyebrows shot up.

Johnny gave him another short jerk of his head and again looked at Addie.

"That's not true, baby," Perry was now coaxing. "I love you. I love Brooklyn. You know that. It's just been tough since the band broke up and—"

"God, spare me," Addie drawled cuttingly. "You're *such* a cliché and I'm *such* a moron for falling for it."

"We got it good, we just gotta get that back," Perry said.

"*You* had it good because you had someone paying your bills and doing all the grunt work taking care of your son so he's nice and clean and fed when you feel like playing with him. *I* didn't have it good. And even after sharing this about seven million times, it didn't sink in that you might wanna give your wife and son better. I know this because nothing changed. I also know this because I walked in on you fucking another woman."

"I'll get in another band soon and then—"

"Do not try to feed me that again, Perry. I believed it two years ago. Do you honestly think I'll believe it now?"

"So, right," Perry clipped out, coaxing gone, he was back to pissed. "Now *you* get to make the decision we're done then *you* clean out the apartment and the bank accounts and take off?"

Johnny's eyes slid to Charlie and he grinned.

Charlie grinned back.

"You cheated on me and we were done so I moved, Perry. I took my stuff. I left yours. That stuff that's mine includes what's in the bank accounts since every penny in them I earned," Addie explained.

"When I got back after you split, there was nothing in the place but my clothes," he returned.

"Which is what you brought to our marriage and all you contributed to our marriage so that's all you'll get out of it."

"It took me a week to get up here because I had to raise the cash for gas since you took it all and canceled our credit cards," Perry complained.

"*My* credit cards. Your name was on them. I paid them."

Perry suddenly raised his hand quickly to his forehead, slamming his fingers against it and then sending his hand flying out, stating, "Can you not see how totally fucked up it is some bitch cleans out an apartment and takes a man's kid then takes off without even a fuckin' note?"

Johnny braced to lock things down.

"You were inside her," Addie whispered.

At that, Johnny instead shifted more toward Adeline.

Izzy became visible as she got up close to her sister's back.

Toby even moved nearer.

"Baby, can we *please* talk about this without an audience?" Perry begged.

"She looked at me. You looked at me. You looked right in my eyes when you were connected to another woman," Addie said, her voice filled with pain.

"I tried to come after you."

"With your dick wet from another woman."

Perry got quiet.

"This is how this is going to go," she said softly. "I'm moving up here. I got a job in the grocery store. I start on Monday."

Johnny cut his eyes to Izzy who cut hers to him.

That answered what she was doing when Izzy was at work.

He looked back to Addie when she kept talking.

"I've already contacted an attorney. She's started divorce proceedings. You *will* pay child support. You *will* take financial responsibility for the child you very enjoyably had a hand in creating. We'll see what part of his life you'll play but *that* will be up to me. But he'll be up here with me and Izzy. And you'll be down there with your broken promises and your ridiculous dreams."

"My dreams aren't ridiculous," he bit off, obviously stung, the selfish ass.

"You wanna be the lead singer of a rock 'n' roll band and no, that's not ridiculous. The ridiculous part is you think that'll happen sitting on a couch, drinking beer."

"You're not going to take my son from me," he threatened.

"Too late, I already did, but just saying, Perry, you never actually had him because you never actually claimed him."

"We'll see how this goes," he snarled.

Johnny tensed when Addie got in his space.

"I know how it'll go so listen up," she hissed. "I'll work until I drop to fight for what's right for my son. I'll sell my body if I need to, to give him not only what he needs but even just a little bit of what he wants. And I'll bleed my last drop before I let you fuck him up. *You know me*, Perry," she stressed. "You know what makes me. You know every word I say is true. And you know you don't have what it takes to fight that. I'll do whatever it takes to beat you, to give my son what he deserves. I was taught how, day in and day out by my mother so I know the way. And I'll take it if you make me and I'll die knowing I gave my boy happy."

"You're gonna have to fight it," Perry hurled at her.

"Only because you're intent on proving how big of an asshole you are and you're gonna make me," she returned.

Perry glared at his wife. He then glared at Izzy, Johnny, Charlie and he turned, stutter stepped when he saw Toby but recovered quickly and started to stalk off.

"Just to let you know," Addie called after him. "My attorney already has three appointments to get sworn affidavits next week. And that bitch you were banging while my son was in the next room got served a subpoena, so she's one of them."

"Kiss my ass, Addie," he yelled toward his car, not breaking stride.

"The time you get that from me, baby, is long gone," she returned in a loud drawl.

They all watched him slam into his car, make it roar and then reverse and peel out in a shower of gravel and a cloud of dust.

"Addie—" Izzy started gently.

But Addie turned and raced down the side of the house, disappearing at the back.

Izzy raced after her.

Johnny looked to Charlie and then he looked to Toby.

"Welcome home, brother," he said.

Inside his thick, black beard, Toby's lips hitched.

"I'm Johnny," Johnny said to Charlie.

"Charlie," Charlie replied, lifting his hand.

Johnny shook it, let go and introduced, "This is my brother, Toby."

"Toby," Charlie said, offering his hand to Johnny's brother.

"Charlie," Toby replied, taking it.

When the two were done shaking, all three men hesitated, then when Johnny started down the side of the house, the two others trailed with only one dog trailing them seeing as Dempsey and Swirl had raced after Izzy.

They walked in the back door hearing Addie saying, "No, Iz. Just put the queso under the broiler and let's get this party started."

But her eyes hit Johnny when he entered then they went behind him after he cleared the door, and the two other men crowded with him into the small kitchen.

She was again holding Brooks tight to her but now she was hovering in a corner of the kitchen like Izzy and Deanna had her blocked in when they were both keeping a distance.

It was then Addie said, "Great. As if that drama being played out in front of Clubber McHotterson," she indicated Charlie with a flick of a hand, "and Magnus McHotterson," she indicated Johnny with a jerk of her head, "wasn't bad enough, now we got Talon McHotterson here to enjoy the show."

She was cracking jokes.

Johnny thought that was good.

"Maybe we should go upstairs and talk, baby girl," Deanna said softly.

"About what?" Addie asked. "About how Johnny's changed more of Brooklyn's diapers after knowing him for a week than his father has after knowing him seven months?"

Deanna closed her mouth and looked to Izzy.

"Doll, how about you let Johnny and Charlie look after Brooks and we girls get a bottle of wine and—?" Izzy tried.

"I saw you two," Addie said, her voice hoarse, and Johnny went on the alert. "In the stable. I saw Johnny doing you against the wall."

"Oh Lord," Deanna murmured.

"Shit," Charlie muttered.

"Hell," Toby mumbled.

Johnny just watched Addie closely.

"He never gave me that, what you two had in that moment," Addie told her sister. "I could have walked right up to you and neither of you would have seen me. I didn't exist, nothing existed. Nothing but him for you and you for him. He never gave me that, Iz. How did I never see that?"

And there they had the answer to why Adeline had been degenerating, outside of the fact that she'd learned without a doubt that her husband was a motherfucking pissant.

She'd had to watch while Johnny and Izzy built all they were building at the same time coming to understand she'd never had

264   KRISTEN ASHLEY

anything like that, no matter how new it was for Johnny and Izzy, or worse, precisely because of how new it was.

She'd not even come close.

"Addie, sweetie," Izzy whispered.

"He gave me this." She cuddled Brooks closer. "That's all he ever gave me. But he gave it to me getting himself an orgasm and honest to God, that was all he was thinking about."

"Addie, please, baby, let's go upstairs," Izzy coaxed.

Addie reared her head like a stubborn mare and snapped, "No. This is a party. We're having a party."

She forged past Izzy, by Johnny, straight to the door where Toby was standing.

"Out of the way, Talon," she ordered.

"Name's Toby," Toby said gently, but he'd read the situation and didn't move.

Addie had been staring at Johnny's brother's chest but her head jerked back. "You're his brother, aren't you?"

"Yeah, darlin'," he replied.

"Of course. You're perfect, so of course. You're probably taken too, aren't you?"

"I—"

"Not for me," she cut him off. "Man like you. Man like Johnny. Man like Charlie. Not for me."

"Honey," Toby whispered. "How 'bout we get you—?"

She tossed her hair and looked over her shoulder at her sister. "I did it, Iz. I did it. What I swore to myself I'd never do. Not the same, but a version. I found Dad. I found a man who was good for nothin' except to break my heart."

And that was when her face dissolved and she started to go down.

"Tobe," Johnny growled, on the move, but Toby was on it.

He caught her in his arms and sank down to the floor with her. Addie's ass hit his inner thigh with Toby's leg at a bad angle, and Johnny saw him wince but he didn't do anything but put his arms around her and tuck her and Brooks close to his chest.

She sobbed into his neck.

Brooks fretted in her arms.

Toby lifted his gaze to Izzy. "Where you want her, babe?"

"My bedroom," Izzy whispered. "Upstairs. I'll show you the way."

Toby nodded, got his feet under him and lifted Addie and Brooks cradled in his arms, walking behind Izzy as she hurried into the hall.

Johnny, Deanna and Charlie watched them go.

When they heard footfalls on the stairs, Johnny turned to Deanna.

"Nice to meet you, I'm Johnny Gamble and that was my brother Toby."

She stared into his eyes.

And then, very slowly, she smiled.

JOHNNY SAT in the wooden chair at the head of the table in Izzy's backyard, staring up at the windows of Izzy's bedroom.

"You need another beer, big man?" Deanna asked.

The one he'd cracked open two seconds after he'd opened one for Charlie while Charlie was pouring Deanna wine, and after he'd tossed one to Toby, was gone in about three gulps.

So yeah.

He needed another one.

He did not share that.

He looked to her. "He had to know. He had to know what they'd lived through. So what I wanna know is, how an asshole could know that and marry her, get her pregnant and then bang some bitch in her fucking bed."

"I do not know the answer to that question, but I do know maybe you should have another beer, which might serve to help you calm down," Deanna said soothingly, studying him closely.

"This is gonna go her way," Johnny stated.

"In your mood, I'm gonna take that as a threat and share with you now that if the authorities ever question me, I heard you make no such threat, and then I'll say again, calm, big man, so you don't commit any felonies," Deanna replied.

Johnny turned his gaze from her to his brother.

Toby was also in a wooden chair (Deanna was the only one in a curlicue one) and his eyes were also aimed at Izzy's bedroom window.

Johnny looked from Deanna to Charlie, pushing out of his seat, asking, "Can you both excuse us a minute?"

Toby's gaze came to him as Charlie murmured, "Not a problem." And Deanna murmured, "Wine ain't gonna cut it, I may need a martini," which Johnny decided to take as a yes.

Toby pushed up and moved to walk beside Johnny as they made their way to a tree that was hopefully out of earshot.

As he took this short trek it hit him that he'd always seen it, but now he was noting that Izzy had an enormous lawn. Everywhere for fifty yards around her house was thick, lush grass mowed up to a line of trees that led to the forest that surrounded her house.

He hoped she had a riding lawnmower in that shed too.

He also hoped she didn't give him too much shit when he shared it was his ass that was going to be on it from that point forward.

Johnny stopped and turned to his brother who'd stopped with him.

He then started.

"You know I'm glad to see you so I don't have to say that. Though still wanna know why you're here."

"Bryce called. Told me Shandra was back in town," his brother told him.

Not this shit.

"Tobe—" he began.

Toby shook his head. "Was just worried about you, Johnny. Her coming back, close to the anniversary of when we lost Dad, thought it'd be a nice surprise to come up and maybe take you fishing, make sure you were okay. Got to the mill, you weren't there. Decided to go to Home and have a beer and some wings to give it some time before I went back. Hit Home, got an earful."

Johnny bet he did.

"And they told you about Iz," Johnny surmised.

Toby grinned. "Lotta people said a lot of things. Including telling me where she lived. Didn't think I'd hit a drama. Thought I'd show and give you shit, and if you weren't around, size up the new girl."

Johnny sighed.

That was when Toby smiled before he asked, "Brother, is a wood nymph gonna materialize and do a dance for us later, or what?"

"Izzy has a certain style," Johnny muttered.

"Can't miss that," Toby replied, still grinning. "Didn't miss that dress she had on either. I could handle crystals hanging from trees too if my woman wore a dress like that."

"You can't miss her dress, but from here on out, how 'bout you keep your mouth shut about shit like that?" Johnny warned.

Toby didn't exactly heed his warning.

He asked, "Then can we talk about you doing her against a wall?"

"No," Johnny growled.

"You're back," Toby said, suddenly quiet.

"What?" Johnny asked.

"That's what they said," Toby shared. "At Home. They said you're back and I see it. You care about something again. You care about her. You care about her sister. Thought you were gonna break that asshole's neck. Since Dad died and Shandra left, you go to work, you do your job. You go home to the mill. You go fishing, mostly out of habit. You go camping just the same. But have you taken an ATV out in three years?"

"Probably."

Toby shook his head. "Back before we lost Dad, then that woman knew you were already on your knees, and still...she gutted you, you worked hard, you played hard. You had plans to open more garages. You wanted to go back to Hawaii. You wanted to eat pizza in Italy. Have you left the state of Kentucky since Shandra took off?"

"Yeah, to drive down to Tennessee to get your ass out of that sling when that woman stole your truck," Johnny reminded him.

Toby ignored that. "You gonna take this girl to Italy?"

If Izzy wanted to go, absolutely.

"She's sweet, she's shy, she's funny—" Johnny started.

"She's got a flair with crystals and a way with wearing a dress," Toby cut in to razz.

This time Johnny ignored Toby and laid the big shit on him.

"And Margot loves her."

"Holy Christ," Toby said, his eyes widening. "It took Shandra two years to win over Margot. And she never liked a single woman I dated."

"Tobe, that's because you don't date. You sleep with women until they get bored of your inability to commit to something like, I don't know...a *date*. Then they dump your ass and you move on like you haven't just spent two, three, four months wasting their time. Like you haven't just spent two, three, four months with them at all."

"None of them complained," Toby returned.

"Not in earshot," Johnny informed him. "But in town you're known as 'Take 'Em and Leave 'Em Toby.'"

"I didn't make any woman any promise and I don't hide how it is with me, so they got nothing to bitch about," Toby shot back, no longer in a joking mood. "Now what I wanna know is, how are we talking about this when I had a brother who was so not over his ex he was *never* gonna get over his ex and now I'm hanging out in the backyard of a woman who's stabling Ben's horse, Ben being your best bud since second grade. And even Sally, whose sister was best friends with Shandra, and far's I know still is, is talking about how awesome this Eliza is."

Johnny looked to the house, the table where Charlie and Deanna were sitting in the sun and back to his brother. "I'm falling in love with her, Tobe."

Toby gave him a look and then that look turned hard.

"You better be."

Johnny's head gave a sharp jerk. "Sorry?"

"She's spoken a handful of words to me and even I know you don't dick around with a woman like that. You say Margot loves her, seals that deal. Now I hate to contradict the people who talk shit about me, but the bottom line is...you're you. You've been hung up on Shandra for years. And even I know if just a little of that is still there, you should steer clear of *any* woman."

"Okay, right now what I want heard, Toby, is enough about Shandra. Shandra's history. Everybody has got to get the fuck over Shandra because I have and I'm the only one who had to do it in the first place."

"You've blown through a few women, brother," Toby replied carefully.

"I made no promises and I didn't hide how it was," Johnny returned.

Toby eyed him a beat before he said, "I hear that."

Johnny dug in his jeans pocket for his keys. "I'm staying tonight with the girls. You can stay at the mill."

Toby grinned. "Excellent."

Johnny twisted his house key off and suggested, "While you're here, you might wanna go out to the shack and see if it's still standing."

His brother was pocketing the key and his grin disappeared. "I thought you were looking after it."

"I am but it's forty miles out so I can't go out there every day."

"I'll head out there," Toby muttered.

Johnny looked to the house when he sensed movement and he saw Izzy coming through the screen door. Her dogs ran to greet her. Ranger lay in the grass where he'd camped out five feet from Johnny and Toby and he didn't twitch.

He watched as she looked for him, found him and he gave her a jerk of his chin.

Then he looked back to Toby.

"Not thinking this is a good time for you to crash a party, Tobe."

"I get that," Toby agreed. "Just hanging around to meet her, say hey and make sure her sister's okay. I'll say that hey and take off."

Johnny nodded before he curled his lips up. "I'll end this saying what I know I don't have to say. It's good to have you home, brother."

Toby smiled back. They moved in, bumped shoulders then moved away and both of them turned to head back to the table.

He saw that Deanna and Charlie were up, doing something, and Izzy was heading toward them.

Her smile on his brother was bright but it still didn't hide the worry.

"Toby, right?" she asked, lifting a hand toward Toby before she got to them. "I'm so happy to meet you and I'm so happy you're here," she said when she stopped, and Toby took her hand. She then went on to babble, "I mean, obviously, what played out with Addie and Perry was unfortunate for all concerned, especially Addie, and I'm sorry you had to witness it. But my sister is my sister. She's bounced back. She's gonna clean up her face and join us. I hope you will too."

"I don't wanna impose," Toby said, squeezing her hand and letting it go.

It was then Johnny moved to her side, slid an arm around her shoulders and claimed her.

He saw his brother's eyes flare with humor at the maneuver but fortunately that was it.

"Family's never an imposition," she replied.

Like she would know. As far as Johnny could tell, she only had two members of hers worth dick, and with the way things were, they needed each other to survive and stop themselves from becoming bitter and twisted.

"Things were kinda dramatic," Toby said softly. "It's really cool if I go and some time later we get together and share a beer or something."

"We can share one now. Honestly," Izzy assured. "Addie got it out and she's fine. That's the way we Forrester women are. Shove us to our knees, we just get back up and keep going."

He felt his jaw get hard at her words and Toby's eyes cut to Johnny's then right back to Iz.

"Really, stay," she continued, throwing an arm out behind her toward the table. "The only thing that would upset Addie now is if you didn't stay because you thought she'd be uncomfortable." She shot him a smile. "And I'm a good cook."

"She's absolutely that," Johnny put in.

Toby looked again to his older brother, assessing if that was Johnny's go ahead to accept the invitation.

When he read correctly it was, he turned his attention back to Izzy. "Then thanks. I'd love to try your cooking."

Izzy beamed.

That was when Johnny gave him a look that told him to take off so he could have a word with his woman.

Toby read that one too, smiled at Iz and then moved toward the table.

Izzy started to make a move too but Johnny held her back.

"Is she really all good?" he asked when she looked up at him.

"Apparently, the dastardly deed was walked in on two weeks ago. Addie and Brooks stayed with some friends while Addie made plans and talked to an attorney. When all was in place, she had her friends show up, clear out their apartment, store her stuff in a variety of different garages, sheds and attics and she came up here."

"She always intending to stay up here?" Johnny asked.

Iz shook her head. "She just needed a break and to be away from there to make some decisions. She got up here and that was her decision but she couldn't exactly make it unless she had a way to feed herself and her son. So she got a job and got Brooks in daycare in town and she does, actually, start Monday."

"Margot can take care of Brooks and she'd be offended if Addie tried to pay," Johnny told her, but she shook her head.

"She'd probably love it if Margot looked after him but she'd never let that happen for free."

"And Margot would lose her mind if Addie put him in daycare

when she's got nothing to do all day but plan coven meetings and boss Dave around, and she'd lose her mind only a little less if Addie tried to pay."

"Johnny—"

He used his arm around her shoulders to curl her into his front. "Let me talk to her to see if I'm even right and she's willing to do it. Then we can take it from there. But at the very least, until Addie gets on her feet, she should consider letting someone with a kind heart lend a helping hand."

She nodded before she told him hesitantly, "She's gonna stay with me for the foreseeable future."

This was not optimal and Johnny knew it was a dick thing to think, and it wasn't even close to the same circumstances, but when he finally found another woman who he wanted in his life and his bed in what could be a permanent way, he wished she didn't have a troubled sibling that took her time and attention from what they were building.

"I'm sorry, I see that—" she began, looking at him worriedly.

Johnny cut her off. "Nothing to be sorry about."

"It's just that, she has a little money saved but the attorney is going to cost a lot, and the grocery store doesn't pay as much as she made in tips so she's going to need a little help."

She was going to get help.

This being Johnny paying for her attorney, if he could manage it, straight up. If she couldn't hack that, then through a no-interest, pay-it-when-you-can loan. He was also putting her and Brooks in one of his properties when a tenant left. He had two small, nice, rental homes in town, closer to the grocery store, big enough for Brooks to grow up in, and when that happened they'd both have their own space.

But that wasn't for now. They'd have that discussion later when there wasn't queso dip to broil.

"She's your sister, babe, and she got burned and bad. Do I want you all to myself? Yeah. Do I get it?" He pulled her closer and dipped his face to hers. "Yeah."

She stared into his eyes and hers were filled with gratitude. "Thanks, Johnny."

"Don't mention it, Iz," he muttered, going in to touch his lips to hers before he pulled away and started to curl her back around but stopped when both her hands that were resting at his waist started to grip him hard.

"Thank you too, for going in...I mean, when Perry showed, you went right up to him and—"

He interrupted her. "Don't mention that either."

"I...Johnny, that meant a lot. You didn't even know who he was. You just felt the vibe and waded in. So it really meant a lot, honey. To both me and Addie."

"I'm glad but I hope you paid attention, Iz, because I'm that guy too. For you and for Addie."

Her eyes went round.

Then they started blinking.

"Oh no, I think I might cry," she whispered, and true to her words, her eyes were getting bright with tears.

He pulled her even closer and whispered back, "Don't cry. There's queso dip to broil, wine to drink, my brother to charm and your friends here for me to make love me like everyone else does."

He saw the bright leave as she started smiling.

So he kept going.

"It happened. It's over. Like you said, baby, you Forrester women get shoved to your knees, you get right back up and keep on keeping on. It's time to keep on keeping on with good company, food and booze, even if there's a danger someone's gonna get their eye poked out by a crystal."

Her head twisted and she gasped, "Oh no! Are they hanging too low?"

He put his hand to her jaw to turn her back to him. "Teasing, *spätzchen*."

"Oh," she breathed.

He kissed her. Not the kiss he wanted to give her but it wasn't a touch of the lips either.

Then he turned her toward the table, but as Charlie and Deanna set it up for Toby to join them, Toby striding off toward the shed, probably to get himself a chair, Izzy and Johnny went into the house.

Izzy put the queso dip under the broiler.

Johnny grabbed another six pack from the fridge to take it outside and put the bottles on ice.

"And then...then...then he said, 'That's the way of it when a badger is in the mix,'" Addie spluttered the end of her story through giggles and everyone burst out laughing.

Including Johnny.

"A badger in the mix!" Deanna hooted and the waning laughter waxed.

But this time, not Johnny's.

Because right then, it hit him like a boulder in the chest.

The sun had set.

The Christmas lights, candlelight and moonlight were dancing off the crystals. Charlie had hauled some curlicue plant stand out and put the drinks bucket on it so they had more room for the diners.

Whether it was because he sat there after the drama, or by design, which was more likely since it seemed Izzy, Deanna and Addie maneuvered him there, Johnny was at the head of the table. He was flanked by Iz and Toby. Charlie sat at the foot flanked by his wife and Addie.

The women had been through four bottles of wine and were on their fifth.

The men, two of them driving, were only on their third six-pack.

They'd been through queso dip, followed by four choices of street tacos with enough for leftovers, Mexican corn, black beans and a southwestern themed salad, and now the table was littered with little pink melamine plates with creamy lace designs on their edges covered in chocolate cake crumbs, vanilla frosting smears and ice cream residue.

The dogs were out dead, snoozing in the grass.

Brooks had fallen asleep in Deanna's arms but was now up in his crib.

There were lightning bugs blinking in and out in the darkened periphery and soft candles were glowing in the screened porch but there was no glaring outside light to disturb the cocoon of friendship, food and magic that Izzy had created.

Johnny understood it all then.

It didn't matter if there was a dent in the drinks tub.

It didn't matter that Perry was somewhere out there, pissed and intent on making trouble for Addie.

Their mother had taught them this was it.

This was the beauty of life.

It wasn't making do.

It was finding the joy in all you had and if you could give it a little sparkle with crystals dangling from trees or just lying side by side, staring at the stars, you did it.

On this thought, still softly giggling, Iz turned bright eyes to him. "I wish Margot and Dave were here."

Yeah, it was finding the joy in all you had, gathering memories, filling them as full as you could, goofing off wearing cheap sandals in front of a horse or sitting under a canopy of Christmas lights and crystals.

"We can invite them next time, *spätzchen*," he murmured.

She shot him a dazzling smile then looked back down the table when Charlie started talking.

Toby leaned his way and Johnny braced in order not to get ticked if his brother teased him verbally rather than just shooting him looks like he had from the first through the several that came after it when he'd called Izzy *spätzchen*.

Tobe knew Shandra never got that.

Toby, like Johnny, knew what it meant that Izzy did.

It had startled him the first time it had come out.

But from that first time, it came out easy.

He looked to his brother just as Toby said under his breath, "I wish Dad was here."

They locked eyes.

There would be no end of the teasing Lance Gamble would dish out about crystals in trees.

But he loved chocolate cake.

And he thought there was no better time, not even fishing, than spending it with friends.

Last, it made him happy when his sons were happy.

"Me too," Johnny muttered.

"...so my Dee-Girl gets on her hands and knees..." Charlie was saying.

"I did not!" Deanna cried. "I just bent over!"

Johnny and Toby looked to the end of the table.

"...in spiked heels and the littlest skirt you've ever seen..." Charlie talked over her.

"Charles!" she snapped.

"...she whips out her phone, turns on her flashlight and shines it into the murk..."

"A lady would never get on her knees in the street. Especially in a skirt."

"...then she looks up at me..."

"Stop!"

"...and says, 'Baby, you gotta go after that,' like I'm gonna be able to pull off a sewer grate and retrieve her freaking earring."

"It was my favorite earring!" Deanna exclaimed through the audible mirth rolling around the table.

He looked to his wife. "How can you have favorites when you got two drawers full of them?"

"I don't have two drawers full of them," she denied.

He arched his brows.

"Okay, but they're small drawers," Deanna muttered.

Everyone again burst out laughing.

Johnny nabbed his cold beer, sat back in his chair at the head of the table and joined them.

SIXTEEN
ALL IN

Johnny

The next morning, after feeding the horses and letting them out to pasture, Johnny walked to the back porch, his gaze on Izzy and Addie sitting on the loveseat there.

He walked through the door and saw that Addie had her long legs stretched out, feet on the coffee table in front of her, and she was wearing a striped cami and short-shorts sleep set. Her mass of hair was an appealing bedhead mess. Her eyes were still shadowed with sleep. All of this further making Johnny wonder what kind of dumb-fuck Perry was. She had a mug of coffee curled in both hands like it was the elixir of life.

Izzy was wearing his Home tee over a pair of his pajama bottoms that she'd cut off at the knees and her hair was also an appealing bedhead mess that had something to do with sleeping but more to do with something else.

Suffice it to say, bottle five moved through bottle six and halfway through bottle seven, so a fun night got more fun.

After bottle seven and a half and everyone leaving, Johnny got to take off her dress, and with Izzy plastered, they'd probably not been as quiet as they should have.

Or at least Izzy wasn't.

Then again, Addie was probably totally passed out, seeing as Iz did the same after he'd made her come, she'd returned the favor, and she'd slipped straight to sleep totally naked without even going to the bathroom to clean up.

Right then Iz looked a lot more alert than her sister, likely due to her practice with early mornings, so she had Brooks in her arms and was giving him his morning bottle.

Seeing her there, looking cute but thoroughly fucked and giving her nephew a bottle, Johnny felt the earth disappear under his feet and he plummeted only to stop and stand solid again.

This was not an unsettling feeling. It was just the first time he took note of it, even though it had been happening in increments for weeks as he kept falling faster and faster, deeper and deeper, even in the time she wasn't around.

No, it wasn't unsettling.

This was a fall he was happy to be taking.

"You want me to get you some coffee?" Izzy asked.

Of course she'd offer to get him coffee even if she was sitting with her sister, feeding her nephew.

"I can get it," he replied, moving toward her.

He bent down and kissed the top of her head.

Then he hesitated, wondering if it was the right thing to do, or if it would be welcome, but then he decided to do it.

So he moved to Addie and did the same thing.

When he was done, her head tipped back, and there was wonder in her blue eyes that were a darker blue than her sister's, and as with everything else, almost as pretty.

"You need a refill?" he asked.

She shook her head mutely.

He turned to Iz, glancing at the coffee table to see her full cup.

She gave him a sweet smile.

It had been the right thing to do.

He went in, got his coffee and came back out, seeing in the meantime they'd been joined by a gray cat who was resting on her belly between the two women, eyes closed, Addie's fingers in the fur of her ruff, and she was purring loudly.

Sabrina had decided to join the girls.

Johnny went to the screen door, leaned a shoulder against the jamb and looked out to the yard.

The table had been cleared but it and the chairs were still out there.

He took a sip and decided he'd see to that next.

"I know I'm cramping your style," Addie announced.

Johnny's gaze went to her as did Izzy's.

She was looking at Johnny.

But it was Izzy who asked, "Sorry?"

"I remember how it is, first blush, all that goodness," Addie said, now speaking to the coffee table. She took a sip and turned to her sister. "But I kinda like that little guy." She indicated Brooks with a tip of her head and gave her sister a small smile. "I like spending time with him. It sucked how in my face it was that I had a husband and he had a father, but we were still on our own. It was that with Perry. It wasn't taking care of my son. I love doing that."

"Of course you do," Izzy replied quietly.

"So you guys should do what you want to do. Go out. Have fun. Spend the night at Johnny's. I'm used to taking care of Brooklyn alone so it's not like I'm in new territory, just," her lips twitched, "in a different place in familiar territory."

"Now you have us," Johnny said, and both women's eyes came to him.

"You don't have to—" Addie started.

This wasn't Shandra and her dipshit brother.

This was Izzy and her strong, smart, funny, loving sister.

So he didn't let her finish.

"No. Now you have us so you don't have to do it alone," he reiterated.

Addie shook her head. "It would really make me feel better if you guys just did your thing."

"We will," Johnny told her. "We *are*," he stressed.

"It's not the same," Addie pressed.

"It's life," Johnny said.

She stared at him a beat before stating, "Okay. I don't mind you guys helping out, only when it fits. But if you don't go camping because I'm on shift and someone has to look after Brooks, forget about it. The daycare does Saturdays but Deanna said she'd pitch in if I need it until I'm settled. And I appreciate you offering to talk to Margot for me but I don't know her that well, and it wouldn't be cool at this juncture to unload my kid on her."

Johnny was going to get into the fact that Margot wouldn't think of it as unloading a baby on her, but before he could, Izzy entered the conversation.

"It's not bad, is it, that for a while we look after you?"

Addie looked to her sister, her face setting firm.

"Like when you warmed up soup for me?" she inquired.

"Ad—" Izzy began.

"Or when you helped me with that report about *The Call of the Wild*?" Addie went on.

"It's what—" Izzy tried again.

"Or when you and Mom made me stay inside when you went out and buried our cat that had died?"

Izzy's face got sad. "Doll—"

"Be with your guy and go camping, Iz," Addie ordered.

"We can—"

Addie leaned into her. "*Be with your guy and go camping, Iz*," she repeated. "I've got this. I'm fine. You're giving us a home. You know how appreciated it is. But when we're here, we *add* to your life, not take from it."

"You never take from it," Izzy returned.

"I've been taking from you since Mom loaded us up in that car in the middle of the night and we left Dad," Addie shot back.

Iz shut her mouth.

Addie looked down to Brooks and back to her sister.

"He's not hard work," she whispered.

"No," Izzy whispered in return.

More whispering when Addie said, "Love you, Iz."

"Love you too, Addie," Izzy replied.

"Be with your guy," Addie urged.

"Okay," Izzy agreed.

Johnny looked back out the window, raising his mug and taking a sip in order to open a throat that had closed.

When he was finished and nothing further had been said by the two sisters, he spoke.

"I'm dismantling that table and putting it and the chairs away, and if either of you two women even look like you're gonna offer to help, I'm wringing your neck."

There was a moment of stunned silence.

And then he heard two women bust out laughing.

"I NEED NEW WINEGLASSES," Izzy muttered.

Johnny turned his gaze from the television show they were watching, lying in his bed, to her beside him.

"And maybe a trip to the Pacific Northwest," she went on.

He looked back to the TV.

They were watching "Big Little Lies." It was funny. It was trippy. Reese Witherspoon was hysterical. And the suspense was excellent.

How Iz got wineglasses out of it, he had no idea.

The Pacific Northwest he could do.

He returned his gaze to her. "What are you talking about?"

"Nothing," she mumbled.

He didn't look back at the screen as he noticed this entire exchange happened with her watching the TV.

It was a great show.

But that wasn't it.

They were both up on pillows, Johnny on his side of the bed, Izzy on hers.

He had his back to the pillows with his legs stretched out in front of him, feet crossed at the ankles, with a bottle of beer in his hand resting on his abs.

She was on her side curled in a wide S, down a little bit with her head on plumped pillows, her glass of wine on the nightstand behind her.

And there was a vast expanse between them.

After a great night and a sweet morning, Johnny felt this vast expanse start widening after the tables and chairs had been put away, they'd shared breakfast then Izzy had showered and come downstairs only for Addie essentially to kick them out of Izzy's house.

Izzy packed to spend the night and get ready in the morning at his place. They loaded up Ranger. They went to the mill. He showed her how to drive an ATV and they went cruising all over his land. But after they got back and had a late lunch, she seemed to be flagging so he suggested she take a nap.

She took him up on that with an eager attitude that he found unsettling.

It was like she was looking for a way to escape him in his (essentially) one-room house.

She slept hard and long, woke up groggy, ate the food he cooked for her like she was in a dream state, and not a good one, and when they decided to camp out in his bed and watch TV, she entered the bed removed from him. Even if she was on her side facing him, she didn't cuddle in or even get close.

She also did nothing to invite Johnny to do it.

At first, Johnny thought she was still groggy or maybe sorting through all she'd learned the day before that was going down with her sister.

But studying her lying beside him watching TV, he knew that wasn't it.

He didn't know what it was but he had a creeping feeling sliding up the back of his neck and he didn't fucking like it.

"What's up, *spätzchen*?" he asked.

"Hmm?" she muttered distractedly.

"Are you okay?"

She lifted just her eyes to him, not her head.

"Sorry?"

"Are you okay?" he repeated.

"Of course," she replied, looking back to the TV.

"You wanna get closer?" he asked.

"I'm good," she said.

"I'm not," he returned.

She lifted her eyes again. "Johnny, I'm watching this."

No, he didn't fucking like it.

That was when he raised the remote.

He hit pause and she glanced at the TV and back to him, now with little lines in between her eyebrows.

"What's up?" he asked again.

"I'm just into this show. It's good," she lied.

They'd never watched TV together.

Maybe she wasn't a cuddler.

However, she'd fallen asleep on top of him with his cum sliding out of her.

She was a cuddler.

"Babe—"

"This is a good show. I'm into it. And maybe still a little hungover."

"You slept for two and a half hours this afternoon and drank more water today than an NFL team during a game."

She got up on her forearm. "Yes, but I drank a lot of wine last night too."

"You did," he agreed.

"So I'm still a little hungover."

"Being hungover means you can't scoot close and watch a show with me?"

"I *am* watching it with you."

"There's three feet of space between us."

She looked down at the bed but again to him when he continued speaking.

"You worried about your sister?" he asked.

"A little," she answered. "Mostly I'm relieved. Perry's always been a loser. I hate how she finally figured that out but I'm glad that part of her life is at an end and she can start fresh without him dragging on her."

He believed at least that.

"You worried about the money it's gonna take for her to get shot of that guy?" he went on.

She shook her head. "We always find a way."

Yeah, he bet they did.

"So what is it?" he pushed.

"It's nothing, Johnny. I'm just a little hungover and into this show."

"Iz, we talk. That's the deal, remember?"

"*Your* deal," she returned.

His brows drew together. "What?"

She turned her eyes again to the TV. "Nothing."

"*Izzy*," he growled.

Her eyes shot to him and she pushed up to a hand in the bed.

"Okay, so, I'm learning the kind of guy you are, maybe you should learn the kind of woman I am," she stated.

"Hit me," he invited.

"Sometimes I need space to sort through things in my head."

"Does this space need to be physical?" he asked.

"I..." She looked around them and back at him. "Sorry?"

"Can't you sort through things in your head curled up to me?"

"I...I..." She stopped there like she didn't know the answer to that question.

He tried something else.

"What did you mean, 'your deal?'"

"What?" she asked, beginning to look panicked.

"You said it was *my* deal that we talk. What did you mean when you said that?"

"I meant that, uh..."

"Spit it out," he prompted.

"Hold your horses!" she snapped, panic gone, she was ticked.

Johnny shut his mouth and stared at her.

The only times he could recall that she'd snapped at him was when she lost it right before he fucked her in her stable and when she got slightly ticked when he'd brought up Shandra on the balcony.

It just wasn't her.

But maybe it *should* be her.

Maybe she *should* feel free to get pissed every once in a while, quit with the stiff upper lip, stop rolling with the punches and *punch back.*

And maybe now was the time to show her that she was safe to do that with him.

"*You* could curl up to *me*," she noted angrily.

"Would you have been good with that?" he asked.

"I...don't know," she said. Then she went back on it and answered, "No."

"So you need space to sort through things, it needs to be physical, but can you let me in on what these things are?"

"That's part of having them to myself to sort through them, so no."

"You ever had anyone to sort them out with?"

"Of course. Mom. Addie. Deanna."

"A man," he clarified.

"What's that matter?"

"Iz—"

"She's my sister, you know," she declared suddenly.

Johnny shut his mouth again.

Izzy didn't.

"Yesterday, when you were asking if it was Addie's plan all along to come up here and stay with me, and I told you no but she was going to be with me for a while, you looked unhappy."

He set his beer aside, turned to her and tried again, "Iz—"

She cut him off. "And she's my sister. We're...we...this is good. What you and I have. It's new but it's good. And it's not habit, me looking out for her. It's family. She needs me. So I need to be there for her. She'd do the same for me."

"I told you yesterday it was all cool."

"Yes, but at first you looked upset about it."

"Because we're new and this is good and I want more of that," he hedged.

It was more than just that. He just didn't want to bring it to his bed with Izzy in it with him.

"That's lovely and all but you were there. Perry didn't just prove himself a loser, he proved himself a total jerk. She's going to be a single mom, a real one now, in a new place and I want more of this too. I mean, you have to know that. I hate that it's true what Addie said, she's cramping our style. But it's true, and I hate that she feels that and I hate that you feel that and I'm stuck in between, not giving the best to either of you."

It was time to shut this down and there was only one way to do it.

He didn't like that way.

But it was the only one.

"Shandra left me because of her brother."

To that, Izzy shut her mouth.

"I can't say why but I'll say me not going to the police to share about shit he did makes me an accessory after the fact. So since I'd rather not be incarcerated, it'd be good you didn't say anything to anyone, including Addie."

Her eyes were now big.

Johnny didn't let up.

"The whole situation was fucked up. So it was a totally fucked decision she made. She had no business going with him. But she felt like someone had to look after him and she was all he had. So she picked him and left me."

"I...don't know what to say," she whispered.

"Nothing to say," he replied. "I was pissed about it at first. Hurt and pissed. It didn't take long to get to a place of understanding and that ended with me not being pissed, just hurt. They were tight. They had to be that way with the parents they had. She felt the bond of blood and obligation, and even if what she was doing was dangerous and downright stupid, she wasn't strong enough to break that bond. So she went."

"Addie's not a criminal on the run," she told him.

"I know that. And yeah, you saw me react to being in another situation that's so good it's great, it feels right, I know there's a future in it and I want that, and I'm also in the middle of a situation with my woman's sibling. But I didn't lie to you then, Eliza. I get the difference and I'm cool with it. That doesn't make me less disappointed when we're at your place I can't fuck you and not bite it back when I come, and I can't listen to the sounds you make that I like a helluva lot when I touch you. That you don't feel totally free to be with me when you want and you're pulled another way. I know it's selfish but this is *that* good. I want all of you. Right now I can't have it. But I want it so I'll take what I can get."

"I like that you want all of it, I want all of it too," she shared softly. "I just can't give it now. Or at least, I didn't feel I could before Addie talked to us this morning."

"And this morning is when I realized where I was at with this. With you. With her. With Brooks. If I want to explore this with you, I have to be all in. I can't hold back like I might in the beginning of a normal situation without any drama, testing the waters, seeing how far in I wanna get. This is no longer about building on what we got. Now, it's about life, learning to have all that's there to have together. And I'm all in. With you comes her. Brooks. Deanna. Charlie. With me comes Tobe. Margot. Dave. Ben and Cait, and whoever else."

She was holding herself very still, staring at him intently, but he wasn't quite done.

"Telling you all this isn't about me getting burned by Shandra and still licking my wounds. Right here and now with this conversation, since I'm already all in, it's about me having a genuine reaction to something, showing it, you internalizing that and not sharing it. I was disappointed because it's disappointing. Life hits you with that too often. But in the end, you being close with Addie and Brooks and being there for them, I wouldn't have it any other way. It's just that I get to have the honor of doing it with you."

"Johnny," she whispered, wonder in her eyes now, like there'd been in her sister's that morning.

Except it was a lot sweeter.

Still.

"Now you need to explain 'your deal,'" he demanded.

The wonder started edging out with the panic beginning to edge back in.

"It's just that it was you that made that decree and like I said, sometimes I need space to sort things out," she explained.

"So you think you not talking to me about this, sitting on it, stewing on it, would have ended up all good?"

"Yes," she replied immediately.

That was completely implausible.

"You're telling me you'd get there on your own," he said with clear skepticism.

"I'm telling you I'd eventually have talked to you about it when I was ready."

"You sure about that?" he pushed.

"Why wouldn't I be sure?"

"Babe, women stew."

"It's not stewing, it's sorting."

"Different words, same meaning," he returned.

"That's not true."

"So I know something's on your mind and I gotta keep my mouth shut, knowing that something is bothering you, not knowing what that is, or how that could affect me, *us,* and wait on you to give it to me?"

"That doesn't make it sound too good," she murmured.

"That's because it's not, Eliza."

"I'm not like that."

"You just snapped at me."

"You were being pushy."

"So we could get through it and fucking enjoy a fucking TV show without anything weighing heavy on either of us."

"I'm not like that," she shot back. "I *do* talk about it. I always get it out in the end and it turns out okay when I do."

"And you can assure me of that," he stated.

"Of course."

"You're sure," he pushed.

"Yes!"

She was snapping again, her face screwing up.

It was cute.

But he still didn't buy it.

"And what if the sorting doesn't go my way and I've had no say in that?" he asked.

"It'll go your way," she answered sharply.

"Right."

"Right," she bit out.

"Now I'm meant to believe that?" he asked incredulously.

"Yes!" she snapped again.

"How?" he pressed.

"Because I'm falling for you!"

Johnny went still.

Izzy did not.

"You're the best thing that's ever happened to me and I'm not stupid. I'm not going to mess that up by being upset about something and letting it fester and get twisted before I talk to you about it. I mean...*yeesh*."

Yeesh?

He had no time to get into the utter adorableness of "yeesh."

He shifted toward her, turning to his side, sliding down, hooking an arm around her waist and hauling her up against him.

Then he kissed her.

At first, he rolled on his back, pulling her on top of him, wanting her weight on him, wanting her anchoring him to his bed.

Then she whimpered in his mouth in that way he always felt in his dick and he rolled them again, Johnny on top of her, giving her as much of his weight as he thought she could take, pressing her into the bed like she could make a dent in it that would never go away.

The kiss started deep and wild and it kept going in that direction as they tore at each other's clothes, devoured each other's flesh any way they could get at it.

By the time he got his mouth between her legs, she was so wet and Johnny was just as ready for her, all he could do was suck her clit hard before surging over her, hand to his cock, guiding the way, finding her and sliding right in.

"Johnny," she breathed when she was full of him.

He thrust, staring at this Izzy, his wild one, his sex kitten, the pink in her cheeks, the haze in her eyes, the swelling in her lips.

She lifted her arms above her head, cocked her knees and let her legs fall wide to the side...

Fuck.

His.

Open for him. Her hips undulating to meet his thrusts. Her body jolting when she took them. Her hair spread all over his bed. Her body his to do anything he wanted.

She trusted him that completely.

And no one else.

She'd never given that to anyone else.

But he had that from the beginning.

He made a noise that he made only for her and pulled out, shifted aside, whipped her to her belly and moved right back in. Hitching one leg, forcing hers up with it, gliding his hands up the outsides of her arms, keeping them straight above her head, wrapping his fingers around her forearms, watching her, one cheek pressed to his comforter, swollen lips parted, breaths coming fast, face flushed, he drove back in, pounding her into his bed.

Connected to her.

Covering her.

Giving her what was in her face at the same time he was her shield against the shit of life, the blanket to keep her warm, the shelter to keep her safe.

That was his to know, to give, to share with her later when she wasn't taking his cock.

But her head arched back, she pressed her temple tight to his jaw and whispered a trembling, "Johnny."

And he knew she knew.

He knew he didn't have to say a word.

But he did have to say something else.

He slid a hand down the soft skin of her arm, her side, over her waist and hip and then in.

He touched her clit, pressed, rolled, she gasped and he said, "I'm falling for you too," in her ear.

She cried out, her pussy rippling tight around his cock, her body shuddering under his, her ass pressing hard to his groin. It was too much, too good, he couldn't ride her through her orgasm so he shoved his face in her neck, drove deep and shot inside his Izzy, groaning against her skin.

When he came out of where Izzy took him and back into the room, he pushed his face harder into her neck and kept her leg hitched as he fucked her gentle, deliberate, memorizing every inch of her inside, over and over slipping his cock out of her silky wet until she only had the tip and then sinking it slowly back in.

He felt her breath in his hair, the ease of her soft body under his. He slid his hand from between her legs and up to cup her breast.

He heard her hand glide over the comforter and press in to cover his.

Finally, Johnny buried himself inside her and stayed there, tracing the line of her neck with his lips.

Her body twitched and her head moved to the side like she wanted to squeeze him out.

He started to pull away but she said softly, but urgently, "Don't. It just tickles. Your beard. But I like it."

He retraced his line at her neck.

She shivered under him.

And it was then he knew.

This was it.

This was all he was ever going to have.

Izzy.

Her body. Her pussy. Her hair. Her neck. Her breasts. Her scent. Her taste.

Her belly would swell with the babies he'd plant there.

Her skin would wrinkle.

Her hair would gray.

He would mourn her when she was gone and there wouldn't be another for him.

Or he would leave this earth knowing she'd do the same.

That was it.

The rest of his life.

Simple.

And unbelievably fucking beautiful.

He'd finished taking the plunge and it ended up being him doing it fucking Izzy wild in his bed.

But he thought that was fitting considering that was how it started.

He nipped her earlobe, kissed it and asked quietly there, "You wanna clean up?"

She spoke no words, just nodded.

He kissed her neck. Her shoulder. Slid out and rolled her around to gather her to him and take her mouth in a deep kiss.

When he finished it, she looked into his eyes, hers blinked lazily, and when she opened them again, they were smiling.

"Be back," she whispered.

He nodded.

She pulled away and he watched her move around naked, searching the floor.

She found what he knew she was looking for when she bent to pick up his tee, straightened and moved toward the hall, pulling it on over her head.

She didn't bother with panties.

Ranger followed her to the bathroom.

Johnny grinned.

They'd left Dempsey and Swirl with Addie and Brooks because Izzy wanted them there for her sister's protection.

So now it was just Ranger.

And it was not lost on Johnny that even in his absence Ranger had always been his dog. It didn't seem he mourned or was even confused about Shandra not in his life anymore.

He was just home.

That said, being all Johnny's, his dog hadn't bonded with Izzy. He liked the attention she gave him when she gave it. He was a dog. That happened.

But he'd never followed her anywhere when he'd be leaving Johnny behind.

Now he was in the bathroom with Johnny's woman.

Still grinning, Johnny angled out of bed, found his shorts, his jeans, tugged them on and then went to Izzy's wineglass.

He nabbed it, took it to the kitchen, got the bottle out of the fridge, yanked out the cork he'd wedged in and refilled it.

He got himself another beer, and when he moved back to the bed, he set her glass on his nightstand with his bottle.

He was just stretching back out in the bed when she and Ranger returned.

She came right to his side. Crawled over him, set her hip beside his, and collapsed onto him, curled close.

He slid a hand over her hip, hiked up his tee, and cupped her bare ass as he found the remote and hit play on the TV.

Ranger dropped his jaw to the side of the bed.

Johnny threw the remote on the nightstand, reached out his other hand and rubbed behind his dog's ears.

In a time in the program where it didn't seem she would miss too much action, he murmured, "You need space, baby, take it."

She pushed farther into him, twisted her neck and kissed his chest then rested her cheek there again and murmured back, "Thank you, honey."

"You have that, feel safe in it," he told her. "But just to say, you need to talk shit out, even if you're pissed at me and we got something to work through, hit me with it. I'm here. I'll listen. If you're talking to me, snapping at me or yelling at me. I'll listen. And we'll get to the other side."

To that, she didn't kiss him.

She turned her head and nuzzled her face against his skin like a sleepy cat or a newborn baby.

Johnny's chest constricted and only did it more when she settled with her cheek back to his chest and whispered, "Okay, *häschen*."

She remembered.

She remembered what his grandmother called him.

And she gave him that back.

He was staring at the TV and not seeing a thing, just trying to remember how to breathe.

When Ranger licked his wrist it came back to him and Johnny murmured, "Right, boy. Down."

Without delay, Ranger slid with a dog groan down the side of the bed and disappeared.

"Want your wine?" Johnny asked Iz.

"In a sec," she answered.

He started tracing patterns on her hip and the cheek of her ass.

She sighed and curled in closer.

This was more like it.

Johnny smiled at the TV.

Then he watched a great program cuddled in bed with his woman.

SEVENTEEN
A NEW MEMBER

Johnny

"You're going to do what?"

Johnny wasn't altogether there.

It was the next morning and they both needed to leave. Him, to go deal with the horses, her, to go to work.

Ten minutes ago, he had heard her heels on his floors as she walked down the hall to appear in his kitchen fully dressed for work.

He turned from scrambling some eggs for her to see Iz in a navy dress that hit her at the knee and had short sleeves.

The thing about it was, it hugged her figure close and had a stripe of sheer navy across her upper chest and another one a couple of inches above her hem taking class and making it sexy.

She was also in beige pumps with spiked heels that looked professional but still called to him to fuck her.

Even though he had that overwhelming desire, since they had to get their shows on the road, he instead launched into his plans for her sister while scraping her eggs on a plate with the toast and bacon he'd made her, handed it to her and made his own plate then stood there shoveling it in while telling her how things were going to go.

She held her plate in front of her while he did this, her eyes on him getting bigger and bigger and he vaguely noted she'd quit eating halfway through him talking. She was just standing there, holding her plate and staring at him. But he needed to get her down with this so they could talk to Addie about it, and when they did, both of his girls could have a couple weighty things off their minds.

The problem was, throughout all this, all he could see was Iz in that dress and those shoes, and in the back of his mind he was thinking about what he'd do to her in them, so he wasn't paying close attention to her eyes getting bigger and bigger and her not eating.

"I'm paying for the attorney," he answered her question.

"She won't let you do that, Johnny," she told him.

"We'll talk to her about it, I'll state my case and we'll see," he said, taking the last bite of his toast.

"No. Really. She just won't let you do that," she said.

"She refuses, then it'll be a no-interest loan. We can work out a payment schedule after she's set that's comfortable for her. But in the meantime, she doesn't have to worry about it."

"She might have a problem with that too," Izzy replied.

He picked up his last piece of bacon and said, "That's where you come in."

"I've not been really successful with talking Addie into things she doesn't want to do. Case in point, I told her to break up with Perry about seven hundred and ten times before he asked her to marry him. And I pleaded with her nine hundred and ten times not to marry him. You can see how that went."

"Let's give it a shot," he suggested.

"You have properties?"

He guessed with the sudden change of subject they were going to give it a shot so he nodded, chewed the last bite of his bacon and put his plate in the sink to run water over it.

"Plural?" she asked, sounding weirdly choked.

Not having her in her sexy work getup as his visual, his mind snapped back to the present and slowly he turned to her to see her standing there with her plate of half-eaten food held up in front of her.

"Yes," he said deliberately, wondering why she was looking at him the way she was looking at him—like he'd sprung a second head and she didn't know whether to stand there and scream in terror or run away as fast as she could.

"How many?" she asked.

"Two," he answered. "Well, three, counting the mill. Actually, four but it's more like three and a half since both me and Tobe own the shack. That said, we did the split. He got the shack. I got the mill. So it's really his. But he's never around, so whenever I need it I go to the shack."

"The shack?"

"A fishing shack we own out at Shanty Hollow Lake."

"Is it a real shack?"

"In a way."

"How can it be a shack *in a way*?"

"It's been taken care of just by guys for the last forty-five years."

"What way is it not a shack?" she asked.

"It's thirteen hundred square feet," he answered.

She looked down at her plate but didn't pick up her fork.

"Izzy, something up with you?"

Her head came up and she looked him right in the eye.

"How rich are you?"

For some reason, this question seemed like it had a wrong answer, and that wrong answer was not the answer any woman he'd ever known would think was wrong.

"That answer is relative," he said as reply.

"Well, I already know you don't own as many places as Circle K," she returned.

"I got money," he told her.

She suddenly looked around. Took it all in.

And her eyes fell on his dining room table.

"Baby, you wanna tell me why this seems to be an issue for you?"

Her gaze came back to his.

"My father's father died in a hunting accident when my father was seventeen. He inherited fifteen hardware stores. He didn't run them. He didn't even work at one. He was a musician. He was going to be bigger than Johnny Cash. But he did take the checks whoever ran them sent him."

Johnny felt his insides growing deathly still.

"Your dad is wealthy?" he asked.

"Yes," she answered.

"Your dad is wealthy." He said it as a statement that time.

"We had a huge house when we were young. That was the only time, until we grew up and moved out, Addie and I had our own rooms. Sometimes we only had a one bedroom place and Mom slept on the couch."

He couldn't process that last part.

Not right then.

He had to stay on target.

"Your dad's got money." He was growling now.

"Y-yes," she stammered, suddenly standing rock solid and staring at him, not like he'd grown two heads, but was a rattler about to strike.

And he was.

He did this taking two strides to her, tearing the plate out of her hand and hurling it underarm into his sink where it exploded, pieces of crockery, strips of bacon and bits of egg flying.

Ranger, who had been sitting beside Izzy while she ate, got to his feet, backed up two steps and barked.

"Johnny," she whispered.

He spun back to her.

"You had plastic sandals," he ground out.

"Sorry?" she asked quietly.

"In those photos in your stable. You with your mom. You were wearing cheap plastic sandals."

She shook her head. "I...I don't remember."

"You were," he confirmed.

"Okay," she said conciliatorily.

"He was fucking *rich* and you had cheap plastic sandals?" he demanded to know.

"We...we were better off without him."

There was a translation to that and Johnny translated it.

"She couldn't go for child support because if she did, he'd fuck with her," he declared.

"Yes," she whispered.

"Try to take you or at least get time with you just to screw with her, not that he cared dick about you, since he proved that being absent from your life and not even being a big enough man to send her some cash. And she couldn't let that happen," he said.

She nodded.

"He ever hurt you?" he asked.

"No, Johnny. No. Not me. Not Addie. Just Mom," she assured him.

"But she was worried it'd come to that."

She shook her head. "I don't know. Maybe. We didn't talk much about him. We just—"

"Kept on keeping on," he clipped, finishing for her.

"Yes," she said softly.

"And now you got an issue with me having money," he stated.

"It's...I'll admit, it's a shock."

"You looked ready to bolt, Iz."

"My, well...Kent is also...he's, well—"

Her creepy ex Kent was rich too.

"Jesus, *shit*," he hissed.

"They're not you," she told him hurriedly. "I should have put it together. You know, that you were, um...comfortable. With all that's been happening I didn't put it together so it was just a shock."

He saw the fear in her eyes and he bit out, "I'd never hurt you, Eliza."

"You threw a plate in the sink," she said quietly.

"Because a man makes two beautiful daughters, he works until he fucking *bleeds* to make sure they don't have to wear cheap plastic sandals. And if he can't make that happen, he's still there to clean their scraped knees, take pictures of them when they go to prom and walk them down the aisle to their future husband. But even when that happens, he doesn't let them go. He *never* lets them go. You and your mother and your sister have eaten shit all your life because first, he's an asshole abuser and second, he didn't sort his shit out when you took off on him. He let you go."

"Yes," she agreed, the uncertain light in her eyes changing to something else entirely.

Johnny couldn't process that either.

"And you've been making do ever since."

She made no reply.

She didn't have to.

He'd made the decision two days ago this shit ended.

Now he'd let her in on that.

"Your sister is gonna take the damn money from me, Eliza," he informed her. "And like I told you, she's gonna move into one of my properties when a tenant moves out. They're nice places. The tenants don't go often. But she's not ready for that yet. Though when one goes, she's got a home, she's safe, her son is safe, and you aren't gonna tell her I'm discounting the rent."

That light in her eyes had fully changed to that something else entirely.

But still, she replied, "It'd be me that wouldn't want you in a bind with that, Johnny, and I'd know."

"I own them outright, Iz, so anything I make off them works."

"We'll talk to her tonight," she said quickly, probably just to appease him.

He was glad she was in to do that.

But he didn't feel very appeased.

"You should find him," he replied.

Her brows went up. "Who? Dad?"

He didn't answer that question.

He announced, "You should find him. You should walk up to his house in that dress and knock on the door, and when he answers, you should tell him who you are. And you should tell him since he wasn't around to take pictures of you when you went to the prom, he isn't walking you down the aisle. He isn't seeing his grandchildren. He's gonna die knowing the woman who gave him his daughters and the precious babies he made lived their lives happier without him in them."

"Johnny, honey, it was a long time ago and we *were* happier without him," she soothed.

"Did you get what happened when I was inside you last night?"

She stared up at him.

"Did you get it, Izzy?" he pushed.

"I think so," she whispered.

"That's the guy I am. *Yours.* Simple. That's it. And you're mine. *Mine*, Iz. And we take care of each other. And we look after those in our hearts and lives. So the Forrester Girls Club has a new member, baby. And he's got a dick."

The tension in her shoulders ebbed, her lips twitched but she asked, "Can I request no future throwing of plates?"

"You can but I can't guarantee that won't happen because I figure I got a lot more to learn about your dad and *Kent*, so anything's game."

"Then can I request that if you learn some of this at my house you don't throw any of *my* plates?"

"Do you own a single plate you bought new?" he demanded to know.

She suddenly looked confused. "I...actually I don't know."

"Guess," he pushed.

"Probably not," she said.

"So no, I can't promise that either. What I can promise is if I hear more about the shit you've eaten and plates go flying, I'll replace them with the finest china that can be had."

That was when her face got soft.

"I don't need fine china, Johnny."

"Then you'll get whatever you want and it'll be goddamned *new*," he returned.

She ignored him and said, "I just need a guy who's mine who cares enough about me to get angry enough to throw plates."

Christ, she was so damned sweet, he wanted to fuck her *all the time*.

"Baby," he growled. "How much trouble will you get in if you're late to work?"

Pink hit her cheeks and she answered, "I'm never late."

"Right, then grab your purse and let's roll."

"We need to clean—"

"*Spätzchen*, we're rolling."

Her brows knit. "You shouldn't leave that egg—"

"Eliza," he bit out.

Her expression changed.

"You want me to be open with you?" she asked tartly.

"Yup. And right now you got about five seconds to do that."

"You can be extremely annoying when you're being pushy. And you calling me 'Eliza' when I annoy *you* further annoys *me*."

"Noted," he replied. "Now get your purse."

She rolled her eyes before she announced, "I need a travel mug of coffee."

"I'll get the mug, you get your purse."

She pointed at the island, which was two feet away from where she was standing. "My purse is right there."

Johnny looked to the ceiling. "Oh for fuck's sake."

She strutted on those freaking heels to the coffeepot, stating, "If we have children and you curse like that in front of them, it'll be *me* throwing plates."

He ignored that since they were having children and he wouldn't curse like that in front of them (at least not the girls, the boys, when they reached a certain age...) and she already knew that (probably).

Instead, he asked, "Your bag in the bathroom?"

"Yes," she answered, grabbing a travel mug.

"It packed or you leaving it?"

"It's packed. But I have to repack it tonight so I need to take it."

"Stock up tonight, *spätzchen*."

"Roger that, Ghostrider," she returned wryly as she splashed cream into the mug.

Yeah.

He wanted to fuck her *all the time*.

Johnny managed not to tackle her at the coffeepot and he and Ranger went to get her bag.

Then he and Ranger walked her and her purse and her travel mug to her car.

He dumped the bag in her back seat.

That done, he allowed himself some time to make out with her, hot and heavy at her car door.

Then he and Ranger loaded up in his truck and followed her down the lane from the mill.

"I'm staying."

Suffice it to say Johnny was thrilled his brother was making this statement.

However, the instant he did, that afternoon after he'd found out Izzy's dad was not just an epic dick, but an asshole of massive proportions, while they stood in the lone bay of the first Gamble Garage (this the only one having one bay, the others had at least two, some of them four), he thought of Toby sitting at Izzy's outdoor table looking up at Izzy's bedroom window.

So he did not share he was thrilled.

He felt his brows draw together and he asked, "Why?"

Toby shrugged.

Shit.

"Tobe—"

"I might not be settling in. I don't know my plans. I just know I'm staying for a while."

"You got trouble somewhere?" Johnny asked.

"Nope," Toby answered, and Johnny watched him closely as he did.

When he saw his brother wasn't lying, he asked, "Feel like consoling a not-so-suddenly single mom after her husband proved how big of a dipshit he is?"

Toby's face changed, a nuance, a nuance only their dad, Margot and Johnny could catch, and he replied, "Nope."

Now that was a lie.

"Hands off, brother," Johnny declared.

It was then Toby got pissed. "I'm not going there," he clipped. "Christ, what kind of ass do you think I am?"

"I don't think you're an ass. I think you're a player and the way you play has nothing to do with me. Unless it's Addie."

"She's pretty."

"She's off limits."

"I'm just saying she's pretty."

"I know she's pretty. And I'm just saying she's off limits."

"I'm not gonna go there, Johnny," he repeated.

"I know you aren't."

"I wanna get to know Izzy better because I'm thinking that's the right call about now with where you two seem to be. And with where you two seem to be, I'll also need to be getting to know her sister, and I don't need you breathing down my neck or treating me like I'm a complete dick who's gonna make a play on a woman who collapsed in my arms because her man is a total tool."

"If that's it then great, awesome, I'm thrilled you're gonna stick around," Johnny said truthfully.

"You know, the time I needed an older brother ended about a decade ago," Toby shared.

"Tobe, you need to get over that because I'm gonna be your older brother until the day I die, and that's just the way it is."

"Terrific," Toby muttered, turning his head to stare at the car Johnny had up on a lift.

"You got plans while you're in Matlock or are you gonna fish and charm women and drive Margot insane because you seem entirely immune to having a healthy relationship?"

Toby looked back to him. "I wanna work with you here, at the garage."

Johnny stood solid and stared.

Toby was good with an engine. He wasn't better than Johnny because Johnny had always been a gearhead like their father and grandfather.

Toby could get stuck in and do great work.

Then Toby could get distracted and take off.

Johnny didn't care. He was used to it and his brother was an adult. He got his checks from the garages. He did his thing. He didn't get into trouble anymore (much). It was his life to live and it wasn't Johnny's place to get involved in it.

Except giving him stick and keeping him away from Addie.

But he'd love having his brother home, working beside him, like the old days.

Like before Dad died.

"You wanna be here, I want you here," Johnny told him. "Long as you want, forever or a week, I don't care. But I don't have to say that. It's yours the same as mine."

"That may be true on paper but it isn't true in practice, and I've been thinking that isn't right."

Johnny again stared.

A healthy relationship with a woman was not Toby's thing.

Responsibility wasn't either.

"I need to do my part," Toby stated. "I don't wanna be managing any mini-marts. But I can change a belt and switch out plugs."

"Then start when you wanna start," Johnny replied. "But if you're here, I manage this bay, brother. You wanna take over your own garage, we gotta work you up to that, and by that I mean, you get one when we lose a man who's managing one. We got great crews in all the garages. That changes, you slide in. But I've laid claim to this one, so it's mine."

"I don't wanna manage anything. I just wanna be rooted for a while."

"Outside of thinking you're not pitching in when you don't gotta pitch in, anything else bring this on?" Johnny asked.

"Grams is dead. Gramps is dead. Dad's dead. And Margot and Dave aren't gonna be here forever. I've seen a lot. Done a lot. Learned a lot. And the biggest thing I learned was that the only place I feel right is in Matlock."

"Then it's really a welcome home," Johnny said quietly.

"Yeah," Toby replied.

"I'll talk to Iz about a good night for you to come over for dinner so you can spend more time with her," Johnny offered.

Toby grinned. "That'd be great."

They stared at each other for long beats.

Johnny ended it, saying, "Dad would be glad."

Toby kept hold on his gaze.

Then he replied, "Yeah."

"Sure," Addie said.

It was after dinner at Izzy's. They were in her living room, a place Johnny wanted to get out of as soon as possible considering spending time with all the white furniture, flower covered pillows and lamp-shades and the flipping bird cage with a pink roof on her white coffee table was making him concerned he'd actually be able to father a child in the future.

He'd just got shot down for paying the attorney straight up.

So he'd pitched the loan.

And that was Addie's response.

Johnny looked from her to Izzy, who was staring at her sister like she'd morphed into someone else, and back to Addie.

"Great," he replied. "Give your attorney's bills to me. I'll cover them. We'll keep track. This is done, we'll sort out a payment plan."

"Done," Addie agreed, giving him a big grin.

"Are you all right?" Izzy asked Addie.

Addie's grin faded and she looked to her sister. "Yeah. Why?"

"You don't have a fever?" Izzy inquired.

Johnny chuckled.

"Put a sock in it," Addie ordered.

"No, really," Izzy said. "Are you sure you wanna do this?"

Addie looked to him. "You gonna screw over my sister?"

"Nope," Johnny answered.

Her gaze returned to Iz. "Then sure, I'm sure." She got up from her place in Iz's slouchy white loveseat, moved to Johnny, dropped Brooks in his lap, Brooks ignored the beard and yanked on his ear and Addie strolled toward the kitchen, asking, "Anyone want leftover cake?"

"Yeah," Johnny called after her.

"Iz?" she prompted.

"Okay," Izzy said.

Brooks grunted as he pulled himself up to Johnny's shoulder.

Johnny spotted him with his hands as he crawled behind Johnny's neck.

The kid hit his other shoulder, threw himself over and slid down Johnny's chest into his lap and giggled.

Johnny then lifted him up, swung him around and planted him on his shoulders, his pudgy legs dangling on either side of Johnny's neck.

He held on to his upper arms.

Brooks tugged his hair.

"If we'd have stayed with him, I wouldn't have met you."

Johnny's attention cut to Izzy to see her face soft, her eyes on her nephew, but he had a feeling that softness wasn't just for Brooks.

"What, baby?"

She dropped her gaze to his. "If he'd gotten it together. If he'd fought for us. If he'd made us stay close, I wouldn't have met you."

"That's sweet, Iz," he said quietly. "But that doesn't erase—"

While he spoke, her eyes darted up and then back down before she cut him off.

"Go through it all again if it led me to you."

He felt his chest start to burn.

Brooks tried to hurl himself over Johnny's head.

So he flipped Brooks over and planted his behind in Johnny's lap.

Brooks squealed.

Izzy smiled and whispered, "You can attack me when we get back to the mill."

"Obliged for the permission," he grunted instead of sharing he didn't need it.

Her smile got bigger.

She knew he didn't need it.

"Ice cream, everyone?" Addie shouted from the kitchen.

"Yeah!" Johnny shouted back.

"Yes!" Izzy yelled.

Brooks let out a shriek and then collapsed into his own lap, giggling.

"The secret room revealed," Izzy murmured in awe.

Johnny had just guided her into the walk-in closet that led off the door at the back of the bathroom.

He'd switched on the lights, which were mostly recessed spots that shone on the railings and shelves as well as on the island in the middle. He'd then walked in and dumped her bag (which was much heavier than yesterday) unceremoniously on top of the island that was covered in sliding glass panels that protected velvet-lined jewelry trays.

All of them empty.

"The secret what?" he asked.

She was wandering around the opposite side of the closet from him like he would suspect she'd wander around a castle. She lifted a hand and ran the tip of her forefinger along an empty slanted shelf, which had a lip that was supposed to display shoes but now was bare.

"Izzy," he called when she said nothing.

She stopped and turned to him. "I always wondered what was in here. I almost looked in that first morning. But I didn't want to snoop."

"It's just a closet," he said.

"It's the biggest, most gorgeous closet in the history of man," she replied, glanced beyond him to the half a rail up top and half a rail under it that were the only rails in the huge place that held clothes. "Though you need more jeans."

His mouth hitched. "I don't need more jeans."

She looked him right in the eye. "You built this for Shandra, didn't you?"

His mouth stopped hitching. "Iz—"

Her head tipped to the side and she interrupted him. "You don't like talking about her."

"I don't like her being any part of us," he corrected.

She gave him a small smile and started walking toward him.

When she reached him, she put a hand on his chest and tilted her head back to look up at him.

"She was a part of your life," she noted quietly.

"I know that," he replied.

"And in your life when you fixed up this place," she guessed.

He put his hands on her hips. "We were gonna move in together. But we didn't do that, Izzy."

"You built this for her. You built the bathroom for her."

"I did but she never used either of them, Iz."

She swayed toward him and asked, "Is that for me?"

He was confused. "Is what for you?"

"All that reassurance, is it for me?"

He gave her the obvious answer. "Well...yeah."

"Okay," she started. "Then let me make it clear that you're not giving me any indication you're still hung up on her. I don't ever even think about it, until you take pains to reassure me you're not hung up on her. Our start was rocky, honey. Then it smoothed out. Notwithstanding, of course, Perry spraying gravel with his angry exit. But that wasn't about us. That was just something we had to deal with." She pressed her hand in his chest. "You can talk about her. You can talk about that time in your life. You can stop trying so hard to protect me from something that happened when I didn't even live in this town."

She swayed even closer so her breasts were brushing his chest.

"I *was* there last night when you were inside me," she told him. "And I *did* get what was communicated, Johnny. You keep trying to educate me but I knew exactly what kind of guy you were from the first moment I met you. So I know you aren't the guy who would lead me on, start something this intense if your heart and mind are with someone else. Shandra is history but that history is *your* history, and I want to know everything about you."

"I love that, baby," he said softly. "And it's me trying to reassure you about that but it's also the fact I know everybody in town is taking sides like there's a chance for Shandra when there isn't, and I know that, I wanna make sure *you* know that, but they don't know that. And I don't want you to hit town and hear shit that makes you doubt where we are. I want you to know where we are and if you hear shit, you can stand strong and know it's just that. Shit."

"I don't care what they think," she returned. "They aren't here.

They don't know. This closet isn't hers. It's yours. The bathroom isn't hers. It's yours. And she's not yours. I am."

He felt those words everywhere. Absolutely everywhere.

But with her that close, her tits brushing his chest, he felt them mostly in his balls and dick.

This meant his, "*Eliza,*" was a growl.

She ignored his tone and ordered, "So stop worrying about it." She then pulled out of his hold, took a step away, but turned her back to him and went on to say matter-of-factly, "Now I nearly dislocated a shoulder trying to get this dress zipped this morning. Can you do me a favor and unzip it?"

If there was nothing else in this world Johnny could do, he could do that.

So he took the step she'd moved away and unzipped her.

She stepped away again, rolled her shoulders so the dress fell off of them and then she slid it over her hips and let it drop to her ankles.

Johnny watched it go and enjoyed the show.

She turned around wearing a black strapless bra, black lace panties and her pumps and gave him a look.

He raised his brows. "Are you trying to seduce me, *spätzchen?*"

"You haven't tackled me yet," she whispered.

He had not.

Johnny didn't hesitate to rectify that mistake.

He lunged.

And Izzy went down without a fight.

EIGHTEEN
MOON IN THE FIFTH HOUSE

Johnny

"You know the constellations?"

"No. Mom did. She was always pointing them out. I never really saw them. Do you?"

"No."

"Then it's good we're not sailors."

Johnny chuckled.

They were lying on their backs on a blanket under the stars. Iz was at a slant to him and had her head on his gut. He was trailing a hand through her hair that flowed over his side. The fingers of his other hand were laced in hers and she had them pressed to the side of her tit.

Opposite Izzy, Ranger was lying with his back plastered down Johnny's leg, head on Johnny's hip.

Johnny's tent was pitched about ten feet away from them. It was a one-man deal but he'd zipped their two sleeping bags together, they were a snug fit, but they fit, and he figured they'd be totally good to make do with the limited space.

The fire was crackling about five feet away in the opposite direction to the tent.

It was the first and only night of their camping trip and the experience had made Johnny decide they'd have a lot more of them.

But even so, he figured he wouldn't need to buy a new tent.

It had been the first time in a while that he'd remembered they hadn't been together for very long.

Mostly this was because Izzy spent the day surprising him.

What he learned probably shouldn't have surprised him. She didn't complain much ever, really. She just got on with it.

And the "it" she just got on with was anything and everything. Not just her doing her thing with her pots and her plants and her friends and her sister and her animals and her land.

That day, she helped him load up Mist and then helped unload him and unhitch Ben's horse trailer before they took off to go camping.

The spot he camped was a mile and a half off the road. He'd packed her backpack and it was half the weight of his, but it didn't weigh five pounds. Since she didn't do this sort of thing, he figured that there would be a possibility that he'd need to shift some things around, take on extra weight with some of the stuff in her pack.

She'd hefted it up and didn't say a word.

She'd then walked a mile and a half with it on her back and she also didn't say a word except to talk about how it was so cool they were going to have good weather, or ask if he wanted her to take a turn with the cooler he was carrying or point out wildflowers and name them by name. "Look, Johnny, there's some yarrow..." "The foxtail is everywhere..." "Awesome, corn poppy..." "There's lupine... this place is filled with flowers. It's *amazing*."

He'd camped at this spot so many times he'd lost count and he'd never once seen the flowers.

Now he could say he liked lupine the best.

While he pitched the tent, he asked her to gather kindling for the fire and she did that, grabbing some small, downed branches when she did, carrying them back to the fire pit he'd created years ago and he knew others used besides him. She stacked it neatly, but far enough away from the pit that the dry tinder wouldn't be in danger of catching a spark.

And then they were there. They were set up. In doing that, they didn't have a disagreement or an argument. Iz was just along for the ride.

And liking it.

The only hiccup they had was when he took her to the edge of the river to teach her how to fish.

She seemed to like fishing and didn't get squeamish about the bait. The fish liked her too, and she caught two bluegill before he got his first fish. They were too small to eat so he showed her how to unhook them and toss them back in.

She didn't get squeamish about that either, to the point she watched her second bluegill swim away, turned to him and said, "This is fun!"

He grinned at her.

She immediately set about re-baiting her hook.

Five minutes later, he caught his first catfish and it was big enough for their dinner. So he immediately moved through spiking it and bleeding it out.

When he threw it aside and looked to her, she was pale and staring at the fish.

Her eyes drifted to his. "Um...you said you brought hotdogs in case we weren't lucky at the lake?"

He tried not to bust out laughing.

But the cooler he had not allowed her to carry had sandwich meat and cheese for their lunch, a six pack for him, a bottle of wine for her, tartar sauce for the fish, cream for their morning coffee, milk, eggs and butter for their morning pancakes and a packet of hotdogs in the very unlikely event he couldn't catch dinner for her.

"Did I just push you closer to vegetarianism?" he asked.

She swallowed and nodded.

He decided against teasing her by reminding her what was in a hotdog and instead leaned toward her, gave her a brush of his lips and moved back. "I got hotdogs."

"'Kay," she whispered.

She gave up on fishing then but she didn't leave him to it and she didn't give him shit about it.

She walked to their camp and came back with the book and pens she'd brought that he'd packed for her.

She then sat close to him, her knees up, her book on them, and she wrote in it, alternating between three pens and the times she'd stop to stroke Ranger, who'd gotten bored with fishing and was flat out at her side with his head in her lap.

Johnny didn't pry when she was journaling. He also didn't say anything when she put it away, stretched out her long legs in her shorts and tipped her face to the sun, focusing on petting Ranger and nothing else, clearly happy to just sit beside him while he was fishing and...be.

Margot never went camping or fishing. She'd cook a cleaned fish one of them caught, but she didn't want to know about it and further detested hiking, outdoor clothing that was "not feminine in the slightest so precisely what is the point?" as well as mosquitos, sleeping on the ground and not being within driving distance of a mall.

According to his dad, his mother had felt much the same way.

Shandra hiked and camped but got bored easily, and a trip couldn't last longer than it took a shower to wear off (her estimation, twenty-four hours) or they had to be in a campground that had showers and toilets, and camping in campgrounds was not Johnny's gig.

It was about being *in* nature. The quiet of it. Life slowing down and your brain slowing down with it. Not being in nature with a bunch of other people, noisy families, kids out just to get drunk and therefore loud, and a lot of people who didn't camp often who did stupid shit that could also be dangerous that drove Johnny right up the wall.

Eliza showed no signs of being bored. She said nothing when he caught his second fish, spiked it, bled it out or when he cleaned either of them (however, she didn't watch, mostly because he took them to a place she couldn't watch).

She helped him build a fire. She roasted her hotdog. He put his fish on aluminum foil and roasted them. They heated up a can of beans and shared them, eating straight from the can.

After they cleaned up, they made s'mores.

They sat through it all close together, Izzy leaning against him, one of each of their legs tangled.

They swapped stories. They laughed. They kissed a lot.

It was Izzy who got up first and put the blanket out for them to stare at the stars.

But Johnny didn't say a word against it.

It was the best day he'd had in a long time.

What made it better was having the understanding it was also the first of many.

Izzy brought him back to the present by sharing, "She was a Mercury in retrograde type of person."

"What's that mean?" he asked.

"I have no idea. But she did. She always talked about what planets were aligned and what that meant. She used to say things like, 'Venus is in the Twelfth House!' That, in particular, meant she'd met some guy she liked. Or, 'Clearly, Mars is in the Third House.' This she'd say when Addie or me were acting like know-it-alls."

Johnny chuckled again, staring at the stars and weaving her hair around his fingers.

"I should look it up, what all that means," she whispered. "I should translate my mom."

"Yeah," he whispered back.

She fell silent.

Johnny did too, staring at the stars, holding hands with Izzy.

"I hate him." She was still whispering but this one was fierce.

The stars blurred and Johnny felt his body get tight.

"Who, baby?" he asked gently.

"Dad," she answered. "I hate him."

He wrapped her hair around his fist like it was him giving her a reassuring hug and started, "Iz—"

"I lied," she stated.

"*Spätzchen*," he murmured.

"We weren't happy. We were poor. Mom worked hard. She dated guys she liked and thought she could love, but they didn't want a woman with kids or they just wanted a piece of ass or they drank too much and became jerks. She wanted to find love again. She wanted someone to help out too. She wanted stability, for her, for us. She wanted *more*. And Addie and me, we had to watch her go through that. Because of him."

Her tone was low but harsh and when she stopped speaking, Johnny said nothing. He didn't move. He didn't prompt her.

He just laid there and waited for her to get more out.

She did.

"Addie was right with what she said in my kitchen. I caught on to it before she did. I saw it. What she found in Perry was what Mom saw in Dad. Dad played the guitar and he was really good. He wrote his own songs and those were really good too. Or as good as I knew, being a little kid. They still seemed good. He was a great singer. He had such a beautiful voice. I remember those times. I remember those being the only good times with him. How he'd get. How he'd be all dreamy and lovey and happy. How he'd put his guitar aside and pull Mom in his lap and hold her close and kiss her. Or catch one of us girls and swing us up and tickle us and shout, 'I make beautiful babies!' But it wasn't that he didn't get the record deal or get discovered and he got frustrated and bitter. He wasn't even out of his twenties. There wasn't time for that. It was just how he was. It was just *who* he was."

Her fingers in his were getting tight, biting into the webbing, but Johnny just held on.

"I think it was the dreamer part of him," she declared. "I think she wanted to be there to watch him build his dream. Live it. I think she liked to think she was his muse. That he'd get off the road and come to us and we'd be his sanctuary against life on the road and his adoring fans. That when he was on tour, he'd step up to the mic and say, 'This is a song I wrote for the love of my life. For Daphne.' I think she wanted to grow tomatoes and string beads and raise his daughters and walk at his side into awards shows being gorgeous and proud and people would say, 'Look at her. The serenity. The beauty. No wonder he writes such amazing music.' I think that was her dream. I think that was the dream he fed her that she swallowed whole. And I think when it didn't happen, when it turned dark and ugly, it broke her in a way that could never be fixed."

Johnny let her give this story to him and the stars and said nothing.

"I think she escaped my grandfather," she continued. "I think my dad was the opposite of him. Free spirit. Romantic. She wanted peace. She wanted adventure. She wanted love. She found hell."

She found that for certain.

Izzy kept going.

"A couple of years after we left, his mother, my grandmother, she showed at the door. That was the only time in my life I saw my mother be ugly. She opened the door to that woman and poison spewed out. She yelled at Mom. Screamed in her face. *'What are you doing? How dare you keep his babies away from him? How dare you run away? He's just troubled! You stand by your man! You never run away!'*"

Izzy dragged in a jagged breath and let more of it out.

"Mom got right up in her face and yelled back, *'Troubled is not hitting your woman in the face with your fist and knocking her down only to kick her in the stomach, you bitch. That isn't standing by your man. That's falling for his shit. That's teaching your queens to be weak and that is* not *what my queens are gonna learn from me!*' She slammed the door in her face, turned to us and said, 'If you ever see that woman again you run. You run away as fast as you can. And you find me.' My grandmother banged on the door and shouted and Mom put us in our room and called the cops. I heard the murmurings. I don't know what happened but that woman never tried to find us again. She never sent money to help out and she was rich too. We never saw her again. She gave up. And that was it."

She fell silent and then started again, quieter.

"She cried that night, Mom did. That night my grandmother came and screamed in her face. I heard her. Woke up like I knew she was doing it and laid in the little narrow bed I shared with my sister because Mom couldn't afford to buy another bed. We were head to feet, the only way we could sleep in it and have room to move. And I listened to her cry. Sob. And I wonder to this day why she was crying. If she missed him. If she was brokenhearted because he'd killed her dream. If she wondered if she'd made the right choice not standing by him. If she thought maybe she should have tried to change him. If she was just angry and that was the way she let it out. Or if she was just tired of it all and she knew we had to pack up and move again the next day and she couldn't face it, which is what we did."

"You'll never know, baby," he whispered.

"No," she agreed. "I'll never know."

She took in a deep breath and Johnny waited.

Then she gave him more.

"So I hate him. I hate him because of cheap sandals and because he hit my mom in the face with his fist so hard he knocked her down and kicked her after she hit the floor. I hate him because I warmed up soup for my sister and me because Mom couldn't be there to cook for us and because all we could afford was soup. I hate him that he wasn't around to bury our dead cat and Mom and me had to do it, tears streaming down our faces. I hate him that he didn't take pictures of me before my prom, and I hate him that it seems like he doesn't even care he missed that or my sixteenth birthday or when I won my scholarship or when Addie broke her wrist showing off on that skateboard of her boyfriend's. I hate him because he broke my mom when she was with him and I hate him because he kept her broke after he was gone."

He heard her take another deep breath, this one hitched, and Johnny tightened, getting ready for what came next.

"We weren't happy. It was fake. We faked happy. My mom died after a life that ran her down because she worked so fucking hard, and one of the things she worked hard at was *faking happy*."

On the last two words her voice broke, so Johnny let go of her hair and hand and did a crunch to grab her under her arms, pulling her up and twisting her until he could lay her torso on top of his.

He rounded her with his arms, laid back.

Izzy shoved her face in his neck and wept.

Johnny stared at the stars and let her, holding her close with one arm, stroking her hair with another.

He gave it time.

Then he told her what he knew. What he saw in those pictures in her tack room.

"You actually were happy, *spätzchen*. You know that, right?"

She nodded with her face still in his neck.

"I...I...kn-know," she pushed out. "I'm just being dramatic."

"You're just being honest," he replied.

"I'm...I'm ruining our camping night."

"No way, Izzy. You ever give that up to anyone?" he asked.

She shook her head this time but didn't say anything.

"Then you just gave me something beautiful, baby. Precious. I'll remember it forever. So you're not ruining anything."

The stars disappeared when she lifted her head, eyes to his.

"You sure?" she asked.

He slid a hand to the side of her head and rubbed his thumb across her wet cheek.

"Yeah," he answered.

She studied him in the moonlight, wiped her hand across her

other cheek then scooted down a little and dropped her head to rest against his pec.

Johnny slid his hand in her hair again.

They lay together in silence for a while before she broke it.

"Mom said we should never hate anyone. But I can't help it, Johnny. I hate him."

"I hate him too and I didn't live through that, Iz. So give yourself a break, yeah?"

She nodded, her cheek and hair moving on his chest.

"Did you ever...I mean, you talk about your dad's folks but not your mom's. Did you at least have them?" she asked, turning the subject to him, he suspected to get it off where they were.

He decided she'd had enough so he allowed that.

"When we were older and we asked, Dad told us that Mom told him the home she grew up in was not a good one so she left the minute she could and never went back. Dad never even met them. He asked us if we wanted him to find them for us, and Toby made that decision, saying if we had her for the time we did and they didn't give a shit enough to find her, and doing that us, then he didn't think Dad should waste his time. I thought that was sound logic so I agreed and Dad honored that."

"It does sound like sound logic," she said.

"Yeah."

She took a deep breath, turned her head and rubbed her face in his chest in that way of hers that was so sweet, then she settled back in.

"What would you do if she came back?" she asked.

"Hear her out and make my decision," he answered then turned it on her. "What would you do if he came back?"

"I'd ask if I had any siblings, and if I did I'd ask where to find them and then I'd shut the door in his face," she answered.

Johnny grinned at the stars, murmuring, "That's my girl."

She sounded like she was smiling when she replied, "Yeah."

They fell into their own thoughts until Iz shifted, putting her chin to his chest. Lifting his head, he took his hand from her hair, put it behind his head and caught her eyes.

"I'm sorry I brought him—" she began.

"Shh," he shushed.

"With Perry showing and you throwing the plate—"

"Baby, did you not hear me say how much it means you gave me that?"

"You make me happy and I...now that I know how it feels when it's real, I guess I just—"

At that, he angled up taking her up with him and dragging her ass into his lap.

"You done with the stars and the moonlight or you wanna fuck out here under them?" he asked.

Her body jerked in surprise at his question.

He waited impatiently for her to answer it.

"I...well..." Her eyes darted side to side before coming back to his. "Is there anyone around us?"

"No clue."

"Well, if there is, do you think they'd take a walk at night?"

"Tent," he decided, surged up and took her with him when he did that too.

He had her hand in his and he was dragging her to the tent.

Ranger followed.

Ranger would have to wait outside for a while.

"Can we go back and gaze at the stars after?" she asked when Johnny had bent low to get into the tent.

He twisted his neck to look up at her. "After, if you can still move, we'll do anything you want."

He could swear he saw her face flush in the moonlight.

Johnny just pulled her into the tent behind him.

She couldn't move when he was done with her, so it was Johnny who had to move to go deal with the fire and let Ranger in.

Then he zipped his woman and himself in their double sleeping bag, she curled into him deep, Ranger arranged himself on their feet, and Johnny Gamble and his woman slept in a tent under the stars.

THAT NIGHT, Daphne Forrester would have said her daughter's moon was in the fifth house.

And she would have been right.

JOHNNY SAT in the grass by Izzy the next morning while they ate the pancakes he'd made for them over the fire.

She was staring at the fire, quiet.

He kicked her sock-covered foot with his.

She turned her head to him.

"Happy?" he asked.

"I have pancakes and Johnny, you have to ask?" she answered.

He felt his face get lazy and he bent in to kiss her.

When he turned his attention back to his pancakes, she whispered, "It's just that...I was thinking...it's not that I'm sad even though it's sad but it's a sad I'm used to. That is, I wanted something for her. Something she didn't really get. A long stretch of time when she didn't have to take care of us. Time when she could just be Daphne. Time when me and Addie could worry about the kids in our lives and she could just spoil them. Time when she could find a man and not have to worry about whether or not he wanted a readymade family, just know in her heart that he wanted Daphne. Time to ride my horses and tend her tomatoes. Time to help Addie show Brooks how to be a good man and time to teach my daughters how to make her facials. Time when she could just be happy."

Johnny didn't look at her.

But he did tangle one of his legs with hers.

She kept whispering.

"She shouldn't have looked for the dreamers. She should have found a man who knows all the different types of motor oil."

Christ, they'd had sex before he made her pancakes and now he needed to fuck her again.

"Iz?" he called.

"Yes, Johnny."

"So I have the strength to hike outta here, stop being sweet."

There was a smile in her voice when she said, "Message received, Ghostrider."

He gave a soft laugh.

"Johnny?" she called.

"Yeah, Iz."

"Can we come camping again?"

He looked at her and caught her eyes.

"Absolutely."

NINETEEN
FRUIT-INFUSED VODKA

Johnny

"Good Christ, woman! What's on your face?" Dave shouted half a second after he walked into Izzy's dining room.

Johnny followed him in, Charlie behind Johnny, Toby coming in after Charlie.

Once in, he saw Iz, Addie, Margot and Deanna sitting around Izzy's round white table, their asses on distressed white chairs. There were two weathered barn doors resting against a wall for some reason and a huge chandelier that was almost bigger than the table hanging low over it that you'd have to look close to see the crystals that were missing.

Johnny had looked close.

There were fifteen crystals missing.

He moved around the table to give all the men room to join them, but also to get to his woman, and he did this with his eyes on Izzy's face, a big smile on his mouth.

Her face was covered in goo.

White goo with bits in.

"This, my girls, is why the magic happens *without* the man in your life bearing witness to it," Margot drawled to the women around the table. She turned to Dave. "And David, please, I beg you for the five hundred and fifteenth time in our marriage, do not take the Lord's name in vain."

"This is not an answer to what you got all over your face, Margot," Dave replied.

She swept a hand along the air at the side of her white goo slathered face like she was a model demonstrating high-end facial care. "It's a facial mask as concocted by Adeline that her mother taught her to make that I already can feel wrings miracles."

Johnny made it to Izzy and he bent toward her as she twisted her neck to look up at him, getting a whiff of yogurt and honey when he got close.

He then made a remark out loud that he thought in his head on more than a rare occasion.

"I don't know whether to kiss you or eat you."

She rolled her eyes.

He decided to kiss the top of her head.

After he did that he looked at her again.

"I'm gooey and you're filthy," she murmured.

It was three Saturdays after their camping trip.

Three Saturdays with three good weeks in between of family and friends, and them just being together punctuated only by the need to sleep in order to keep going and work in order to afford to eat (or Izzy's work was that, Johnny was stinking rich and could have quit but then he'd be bored stiff and working on cars anyway so he might as well do it and make his garage more money).

Addie was off work at the grocery store that day so the women decided to have a girls' day out, which meant the men could have a boys' day.

They'd all started it meeting at Izzy's and going their separate ways with the plan to meet back and mix genders for dinner.

Brooks was the odd man out, considering he couldn't reach the grips on an ATV, so he had to stick with the women.

"Too bad with all this company we can't take a shower," he murmured back.

"Johnathon, please. No sexual innuendo at a lady's dining room table," Margot scolded. "It's crass."

Johnny straightened and looked at her. "It wasn't innuendo, Margot. It was just sexual."

Toby busted out laughing. Charlie chuckled. Dave shook his head at him, but did it grinning. Deanna and Addie smiled at each other.

Margot's eyes narrowed. "We're sampling Eliza's excellent infused vodkas and I'm in a chipper mood. I'd thank you not to upset that."

"I'd thank you too. My woman's gonna feel good about her skin and be drunk, this bodes good things," Dave delivered his own sexual innuendo, leaning into the table, grabbing the bottle that was closest that looked like it had strawberries and mint leaves in it, pouring a healthy dose into the glass in front of Margot and then he leaned back and shot the whole thing.

"David, you *sip*," Margot snapped.

Dave put the glass down, ignored his wife and winked at Izzy. "I don't even know what that was but you got my approval, child."

Izzy beamed at him.

"I hope you all have changes of clothes seeing as you all need showers before we feed you," Margot declared. She then turned to Izzy. "Take note of this, darlin'. In case you weren't aware, ATV stands for *all-terrain vehicle*, and when they're on one, they attempt to discover every type of terrain they can, the muddier, the better."

Izzy, apparently unaffected by her man having dried mud caked up to his hips, just nodded and replied, "So noted, Margot."

"I'm gonna go home and shower," Charlie said then bent and kissed Deanna under her ear. "I'll be back for dinner."

"Iz, can I jump in your shower?" Toby asked.

"Sure," Izzy answered.

"It's my shower at this juncture so you should ask me," Addie put in. "Unless you're going to the master."

"I'm in the master," Johnny stated.

"Adeline, can I use your shower?" Toby asked.

"Sure," she answered on a big grin.

He shook his head at her and strolled out, Charlie following him.

Dave took a chair that was against the wall and started twisting it to the table.

"*Halt!*" Margot shouted.

Dave froze.

"Do you think you're sitting in your muddy jeans in Eliza's chair?" she asked.

"It's chipped and dented and has no pad," he stated.

"It's *shabby chic*," Margot returned with emphasis on words Dave didn't understand and even if he did, he wouldn't give that first shit about.

"It's fine, really. I have cats, dogs, and these chairs cost me four dollars each," Izzy entered the conversation. "Except the one Deanna's sitting in had a missing leg so I got that one thrown in for free. Anyway, a home is a home, not a showplace. Everyone is welcome, muddy jeans and all."

"See?" Dave asked his wife.

"You'll remain standing until you're showered," Margot returned.

"Both showers are taken 'cause Tobe has no respect for his elders," Dave shot back. "And I'm sitting," he declared, finished twisting his seat and then he put his ass in it.

Margot turned to Izzy. "You should take note of this as well, my beautiful girl. He's quite right. Tobias should have let David go first. He's also demonstrating how he doesn't respect *me* by sitting in that chair. Don't let that start. If you do, it never stops."

"I respected you enough when I paid that credit card bill yesterday," Dave retorted and looked at Johnny. "Take note, son. Seven-hundred-dollar shoes. And I'm not even kidding."

He felt Izzy's gaze and looked down at her.

"I'd never buy seven-hundred-dollar shoes unless they were seriously on sale," Izzy told him.

"It comes to a time I'm paying our credit card bill, feel free to buy as many seven-hundred-dollar shoes as you want," he replied.

"I love him," Deanna declared.

"Easy for him to say, he's a millionaire," Dave muttered.

Izzy's eyes in the goo got huge.

Fuck.

"You're a millionaire?" she whispered.

Damn.

"Yeah," he grunted.

"Oh...my...God!" Addie shouted. "I take it back! I'm totally letting you pay my attorney's fees!"

Brooks, in his mom's lap, squealed with glee.

"Iz?" he called when she just stared at him.

"I've always wanted a pair of Louboutins," she said softly.

He grinned, bent his head and kissed her hard.

He got goo all over his mouth and chin.

But she tasted great.

After dinner, Johnny stood at the back door in the kitchen looking out the window.

Izzy was on the porch, standing as well, directly opposite him, and watching what was happening in the backyard through the screen.

She was goo-less, in a pretty sundress, arms and legs tanned, no shoes, no makeup, hair in a ponytail at the base of her neck streaming down her back, and he only had her profile but he saw a small, happy smile on her face.

He looked beyond her to what was making her happy.

In the yard under the tree that still was hung with crystals and strung with Christmas lights that were not yet turned on because the sun was just beginning to set, Toby had hold of Brooks and was swinging him around, dipping him down, lifting him up, like he was flying.

The kid had a look on his face like he was frozen in laughter, experiencing bliss.

Addie was ass to the grass close by, Frisbee in hand, winging it, after which Swirl, Dempsey and Ranger took off after it.

But she didn't watch to see which dog got the Frisbee.

She looked right at Toby and her son.

Shit.

"I don't know who's falling faster. Her for him or him for that baby boy," Margot said from his side.

Johnny turned to her.

"Or him for her," she finished. "It's a tossup."

"She's in the middle of divorcing her husband, who it's my understanding she loved," Johnny informed her.

"Time moves on, my sweet Johnathon," she replied. "And love never really dies, but it does fade, as you well know."

He looked back at Izzy.

"And when it fades, the part that remains teaches us how to love better the next time," she said softly, putting her hand on his forearm.

He pulled it away but only to catch her fingers and lift them up to press to his chest.

But he didn't reply.

He set his eyes back to the yard.

"Tobe doesn't do relationships," he said.

"People change."

Johnny looked back to her. "He's not going to take his first test drive with Adeline."

Her gaze drifted to the window. "He's going to do what Tobias has always done. Whatever he wishes."

"Margot—"

She cut her gaze back to him. "My love, he would tear out his own heart before he did anything that might harm yours." Her fingers squeezed his. "You have nothing to fear."

"I don't like it," he shared.

"Well, first, it's your job as his big brother not to like pretty much everything he does until he proves to you that he can do it well. It's both your lots, I'm afraid, and there's no escaping it. And second, you're so blind in love with Eliza it's taking everything you have not to hammer a wall made of iron around her to protect her from anything that might hurt her. And something that might hurt her sister will hurt her. So you've got twice as much to get over when that," she tilted her head to the window in the door, "takes root."

"He doesn't even know if he's staying in Matlock," Johnny said.

She raised a brow. "And he can't take her and Brooks with him should he decide to go?"

"That would devastate Izzy. She loves having her sister close."

She smiled. "Ah, there's that iron wall."

Johnny felt his lips hitch, but he shook his head and looked back to the yard even as he pressed her hand closer to his heart.

After a turn around the yard, probably just to get some alone time since they hadn't seen each other most of the day and Johnny had noticed the two were not just a married couple, but a *couple*, Deanna and Charlie were strolling up to Toby. Deanna had again worn heels that day, but she was walking barefoot in the grass now, though the straps of her sandals dangled from her husband's fingers.

Johnny took note of that.

Dave was latching the gate on the stables. He'd just brought in Izzy's horses while Margot and Johnny did the dishes and the rest Margot had ordered, "Had done enough...so *get*."

This, even though she didn't let anyone do anything. She'd pushed out the women so she could cook, and then she'd pushed out everyone except Johnny so they could clean up.

No one said dick. Even if most of them knew her a short time, they'd all learned this was Margot's way.

Toby now had Brooks around his neck, walking toward Dave with Deanna and Charlie closing in.

Addie was watching Johnny's brother and her son go.

Izzy was pushing through the back door.

He felt it as Margot moved closer to him and he felt it as she curled the fingers of her other hand over both of theirs.

"It will be just fine."

"When we were camping, she told me a lot about her mother and father. I already knew he beat her mother and her mom's parents refused to let her come home so they were on the run and had nothing. They never got anything either, no matter how hard Iz's mom worked. They only had each other. Daphne, Izzie and Addie. That was all they had."

"That's terrible," Margot murmured her understatement, the timbre of it sharing just how terrible she thought it was.

"Thank God for you," he whispered.

"Pardon?"

He turned his head and looked her direct in the eyes.

"Thank God for you. Dave and you. Thank God Dad had you so he could give you to us. If he hadn't, I wouldn't have a lot of things, Margot. Too many to name. It'd take a week just to get through table manners. But there's a new one now. And that would be, if I didn't have you, I wouldn't know how to love her like she needs me to do it."

Tears brightened her eyes and she tried to slip her hand away, because Margot was the kind of woman who left the room to have her emotion in private, probably because she'd spent most of her life around men and she thought they had no clue how to deal with it.

Except those men had her too so she was wrong about that.

In other words, Johnny's hold only got tighter so she wouldn't slip away.

"She lost her mom and mourns her like that happened yesterday. She blossoms when she's anywhere near you. You try to act the diva, sweetheart, but you can't help but just give and give. Thank you for giving that back to Izzy."

"Stop," she whispered.

He didn't stop.

"Mother-son dance," he said softly.

Her eyes got brighter.

"You've already done it three times, you up for a fourth?" he asked.

She swallowed.

She sniffed.

She squared her shoulders.

Then she declared on a tight squeeze of his hand, "Most certainly."

She gave him that and it was not the first time she gave him something for which he'd be forever grateful.

But she was Margot.

So she wasn't done.

"However, as I also intend to stand in for another important role, you best prepare Eliza. Because everyone knows, a girl's wedding is not her own. It's the dream wedding her mother always wanted, and if not that, it's the wedding her mother determines she should have. And I birthed three boys and helped raise two more. The first three's women had mothers. Now, it's my turn."

To that, Johnny busted out laughing.

THE SUN WAS DOWN.

The Christmas lights in the tree were on.

The infused vodka had again been unearthed.

Blankets had been brought out and spread in the grass.

So they sat under moonlight, Christmas lights and crystals, one couple each to their own blanket, sucking back vodka, talking and laughing, both quietly because Addie was giving her son his night-time bottle.

Johnny was frowning at his brother who was stretched out on

Addie's blanket with her, watching her feed her son like he'd never seen anything more beautiful.

"Johnny, honey, can you pass me the ginger and peach bottle?" Izzy asked softly.

He reached to the bottle of vodka he guessed was ginger and peach because it had peaches in it as well as something that looked like cut up garlic cloves (a bottle he had, until she just said that, avoided because he wasn't thinking he'd be a big fan of peach and garlic).

He turned and handed it to her.

She took it with a, "Thanks, *häschen*."

He said nothing.

He just stared at Izzy's face in the moonlight and Christmas lights, seeing right then, next to him on a blanket, with their people around them, she was not happy.

She was what she thought her mother wanted to be.

She was in her place.

She was where she'd always wanted to be.

She was serene.

He'd thought he'd never seen a more beautiful woman than the woman he'd seen with her daughters in those pictures in Izzy's stables.

But that changed right then.

Eliza set the bottle in the grass by their blanket and lifted her eyes to his.

She tipped her head to the side. "You okay?"

"Best ever, baby."

She smiled.

And there was the happy.

So Johnny forgot his brother on Addie's blanket.

Izzy was happy.

Therefore so was Johnny.

AND THEY'D RIDE that the next day, Sunday, when he loaded up Izzy and his dog in the morning and he spent the entire day with her in bed at the mill.

And they'd keep riding it, falling asleep together and waking up together the next morning.

It wouldn't be until Monday afternoon when Izzy's serenity was shattered, when her world of moonlight and crystals and fruit-infused vodka and good people all around that Johnny knew she'd worked her entire life to find her way to fell apart.

And when it did, everyone on those blankets plummeted straight into hell.

TWENTY
CAN YOU GO FASTER?

Johnny

Monday afternoon, Johnny was washing grease off his hands when his phone in his coveralls rang.

Normally he would ignore it.

Izzy in his life, he did not.

He grabbed some paper towel, did a quick swipe, and with still mostly wet hands, he pulled out his phone.

It was Iz.

He took the call, put the phone to his ear and answered, "Hey, spätzchen."

"Johnny."

A red-hot iron spike rammed down his back and his head jerked around until his eyes found Toby, who was bent over a car.

As if he felt it, felt what Johnny heard in Izzy's voice, his brother's head came up and they locked eyes.

"Iz, what's going on?" he growled.

"Johnny," she repeated in that awful voice.

"Talk to me," he demanded as Toby pulled out from under the hood.

"I...I—" She was losing it.

"Give it to me, baby girl," he heard Deanna say.

Deanna.

Deanna was with her.

They worked together.

But he did and did not like knowing Deanna was with her when she sounded like that.

The good part was that Deanna was with her.

The bad part was *she sounded like that.*

Johnny thought his head would explode as he waited and listened to the phone jostle while watching Toby move quickly toward him.

"Johnny?" Deanna asked.

"Deanna, what's happening?" he bit out.

"Okay, now, okay, *damn,*" she replied, sounding freaked and tortured at the same time.

"Deanna," he said warningly.

"Okay, no way to say this easy so I'll say it fast. Someone took Brooks from the daycare center."

Johnny tore the shoulder on his coveralls down his arm, ripping the buttons at the front clean off.

"It was naptime," she continued. "The lady minding them got called out of the baby room. When she got back, she didn't notice at first. Then she did. They looked around for him, but the lady that runs the place right away called the cops because all the babies are in cribs so they shouldn't be able to get out. They called Addie at the grocery store. She came straight away. He's...he's...Johnny." Her voice dropped. "No one knows where he is."

He heard Izzy's sob in the background as he stepped out of his coveralls, kicking them away. "Where's Addie now?"

"*Fuck,*" Toby hissed.

"That's why we're calling 'cause we're trying to get there fast but you can get there faster and she's lost it, Johnny. She's a mess. You gotta get to the daycare."

"On my way," he said, sprinting toward the door of the bay, feeling Toby on his heels. "Tell Izzy I'm on my way. I'll be there in five minutes. Yeah?"

"I'll tell her, Johnny."

"See you soon," he said.

"Soon," she said back, her voice cracking.

Fuck.

Deanna wasn't hard but she was strong and she was one of the most together women he'd ever met. She wouldn't break down in any situation.

Except this one.

He shoved the phone in his back pocket and dug his keys out of the front.

"Johnny!" Toby shouted from close at his back.

He stopped at his truck door and turned back to his brother. "Tell Ray we're closing down the bay. The Meyers aren't getting their car today. Then close down the bay, get in your truck and meet me at the daycare center."

Toby's face, already alert, blanked as he prepared to get shitty news.

"Brooks okay?" he asked.

"Brooks is missing."

That was when he watched Toby's face get hard.

Johnny didn't hesitate longer.

He hauled open his door, knifed into his truck, started it up and took off.

ADDIE RACED to him the minute she saw him enter the front doors of the daycare center, crying an agonized, "Johnny!"

When she made it to him, she hit him so hard he nearly went down and to stop it had to step back on a foot.

He put his arms around her, hers were around him, but she yanked them free and latched onto his neck so tight, her nails dug into the flesh. She snapped her head back and the first close look at her face cut through him like a blade.

"Someone took my baby," she whispered.

"Okay, *mäuschen*," he murmured. "I got ya. Hang tight."

"I should have...I should have let Margot watch him," she said.

"This is not your fault," he returned firmly.

"I didn't want to take advantage."

"Addie, this is not your fault."

"I didn't...things were going so great with you and Iz, I didn't want your family to think I was a freeloader.'"

Christ, the Forrester Girls.

"Adeline, listen to me," he demanded. "*It is not your fault.*"

"They said, the staff said...they think he came in and hid. Waited for his chance."

Shit.

"See, sweetheart, not your fault," he told her. He lifted his eyes to the cops who came his way. "What's happening?" he asked.

"This your girl, Johnny?" Cary, one of the cops and someone Johnny had known and liked since high school, asked with surprise in his voice, but also something deeper.

"Her sister," he clipped. "Now what's happening?"

Cary nodded. "Okay, just to assure you, we have men out looking."

"Looking for what?" Johnny demanded.

"A man was seen entering the daycare. The way he did, the woman who saw him thought he was a dad. Though interviewing the staff, no one recognized his description. Also interviewing the staff, no one saw him. Not anywhere. But this woman, a lady that lives across the street, she hangs out on her porch. She saw him come in, and about twenty minutes later, she says he exited with a little boy. A baby. She thought it was peculiar because he didn't have, well..." his gaze flicked to Addie, "a baby seat in his car."

Addie's nails dug in deeper and ice filled Johnny's veins at the thought of Brooks unrestrained in a car.

"And this man? What's he look like?" Johnny asked but didn't wait for the answer. He looked down at Addie. "Did you tell them about Perry?"

She nodded.

"Kent?" he asked.

She blinked. "Kent?"

"Izzy's ex."

"Oh my God," she breathed, brightened, took her hands from him and turned to the cops, babbling, "Kent. Kent's crazy. Kent's got a restraining order. Kent's my sister's ex. He's tall. Not as tall as Johnny. Blond. Dark blond, not light. Like, almost red but not red. Blond. Mostly. And...and..."

"Text your sister, sweetheart," he murmured. "Get her to send a picture of Kent."

She nodded and dug her phone out of her pocket.

"The guy was redheaded," Zach, the other cop, muttered. He was a man Johnny knew from having the occasional beer with him at Home but he was younger, younger than Toby, so he didn't know him well.

Jesus, Izzy's creepy ex kidnapped her fucking nephew.

Jesus, now he had to stop himself from murdering Izzy's crazy fucking ex who had kidnapped Brooks.

"Johnny, can I have a sec?" Cary asked.

Johnny looked at him and did it closely.

What he saw made him turn back to Addie. "Gonna have a chat, sweetheart. You get that text, you show this man, yeah? I'll be right back."

She nodded again.

He curled his fingers around the back of her neck, gave it a squeeze, and hoped to Christ Toby was quick with closing that bay so someone would be with her that wasn't a cop.

Then he followed Cary down a hall under the gaze of hovering staff members of the daycare center, most of their eyes red, all of them terrified.

When they were out of earshot, Cary stopped and turned to Johnny in a way that Johnny didn't like because he had his back to Addie.

Cary didn't fuck around.

"Because of her concern about the car seat, the lady took note of the make and model of the car and she got a partial plate. We ran what she got and the car that popped up was reported stolen in Missouri two weeks ago."

Shit.

Was Izzy's creepy ex that crazy?

"Also, Johnny," Cary continued, "the description of the man given describes Stu."

Johnny felt his gut drop, his heart constrict, his throat close and his hands form into fists.

Even though he couldn't see most of it, Cary didn't miss any of this.

"Keep it tight, Johnny," he warned.

Stu.

Stuart.

Stuart Bray.

Shandra's brother.

"You hear from him?" Cary asked.

"No," Johnny forced out.

"Seen him?" Cary went on.

"No," Johnny repeated tightly.

"Shandra?" Cary continued.

Johnny gave his head a short shake.

"Guy's always been trouble," Cary noted.

"Ransom," he pushed out and saw Cary perk up.

"Say again?"

"He knows I got money. More than once Shandra came to me to get his ass out of a sling. I didn't see him but that doesn't mean he wasn't out there, watching me. Half the time, before you step on it, you don't see the snake in the grass. It's only when you get too close does the copperhead give you warning."

"That's your girl's sister. Her son—"

"Her son's gonna grow up my nephew," Johnny cut him off to say. "So yeah, he means something to me. He's family. That would be hard to miss. We all go out together. We were out at JerryJack's Diner for burgers just this last Thursday, me, Tobe, Iz, Addie and Brooks."

They were.

Toby had Brooks most the time so Addie could eat.

But Johnny and Izzy had had him too.

He wasn't passed around, as such. He crawled around because he could get away with that because he was a baby with four adults who thought he turned the world.

Cary's eyes had wandered and Johnny twisted at the waist to see Toby was there and had Addie tucked tight to his body, her face buried in his chest.

"I see," Cary muttered, and Johnny twisted back.

"She needs to get home and we need to get out there looking for him," Johnny stated, and Cary's gaze cut back to him.

"Johnny, take her home and let us worry about this."

"Your nephew was kidnapped would you stay home with his mother?"

"I'm a cop," Cary pointed out.

"And as such you would have no business working a case that personally involves you but you'd do it anyway, wouldn't you?"

Cary gave him a squinty-eyed look, it cleared and he muttered, "Fuck."

Johnny turned on his boot and stalked to his brother and Addie.

"You take her home. I'll call Iz and Deanna and tell them to reroute there. Then I'll call Dave and Margot to come over."

"You wanna give me the lowdown?" Toby formed a question that was a demand.

"At Izzy's. Let's get her somewhere safe and familiar."

Toby gave him a glower before he nodded and started to move Addie.

She stood solid and grabbed on to Toby's tee. "What if they bring him back here?"

"They're not gonna bring him back here, honey," Toby whispered. "When he comes home, he'll come *home* so let's get *you* home. Yeah?"

She stared at him, her face searching then it set, and Johnny knew she was going to dig in but then it went slack and she said, "Yeah, Toby."

Toby gave Johnny a look and led her out.

Johnny yanked his phone out of his jeans and followed them.

HE MADE his first two calls quick, on the road, tailing Toby and Addie.

The last call he made, they were out of town, close to Izzy's, and he pulled off to the shoulder to do it.

She answered after two rings.

"Johnny?"

"Cops at the daycare center where Eliza's nephew was kidnapped this afternoon say the kidnapper looks like Stu."

"Mother of God," she whispered.

"You get 'hold of your *fucking* brother, Shandra, and you make him bring that boy to me."

"Stu wouldn't—"

"He would."

"Not a baby."

"*He would.*"

"And not you. He wouldn't hurt you."

"I'm not to you what I was before."

"He still loves you and he knows I do too so he would never—"

"He needs money and he's desperate and he'll do anything he has to do to make sure one person is all right. *Stu*. Now you fucking *call him*, Shandra, and get me back my *boy*."

"I'll call him, Johnny. Right now."

He didn't thank her and he didn't say goodbye.

He disconnected, checked his mirrors, pulled back on the road and drove to Izzy's.

"You'll get him?"

"I'll get him."

"You'll bring him back?"

"I'll bring him back."

"You'll bring him home?"

"I'll bring him home, *spätzchen*."

Eliza had hold on him almost like her sister except her hands were gripping his head right behind his ears and her body was pressed tight to his.

Her face was pale. Her eyes were haunted. And her hold was so hard, if she had it in her, she'd crush his head.

He'd had to tell her. He'd had no choice. When this was over, that was something he couldn't keep from her and still keep her. So while Margot and Deanna saw to Addie in the kitchen, he'd taken her aside and told her. It was up to her if she shared.

But Eliza, like Toby and Dave, both he'd shared it with before she got home, knew he suspected Shandra's brother.

That did not rock her or make her look at him with revulsion.

It made her visibly fill with hope.

But even if she could get past it, when he found Stu and beat him bloody, he'd still get another few licks in just for Johnny having to tell his woman his ex's brother kidnapped their boy.

She yanked his head down so his forehead collided with hers.

Staring him in the eye, hers burning, she forced out a guttural, "*Go.*"

Then she released him.

He bent in quick to touch her mouth with his and he turned.

His eyes slicing through Toby, Dave and Charlie, who had arrived five minutes earlier, all of them standing close to Johnny and Izzy in her front hall, he growled, "Let's roll."

They followed him out of Izzy's front door, across the porch and down the steps.

"Charlie, you're with me. Dave, you're with Toby," Johnny ordered.

"We can spread out, cover more area if we all take our own trucks," Toby returned.

He stopped and looked at his brother. "You know him. Before he went bad, you were friends with him. You know his hangouts, his friends, the women he's been with, they don't. You cover the ones east and north. We'll cover the ones south and west. You run out of options, you call me and I'll give you more. Ben's out with a bud, he's heading to that hunting cabin Shandra's dad had. But this way, we get in a situation, it's better two men against one than one man alone against whatever he's got going on in his head. Be smart. Let Dave drive. You navigate. Now roll out."

What he didn't say was that it was also better that they found him. God only knew what Stu Bray would do if cornered by cops, and Johnny didn't want Brooks anywhere near that situation. He was already having severe difficulty dealing with the situation as it stood. Stu trapped and desperate and Brooks with him, Johnny couldn't even allow himself to contemplate.

Toby took a beat before he nodded then sprinted toward Dave's truck, a truck Dave was already in and had running.

Johnny turned to Charlie. "You drive."

"Gotcha," Charlie grunted, not hiding he was keeping his shit together by a thread and that thread was unravelling.

They jogged to Charlie's truck and both of them angled in.

Charlie was kicking up dust and gravel when he asked, "South or west first?"

"South," Johnny told him. "Toby fill you in on who we're looking for?"

"Yep."

"Right. There's a dive bar down south Stu hung out at."

"He'd take a kidnapped baby to a dive bar?"

"He banged the owner on and off. She lives over it and he'd take Brooks there."

"Right."

Charlie peeled down Izzy's drive.

When they made it down the lane to the road, he turned south.

"Jesus Christ, seriously?"

Her name was Sharlane. She still owned the dive bar. And as Johnny had thought practically every time he'd seen her, she'd be very pretty if she wasn't so obviously hard as nails.

"Would I joke about that shit?" Johnny growled.

"The cops came by before you but they didn't say *why*. Fucking hell." She ended that on a mutter.

"Sharlane, his mom has known he's been missing now for nearly two hours. If you got anything on Stu—" Johnny said.

She whipped out her phone. "Give me your number. I see him, I'll call you, Johnny."

"I walk out of here, I can trust that?" Johnny asked.

She pinned him with a look. "Left me high and dry with a bun in the oven, an abortion bill to pay and did it stealing seventy-three bucks from my wallet. He's not gonna come back here. But if he's stupid enough to do that, I'll give him a place to hide out. Then my first call will be you. You'll have five minutes, Johnny. Because my second call will be the cops."

Right.

He could trust that.

And Johnny wondered briefly if Stu knocking up Sharlane was the reason he'd knocked over a bank three years ago.

If it was, he'd have taken her with him, not Shandra, or at least have left her some cash to cover the medical bills.

So Johnny figured he was doing what Stu did.

Fucked-up shit that was just about Stu.

He gave her his number and then said, "Obliged, Sharlane."

"It goes down, it'll be my pleasure, Johnny."

Johnny gave Charlie a look and they headed out.

"He was seeing a single mother who worked at the bank in Bellevue," Johnny told him when they were in the truck. He didn't tell him the part about Stu seeing her to get intel on how to rob her bank. "Let's head there."

"Jesus, how many stupid bitches did this jackass bang?" Charlie asked, pulling out of the parking lot.

"We'll just say it could be long night," Johnny said as answer.

"We got a problem," Charlie stated.

Johnny looked his way. "A bigger problem than Brooks missing?"

"No, but see, we actually find that jackass before the cops do, ain't no way I'll keep my hands off him and ain't no way you'll keep your hands off him. I think this same situation is happening in Dave's truck. Dave's an old guy but I figure he can haul out a can of some whoop ass, anyone harms anyone that you boys got in your hearts. Plus, he's a dad. He cares about Brooks and Addie *and* he feels her pain. So we gotta make a pact and hope to Christ they're making one in Dave's truck too. But the way Toby is with that boy, I'm thinking there's no prayer of that happening. But we can't think on that. We gotta have a plan. So if I get there first, you gotta stop me from murdering him. If you do, I'll stop you."

"Don't wade in too soon," Johnny replied.

"Oh, I won't," Charlie promised.

They drove.

Johnny's phone rang.

He pulled it out and his mouth got tight at the name on the screen.

He took the call and put the phone to his ear.

"Norma," he began, "not sure what this is but—"

"I know," she cut him off, "everyone knows, word about what's happening spread through Home like a wildfire, 'spect it's doing the same all through Matlock. So I'll make this quick, son."

"Obliged," he muttered.

"I'm in my car. Sally's in hers. We're on the way to your woman's place."

Johnny did not like that at all.

"Norma—"

She spoke over him. "Folks are thinkin' best way to help is get on the roads lookin' for Stu. I can't stop that. Others think best way to help is go see to your women. Sally and me disagree so just to say, we're heading out to Eliza's acres and we're gonna park across her lane and send people on their way. Make sure they got privacy while you're handlin' this situation."

Johnny hadn't thought about word getting out or what that would mean.

But now confronted with it, he decided Sally was going to get much bigger tips from now until the last drink he drank at Home, and he didn't know what he'd do for Norma, but it would be something.

"That'd be appreciated, Norma," he replied. "But you hear anyone talking, they find Stu, they call me first. Don't know what's in his head, never did, but think he'll react better he sees me or I can call Shandra in and he'll listen to her."

"Gotcha," Norma replied. "I'll spread that word. Find him, Johnny. Now letting you go."

And then she did just that, disconnecting.

When Johnny took his phone from his ear, Charlie asked, "What was that?"

"Townsfolk of Matlock are getting in the hunt, which I can't think about right now. But some are also thinking of heading out to make sure Adeline and Eliza are okay. Norma, woman who owns Home, is heading out with her bartender to barricade Izzy's lane and shut that down."

"Good," Charlie murmured.

He drove.

Johnny sat next to him, trying to keep his shit together.

His phone rang.

Johnny lifted it and his heart squeezed at the name on the screen.

He took the call and put the phone to his ear.

"This better be what I want to hear."

Mercifully, Shandra told him what he wanted to hear.

"Meet me at the shack. I have the baby. I'm so sorry, Jo—"

He cut her off. "My shack?"

"Yes," she said softly.

"Stu took him to *my shack?*"

"I'm so, *so* sorry, Jo—"

"He there?"

"No."

This was probably good.

"We'll be there in twenty," he told her.

"Okay."

He hung up. "Swing a left at the first light in Bellevue. Shandra's got Brooks. I'll make the call to Dave and Toby but I'm not calling Izzy or the cops until we've got Brooks."

"Jesus. Holy Christ. Lord, Lord, Lord," Charlie whispered.

Johnny closed his eyes and focused on settling his heart.

This failed so he opened his eyes and said, "Can you go faster?"

CHARLIE WAS BIGGER than him and driving, so even though they both ran flat out, Johnny had his door open and was out of the truck before Charlie had come to a full stop, which meant he beat him to the porch.

He vaguely noticed the glass in the window of the door of the shack was busted.

He just ran in.

Shandra was standing five feet in, holding a fretting Brooks.

Johnny went right to her and pulled him out of her arms.

Brooks looked at him, hooked an arm around one side of his neck and buried his face in the other side.

He might be eight months old but he wasn't dumb.

Johnny wrapped both arms around him and held him close.

"You're home, son. It's good," he murmured.

Brooks nuzzled his face in Johnny's neck like Izzy did to his chest.

And only then did Johnny's heart settle.

Charlie was standing behind him and Johnny turned to him.

"Call them. Tell them he's safe and we're bringing him home."

Charlie nodded, shot a dark look at Shandra and walked out.

"Johnny," she said.

He turned to her.

"This isn't on you," he said.

"I still feel—"

"But swear to Christ, Shandra, if you don't impress on him that me, Izzy, Addie, Toby, Margot, Dave, anyone who has dick to do with me as well as the entire town of Matlock is off limits to him, I will hunt him down myself and I'll make sure that message is received and then I'll deliver his ass to the goddamned police."

"He's in a spot."

Was she fucking serious?

"I don't give a fuck."

"I'm not defending him," she returned. "I told you we were done. This wasn't the last straw. That already happened. I've already called the police and told them what happened and where I suspect he'll go. He handed over the baby and took off. If I thought I could get the baby safe and keep him here, I would have done it so they could arrest him here. But I had to look after the baby and he knows you. He didn't hang around."

"Your brother kidnapped a baby to hold him for ransom."

Her eyes filled with tears.

"Get out of Matlock, Shandra. Not for me. Not so you won't have to watch what's gonna happen next with me and Eliza. For you. Scrape your brother off, your folks off and find something for you. You don't, they'll find ways to keep dragging you down while tearing pieces from you and you'll be buried in shit with nothing left."

"I should never have gone with him," she whispered, tears wetting her cheeks.

"No, you shouldn't have," Johnny agreed.

And still holding Brooks close, he turned and walked out of the shack.

NORMA SAW them coming and she ran to her truck while Sally jogged to her car to jump in and then pull them back so they could drive right in.

Toby and Dave were already there.

Everyone was hanging on the front porch, but it was only Addie who came racing off it toward Charlie's truck.

Charlie swung a sharp left and stopped a truck-length away from the other vehicles in order not to hit her.

Johnny opened his door and had barely stepped out before Brooks was pulled from his arms.

Brooks did exactly what he did with Johnny to his mother as she cupped the back of his head, held him tight, and swung him side to side, her lips to his baby fuzz, tears streaming down her cheeks.

"Come on, darlin', come on, child," Margot whispered, arms around Addie, gently pulling her around. "Let's get this precious bundle inside, give him a once-over and get some food in his belly. Come, come, come on, my beautiful girl."

Addie moved with her and Margot's gaze lifted to Johnny's. Relief and pride were stamped in it.

They walked away and Izzy touched her sister's hair as Addie passed her.

Johnny slammed his door, walked to his woman and stopped.

He looked down at her face.

Tears were streaming down her cheeks too.

"I love you," he said.

Sunlight and moonshine and honey and song and love shone in her face.

"I know," she replied.

Right then, a police car pulled up the lane.

"Right, out," Cary said into the speaker at his shoulder.

He looked back to Johnny.

They were alone outside Izzy's house.

"They caught him on 36. High speed chase. He lost control, ended up in a ditch, tried to run through a field, they ran him down. He's in custody. And to get back to what we were talking about, he'll be goin' down for kidnapping, vehicular theft as well as bank robbery, Johnny. But he'd have been doing that last before you shared what you just shared. We knew."

Johnny stared into his eyes.

"The bank teller he was doing came in the day after. She wasn't sure, but since he wrote her a note she thought was about him disappearing, but then reconsidered, she suspected. Shandra took off, leaving you, we looked into shit, gathered the evidence, of which that moron left plenty, we knew," Cary went on.

Johnny jerked up his chin.

"But I'm glad you told me," Cary said low, referring to the conversation Johnny had been having with him before his radio squawked. "It wouldn't have meant anything. Hearsay. You had no physical evidence. It would have just sealed a deal on a slippery felon who'd already had the deal sealed on him. Though I wish you'd have come forward earlier."

"Shandra gonna get fucked in this?" he asked.

"That's for the DA to decide. She aided and abetted a bank robber. But no one was harmed during the robbery and everyone knows how screwed in the head that family is. Shandra's the only decent one in the lot. Everyone thought she'd make her way clear bein' with you. Pretty much everyone reckoned, Stu disappeared, she did too, he dragged her down all the same."

"For what it's worth, she tried to get him to turn himself in."

Cary nodded. "I'll talk to the chief and the DA. Chief's lived in Matlock thirty years longer than me. I reckon he knows the tale of woe of Shandra and Stuart Bray. She might get slapped on the wrist. Worst, community service. But I doubt that, since she got Brooks Forrester and called it in, giving up her brother. Two wrongs don't equal a right. But one wrong and one right makes you even."

It was Johnny who nodded then.

Cary looked to the house. "Glad this had a happy ending."

"Yeah, me too," Johnny muttered, even though "glad" was not the word he would have used.

Cary looked back at him. "No, Johnny. For that baby, goes without sayin' I'm glad he's home safe. But I'm also talking about another happy ending."

Johnny just stared at him.

Cary grinned. "She as sweet as they say?"

"She's the world."

Cary blinked.

Then he smiled.

Then he clapped Johnny on the arm and headed to his cruiser.

Johnny watched him get in and drive away.

And he watched Izzy's empty lane, assessing the calm of his heart, making sure it was still there.

He felt her arm curl around his waist and her weight lean into him.

He lifted an arm to wrap around her shoulders and kept his eyes on the lane.

"You told him, didn't you?" she asked.

Fuck yes, he did. If it meant just a month more on Stu's sentence, he was going to spill.

"Yup."

"Are you gonna get in trouble?"

"Nope."

"Angry you didn't get the chance to beat the crap outta him?"

"Yup."

"Me too," she whispered.

That was when he looked down at her.

She lifted blue eyes up to him and gave his waist a squeeze.

"It's all good, *häschen,* let's go inside."

"All right, baby."

She didn't move.

She called, "Johnny?" like she wasn't staring straight at him.

"Yeah?" he answered anyway.

"*Ich liebe dich auch.*"

He kept looking at her.

Then he busted out laughing.

But while doing it, he curled his Eliza to his front and he kissed her.

EPILOGUE

I'M A DREAMER

Johnny

It took a lot out of Johnny to watch the man walk into the room in his shoelace-less sneakers and orange jumpsuit.

And bile raced up Johnny's throat at seeing the excitement in his face as his eyes darted back and forth between Johnny and the woman standing beside him.

He sat in the seat on the opposite side of the glass and swiftly yanked the telephone that was there out of its cradle.

Slowly, Johnny sat in the chair in front of him and lifted the phone at his side.

He put it to his ear, and Stu said instantly, "Are you guys back together?"

Christ, it was like the guy didn't remember he'd kidnapped Brooks just a week and a half ago and just how insanely messed up that was.

Johnny didn't get into that.

"Do the right thing," he stated.

Stu blinked at him.

Then his face got shifty. "Johnny, I was in a bind. You know me. I get that was extreme. But I had no choice. If there was another way, I'da—"

He wasn't going to listen to this shit.

"Do the right thing," Johnny repeated.

Stu leaned into the glass and whispered desperately into the phone, "I'm dyin' in here, brother."

"Do the right thing, Stu."

"Been trapped all my life, my parents, their shit. I can't be trapped, man."

"Stu, fucking *do the right thing*."

Suddenly, as it was with Stu when he wasn't getting what he wanted, his demeanor changed.

He sat back and started sneering.

"You don't get it," he spat. "Johnny Gamble of Gamble Garages. Hot shot. Big man. Money to burn. Dad that thought his shit doesn't stink. You never felt trapped. You've never been fucked over in your whole life."

"Let her be free."

Stu fell silent.

"She's the principal witness in your case," Johnny told him something he knew. "She can't leave town. She can't get clear. She can't be free. And you're forcing her into a situation where she has to testify against her own brother."

He was.

Stu had pled not guilty to all charges.

He'd done it even though there were witnesses everywhere. The lady across the street at the daycare center. A female clerk in a Gamble Garage, of all fucking places, where he bought a jar of baby food, holding a crying Brooks to him, this caught on security film.

There were also his fingerprints at the shack. And getting in a high-speed chase in a car he'd stolen. Not to mention, striking up a relationship with a bank teller in a town where he didn't live, but he did have enough good in him (and stupidity) to write her a fucking note that said, *I'm sorry, baby*, before he fucked her and her kid over, robbed her bank and skipped town.

Last, there was his sister who he forced to be a material witness to all of that...and more than likely a lot more Johnny and the cops didn't know about.

Shandra stood at Johnny's back for one purpose.

To put the heat on her brother to do the right thing.

For once.

"You fight this, I talked to Cary. They're pissed at your plea, Stu," Johnny told him. "You take county resources to try you, you're gonna lose and the judge is gonna throw your ass in the joint for a sentence that'll mean you're trapped for a long fucking time."

"I'm comin' out of my skin in here, Johnny," Stu whined.

"Then you shouldn't have robbed a bank, stolen a car and kidnapped a baby, Stu," Johnny pointed out the obvious.

Stu did the darting of the eyes thing again between Johnny and Shandra standing behind him then said, "I screwed you over. You and her. But she's the only thing I got."

"She *was* the only thing you had but just like you made it for me, you lost her."

Stu read the wrong thing in that and leaned in again, eager, fierce. "She loves you," he whispered in the phone. "She never quit."

"We're not talking about that."

"At least I can go down knowin' I fixed one thing I broke."

Johnny felt his jaw tighten, he gave it a beat, and only when he had it together did he speak again.

"This world, Stu, does not revolve around you and your hurts and your bullshit and your anger and your fuckups. This is not about you. This is about your sister. She has to get out of this town. She has to get out from under your shit and your history and your anger. She has to get away from those two predators who call them-selves your parents. For once in your miserable life, think about someone other than you. Think about someone who laid it all on the line *for you.*"

Stu sat back. "So you want me to think all this," he swept his hand in front of him to indicate Johnny with Shandra, "isn't about that new piece you're tagging."

Johnny fought his jaw tightening and bit out, "No. You're in there and you're going down whether you fight it or not and the nightmare you forced them to endure is done. Yours is just beginning, and as usual you're dragging your sister right along with you. Now you got a choice and I'll put this in terms you'll understand. Cary says if you change your plea, they're still open to bargain with you. It'll mean a reduced sentence. You got an hour to make that call. That hour's up, you go on trial and the cops and the DA are so pissed, Stu, they're gonna come at you with everything they've got and they've got a lot. They've shared with me that the kidnapping charge will get you twenty years. The robbery charge, since you used a gun, will get you twenty-five. And the DA is gonna push for those being served non-concurrently, which, not taking into account the car you stole, means you'll get out when you're seventy-seven years old."

Dread filled Stu's face but Johnny wasn't done with him.

"And not that you give a shit, but they're so pissed, they'll consider Shandra going on the run with you as her not only receiving but concealing money taken from that bank, and she'll go on trial and face ten years."

Stu jerked forward in his seat so violently, the cop at the door watching him went on alert, putting his hand to the baton on his belt.

"They can't do that!" he shouted.

"An hour," Johnny said. "Your call."

He started to put down the receiver but heard Stu shouting agitatedly, "Johnny! Johnny! Johnny!"

He put the phone back to his ear.

"Let me talk to my sister," he demanded.

"She's done with you."

"Please, brother, let me talk to my sister."

Johnny stared into his eyes. "You're wasting time."

Stu stared back, he did it almost desperately, like looking at Johnny could make all he'd done disappear.

Then he said, "I'll change my plea."

Thank Christ.

Johnny nodded.

He put down the phone.

He got out of his chair.

He turned to Shandra, put a hand to her elbow and guided her out of that room and the jail.

They stopped at the front steps and turned to each other.

"He's gonna change his plea," he told her.

Her shoulders sagged and he had a feeling they sagged not because she was now free, but because Stu would suffer less.

He got that. He loved Toby that much, if Toby had turned like Stu had done he'd feel the same way.

Those desperate hours not knowing where Brooks was, he also didn't get it at all.

"I gotta go," he told her.

She tensed and seemed to lean toward him.

"Johnny."

"This gets sorted, Shandra, get outta town. Find your happy."

She shook her head and said solemnly, "You have to know how sorry I am for everything. Really everything, Johnny." Her face started to crumble but she was Shandra. She'd lived through a lot, too much. She didn't crumble easy. So she sniffed through her nose, pulled it together, and whispered, "Everything."

"I know that, Shandra," he said quietly.

"I really did love you," she told him.

"I know that too," he replied.

"Not to...I mean, I know you've moved on, so not to make this anymore awkward than it already is, which seems impossible, but here it is. I always will. I'll always love you, Johnny Gamble."

He dipped his chin and whispered, "You get out from under all of this, start somewhere fresh, find your happy, you'll find someone else to love."

"Maybe."

"Definitely. Just..." he drew in breath and put his face closer to her, "use what we had and do it better next time."

She rubbed her lips together and nodded, and he remembered he used to think that was cute. If he had his shot, he would always kiss her after she was done doing that.

It was still cute.

And he hoped the guy that came next would think that too.

"Stay safe and be happy, sweetheart," he murmured.

"You too, baby," she murmured back.

He looked into beautiful eyes, what seemed a very long time ago he thought he'd be looking into until his dying day.

Then he smiled at her and walked away.

Twenty minutes later, he drove up Izzy's lane to see her rocking in her wicker chair on her front porch with three dogs lazing around at her feet.

She had a chilled glass of something on the table next to her, her colored pencils out and a book on the knees she had lifted up with her heels in the seat.

He knew that book.

His Izzy was coloring.

That was Izzy. She didn't rock away the time, anxious for his return, worried about him knowing what he had to do, waiting for him in quiet reflection, wasting time where she could be using it, even if she was using it to color in the lines.

She had to be doing something.

The dogs raced to him, Ranger in the lead, as he stopped his truck beside her dusty Murano.

He got out, handed out pets, and walked slowly to her with his eyes on her.

She didn't move from her chair and she also didn't move her gaze from him.

When he was standing on her porch two feet away, looking down at her, she asked, "How'd that go?"

"He's changing his plea."

She grinned up at him.

Now that...

That was kissably cute.

"Can you do anything, Johnny Gamble?" she asked.

He just shook his head and hitched his lips.

Her face got serious. "How's Shandra?"

"If she's smart, finally free."

She nodded gravely.

Then her head tipped to the side. "We had rather a drama fifteen minutes ago when Brooks decided he would prefer Kelly's fur yanked *out* of her furry kitty body and Kelly decided she liked her fur where it was, so she swatted at him and caught him with a claw. The scratch is about half an inch long so not bad but she drew blood. Brooks wasn't a big fan. Addie bathed it and shared with him that some lessons need to be learned the hard way. I have a feeling Brooks can't understand English, but he understood that. Kelly's still miffed."

"Addie's right," Johnny declared.

"Yes," Izzy agreed.

"Iz?"

"Yes?"

"It gonna take until we're eighty for you to get with the program?"

She looked confused for a second before she set her book aside, pushed out of her chair, moved her body into his and slid her arms around his neck.

"Sometimes *you* can kiss *me* when you get home, you know," she whispered, eyes to his lips.

"You're right," he replied.

And then he did just that.

Izzy

"That is absolutely, one hundred percent not going to work," I said decisively.

"Are you serious?" Johnny replied, not hiding he was getting angry.

I threw up both my hands. "Yes, I'm serious." I leaned toward him where he was standing five feet away from me in front of his couch in his living room/bedroom/dining room/kitchen (part of the point!) and reminded him, "I have horses, Johnny."

"That isn't lost on me, Izzy," he retorted.

"And I kinda like them," I went on. "I also like having them outside my back door, not fifteen miles away."

"Iz, you got three acres. I got twenty-seven."

I felt my eyes get big at this news. "You have twenty-seven acres?"

"Baby," he growled, "you have got to get over me being loaded."

I felt my eyes narrow. "I had no problem with you being loaded last week when I came home and you handed me that box with brand-new, nude Louboutin pumps in it."

His head twitched and his brows came together. "You call that beige color nude?"

"Yes."

"It's beige," he replied.

"It's *nude*, Johnny."

"*Christ!*" he exploded. "We're not gonna fight about the color of your shoes when we're fighting about where we're gonna live when we move in together."

That was what we were doing.

I'd barely walked through the door after work and we were

fighting over where we were going to live when we moved in together.

I didn't know when that would be, we hadn't made that decision.

But we were fighting over it anyway.

It was October. We'd now officially been seeing each other for five months (I was starting from the day we hooked up, which I considered our beginning).

Some might think this was too soon to be discussing moving in.

Though my mom wouldn't.

And Addie just plain didn't because she told me so.

Neither did Deanna (she'd told me so too).

And Margot, just the other night at dinner at The Star said chidingly, "You two children and this back and forth, and packing and repacking bags and extra expense on toiletries. It's ridiculous. You need to *settle*, for goodness sakes."

So I had a feeling she didn't either.

But Johnny had just declared no way *in hell* he was moving into the acres.

My response, as noted, was decisive.

"I need stables, Johnny," I pointed out, deciding to save the fact that I also might need rooms and use that if I needed to turn to another weapon in my arsenal for our argument.

"I got twenty-seven acres, Iz. I can build you stables and you got a lot more space to ride. When we were riding last weekend it felt like we barely left before we were home. We'll need them and an outbuilding to put the ATVs, snow mobiles and bikes in, as well as a garage since you're not parking your vehicle outside when it gets cold or rains. When that's all cleared out, we can finish the downstairs with bedrooms for the kids we're gonna have, and a family room so they can have their own space and do it all being far away so I can fuck you like you like it. We'll redo up here so we got common area for the family and a master with a killer closet you can fill with your dresses and shoes and we got plenty of space for me to do you on the floor if I happen to see you get dressed, or undressed, however it happens."

I was standing frozen, staring at the perfection of Johnny Gamble.

Johnny was not frozen.

Johnny was on a roll.

"You got three bedrooms and you want fifteen kids. I want two. I'm willing to compromise to bring that up to four, but four kids and two adults at the acres means we'll be living on top of each other and that's not what I wanna give my family. Plenty of room to put four bedrooms with two Jack and Jill baths downstairs and a family room. And just to say, *spätzchen*, it comes that time I start planting my babies in you, my sperm count cannot be eradicated by living in a place that has pink walls, flowered pillows and a fucking birdhouse with a pink roof on the coffee table in the family room."

"Are we...are we...moving in together or getting married?" I asked breathlessly.

His heavy brows shot together in that ominous way he had.

"We're moving in together *then* we're getting married."

I stopped breathing entirely.

"And, babe," he stated warningly, "I already picked the ring. It's kickass. Guy said cushion cut and called it a halo. I have no clue what that means but it fucking rocks. It's also four carats. If you balk at that because someone could buy a truck with the cost of it, I'll lose my fucking mind."

Four carats.

An engagement ring that cost the same as a *truck*.

"And while we're fighting," Johnny carried on, "might as well share now that Margot's already planning our wedding. When I went over there the other day because Dave needed a hand putting in that new farm sink Margot ordered off some website, she had bride magazines with about seven hundred Post-it notes sticking out of them on her kitchen table. She told me you were either gonna have the wedding she'd always wanted or the wedding she was determined you were gonna have. With Margot, my guess is it's the last but they'd both be the same. So strap in, *spätzchen*, because it's a guarantee any wedding Margot plans is gonna get outta hand."

"You're okay with four kids?" I whispered.

He flipped out a hand. "You wanna push that to five, I'll consider it. But let's make sure there are no Tobys in the bunch with the first four."

"Your brother is wonderful, Johnny," I said.

"Pretty much all women think that, Izzy, so you thinking it doesn't surprise me."

I really had nothing to say to that so I said nothing.

At this point, Johnny seemed to note my mood had changed and the irate way he was looking at me changed too.

"Iz?" he called.

"I like my birdhouse."

"Iz," he whispered, lips hitching at one side.

God, I loved the way he grinned.

"But if you don't, I'll put it in the yard sale it seems I'll be having."

"Your sister and Brooks can live there. They love it there," Johnny told me.

"Yes," I agreed.

"And this place was my dad's."

"I know, *häschen*."

His face grew soft, and God, oh God, just that much more beautiful.

"You got a dream wedding you want, baby, I'll intervene with Margot," he told me gently.

"I have a feeling my dream wedding would be whatever Margot wants for me."

"Yeah," he agreed.

"Mom would love your water wheel," I shared.

"Good," he replied.

"She'd love you more."

And his face grew even softer, and God, oh God, so much more beautiful.

"Good," he whispered.

"Can I tackle you now?" I asked.

He smiled.

"Hit me, baby," he invited.

I lunged.

And Johnny went down without a fight.

"Iz."

I pulled him out of my mouth, wrapped my hand around him and stroked hard as I lifted up between his legs and looked at him laid out diagonal on his bed, his muscles flexing, his knees up, feet off the bed, long, powerful legs falling to the sides, his rock-hard cock flushed and distended, the veining I felt pulsing in my mouth I could feel doing that now in my hand.

"I wanna watch," I whispered.

He lifted his head from the mattress, his hands moving, one shoving mine aside, his other going low to cup his balls, and he growled, "Then settle in for the show, baby."

I settled in for the show, panting, restless, my palms sweaty and itching, wanting to touch him as I watched him jack off for me, massaging his balls, pulling at his cock, noises rolling up his chest, his hips lifting to thrust in his hand.

I gave a small cry right along with his low groan as he dug his dark head into the mattress, exposing the strong line of his jaw through his beard, the cords of his throat taut, and the creamy stream jetted from his cock up his chest.

He was milking himself when I could take no more.

I crawled up him and plastered myself to him, taking his head in my hands and driving my tongue in his mouth even through his labored breathing.

He recovered enough to kiss me back and force his arms out from where I'd trapped them between us. He latched onto me around my hips with one, holding me steady as his other hand dove between my legs, two fingers thrusting right in.

I moaned into his mouth as he gathered my wet, pulled his fingers out and circled my clit hard.

It took perhaps ten seconds before I sank my teeth in his lower lip, heard him grunt, felt his arm around my hips tighten, slide, his hand going down, in. He again coated his fingers with my wet and slid them up, gliding one into my ass.

I released him as my head shot back and I cried out as I came.

He worked my clit through my climax and kept stroking me tenderly, fucking my ass the same, as the jolts turned to shudders then to trembles and I collapsed on top of him, my face in the side of his neck.

Johnny slid his finger out, gliding that arm up my back and his hand between my legs traced around so he could wrap that arm around my waist.

I caught my breath against his skin.

After I was sated and settled on top of my man, he started trailing his fingers down and up the back of my thigh.

"When we get down to making babies, *spätzchen*, I'm thinking I'll need my cum to find its way inside you, and I don't mean you absorbing it through your skin," he teased.

"You come inside me plenty," I muttered, and he absolutely did.

One could say five months of togetherness had not affected the intensity of our attraction to each other.

In fact, one could say the exact opposite.

"When we get down to making babies, Iz, we're gonna be serious about that and step up our game."

That comment forced my face out of his neck so I could look down at him.

"More sex?" I asked, astonished.

He grinned. "Definitely. A *lot* more."

"We have a lot of sex now."

"I'm a guy who's thorough when he does a job, Iz, but I'm thinkin' with that job, I'll be meticulous."

I rolled my eyes and let my head plop down again.

Johnny chuckled under me and kept stroking the back of my thigh.

We lay together for a lovely while before he said quietly, "Now we got that sorted, when you wanna move in?"

"Tomorrow?"

His arm around me went tight and his hand at my thigh quit stroking and gripped hard.

Johnny's way of saying he liked my answer.

"Though I probably should talk to Addie," I continued, "and sort some things out. So how about the weekend after next?"

He curled his hand around the inside of my upper thigh and held on as he replied, "Works for me. I'll start making calls. Get some plans for stables drawn up."

I lifted my head, looked into his eyes and began, "The cost of that, Johnny—"

His hand left my thigh and cupped my face, his thumb pressing against my lips.

"Never again," he growled. "Don't ever mention that again, Izzy. I'm not stupid with money and God knows you aren't. I wouldn't do it if I couldn't do it or I didn't want to do it, even if me wanting to do it is doing something that's for you. But I like horses and you have horses that I like and I'll want our kids raised around animals, including horses, so now's the time. We get stables. And I'll buy you shoes and give you a huge-ass diamond ring and build this mill into a house you love and you'll know I'm doing it smart. You'll know I'm doing it because I can afford it and because I want to. And I'll know the days you had to make do, you had to eat shit, ended the night you met me. It's not gonna be about four-dollar dining room chairs and taking someone else's castoffs and making it into something that works anymore. And if you got trouble swallowing that, right now, know to your soul that I know to mine I was put on this earth to do exactly that for you. So I'm gonna do it and you, Izzy, you're gonna let me."

"I'll want a garden," I whispered, my voice thick with the emotion that was welling inside, put there with all Johnny just said to me, and he moved his thumb from my lips.

"We'll pick the spot this weekend and I'll turn over the dirt in spring."

Of course he would.

"And I'm gonna be buying new wineglasses before I move in," I shared. "Yours are nice and all, but they're kinda...utilitarian."

He grinned at me. "Go crazy."

"I'd bring mine but they're a little too...girlie for the mill."

"I think the mill might shatter those glasses through angry vibes if you tried," he joked.

I was not joking when I asked, "If you were put on this earth to take care of me, what was I put on this earth to do for you?"

His brows knit.

"To make me happy," he said, like I wasn't quite all there.

"Johnny—"

"To make me laugh."

I shut my mouth.

"To help me make babies."

I started to draw circles on his neck with my thumb and I did this in an effort to distract me from needing to cry.

"To give them a good mother because you learned from the best," he went on.

Okay, now he was totally going to make me cry.

And yet, he wasn't done.

"To give me a wife made of iron and steel and everything strong all bound up in feathers and kitten fur and everything soft. One I'll always know loves me. One I'll always know will never leave me. The going will get tough, and you'll stick. We'll fight, and you'll stick. Our world could rock, Eliza, and there's one thing I'm certain about, you'll stick."

The tear that fell from my eye dropped into his beard.

Johnny moved his thumb to my cheek to sweep the trail of wet it left behind away.

"Have I mentioned the sex kitten who lets me do what I want with her and doesn't mind lying on me, covered in my cum?" he asked quietly.

I swallowed and replied huskily, "No, you hadn't mentioned that yet."

He gave me a gentle smile. "Well, there's also that." The smile ran away and he whispered, "He didn't come back for you because he's a mammoth asshole, not because you weren't worth coming back for. And if it takes until you die, baby, and if it takes every dime I have, I'll do everything I can so you die knowing just how fucking amazing you are and that's worth anything and everything."

I could take no more so I shoved my face in his neck.

Johnny slid his fingers in my hair and cupped the back of my head.

It took me some time, but when all he said had settled deep, I asked, "Did you buy the ring?"

"Oh no, *spätzchen*, doing that up big. You don't get to know when and you don't get to know how. It could be dinner and candlelight and champagne, and I might even be moved to get down on a knee. It could be we're at the shack right after I come back from fishing, bringing up dinner you're not gonna eat. It could be after I make you come and you're all soft and wet and sweet for me. It could be over the eggs I make for your breakfast. It could be anytime, but you won't know the time. I can just promise it'll be the perfect time. A time I can be sure I'll remember the look on your face so I can tell our kids the story of when their daddy gave their momma her ring. So right now you know you're my world and I'm holding on to that for always, but you aren't gonna know when I'm gonna ask you to marry me."

"I'm all right with that," I muttered.

His voice sounded amused when he replied, "Well, that's good. Now you think we should hit the shower and then maybe eat some dinner?"

I lifted my head. "Can we take a bath instead?"

He looked in my eyes and continued to be the only thing he could be.

All that was Johnny.

"We can do whatever you want, Izzy."

I smiled at him.

And he smiled back at me.

Then we got out of bed and took a bath.

I MOVED in with Johnny a week and two days later.

Addie and Brooks stayed at my place rent free for the next month, and the month after that, when her attorney that Johnny paid trounced Perry, she started paying the mortgage.

Perry was awarded one weekend a month of visitation.

He came and got Brooks twice and then never came again.

He also paid child support twice and never paid it again.

During this time, Addie very poorly hid she was falling in love with Toby.

For his part, Toby very poorly hid that he was falling in love with Addie.

Brooks, however, didn't bother hiding he'd gone head over heels for both the Gamble men.

And just to say, all that was very fun to watch play out.

Deanna and Margot thought so too.

Though Johnny didn't agree with us.

JOHNNY DIDN'T GET DOWN on a knee.

But there was champagne and roses on his dining room table and the steaks he made with the garlic and herb cheese I loved so much.

He'd duped me.

First, he cooked all the time. He cooked because he was home first and said he was hungry.

But I knew he did it for me.

Steaks were special but he was a good cook so everything he made was fantastic.

Also, when I moved in, he found out I hit Macy's Flower Shop every Friday. So he started to have flowers delivered every Thursday.

That was Johnny Gamble.

Yes.

That was my Johnny.

They'd broken ground on the stables that day. The day he proposed. We'd approved plans within a week of him finding a contractor he wanted to go with. They didn't have a lot of time before there was a danger the ground might freeze so Johnny was paying for double the manpower so I could have Serengeti and Amaretto with me.

I didn't say a word.

I should have known when I came home and there was a pink shoebox sitting on the island that contained the pair of tie-strap, suede Alexandre Birman sandals I'd been rhapsodizing about on the laptop when Deanna was over the week before.

He was trying to throw me off the scent by being doubly generous.

It worked.

After I put my new wineglass down and was about to pick up my fork and knife to resume eating my steak, he'd murmured, "Give me your hand, *spätzchen*."

I'd looked at him and reached out my right hand.

"Other one, Izzy."

My breath caught and I gave him my left.

He was right.

The ring was extraordinary.

I loved it.

So much, we didn't finish dinner.

THAT NIGHT, the night of the ring, I didn't know what woke me.

But I woke.

I realized I was alone in the bed instantly.

I turned.

Johnny was outside, bathed in moonlight, wearing sweatpants and a half-zip sweatshirt with a high collar.

He was standing at the railing, staring through the dark at the creek.

I pulled back the covers and walked down the hall to the bathroom and into the closet with three dogs trailing me (Toby had given Addie and Brooks a rescue, half ridgeback, half we didn't know. See? Poorly hiding the falling-in-love thing).

I yanked on a pair of Johnny's thick socks, moved to a different drawer and tugged another of his sweatshirts over my head to cover his tee I was already wearing.

Then me and our dogs headed back out, down the hall, to the door.

We also headed out of it to see Johnny looking our way, frowning.

"Eliza, your legs."

It was cold, for certain.

I assumed.

I didn't feel it.

It was then I discovered his ring held magical powers.

It warmed me through and through.

I just walked up to him, fit myself to him and wrapped my arms around him, feeling the alien feeling of my ring shifting on my finger due to the weight of the stone.

I liked that feeling.

He just did the wrapping his arms around me part.

"Why can't you sleep?" I mumbled into his chest.

"I'm too happy."

I didn't know what his answer would be but that was not an answer I'd ever expect.

My head tipped back. "What?"

"I'll get used to it," he said to the creek.

"You can't sleep because you're too happy?" I demanded his confirmation.

He looked down at me and shook his head. "You're still not with the program."

"I always wanna kiss you, Johnny, but right now I wanna know more why you're standing out in the cold instead of in bed with me."

"That's not the program I'm talking about."

I closed my mouth.

"Never know whether to clue you in," he muttered.

"It's always the right thing to clue me in." I did not mutter.

"I'm a dreamer."

I stared up at him.

"Always been a dreamer. Always." He paused then socked it to me. "Since she left. That she being Mom."

I kept staring up at him but now I was doing it with my chest feeling tight.

"You wanna know what I dreamed, Izzy?"

Unable to speak, I nodded my head.

"I dreamed of winning a pretty woman and making her love only me. I dreamed of living with her at this mill and filling it with babies. I dreamed of keeping those garages strong for my sons to take over when it was their time. I dreamed of living my life knowing things would come and go. My children would be born, my woman and I would raise them and love them, and then they'd move on to live their own lives and be happy. But that pretty woman, my pretty woman, would always be with me. Now tell me, *spätzchen*, how does a man sleep when he's living his dreams?"

"I...I honestly don't know," I replied.

"Obviously, me either," he said.

"I seem to be able to do it," I shared.

He stared down at me.

Then he made that noise, his muted roar.

After that, Johnny was kissing me.

I didn't know how we made it back to the bed.

I did know how I was able to fall back to sleep almost instantly after Johnny was finished with me.

So I obviously didn't know he didn't fall back to sleep.

He also didn't go stand under the stars and stare at the creek.

He lay in bed, holding me.

And he stared at the dark ceiling.

Smiling.

The End

MOONLIGHT &
DISCUSSION & REFLECTION
Questions
MOTOR OIL SERIES

DISCUSSION & REFLECTION QUESTIONS

1.The author has stated the idea that generated *The Hookup* was to explore what a hero does after he's lost "the love of his life." Normally in romance novels, she returns to a fraught reunion and they rekindle their love. In *The Hookup*, that doesn't happen because Johnny meets Izzy before his "great love" returns. Izzy, in many other romance novels, is essentially the *other* woman who will need to be let down easy as the hero returns to his true love.

This book does not go down the "normal" romantic-reunion path, but instead examines the possibility that there is no such thing as "the love of your life." You don't get just one great love. What did you think about this? Do you believe in the concept of "one love of your life?"

2. Even though Izzy's mom, Daphne, did everything she could to make her daughters comfortable, Izzy and Addie clearly had a difficult childhood. Children can seem oblivious to how hard things are, but in reality they feel them on some level and eventually grow old enough to recognize and name their hardships. Izzy certainly suffers

from this, but also learns valuable lessons and uses them to build a comfortable home and a stable financial position. What did you think about how Izzy used the lessons she learned in her youth? Do you think it might be good for children, perhaps not on this level, but on some level to face adversity and learn how to manage? How much of that hardship do you think shapes a child's memories of their youth?

3. On that note, in the scene when Johnny and Izzy go camping for the first time, Izzy shares that they "faked happiness." Do you think that's true? Or do you feel Johnny was right, Izzy was having a vulnerable moment and finally embraced the difficulty of her childhood for the first time as an adult?

4. It's clear in this story that our past tends to help shape our future – in big and small ways. Our parents' relationship, our relationship with our parents/family and the circumstances surrounding our childhood. Shandra is not immune to that. Johnny and Shandra were good together and very much in love. Shandra did what she'd been conditioned to do, and in doing it, broke Johnny's heart. Shandra might not get a lot of page time but she looms large and is integral to the plot so let's discuss what now for Shandra? Were you curious to know about her? Do you hope she finds a new love of her own?

5. Sex in romance is a great thing. Sex in a romance book is also great, but it should move the story forward in some way. Johnny and Izzy each in their own ways express how incredible they feel their love-making is. For Izzy, she explains that she's never been as free as she is when she and Johnny have sex. They are open, vulnerable, sweet and a little kinky. Did you have a favorite sex scene and why? Did the sex between Johnny and Izzy seem different in any way from other sex scenes you've read?

5. Found family vs. biological family is always an interesting discussion. In *The Hookup* Johnny and Izzy equal each other out.

Johnny had a great dad and a deadbeat mother, Izzy had a great mom and an abusive father. What Izzy didn't have was a Margot and Dave in her life. Discuss (or consider) the bond Johnny has with Margot and speculate on what his life would've been like without her influence. On the other hand, do you think having a Dave in their lives would've changed anything for Izzy and Addie?

6.Taking that deeper, Daphne was never in the position, either financially, or in a way she felt it was safe, to lay down roots for herself and her girls so she could create a social circle that would offer more to her daughters. How did you feel about how the enduring tentacles of her husband's abuse affected her and the girls' lives? Addie goes so far as to blame the cancer that killed their mother on their father. Do you think this is an apt metaphor, considering how vulnerable his abuse made all the Forrester girls and how hard Daphne had to fight to keep them safe, fed, housed and raise them well?

7. Which would you pick to live in, the mill or the farmhouse?

8. Did you have a favorite outfit of Izzy's?

INTERESTED IN READING MORE MOONLIGHT AND MOTOR OIL?

Read on for more in Book Two
The Slow Burn

Tobias Gamble knew from a young age precisely the kind of woman he was going to make his. She was not going to be like his mother. She was going to be like the mother he claimed.

In other words, she was going to be just right.

And when Toby returns to his hometown of Matlock, Kentucky and claps eyes on Adeline Forrester, he knows she's the one.

The problem is, his brother Johnny has a new girlfriend. And Addie is her sister. Last, Toby would do nothing to hurt Johnny's chance at happiness.

Toby hangs around town to get to know the woman Johnny fell in love with. He also hangs around to get to know Addie.

But he's fallen hard, and he knows the best thing for him—and Addie—is for him to leave.

Addie Forrester is thrilled her sister Eliza found a good, solid man. Johnny Gamble is the salt of the earth. The best guy in the world.

The best except for his brother, Toby.

Toby doesn't know it, but Addie's fallen hard too. He's perfect, except for the fact that he's hands off and it's torture, being friends with Toby when she wants so much more.

Addie also has a lot on her mind. She's got bills to pay, her young son needs food, Christmas is coming and her job at the grocery store just isn't cutting it.

Toby is steering clear of Addie. Addie is steering clear of Toby. But everyone around them knows this is the slow burn.

Because just like Eliza and Johnny, Addie and Toby were made for each other.

Read the Prologue of *The Slow Burn* now.

THE SLOW BURN

MOONLIGHT AND MOTOR OIL BOOK TWO

PROLOGUE

SHE WAS GOING TO BE JUST RIGHT

Toby

T*hirty Years Ago...*

TOBY SAT on his rump in the middle of the room and stared.

His big brother Johnny was standing by their daddy's leg and patting it.

Daddy was sitting on their couch, bent over, head in his hands, his shoulders heaving.

He was crying.

Toby had never seen his daddy crying.

"Daddy," his big brother said, his voice funny.

Their daddy lifted his head, his face red, and looked at Toby's big brother.

Then he lifted one of his big hands and wrapped it around Johnny's neck.

"It's okay, son," he said, his voice funny too. "It's okay," he repeated.

His eyes strayed to Toby.

Toby felt his lip wobble, his belly all funny when he saw his daddy's face.

"We'll all be okay," his father whispered.

Toby didn't believe him.

He didn't believe him at all.

This was Tobias David Gamble's first cognitive thought.

It was also his first memory.

He was three.

And when it came to his dad, Toby's thoughts on that particular subject would turn out to be right.

Ten Years Later...

"She's ruined him," Margot snapped.

Toby was about to go in the back door.

It was after school.

His dad and brother were at the garage.

If Toby didn't feel like working on some car, and sometimes he didn't, he'd go to his Grams and Gramps's after school.

That is, if he didn't sneak out to the mill and pretend he was a fugitive from justice. Or a cop hunting a fugitive from justice. Or a scientist discovering a new kind of moss that would cure cancer. Or a sailor stranded from his ship on a desert island (that had a mill with a water wheel).

Everyone had freaked the first time he'd walked all the way out to the mill to do his own thing.

He'd been eight.

Now, if he was in the mood, he just went. And if they didn't know where he was, they went out there to get him.

But Grams and Gramps were in Germany for a vacation, visiting Grams's family.

Since he didn't want to go to the garage, like always when his Grams and Gramps were busy, Toby went to Margot and David's after school.

David was his dad's best friend.

Margot was Dave's wife.

She was also a pain in the butt.

This was because she was super strict. It was always, "A gentleman does this," or, "a decent man does that," or, "you offer a lady a cookie first, Tobias, before you eat fifteen of them."

Her cookies were *the best*.

Who wouldn't eat fifteen of them?

And if you offered them to some girl first, *she* might eat fifteen of them, not leaving you enough when she was done.

But okay...

He'd never tell anyone this, not anyone in the whole world, but he liked it when Margot got all cuddly with Dave, her eyes getting soft, like he built some big cannon and pointed it to the sky and lit that thing, filling the heavens with stars.

He wished his mom had thought that about his dad.

But he liked it that Margot gave that to Dave.

He wouldn't tell anyone this either, but Toby liked it when she got all soft in the face sometimes, when she looked at him when he got an A on some paper or after he helped his team win a game (and she'd know, she always went to his games, Dave too) or after he made her laugh.

And he liked it a whole lot when she'd run the backs of her fingers down his jaw.

But right then, Toby didn't turn to the screen door and push it in when he heard Margot in the kitchen talking on their phone.

He stood at the side of the door and listened.

Margot'd get ticked, she knew he was there. She was big on manners, and eavesdropping was not something she was keen on. So eventually he'd have to retrace his steps, give it time and come back.

But now he was gonna listen.

"I can't begin to imagine what's wrong with Rachel, except for the fact she's not Sierra."

Toby's eyes closed and his shoulders slumped.

His dad was scraping off another girlfriend.

That sucked.

His dad seemed better when he had a lady around.

This time it sucked more because Toby really liked Rachel.

He'd learned not to like them. They never lasted long.

A lot of them tried real hard to last as long as they could, and Toby could see this. His dad had money. He was a decent-looking guy. And he had that low voice Toby had overheard one of his father's girlfriends say was "sexy."

Lance Gamble was a catch.

A lot of them tried to get to Lance through his sons.

Most of the time it was sickening, and it bugged the crap out of Toby and Johnny (it was just that Johnny was the kind of guy who'd learned to keep his mouth shut about stuff that bothered him or find a time he could talk it out with Dad so it wouldn't tick Dad off, Toby... not so much).

But Rachel was real. She was pretty and she was sweet. She didn't give off that fake vibe.

And she cooked awesome.

He'd wanted her to stick around.

Apparently she wasn't going to do that, and as usual with his dad and his girlfriends, that was not her choice.

"If that woman ever came back, I'd slap her right across the face," Toby heard Margot go on. "That is, before I tore her hair out, scratched out her eyes and ran her right back out of town on a rail."

Now Margot was talking about Sierra.

Dad's wife.

Johnny and Toby's mom.

She was still his dad's wife, as far as Toby knew.

Even though his dad tried to hide it from the boys, he'd tried to find her, but she was nowhere to be found. A couple of years ago, when an effort at this had failed, Toby had heard Dave suggest he get an *ex parte* divorce (whatever that was). But his dad had said, "Just gonna give her more time. If I know my Sierra, she won't be able to stay away from her boys for too long."

He was wrong, seeing as she'd stayed away by that time for eight years.

Toby still didn't think his mother needed more time. She'd had enough time. Now it had been ten years.

She hadn't come back.

Because she wasn't gonna come back.

And if she did, no one wanted her back.

Except his dad.

And Toby.

He didn't remember a lot about her. He'd been too young when she'd gone.

Except he remembered her being pretty. He remembered her smelling good.

He remembered how happy she made his dad.

Though Toby wasn't feeling that so much anymore.

Mostly in this moment because he liked Rachel.

"I don't know," Margot was saying. "David will talk to him, I'm sure. But he won't listen. I think he thinks he has to be available when she comes home. But that woman is never coming home. Dave knows it. I know it. The whole town of Matlock knows it."

As Toby had noted, he knew it too.

"No," Margot snapped. "I can't even *begin* to understand what was in her head. But I'll tell you this, we're all having the last laugh."

Toby straightened after she said this.

How were they all having the last laugh when his mom had up and left them?

Margot told him.

Well, not him. Whoever she was talking to.

"Johnathon is fifteen and he's already one of the finest men I know. Good. Decent. Kind-hearted. Strong. Knows his own mind and how to speak it. Sharp as a whip. And she'll never know what a fabulous man her boy turned out to be."

Yeah.

Well, sure.

Johnny was awesome.

Everyone knew Johnny was awesome.

Everybody.

Even Toby, and sometimes Tobe wanted to hate his big brother, but Johnny was just that guy.

You couldn't.

No one could hate Johnny Gamble.

"And Tobias..."

Toby perked up.

"He has no idea his potential..."

Right.

His *potential.*

"But when he learns..." she trailed off for a sec before she carried on. "I find myself struggling with him. Do you rein in all that audacity? Is it right to try to stop a boy from *devouring* life? He's so bold, Judy, it sometimes takes my breath away. In another time, he'd be the first to walk on the moon. The first to corral fire. Johnathon will find a sweet girl, make babies with her, work in his father's garages and live a good life, quiet and happy. Tobias will find a spitfire who challenges him and drives him insane, and they'll go off and tear through the world, running with the bulls in Pamplona or uncovering hidden treasures in Egypt or something."

Toby blinked in the sun.

Margot thought all that?

About him?

"And then what do I do?" Margot asked her friend Judy (who did not make cookies as good as Margot's, but they were all right). "My last, not born of me, but my last boy? How does a woman handle her baby trekking through the Amazon or deep-sea diving to explore sunken pirate ships? I fear I'll spend the rest of my life waiting for the phone to ring just to hear he's all right. Lord, I hope he finds a woman who can communicate. At least she'll check in."

Without him telling it to do it, Toby's body slid down the siding of Dave and Margot's house.

All the way down.

Until he hit his rump.

Because she thought all that.

About him.

"And Sierra doesn't get that," she continued. "She doesn't get the solidness of Johnathon or the fearlessness of Tobias. She'll never know that. She'll never hold the grandchildren Johnathon will give her in her arms. She'll never hear the breathless excitement of Tobias's children over the phone when they call and share what their father's up to now."

Toby felt something hit his stomach, and it wasn't what usually hit it whenever anyone mentioned his mom.

It was something a whole lot different.

"So I suppose I should thank her," Margot declared. "Because she left and I got all that. She left and that became mine. And I suppose I shouldn't be angry with Lance for breaking it off with Rachel. Because if he found a woman, she might claim those boys. Because what woman, outside Sierra, who's no woman at all, wouldn't claim those boys? And then where would I be?"

Again, without him telling it to do it, his body got off its rear, took its feet and turned right to the screen door.

Margot never missed a trick.

So even though she was standing at the kitchen counter with the wall phone, with its long cord, held to her ear, her side to the door, she sensed him and turned.

Toby didn't move.

He just stared at her with her pretty light-red hair and her big eyes, wearing one of her nice dresses (she was always in nice dresses) and he felt that feeling in his stomach.

"I have to go, Judy. Tobias is home from school and if I don't get him an after-school snack, his stomach will eat through him." She paused. "Okay. Yes, of course. See you then. Ta, Judy."

With that, she hung up the phone.

But all Toby could think was she'd said he was "home."

And he was.

He had three homes.

His dad's.

His Grams and Gramps's.

And Margot's.

And she'd make him a heckuva after-school snack.

She always did.

Anytime he came to her for as long as he could remember.

His mom gave him that. All of that.

And she did it by leaving.

Unmoving, he watched her walk to him.

He only shifted when she pushed out the screen door.

She held it open, stood in the door and studied him.

"How much did you hear, darlin'?" she asked quietly.

"A lot," he answered.

Her pretty face got that soft he liked so much before she whispered, "Child."

Toby said nothing.

"I know you liked Rachel, Tobias, but—" she started.

"I like you."

She stopped. Blinked.

Then her hand crept up in front of her to cover her throat so he wouldn't see it move as she tried not to cry in front of him, because ladies did not give in to tears or hysterics in front of others. It was rude.

According to Margot.

"When I find a woman, she's gonna be like you," Toby told her.

"My beautiful boy," she said quietly.

"Though she's gonna hafta be able to wear pants if she's gonna run with some bulls or somethin'."

Her face got even softer, but she said, "Someth*ing*, Tobias. Don't drop your 'Gs.' You're not a hillbilly."

"I'm totally a hillbilly. Everyone from Kentucky is a hillbilly, don't you know."

Her mouth did that thing it did with him a lot. It got all shaky, like she was trying not to laugh, before it got stern.

"I am not a hillbilly and I'm a Kentuckian born and bred. And *you* are not a hillbilly either," she stated.

"Are you gonna feed me, or what?" he asked.

"'Margot, I'm famished. Will you please make me a snack?'" she corrected.

"I'm never sayin' that famished word *in my life*," he returned.

She didn't quite beat the smile before she replied, "Say*ing*, Tobias." Then she shifted aside so he could get in, murmuring, "Lord, child, what am I going to do with you?"

"Feed me?"

She rolled her eyes, but he saw before she did, they were smiling.

He walked in.

She made him wash his hands then get out his books at the kitchen table while she fixed him a roast beef sandwich with melted muenster on top, slathered in mayo with a ton of ridged Ruffles stacked on the side.

In fact, there were so many chips, the sandwich was almost covered in them. It was like she was making him a full meal, even if he'd had lunch and it was near-on dinnertime.

He didn't care. It was awesome and he was, well...*famished*.

He grinned and got down to his geometry because he knew she

wouldn't let him go home until he was done with his homework.

Toby was half through the sandwich, had made a dent in the chips, and was almost done with geometry when he looked at Margot at the stove, doing stuff with a big hunk of meat in a pan she was gonna roast for Dave for dinner.

Their boys were all in college. Well, Lance, the oldest one, was an engineer out in Oregon, but Dave Junior and Mark were in college.

So it was now just Margot and Dave.

She didn't have all her boys to look after anymore.

Dad had said it made her sad. And Toby'd seen that, for sure.

And when he did, even if Grams or Gramps were home, or the mill was calling, he came after school to her, and not just because she did great snacks (Grams did great snacks too).

Now she seemed to be doing better.

And he was glad.

Still.

He was looking at her because that feeling in his stomach had turned and it did it so bad, he had to get it out.

"Only thing I care about..." he started.

Margot turned her head to him.

"Is you not goin' away," he finished.

She straightened from her beef and rotated fully to him.

"I'm not going anywhere, Tobias."

"I like Rachel fine," he said. "And I don't care about Mom," he lied. "But don't you go anywhere."

"I'm not going anywhere, darlin'."

He stared at her.

She let him and stared right back.

This went on awhile.

When it lasted long enough to make that feeling start to fade, he looked back to his books.

Margot went back to her roast.

When Dave, Dad and Johnny got home (Dave worked at the garage too), Margot demanded the Gambles stay for dinner.

And when Margot demanded something, the men in her life did it.

Toby didn't mind.

Her roast was almost as good as her cookies.

And they all got to give her stuff during dinner and she got to pretend it annoyed her.

Like always with his family the way it was...

It was awesome.

And like always when he was over at Margot and Dave's he went home with a full stomach.

And that felt good.

FIFTEEN YEARS LATER...

TOBE LAY with his back to the headboard of his bed, his phone to his ear, listening to it ring.

It was late and there was a three-hour time difference.

He knew they'd answer.

They did.

Or Dave did.

"Hello?"

"Hey, Dave," Toby replied quietly.

"Son, do you know what time it is?"

"Tell Margot I got my pilot's license today."

"Oh hell," Dave muttered.

Toby grinned.

"What?" he heard Margot in the background. "Is that Tobias? Where is he? Is he all right?"

"I'll let you handle that," Toby said to Dave, still quiet. "Love to you both."

Then he disconnected.

He looked at his watch and timed it.

It was one minute and twenty-three seconds later when his cell phone vibrated.

"Hey, Margot," he answered in a soft voice.

"I have a mind to—"

"I got all my hours in. I aced the test," he assured her. "My instructor said I was a natural."

"When you were learning to teach golf, your instructor said you were a natural at that too," she returned.

"Well, I was."

"And when you were up in Alaska logging, your foreman told you he thought you'd been born in the north, you were such a natural logger, when you're *southern* through and through."

"Well, there was that too."

She sighed before she announced, "All I can say is that I'm glad you're not doing that anymore. Did you know that logging is the number one most dangerous job in America?"

He did not know that.

Though, having been a logger for two years, he wasn't surprised.

She kept at him.

"And I suspect being a pilot is number *two*."

He had no idea.

He also didn't care.

"You'll be the death of me," she declared.

He cared about that.

"You're gonna live to be a hundred and twenty and bounce my grandchildren on your knee," he said low.

Margot had no reply.

"Don't tell Dad. I'll call him tomorrow and give him the news," Toby instructed.

"Oh, so your father gets a phone call that's *not* after one in the morning?" Margot replied.

He lowered his voice further but didn't pull the smile out of it. "Just makin' sure I check in with my girl."

Margot again said nothing.

"Come out to Phoenix, I'll take you up," he offered.

"That will happen when hell freezes over, Tobias."

Tobe fought back busting out laughing.

Though he couldn't beat back a quiet chuckle.

"Now that you've bested the skies, can I expect a call to share you've spent your time looking for, and finding, a special someone?" she asked through his humor.

She wanted him settled and happy.

Okay, maybe not settled. She liked he was a rambling man (though she'd never admit it out loud).

She just wanted him happy.

"Not sure that'd be a good idea, sweetheart. I'm missing green. I'm thinking of hitting Tennessee next. Always wanted a spell in Nashville. Wouldn't be a good idea to find a woman, then expect I could drag her across the country."

"Dear Lord," she murmured.

It drove her nuts he hadn't met anyone yet.

Johnny had met someone.

Of course.

It took Margot ages to like Shandra, or trust her, and Toby still didn't know if she really did.

Of course.

No one was good enough for her boys.

Not a soul.

Then again, as far as Toby was concerned, she was right.

He hadn't found anyone good enough for him.

Because there was no one like Margot.

Not a soul.

"Gonna let you get back to sleep," he told her.

"That'd be nice," she replied, but he could tell she didn't want to let him go.

"I'll phone at a decent hour next time."

"That'd be nice too."

"Love you, Margot," he said softly.

She only hesitated a second, and he knew that second was to get her shit together, before she said, "Love you too, my beautiful boy."

Toby was grinning when he disconnected.

"Maybe not make a phone call to check in with *your girl* when I've just let you fuck me twice and I'm trying to sleep."

That came at him groggy as well as unmistakably ugly.

Toby looked down at the naked woman beside him in his bed.

They'd been drinking (a lot) and then they'd been fucking (a lot).

He thought she'd passed out.

Then again, obviously she had, though not for long since he hadn't even turned out the lights, but also obviously she wasn't a huge fan of being woken up and had no issue sharing that.

She had a great ass. Nice hair.

But nope.

And again...

Not good enough.

From what she said, and how she said it—clearly thinking he was the kind of guy who'd talk to some other woman when he had one naked beside him in bed—she was not good enough by a long shot.

"Maybe it's time we get you home," he suggested.

She blinked and the ticked look on her face changed to coaxing. "Baby, a girl just needs some rest for round two, or, uh, in this case...three."

"Sorry. I got an early morning." Lie. "So I'll take you home."

And that, as far as he was concerned, was that.

He shifted his legs off the bed and reached for his jeans.

"Toby—"

He yanked on his jeans and looked at her face.

Pretty too.

Still, not close to the one.

"I was talking to my mom," he shared.

"Oh," she whispered, now up on a forearm. "You call your mom Margot?"

He was not gonna get into that, so he answered simply, "Yep."

"That's sweet, I guess."

"You know something big happened today," he reminded her.

And she did.

They'd met that night at a bar, and when he'd told her, she'd been all in to celebrate with him. If her celebrating with him meant him buying her a lot of drinks, a late dinner since she was getting loaded and he wasn't a big fan of sloppy, drunk women, then coming home with him and getting it on.

"I went out to celebrate, met you, so I hadn't had a chance to tell Margot yet," he finished.

"Yeah, okay. But it's still uncool to make a phone call when someone is sleeping," she responded. "Even if it's your mom."

It was also uncool to be a bitch about it when you'd been asleep for maybe ten minutes.

And he'd been quiet. It wasn't like he'd had a forty-minute conversation with someone he had to shout at because they were on a helicopter.

He shared all that by saying, "Babe, get dressed."

"But I didn't know it was your mom."

No, she thought he was a colossal asshole and was chatting with some other woman while she was beside him after he fucked her in his bed.

He was not going to get into that either.

He bent to nab his tee, straightening and repeating, "Get dressed. Let's get you home."

He pulled on his tee when she began, "Toby, I was just—"

"You're right," he cut her off again. "It was rude. I should have left the room to make the call. I didn't. Sorry about that. I was trying to be quiet. I didn't know you were a light sleeper. But I got shit to do tomorrow, I 'spect you got work tomorrow, and you're up, so might as well get you home so we don't both have to get up early for me to drive you there."

"God," she muttered, turning her head and sliding toward the edge of the bed. "What a dick. Always the way with the hot ones. Total fucking dicks."

So totally not the one.

"You know, you wanna stay, hang, sleep with me, wake up with me, the way to do that is not act like a bitch when I wake you up after I call my mom when I accomplished something that means something to me and I wanna share that with her and then call me a dick," he advised.

"What am I supposed to do?" she snapped, yanking up her panties. "Thank you for waking me up when you made a phone call *right next to me* while *I was sleeping?*"

"It's my bed, Kristy," he pointed out. "And you were out for maybe ten minutes. It wasn't like I woke you up from a deep sleep when you gotta perform neurosurgery tomorrow."

"And it was *my* pussy I let you eat an hour ago in *your* bed, Toby," she shot back, now angrily snapping on her bra.

With that, he was done.

Really so totally not the one.

"You know, a woman gives it up," she kept bitching, "a gentleman doesn't kick her out of bed."

That made him still in doing his belt.

Because Margot drilled being a gentleman into him since he could remember.

And Kristy was not wrong.

"And don't give me any shit about giving it up," she kept going, now yanking on her short skirt. "'Cause you were there and you gave it up too. Though most men don't see it that way," she ended on a mutter.

"We met five hours ago. And in that five hours, babe, I didn't make any promises," he reminded her, doing it going careful because he hadn't, but he had been a dick (though that was a stretch, but if he stretched it he could see where she was coming from, he wasn't a huge fan of sleep, there was too much living to do, but he got others were) and now she had a point.

"Oh no, they never do," she sniped.

Hang on a second.

"You give it up, I give it up, I make you go twice. Tell me, Kristy, where do you think that puts us?" he asked. "Not bein' a dick now, babe. Really wanna know so I don't run into this shit again." He flung an arm out her way. "I mean, it's clear you don't want me to think you're easy when I'm just as easy. So a woman can bang a man all easy. But a man bangs a woman, there's some inherent promise in that?"

She didn't have an answer to his question and she shared that by replying, "Fuck you."

"Great," he muttered, bending and reaching for his socks.

Boy, he could pick them.

Just like his dad.

He turned his back on her to sit on the bed and pull his socks on.

"You know, maybe I thought we were starting something," she said to his back.

He twisted to her. "And maybe we would have been if you didn't call me a dick."

She threw out both arms. "So it's me calling you a dick and not you kicking me out of your bed that puts us here?"

He stood again and turned to her. "No, it was me actually *being* a dick and making a call when you were sleeping, 'cause, you see, Kristy, I live alone so I'm not used to having a woman sleeping beside me in bed. Especially that woman bein' you, since I only met you tonight, so I didn't think, and I should have because that was a dick move. But me waking you up and you not sayin', 'Who was that, baby?' Then saying, 'It's sweet you called your mom to celebrate the news, but next time, do you mind not doin' it in bed when I'm sleeping? I'm a light sleeper.' Instead, you give me shit like I'm phonin' some other woman when I'm with you, *that's* what put us here."

"Thanks for the lesson in consideration, Toby. Next time a guy's an asshole, I'll be all sweet instead of just pointing out he's an asshole."

"What I'm saying, Kristy, is a man might not know he's *bein'* an asshole, or you think he's bein' an asshole, so maybe bein' a modicum of cool in pointing it out, he'd learn the way with you and not do it again."

She snapped her mouth shut.

She opened it to clip out, "I'll call a friend to give me a ride."

"Takin' you home," he murmured, turning back to sit on the bed and pull on his boots.

"Don't do me any favors."

"For fuck's sake," he muttered, and pulled on his boots.

When he got up, he found she was dressed.

He also saw by the look on her face she was in a different mood.

"You know, you want me to cut you some slack in being a dick, maybe you should do the same. I mean, I did just wake up, Toby."

Yeah.

After ten minutes.

Jesus.

She gave him that, he gave it back to her.

"And then you called me a dick and gave me shit about eating your pussy and kicking you out of my bed. I'd give you a blow by blow, but it just happened, and you were there. You think when we got zero foundation but a couple of orgasms, after all that ugly we can resurrect something that hadn't even gotten off the ground?"

"Probably not," she mumbled.

Definitely not.

He moved to the bedroom door.

He was at it when she called, "You know..."

Toby turned to see she was still standing at the side of the bed, the only move she'd made was to shift around to face him at the door.

"...I get it," she finished.

He beat back a sigh and asked, "You get what?"

"You want the sweet ones. All guys want the sweet ones who are all understanding, even when they're being jerks, and don't point out you let them go down on you, much less fuck you, *twice*, and that means there's been a connection. You can't handle it being real. They say girls want the fairytale. But boys want it more and they have the power, so a girl has to twist herself into that fantasy to land a guy."

"No, Kristy, that isn't how it is," he returned. "Maybe for some guys, but not me."

"And you're not taking me home right now because I wasn't how you wanted me to be?"

"Yeah, I'm takin' you home right now because you weren't how I might want you to be. But this is the gig, babe. You give your shit to me, you don't cool it and attempt to handle the situation, not only might I have a lifetime of that if I eat it now, that's what you'd give our kids, if we got that far."

Her head jerked and her eyes got big.

But Toby kept talking.

"And that isn't okay. I actually *don't* want a sweet one. I want one who'll give as good as she gets, stick up for herself, stick up for me, and stick up for the babies we make. And when shit goes off the rails, and I admit I've been a dick, what I *don't* want is her to shut her mouth and not admit she's been a bitch, so we can take it from there. That's what I don't want, Kristy."

"Okay, I've been a bitch," she admitted.

"And what do I do with that?" he asked.

She again threw up both hands. "You just told me to admit it."

Now he was curious.

"Why are you fighting for this?"

"Well, duh," she said. "Because you're all kinds of hot and insanely good in bed."

He shook his head.

"Oh please," she drawled. "Don't act like I'm not right here because you didn't like the looks of me and wanted to get in my pants, but instead you liked my *smile*, or some shit, and I made you laugh."

She had not, he just realized, made him laugh.

With her looks, ass, legs and come on, she'd made him fight getting hard.

That was why she was there.

And now Tobe was beginning to realize where he'd gone wrong from his very first girlfriend, the one he'd asked to "go with me" at fourteen to the woman standing in front of him right now.

She wasn't finished.

"The ones who look like you don't go for some fat bitch who cooks good and worships the ground they walk on. The ones who look like you go for ones that look like him, gorgeous, and they still worship the ground he walks on."

"Yeah, I totally want my woman to worship the ground I walk on," he shared.

"See," she retorted.

"And she'll do that because I'd die for her."

Kristy again shut her mouth and her eyes got big.

"She has to have that fire for me too, babe," he told her. "And yeah, she'll probably be gorgeous because I'll want that fire for her when I'm eating her pussy. But this," he indicated the room with a tilt of his head, "this is just a pain in my ass."

Her voice was small when she shared, "I heard you tell your mom you're moving to Nashville and it wouldn't be good to meet a woman now and drag her there."

And it comes out.

Why didn't she lead with that?

Why hit him with a load of shit when she was clearly more into him than he knew and wanted him to be into her?

"I was just messing with her, though I wouldn't mind heading to Nashville. That's not the point. You've got no idea my relationship with Margot or my plans for the future, immediate or otherwise. But just to say, if I'm willing to die for a woman, Kristy, when I meet her, it goes without saying I'd be willing to stick. And if I feel I gotta bounce, I'll be willing to put the effort into talking her into coming with me," he explained, what he considered unnecessarily.

"And obviously I'm not that girl."

Was she out of her mind?

Toby didn't field that one.

She read his silence correctly.

"Right. Great. Just sayin', not in the mood to spend more time with you. So I'm gonna call a taxi," she snapped.

"Maybe that's a good idea."

She strolled his way, going all out with the sway of her hips to the point he worried she'd take herself off balance.

"Good luck finding your fantasy girl," she bid acidly.

"Thanks," he muttered, getting out of her way.

He let her pass him but followed her out.

He didn't lock his front door when she slammed it behind her.

But he did look out his window to watch her dig her phone out of her bag and bend her head to it.

And he kept watching as she stood out there until a taxi pulled up.

He didn't go for the door to walk out with her and pay for the damn taxi when she turned to him and flipped him off through the window, mouthing, *Fuck you, dick.*

Toby sighed again.

Yeah, he could pick them.

He still continued to watch until she folded into the taxi and it took off.

She'd get safe home.

So Toby stopped watching and went to lock the door.

He went back to his bedroom thinking that it was going to be just him and his fist for a good long while after that.

After he got undressed and stretched out under the covers, Kristy was already barely a memory.

All the ones who came before, who acted like bitches or nagged incessantly, or decided he was going to marry them before he even knew their middle names or how they took their coffee, were memories.

Tobias Gamble was not going to be his father.

He was not going to pick the wrong one and end up broken in a way no woman—or no child, not even his own blood—could fix.

She was going to be just right.

She was going to love the children they made more than anything in the world.

She was going to worship the ground he walked on.

And she was going to be so spectacular, he'd be willing to die for her without even a blink of an eye to think.

So yeah, Kristy was a memory.

And therefore, Toby had no problem getting back to sleep.

FOUR YEARS LATER...

Toby pulled up to the house in his old red Chevy truck with the silver panels.

The house was cute-as-fuck, totally the place where whoever the new woman his brother was seeing, after Shandra got done grinding him to ash, would live.

But Toby didn't have a mind to the house.

Toby didn't even have a mind to the fact this was the first time he'd seen his brother in months, since he hadn't been back to Matlock in months.

He didn't have a mind to any of this seeing as there was clearly a drama playing out beside that cute-as-fuck house.

A drama Johnny was involved in.

Johnny and some strung-out-looking dude, some huge black dude, and two of the prettiest women Toby had ever seen in his life.

Yeah, one of those women was Johnny's new girl.

And that figured.

House cute as fuck.

Women pretty as hell.

Toby got out of his truck and saw Johnny give him a short shake of his head before Tobe began to make a slow approach.

The strung-out dude was speaking.

"You know I've been lookin' for gigs," the dude announced.

"I'm not sure how you'll find gigs camped out on the couch with a six pack or humping some chick in my bed," the blonde woman (or one of the two) with all the hair, fantastic ass, long legs and clear attitude replied.

Right.

That probably wasn't Johnny's girl.

Though she was the prettier one.

Christ.

Coming closer, Tobe saw she was gorgeous.

"Addie, don't lay this shit on me," the dude returned. "You haven't been giving it up for months."

"That's because I'm *tired*, Perry," she shot back. "I'm *exhausted*. I'm a single mother of a baby boy with a deadbeat dad who *lives with me.*"

Great.

Just fucking fabulous.

This strung-out dude was *her* dude.

"I love my kid," the Perry guy hurled back.

"He's a toy, like I was a toy before I wasn't shiny and new anymore and life became a drag. But you didn't give me away, you tossed me aside and looked for a new toy just like I know you'll do with Brooklyn when he's not fun anymore," the gorgeous chick called Addie replied.

Toby saw Johnny turn his head and watch his approach.

Toby lifted his eyebrows toward his brother.

Johnny gave him another short jerk of his head and again looked at Addie.

"That's not true, baby." Perry was now trying to wheedle. "I love you. I love Brooklyn. You know that. It's just been tough since the band broke up and—"

"God, spare me," Addie drawled bitingly. "You're *such* a cliché and I'm *such* a moron for falling for it."

"We got it good, we just gotta get that back," Perry said.

"*You* had it good, because you had someone paying your bills and doing all the grunt work taking care of your son so he's nice and clean and fed when you feel like playing with him. *I* didn't have it good. And even after sharing this about seven million times, it didn't sink in that you might wanna give your wife and son better. I know this because nothing changed. I also know this because I walked in on you fucking another woman."

What was happening sunk in.

That beautiful woman had a baby with this asshole guy.

They were *married.*

And this fuckwad cheated on her.

She'd seen him do it.

Shit.

"I'll get in another band soon and then—" the asshole guy started.

"Do not try to feed me that again, Perry. I believed it two years ago. Do you honestly think I'll believe it now?"

"So, right," Perry bit out, not trying it on anymore. He was again pissed. "Now *you* get to make the decision we're done then *you* clean out the apartment and the bank accounts and take off?"

"You cheated on me and we were done so I moved, Perry. I took my stuff. I left yours. That stuff that's mine includes what's in the bank accounts since every penny in them I earned," Addie explained.

Toby could not believe this moron had cheated on her.

Jesus.

Was the man blind?

"When I got back after you split, there was nothing in the place but my clothes," the moron retorted.

"Which is what you brought to our marriage and all you contributed to our marriage, so that's all you'll get out of it."

"It took me a week to get up here because I had to raise the cash for gas since you took it all and canceled our credit cards," Perry complained.

"*My* credit cards," she fired back. "Your name was on them. I paid them."

Man, this woman had some serious sass.

And she was laying his ass out.

It would be really fucking righteous, if what was happening didn't suck.

Perry raised his hand quickly to his forehead, slamming his fingers against it and then sending his hand flying out, and Toby braced to lock things down because if this dude was stupid enough to cheat on his beautiful wife with all her righteous attitude, he'd be stupid enough to do something even more dickish to her surrounded by three men.

The asshole made this irate move, stating, "Can you not see how totally fucked up it is, some bitch cleans out an apartment and takes a man's kid then takes off without even a fuckin' note?"

Toby found himself swallowing a growl that the man had called her a bitch.

"You were inside her," Addie whispered.

At that, precisely the way she said it, Toby's focus locked on her, and like it had a mind of its own, his body moved nearer to hers.

"Baby, can we *please* talk about this without an audience?" Perry begged.

"She looked at me. You looked at me. You looked right in my eyes when you were connected to another woman," Addie said, her voice dripping with hurt.

"I tried to come after you."

"With your dick wet from another woman."

The moron went silent.

Toby still didn't look at him.

His attention was riveted to her.

How could she be even more beautiful showing her pain?

"This is how this is going to go," she said softly. "I'm moving up here. I got a job in the grocery store. I start on Monday. I've already contacted an attorney. She's started divorce proceedings. You *will* pay child support. You *will* take financial responsibility for the child you very enjoyably had a hand in creating. We'll see what part of his life you'll play, but *that* will be up to me. But he'll be up here with me and Izzy. And you'll be down there with your broken promises and your ridiculous dreams."

"My dreams aren't ridiculous," Perry clipped out, clearly insulted by that, and not all the shit she'd been saying about him being a dick of a partner, a cheat, and shit at being a dad.

The selfish ass.

"You wanna be the lead singer of a rock 'n' roll band and no, that's not ridiculous. The ridiculous part is you think that'll happen sitting on a couch, drinking beer," Addie told him.

"You're not going to take my son from me," he threatened.

"Too late, I already did. But just saying, Perry, you never actually had him because you never actually claimed him."

"We'll see how this goes," he snarled.

It was then Toby tensed when Addie got in his space.

"I know how it'll go so listen up," she hissed. "I'll work until I drop to fight for what's right for my son. I'll sell my body if I need to, to give him not only what he needs but even just a little bit of what he wants. And I'll bleed my last drop before I let you fuck him up. *You know me*, Perry," she stressed. "You know what makes me. You know every word I say is true. And you know you don't have what it takes to fight that. I'll do whatever it takes to beat you, to give my son what he deserves. I was taught how, day in and day out by my mother, so I know the way. And I'll take it if you make me, and I'll die knowing I gave my boy happy."

Toby felt something he hadn't felt in years slide into his stomach as he stared at her while she said these words.

But even at its strongest in the past, it had never burned as deep as it did right then.

"You're gonna have to fight it," Perry hurled at her.

"Only because you're intent on proving how big of an asshole you are and you're gonna make me," she returned.

That asshole glared at his wife. He then glared at the other blonde, Johnny, and the African American guy before he turned and

stutter-stepped when he saw Toby. He recovered quickly and started
to stalk off.

"Just to let you know," Addie called after him. "My attorney
already has three appointments to get sworn affidavits next week.
And that bitch you were banging while my son was in the next room
got served a subpoena, so she's one of them."

She didn't even know his name, but Toby wanted to bump fists
with her for being so fucking badass.

That or kiss her.

At that juncture, the second option was seriously inappropriate.

But that didn't mean he didn't want to do it.

"Kiss my ass, Addie," Perry yelled, not breaking stride.

"The time you get that from me, baby, is long gone," she returned
in a loud drawl.

Only then did Toby wrench his eyes from her so he could watch
her hopefully soon-to-be-official ex slam into his car, make it roar and
then reverse and peel out in a shower of gravel and a cloud of dust.

Toby twisted back when the other blonde started carefully,
"Addie—"

But Addie turned and raced down the side of the house, disappearing at the back.

The second woman raced after her.

Toby felt his brother's eyes and tore his away from the area where
the women had disappeared, doing this fighting running after them,
and put them to Johnny.

"Welcome home, brother," Johnny said.

God.

Johnny.

Toby felt lips hitch.

"I'm Johnny," Johnny said to the black dude.

Say what?

They didn't know each other?

"Charlie," the guy replied, lifting his hand Johnny's way.

Johnny shook it, let go and introduced, "This is my brother,

Toby."

"Toby," Charlie said, offering his hand to Toby.

"Charlie," Toby replied, taking it.

When they were done shaking, all three men hesitated, then when Johnny started down the side of the house, Toby and Charlie trailed with Ranger, Johnny's dog, walking with them.

So rumor in town was true.

Shandra, Johnny's ex-bitch who destroyed him was back in Matlock, because there was Ranger. The dog he'd given her to look after her after she'd kicked his brother in the teeth (this being about a nanosecond (slight exaggeration) after their father died) and took off.

But Ranger was here.

With two blondes and a cute-as-fuck house with ugly drama playing out in the side yard.

Jesus.

So Johnny walks his ass into that kind of drama, setting himself right up to be the hero, which Tobe so totally knew Johnny would wait about an hour to do.

And when Toby had tried to intervene with some chick whose brother had some medical bills she was trying to help pay, she decided he was her prince charming. She then rented some hall for their reception when he had no intention of buying her a ring. And when he tells her that last, even though he goes gentle, she loses her mind about losing her deposit and takes off in his truck.

Johnny found the righteous blondes who'd go to the mat to take care of their kids.

Toby found the nutcases.

Good to know things didn't change.

They walked in the back door hearing Addie saying, "No, Iz. Just put the queso under the broiler and let's get this party started."

But her eyes hit Toby's brother when he entered then they went behind him after Johnny cleared the door, and Tobe and Charlie crowded with him into the small kitchen.

She was holding an adorable baby tight to her and hovering in a corner of the kitchen like the two women in it had her caged in (the blonde, clearly Eliza, who everyone in town was talking about being the girl who mended Johnny Gamble's broken heart) and an African American woman, who probably belonged to Charlie.

Though, to Toby, they seemed to be giving her space.

It was then Addie said, "Great. As if that drama being played out in front of Clubber McHotterson," she indicated Charlie with a flick of a hand, "and Magnus McHotterson," she indicated Johnny with a jerk of her head, "wasn't bad enough, now we got Talon McHotterson here to enjoy the show."

All the drama with that dickhead outside and she was cracking jokes.

Fuck.

Fuck.

Toby again couldn't take his eyes off her.

"Maybe we should go upstairs and talk, baby girl," the black lady said softly.

"About what?" Addie asked. "About how Johnny's changed more of Brooklyn's diapers after knowing him for a week than his father has after knowing him seven months?"

Yeah.

That was Johnny.

And it just sunk in that her kid was called Brooklyn.

Kickass name.

"Doll, how about you let Johnny and Charlie look after Brooks and we girls get a bottle of wine and—?" Eliza tried.

"I saw you two," Addie said, her voice hoarse, and Toby, already alert to everything about her, went more so. "In the stable. I saw Johnny doing you against the wall."

Well, shit.

That he did not have to hear.

"Oh Lord," the black woman mumbled.

"Shit," Charlie muttered.

"Hell," Toby murmured.

"He never gave me that, what you two had in that moment," Addie told the woman who had to be her sister, they looked so much alike. "I could have walked right up to you and neither of you would have seen me. I didn't exist, nothing existed. Nothing but him for you and you for him. He never gave me that, Iz. How did I never see that?"

That made Toby look to his brother.

With relief.

Shandra had torn him apart.

Apparently, town talk was right, and this Eliza had put him back together.

His brother had that. And Tobe was glad he did.

And he was glad even thinking he wanted the same.

His eyes moved back to Addie as Eliza whispered, "Addie, sweetie."

"He gave me this." She cuddled Brooks closer. "That's all he ever gave me. But he gave it to me getting himself an orgasm and honest to God, that was all he was thinking about."

"Addie, please, baby, let's go upstairs," her sister coaxed.

Addie reared her head like a stubborn mare, and it was inappropriate as hell in that moment, but that didn't change the fact that move was hot, before she snapped, "No. This is a party. We're having a party."

She forged past her sister, Johnny, straight to the door where Toby was standing.

Yeah.

Totally gorgeous.

But holding that baby and doing everything in her power not to fly apart...

The most beautiful thing he'd ever seen.

"Out of the way, Talon," she ordered.

"Name's Toby," he replied gently, but he didn't move.

Her head jerked back, and her tortured blue eyes caught his.

Christ, yeah.

Spectacular.

"You're his brother, aren't you?" she asked.

"Yeah, darlin'," he replied.

"Of course. You're perfect, so of course. You're probably taken too, aren't you?"

If he was taken, which he wasn't, he wouldn't be in about half an hour.

Fortunately, he wasn't.

"I—" he started to tell her that.

"Not for me," she cut him off. "Man like you. Man like Johnny. Man like Charlie. Not for me."

Right.

She'd been holding it together.

But he sensed she was about to fall apart.

"Honey," Toby whispered. "How 'bout we get you—?"

She tossed her hair and looked over her shoulder at her sister. "I did it, Iz. I did it. What I swore to myself I'd never do. Not the same, but a version. I found Dad. I found a man who was good for nothin' except to break my heart."

And that was when her face melted, and she started to go down.

"Tobe," Johnny growled, on the move.

But Toby was all over it.

He caught her in his arms and sank down to the floor with her. Addie's ass hit his inner thigh with Toby's leg at a bad angle and that didn't feel too hot.

He winced, but ignored it, putting his arms around her and tucking her and her kid close to his chest.

She shoved her face in his neck and started sobbing.

All he could think was she felt good, especially her hair against his skin, so fucking soft.

Also, she smelled great.

Her baby started fretting.

Right.

Time to get her to a safe place.

Toby lifted his gaze to her sister. "Where you want her, babe?"

"My bedroom," she whispered. "Upstairs. I'll show you the way."

Toby nodded, got his feet under him and with great care lifted Addie and her baby cradled safe in his arms, walking behind the sister as she hurried into a hall.

He walked them up the stairs as Addie cried in his neck.

And he walked her down the hall into a bedroom where he placed her in the bed while she kept crying in his neck.

Eliza moved in the minute she was in bed, so Toby took a step back.

Another step.

Then he stopped and watched.

Eliza soothed Addie, and with the two sisters' heads so close, Toby thought another man might not be able to tell their hair apart.

But he could.

Already.

Because Jesus Christ, fuck...shit...

He'd fallen in love.

Fallen in love with a spitfire with a baby and a cheat of an asshole husband she was trying to make her ex...

A spitfire who just happened to be the sister of his brother's new woman.

Something Toby could not fuck with.

Johnny, who had retreated from life when the love of his had torn his heart from his chest, was back. Healed. Moving on with a pretty woman with a cute-as-fuck house who obviously loved her sister, and who his brother connected with so much, someone had seen him fucking his girl and he hadn't even noticed.

So yeah.

Toby could not fuck with this.

And again yeah.

To put it simply...

Fuck.

On that thought, reluctantly, Toby walked out.

ABOUT THE AUTHOR

Kristen Ashley is the *New York Times* bestselling author of over eighty romance novels including the *Rock Chick, Colorado Mountain, Dream Man, Chaos, Unfinished Heroes, The 'Burg, Magdalene, Fantasyland, The Three, Ghost and Reincarnation, The Rising, Dream Team* and *Honey* series along with several standalone novels. She's a hybrid author, publishing titles both independently and traditionally, her books have been translated in fourteen languages and she's sold over five million books.

Kristen's novel, *Law Man*, won the *RT Book Reviews* Reviewer's Choice Award for best Romantic Suspense, her independently published title *Hold On* was nominated for *RT Book Reviews* best Independent Contemporary Romance and her traditionally published title *Breathe* was nominated for best Contemporary Romance. Kristen's titles *Motorcycle Man, The Will*, and *Ride Steady* (which won the Reader's Choice award from *Romance Reviews*) all made the final rounds for Goodreads Choice Awards in the Romance category.

Kristen, born in Gary and raised in Brownsburg, Indiana, was a fourth-generation graduate of Purdue University. Since, she has lived in Denver, the West Country of England, and she now resides in Phoenix. She worked as a charity executive for eighteen years prior to beginning her independent publishing career. She now writes full-time.

Although romance is her genre, the prevailing themes running through all of Kristen's novels are friendship, family and a strong sisterhood. To this end, and as a way to thank her readers for their support, Kristen has created the Rock Chick Nation, a series of programs that are designed to give back to her readers and promote a strong female community.

The mission of the Rock Chick Nation is to live your best life, be true to your true self, recognize your beauty, and last but definitely not least, take your sister's back whether they're at your side as friends and family or if they're thousands of miles away and you don't know who they are.

The programs of the RC Nation include Rock Chick Rendezvous, weekends Kristen organizes full of parties and get-togethers to bring the sisterhood together, Rock Chick Recharges, evenings Kristen arranges for women who have been nominated to receive a special night, and Rock Chick Rewards, an ongoing program that raises funds for nonprofit women's organizations Kristen's readers nominate. Kristen's Rock Chick Rewards have donated hundreds of thousands of dollars to charity and this number continues to rise.

You can read more about Kristen, her titles and the Rock Chick Nation at KristenAshley.net.

Connect with Kristen Ashley

facebook.com/kristenashleybooks

twitter.com/KristenAshley68

instagram.com/kristenashleybooks

pinterest.com/KristenAshleyBooks

goodreads.com/kristenashleybooks

bookbub.com/authors/kristen-ashley

ALSO BY KRISTEN ASHLEY

Rock Chick Series:

Rock Chick

Rock Chick Rescue

Rock Chick Redemption

Rock Chick Renegade

Rock Chick Revenge

Rock Chick Reckoning

Rock Chick Regret

Rock Chick Revolution

Rock Chick Reawakening

Rock Chick Reborn

The 'Burg Series:

For You

At Peace

Golden Trail

Games of the Heart

The Promise

Hold On

The Chaos Series:

Own the Wind

Fire Inside

Ride Steady

Walk Through Fire

A Christmas to Remember

Rough Ride

Wild Like the Wind

Free

Wild Fire

Wild Wind

The Colorado Mountain Series:

The Gamble

Sweet Dreams

Lady Luck

Breathe

Jagged

Kaleidoscope

Bounty

Dream Man Series:

Mystery Man

Wild Man

Law Man

Motorcycle Man

Quiet Man

Dream Team Series:

Dream Maker

Dream Chaser

Dream Bites Cookbook

Dream Spinner

Dream Keeper

The Fantasyland Series:

Wildest Dreams

The Golden Dynasty

Fantastical

Broken Dove

Midnight Soul

Gossamer in the Darkness

Ghosts and Reincarnation Series:

Sommersgate House

Lacybourne Manor

Penmort Castle

Fairytale Come Alive

Lucky Stars

The Honey Series:

The Deep End

The Farthest Edge

The Greatest Risk

The Magdalene Series:

The Will

Soaring

Wild and Free

The Unfinished Hero Series:

Knight

Creed

Raid

Deacon

Sebring

Wild West MC Series:

Still Standing

Other Titles by Kristen Ashley:

Heaven and Hell

Play It Safe

Three Wishes

Complicated

Loose Ends

Fast Lane

Printed in the USA
CPSIA information can be obtained
at www.ICGtesting.com
CBHW021219111223
2545CB00034B/77